Sheltering
Rain

SHELTERING RAIN

JOJO MOYES

Bookspan Large Print Edition

WILLIAM MORROW

An Imprint of HarperCollins*Publishers*

**This Large Print Book carries the
Seal of Approval of N.A.V.H.**

For Charles Arthur and Betty McKee

Acknowledgments

This book would not have been written were it not for the crystalline memory of my grandmother, Betty McKee, whose extraordinary romance with my late grandfather, Eric, and colorful recall of it I have shamelessly plundered in order to bring my own characters to life. I would also like to thank Stephen Rabson of P&O's archive department, for helping paint a vivid picture of passenger life on board ship during the 1950s and Pieter Van der Merwe and Nicholas J. Evans of the National Maritime Museum in London for their help with naval history. Thanks also to

Brian Sanders for his imparted knowledge of the Suez Canal.

My heartfelt gratitude goes to Jo Frank at APWatt for finally getting me into print, and for all her encouragement, advice, and tremendous lunches in the (long, long) lead up to it. Equal thanks to Carolyn Mays and the wonderful team at Hodder U.K. and HarperCollins U.S. for their alchemists' skills, and to Vicky Cubitt for her seemingly endless enthusiasm. I'd like some of what you're on.

I'm immensely grateful to Anya Waddington and Penelope Dunn for their advice and contacts, and for not ever raising an eyebrow when I told them I had written something else "that I'd like them to take a look at." Also to David Lister and Mike McCarthy at the *Independent* and Ken Wiwa for their boundless generosity and encouragement during our various literary adventures. Good luck with the next ones, guys.

Thanks to my parents, Jim Moyes and Lizzie Sanders, for passing down if not a genetic storytelling ability, then a certain bloody-minded determination. But most to my husband, Charles, for the uncomplaining babyminding, considered criticisms, and faith that I could do it. To him, and everyone I've ever bored rigid with yet another story idea, thank you.

SHELTERING RAIN

Prologue

Then shall the Archbishop kiss the Queen's right hand. After which the Duke of Edinburgh shall ascend the steps of the Throne, and having taken off his coronet, shall kneel down before her Majesty, and placing his hands between the Queen's shall pronounce the words of Homage, saying:

I, Philip, Duke of Edinburgh
do become your liege man of life and limb,
and of earthly worship;
and faith and truth will I bear unto you,
to live and die, against all manner of folks.
So help me God.

And arising, he shall touch the Crown upon her Majesty's head and kiss her Majesty's left cheek.

In like manner shall the Duke of Gloucester and the Duke of Kent severally do their homage.

FROM THE FORM AND ORDER OF THE
CORONATION SERVICE, 1953

It had probably been rather rude, Joy thought afterward, to meet one's future husband on what was really meant to be Princess Elizabeth's day. Or Queen Elizabeth II, as she would more grandly be known by the end of it. Still, considering the momentousness of the occasion for both of them, it had been quite hard (for Joy at least) to work up the appropriate feeling of excitement.

It was a day portentous of rain, not divine appointment. The skies over Hong Kong harbor had been humid and iron gray, and walking slowly around the Peak with Stella clutching a folder of damp song sheets, her armpits sliding as if greased and her blouse already sticking to her back like icing, Joy had felt something less than monarchist fervor at the thought of the Brougham Scotts' coronation party.

There was her mother, already fluttering at home, a taut string of anticipation and dissatisfaction, largely due to the presence of her father, back from one of his China trips. Her father's visits always seemed to coincide with a swift downturn in Alice's moods, anchoring her hankerings for a better life, somewhere else, into something meaner and darker. "You're not wearing that," she had said, and frowned at Joy, her mouth a scarlet moue of disapproval.

Joy had eyed the door. She was desperate to meet Stella, and avoid having to walk to the Brougham Scotts' villa with her parents and had fibbed, telling them that the hosts had requested the sheet music early. Journeys with her parents, even by foot, left her feeling seasick.

"You look so plain, darling. And you're wearing your heels. You'll tower over everyone." That "darling" was a familiar sweetener to disguise the unpleasantness of what Alice was saying.

"I'll sit down."

"You can't sit down all evening."

"I'll bend my knees then."

"You should wear a wider belt. It'll shorten you."

"It'll cut into my ribs."

"I don't know why you have to be so difficult. I'm just trying to make the best of you. It's not as if *you* try to make yourself look nice."

"Oh, Mummy, I don't mind. No one else will mind. It's not as if anyone's going to notice me. They'll all be listening to the princess saying her vows, or whatever it is she does." Just let me go, she willed. It would be bad enough to have to suffer Alice's corrosive temper for the entire party.

"Well, I mind. People will think I've brought you up not to care."

What people will think was very important to Alice. Hong Kong is a goldfish bowl, she would say. There was always someone looking at you, talking about you. What a very small and boring world they must live in, Joy wanted to answer. But she didn't, largely because it was true.

There was her father, who would doubtless drink too much, and kiss all the women on their mouths instead of their cheeks, so that they glanced around anxiously, unsure whether they had missed something. Just letting his hair down a bit, he would shout back at Alice later. What kind of a wife would deny her husband a bit of fun, after weeks of exhausting work in China (and we all knew the horrors of dealing with *the orientals*)? He hadn't been the same since the Japanese invasion. But then they didn't talk about that.

There were the Brougham Scotts. And the Marchants. And the Dickinsons. And the Alleynes. And all the other couples who lived in that particular class that resided just below the Peak, but not below Robinson Road (midlevels were really for the clerical classes these days), and saw one another at every drinks party at the Hong Kong Cricket Club, and met one another at the race meetings at the Happy Valley Race Course, and shared company junks on sherry-fueled boat trips around the outlying islands, and moaned about the difficulty of getting milk, and the mosquitoes, and the cost of property, and the shocking rudeness of the Chinese help. And talked about England, and how much they missed it, and about those visitors from England, and how pale and boring their lives seemed, and how *drab* England seemed to be even though the war had been over for simply ages. But most of all they talked about one another: the services men, a whole separate language of in-jokes and barrack-room humor; the merchant men, discussing and disparaging their rivals' performances; their women, grouping and regrouping in endless bored and toxic permutations.

Worst of all there was William. William who was omnipresent at any social gathering with his receding chin and his blond hair as fragile and wispy as his strangled, high-pitched voice, placing his clammy hands on the small of her back to propel her into places she had no desire to go to. While pretending, politely, to listen, she could look down on the top of his head, and consider where it was going to thin next.

"Do you think she's nervous?" said Stella. Her hair, glossy as wet varnish, had been pinned back in a chignon. There were no stray hairs to frizz in the damp air, unlike Joy's, which launched a chaotic bid for freedom within minutes of being pinned back. Bei-Lin, her amah, would scowl and tut at Joy when she was pinning it, as if it were due to some deliberate unruliness on Joy's part.

"Who?"

"The princess. I would be. Think of all those people watching."

Stella, resplendent in a red skirt, white blouse, and blue cardigan, especially for the occasion, had displayed what Joy considered a rather unhealthy interest in the Princess Elizabeth for the past weeks, speculating upon her choice of jewels, her outfits, the weight of her crown, even how her new husband was likely to feel jealous about her title, seeing as he didn't get to be king. Joy was beginning to suspect a rather unhumble-subjectlike sense of identification going on.

"Well, they won't all be seeing her. There'll be lots like us, who'll be listening only on the wireless." They both stepped aside to let a car pass, glancing briefly inside to see if it was anyone they knew.

"But she could still get the words wrong. I would. I'm sure I would stutter."

Joy doubted this, as Stella provided the template for just about everything ladylike. Unlike Joy, Stella was the proper height for a young lady, Stella always wore elegant clothes that her Tsim Sha Tsui tailor made up in the latest Paris fashions, Stella never tripped over her feet, or was sulky in front of company, or got tongue-tied talking to the endless line of officers who, passing through, were commandeered to the "receptions" designed to take their minds off their impending arrival at the Korean War. Joy often thought that Stella's public image might have been slightly dented if her ability to belch the entire alphabet had been as visible.

"Do you think we'll have to stay for the whole thing?"

"What, the whole ceremony?" Joy sighed, kicking at a stone. "It's bound to take absolutely hours, and they'll all get tipsy and start talking about one another. And my mother will start flirting with Duncan Alleyne and start on about how William Farqhuarson is related by marriage to the Jardines and has the right sort of prospects for a girl of my standing."

"I should think he's rather short for a girl of your standing." Stella also had wit.

"I've worn my high heels specially."

"Oh, come on, Joy. It's exciting. We're going to get a new Queen."

Joy shrugged.

"Why should I be excited? It's not even as if we live in the same place."

"Because she's still our Queen. She's

almost the same age as us! Imagine! And it's the biggest party for simply ages. Everyone will be there."

"But they're all the same people. It's no fun going to parties if it's always the same people."

"Oh, Joy, you're determined to be miserable. There are lots of new people if you'd just talk to them."

"But I don't have anything to say. They're only interested in shopping and clothes and who's being disgraceful with whom."

"Oh, excuse us," said Stella, archly. "And what else is there?"

"I don't mean you. But you know what I mean. There must be more to life. Don't you ever want to go to America? or England? Or travel the world?"

"I've been. Lots of places." Stella's father was a naval commander. "Frankly, I think people are interested in the same things wherever you go. When we were in Singapore it was just one big blur of cocktail parties. Even Mummy was bored," said Stella. "Anyway, it's not *always* all the same people. There are officers. There'll be lots there today. And I'm sure you won't have met them all."

There were lots of officers. The Brougham Scotts' wide palazzo terrace, which over-looked Hong Kong harbor in the rare moments when the mist at the top of the Peak cleared, was a sea of whites. Inside the house, under fans whirring like huge pro-pellers, Chinese staff also dressed in white topcoats moved silently between them in soft shoes, proffering long iced drinks on sil-ver trays. Murmuring voices rose and fell above the music, which itself seemed muf-fled by the heavy, wet heat. The Union Jack pennants, strung across the ceiling points, hung like wet washing, barely moving despite the contrived breeze.

Pale and luscious, and seemingly as limp, Elvine Brougham Scott was reclining on a damask-clad chaise longue in the corner of the marbled drawing room, surrounded, as was habitual, by a corps of attentive officers. She wore a plum-colored silk dress with a sweetheart neckline and a long, gathered skirt that fell in folds around her long, pale legs. (There were no sweat marks under her arms, noted Joy, pressing her own close to her sides.) One of her shoes—trimmed with a joke ermine—had already been kicked onto the floor below, revealing Elvine's scarlet toenails. Joy knew what her mother would say, when she saw her, while biting back her own frustration at not being Barbara Stanwyck enough to wear it herself. Scarlet Woman lipstick was as close to vampish as Alice got, although it wasn't from lack of longing.

Joy and Stella deposited the song sheets and nodded a hello, knowing Mrs. Brougham Scott would not want to be interrupted. "How will we hear the ceremony?" said Stella, anxiously, glancing around for the wireless. "How will they know when it's begun?"

"Don't worry, my dear, hours to go yet," said Duncan Alleyne, bowing as he passed, in order to check his watch. "Don't forget they're seven hours behind in Blighty." Duncan Alleyne always spoke like the R.A.F. hero in a war film. The girls found it laughable, but Alice, to Joy's disgust, seemed to think it turned her into Celia Johnson.

"Do you know she has to accept "the lively oracles of God?" said Stella, rapturously.

"What?"

"Princess Elizabeth. In the ceremony. She has to accept the "lively oracles of God." Haven't a clue what they are. Oh. And she has four Knights of the Garter attending her.

Do you think they might possibly look after her real garters? She does have a Mistress of the Robes, after all. Betty Warner told me."

Joy stared at the faraway look in Stella's eyes. Why couldn't she feel as transported by the occasion? Why did the thought of the evening ahead fill her only with dread?

"Oh. And you'll never guess. She has her breast anointed with holy oil. Her real breast. I wish it wasn't the wireless so we could see if the Archbishop actually touches it."

"Hello, Joy. Gosh—you look—you look—actually, you look rather warm. Did you have to walk here?" It was William, blushing at his own approach, his hand extended limply in an unconvinced attempt at greeting. "Sorry. Didn't mean—I mean, I walked. Too. And I'm terribly damp. Much damper than you. Look."

Joy swept a tall pink drink from a passing tray, and gulped at it. It wasn't just Princess Elizabeth laying down her life for her country today.

There had been rather a few tall pink drinks by the time coronation hour approached. Joy, who tended to get dehydrated in the humidity, had found the tall pink drinks slipped down rather easily. They didn't taste alcoholic, and her mother's attention had been elsewhere—torn between the rictus Toby Jug grin of Duncan Alleyne, and her fury at her own husband's apparent enjoyment—so it was rather a surprise to her when Princess Elizabeth's face, fixed high on the dining room wall, suddenly multiplied, and appeared to be grinning in complicity at Joy's attempts to walk a straight line.

Over several hours the noise of the party had gradually risen and swollen, filling the hosts' substantial ground floor, their guests' voices greased and elevated by the copious supply of drinks. Joy had grown progressively more withdrawn as the evening had drawn on, lacking the social skills for talking about nothing that these events seemed to require. Joy was apparently good only at losing people, not captivating them. William she had finally shaken off, telling him she was sure Mr. Amery had wanted to talk to him about business. Stella had disappeared, swallowed into a ring of admiring naval officers; Rachel and Jeannie, the other two girls of her age, were seated in a corner with their twin Brylcreemed beaux; and so freed from the opprobrium—or even attention—of her peers, the tall pink drinks and Joy had become rather good friends.

Realizing her glass was somehow empty again, she glanced around for another houseboy. They appeared to have vanished—or maybe it was just that she was finding it hard to distinguish their bodies from anyone else's. They should have all worn Union Jack jackets, she decided, giggling to herself. Union Jackets. Or little crowns.

She was dimly aware of a gong banging, and Mr. Brougham Scott's laughing tenor attempting to summon everybody around the wireless. Joy, leaning briefly against a pillar, waited for the people in front of her to move. When they moved, she would be able to walk out onto the terrace and breathe in the breeze. But at the moment their bodies kept swaying and merging, forming an impossible wall.

"Oh, God," she muttered. "I need some air."

She had thought these words had been spoken only in her head, but a hand suddenly took her arm, and muttered, "Let's get you outside then."

Joy, to her surprise, found she had to look up. (Joy rarely had to look up—she was taller than nearly all the Chinese, and most of the men at the party.) She could just about make out two long, grave faces looming at her, swimming above two tight, white collars. A naval officer. Or two. She couldn't be quite sure. Either way, one of them had her arm and was steering her gently through the crowd toward the balcony.

"Do you want to sit down? Take deep breaths. I'll get you a glass of water." He sat her on a wicker chair and disappeared.

Joy gulped in the clean air, as if it were water. It was getting dark, and the mist had descended on the Peak, shrouding the house from the rest of Hong Kong Island. The only clues that they were not there alone were the distant, rude honking of barges travelling through the waters below, the rustle of nearby banyan trees and a faint waft of garlic and ginger, whispering through the still air.

It was this smell that suddenly did Joy in. "Oh, God," she muttered. "Oh, no . . ."

She glanced behind her, noting with relief that the last of the partygoers were disappearing into the room with the wireless. And then she leaned over the balcony and was lengthily and noisily sick.

When she finally sat up, her chest heaving, and her hair stuck sweatily to her temples, she opened her eyes to find, to her horror, the naval officer standing in front of her proffering a glass of ice water.

Joy couldn't speak. She simply looked at him in mute horror, and then buried her face, now flooded with embarrassment, in her glass. Perhaps, she prayed, suddenly, uncomfortably sober, when she looked up, he would be gone.

"Would you like a handkerchief?"

Joy kept her face down, staring grimly at her too-tall shoes. Something unmentionable was stuck in her throat, refusing to descend despite her repeated attempts to swallow.

"Look. Here. Take it."

"Please go away."

"What?"

"I said, please go away." Oh, God, if she didn't leave soon, her mother would come out to find her, and discover her. And then all hell would break loose; she could hear the chapters ahead: 1. She Was Not Fit to Be Taken Anywhere; 2. The Shame of Her Behavior, or Why Couldn't She Be More Like Stella?; 3. What Would People Think?

"Please. Please just go."

Joy was aware that she sounded rude, but the horror of possible discovery, as well as being stuck there having to make polite conversation while there might be goodness-knows-what splashed on her blouse—on her *face*—made it seem a lesser ill.

There was a lengthy pause. The sound of loud exclamations, overlapping, rose and fell from the dining room.

"I don't think—I think it would be better if somebody kept you company for a bit." It wasn't a young voice, not the excitable braying tones of most of the officers; yet it didn't have the basso profundo of a lengthy association with power. He couldn't be higher than officer rank.

Why doesn't he go? thought Joy.

But he just stood there. His immaculate trousers, she noted, had a small splash of something orange on the left shin.

"Look, I'm much better now, thank you. And I really would rather you left me now. I think I might go home." Her mother would be furious. But she could say she had felt ill. It wouldn't be an outright lie. It was only this man who would know the truth.

"Let me escort you," he said.

There was another buildup of noise from inside, and some high, slightly hysterical laughter. A jazz recording began and ended just as abruptly.

"Please," he said. "Take my hand. I'll help you up."

"Will you please just leave me alone?" This time her voice sounded harsh, even to her own ears. There was a brief silence, and then, after a never-ending, breathless pause, she heard the sound of his footfall on the terrace as he walked slowly indoors.

Joy was too desperate to feel ashamed for long. She stood, took a long draft of the ice water, and then walked briskly, if a little shakily, toward the house. With a bit of luck, she could tell the staff and escape while they were all listening. But as she walked past the doorway of the drawing room, guests were already beginning to filter out. A teary-eyed Stella, the corners of her eyes drawn down in disappointment, was among the first.

"Oh, Joy, can you believe it?"

"What?" said Joy, dumbly, wondering how quickly she could walk past her.

"The bloody, bloody wireless. What a day for it to break. I can't believe they've got only one in the house. Surely everybody's got more than one wireless."

"No need to fret, Stella, dear," said Duncan Alleyne, one hand fingering his mustache, the other lingering on Stella's shoulder just a little too long for his professed brand of paternal interest. "It won't take long for one of the men to go and fetch one from the Marchants' house. You'll hardly miss a thing."

"But we'll miss the whole beginning. And we'll never get to hear it again. There probably won't even be another coronation in our lifetime. Oh, I can't believe it." Stella was properly crying now, oblivious to the guests around her, some of whom had evidently regarded the sacred ceremony of kings as a rather irritating interruption to a perfectly good party.

"Stella—I've got to go," Joy whispered. "I'm really sorry. I'm not well."

"But you can't—at least stay until they've got the wireless."

"I'll call for you tomorrow." Swiftly, seeing that her parents were still in the group that sat unnoticing around the dead wireless, Joy ran for the door. Nodding briefly to the boy who let her out, Joy was out, alone in the damp night air, with only the whining dive-bomb of the mosquitoes to keep her company, and the faintest of misgivings about the man she had left behind.

The expatriates of Hong Kong were used to living well, with an almost nightly schedule of drinks and dinners, so it was not uncommon for there to be few *gweilo* faces around first thing in the morning. But Joy, whose unfortunate accident with the pink drinks had left her feeling remarkably clearheaded on waking, found herself in the rare position of being a minority of one.

It was as if the whole of the Peak were suffering a hangover. While pairs of Chinese men and women trod softly past, some bearing heavy baskets or dragging trailers of rubbish, there was not a white person to be seen. Outside the white-painted houses, set back from the road, streams of colored bunting hung apologetically, and pictures of the smiling princess curled from windows, looking themselves exhausted from the excesses of the night before.

Padding around the teak-floored apartment, both she and Bei-Lin communicating in whispers (neither wanted to wake Alice

and Graham, whose feverish, rambling arguments had stretched long into the early
hours), she had decided the only thing for it
was a trip to the New Territories so that she
could go riding. Everyone would be spiky-
headed and miserable today; and the wet
heat pressed down harder than ever, magni-
fying hangover headaches, and ensuring
that the day would be spent in a bad-
tempered torpor, stretched out under fans
on the soft furnishings. It was not a day to be
in town. The problem Joy faced was that this
was the one morning in which there was no
one around to take her out of it.

She had walked to Stella's at around ten,
but the curtains had been drawn, and she
hadn't liked to call in. Her own father, who
could usually be relied upon to drive his
princess, would be unlikely to rise before
midday. Not having many friends, there was
no one else she felt comfortable calling
upon. Seated on a wicker chair by the window, Joy toyed with the idea of taking a tram
to the center of town, and then catching a
train, but she had never done it alone and
Bei-Lin had refused to accompany her,
knowing that the mistress would be in an
even fouler temper if she awoke to find the

help had gone off on a "jaunt." "Oh, God save the bloody Queen," muttered Joy at her retreating back.

Not for the first time, Joy felt mutinous at the restrictions of her life, both geographical and physical. In the short time she and her mother had lived in Australia, shortly after the Japanese had invaded and the women and children had left the colony, Joy had found herself the recipient of unheard-of freedoms. They had stayed with Alice's sister, Marcelle, the doors of whose beachfront house had seemed permanently open, free for Joy to walk out, and for a variety of neighbors, all of whom seemed so relaxed and cheerful compared with those in Hong Kong, to walk in.

Alice had been relaxed there, too, had blossomed in the dry heat, where everyone spoke her language and the tall, bronzed men flirted disgracefully. There, Alice's manners had been the peak of refinement, her clothes so far beyond anything they had seen, and she could appear as she had wanted to appear: chic, cosmopolitan, exotic by way of her exile. Plus, Marcelle was younger than Alice, and enjoyably deferential in all matters of taste and style. This elevated sense of goodwill had meant that Alice had been much less "bothered" by Joy than usual, had waved her off to the beach or to the mall with barely a backward look, unlike in Hong Kong, where she was permanently preoccupied with the deficiencies of Joy's appearance, manners, and the potential dangers, in an uncivilized country, of letting her out on her own.

"I hate my life," she said out loud, letting her thoughts flood out and hang, like brooding clouds, in the air before her.

"Ma'am?"

It was Bei-Lin, standing in the doorway. "There is a gentleman to see you."

"For my mother?"

"No, ma'am. He ask for you." She grinned, meaningfully.

"You'd better show him in."

Frowning, Joy smoothed back her hair and stood. Company was the last thing she wanted.

The door opened, and in walked a man she had never seen before, dressed in a white, short-sleeved shirt, and cream-colored trousers. He had short, neatly cut, reddish hair, a longish, patrician face, and pale blue eyes. He was also tall, and stooped unnecessarily, seemingly out of habit, as he came through the door. Naval, she thought, abstractly. They always stooped through doorways.

"Miss Leonard." He held a straw hat in front of him, clutching it with both hands.

Joy looked blankly. She couldn't work out how he might know her name.

"I'm Edward Ballantyne—sorry if this is an imposition. I just wanted—I just thought I'd see how you were."

Joy gazed at his face, and suddenly flushed with appalled recognition. She had seen that face only in duplicate before. Her hand rose unconsciously to her mouth.

"I took the liberty of asking your friend your name and address. I just wanted to make sure you got home safely. I felt rather guilty about letting you go on your own."

"Oh, no," said Joy, looking determinedly down at her feet. "I was fine. You're very kind," she added, after a pause, aware that she was being rude.

They stood for some minutes, until Joy realized uncomfortably that he wasn't going to offer to leave. She felt so uncomfortable that her skin had begun to prickle. She had never been so embarrassed as she had been last night, and now it was repeating on her, like a too-strong taste. Why couldn't he just leave her alone? Leave her to her private humiliation? Bei-Lin kept loitering anxiously in the doorway, but Joy studiously ignored her, damned if she was going to offer him a drink.

"Actually," he said, after a lengthy pause, "I was wondering whether you would like to go for a walk. Or a game of tennis. Our commander has been given special permission to use some courts down by Causeway Bay."

"No, thank you."

"Perhaps I could ask you to show me some of the local sights? I've never been to Hong Kong before."

"I'm very sorry, but I was just on my way out," said Joy, who found she still couldn't look at him.

There was a long pause. He was definitely staring at her. She could feel it.

"Anywhere nice?"

"What?" Joy felt her heart thumping against her chest. Why wouldn't he go?

"You said you were going out. I just wondered . . . well, where?"

"I'm going riding."

"Riding?" Here she looked up, hearing the

eagerness in his voice. "Are there horses here?"

"Not here," she said. "Not on the island, anyway. In the New Territories. A friend of my father's runs a stables up there."

"Would you mind if I tagged along? I ride a bit back home. Miss it terribly. In fact, I haven't seen a horse for nine months."

He said it in the wistful way that most servicemen talked about their families. His whole face, she realized, had sort of opened out, all the rather severe planes of it softening and lifting. He was, she had to admit, terrifically handsome, in a grown-up sort of way.

But he had watched her disgracing herself over the balcony.

"I've got a car. I could drive you. Or, just follow you, if that was more—er—convenient."

Joy knew her mother was bound to be horrified when Bei-Lin told her that Miss Joy had disappeared in a car with a strange man, but the aftershocks probably wouldn't be that much worse than if she had stayed under her feet all day, providing a verbal punching bag for Alice's hangover. And there was something rather delicious about skimming along the quiet roads with this strange, tall, freckled man, who, rather than making her feel awkward and clumsy with words, as most officers did, simply talked and talked himself, about his horses in Ireland (curiously, he didn't have an Irish accent), the wildness of the hunting country where he lived, and, by contrast, the endless claustrophobic boredom of being confined to ship, stuck in the same tiny world, with the same people, for months and months at a time.

She had never heard a man talk as he talked, free of the endless clipped observations that characterized most of the officers she spoke to. Edward's speech was uncluttered and frank. He spoke like someone deprived of language for a long time, whole sentences coming out in gasps, like a drowning man gulping at air, and his laughter punctuated his sentences with huge, bellied guffaws. Then periodically he would stop, glance at her as if embarrassed by his own lack of reticence, and be quiet until the next thought bubbled out of him.

Joy found herself laughing, too, at first shyly, her own self gradually liberated by this strange man, so that by the time they arrived at the stables she was glowing and giggling in a way totally alien to her. After a forty-minute absence, Alice would not have recognized this daughter at all. In fact, Joy hardly recognized her, sneaking glances at the man next to her, averting her eyes coyly when he met hers, generally behaving—well—like Stella.

Mr. Foghill said he would let him ride. Joy had been secretly hoping he would, and once Edward had stood in the small yard with him, talking in reverent tones of great hunters he had known, and agreeing on the evident superiority of Irish bloodstock over English, the little widower had lost all his initial stiffness, and even recommended his own horse, a towering young chestnut with a crafty buck. He had demanded Edward take him around the manège for a couple of circuits, just to check on his seat and hands, but what he saw evidently satisfied him, for they were then riding slowly out of the gates, and up the road toward the open country.

By this stage, Joy didn't know what had come over her. She found it impossible to stop smiling, and nodding, and yet was struggling to properly hear anything he said, above this unfamiliar pounding in her ears. She was grateful to be able to hold on to the reins, and legitimately gaze at the long gray neck in front of her, stooping and rising in time with the sound of hoof fall, because she couldn't quite concentrate on anything. She felt simultaneously distant from everything around her, and acutely aware of the smallest thing. Like his hands. And his freckles. And the way he got two lines in the side of his jaw when he smiled. She didn't even notice when the mosquitoes zoomed in back on her neck, trapping themselves under her tied-back hair, and feasting on pale and tender flesh.

Best of all, he could ride. Properly ride, in that he sat tall and relaxed in the saddle, his hands moving gently backward and forward so that his reins didn't pull back against the horse's mouth, one occasionally reaching forward to stroke, or to bat an unsuspecting fly away. Joy had been to the stables only with one other man she had liked, a shy banker friend of her father's, and her fragile crush had dissipated like smoke on the wind when she saw him lurching around on the horse's back, unable to hide his fear when the horse moved into a slow trot. William she didn't even want to bring near. There was nothing to put you off a man like seeing him on a horse. It was only now, however, that Joy realized the potent appeal of a man who could ride well.

"Ever been to Scotland?" said Edward.

"What?"

"These mosquitoes. They're like midges," he said, slapping the back of his own neck. "Bite you anywhere."

Joy blushed and looked down. They rode on.

The sky grew darker, and sank lower, so that Joy was unsure whether it was the damp air or sweat soaking her clothes and making stray pieces of grass and seeds stick to her skin. The atmosphere seemed to muffle everything, cloaking the sound of the horses' hooves as if they were wrapped in flannel, enclosing them both in a warm, wet blanket. Above them, high against the backdrop of Lion Mountain, even the buzzards seemed to hang in the air like black drops of moisture, as if movement itself were too much of an effort, while the leaves that brushed against her boots left trails of water, despite the lack of rain.

If he noticed her thoughts careering chaotically, or picked up on the fact that she blushed repeatedly, found it hard to speak, or that her horse kept taking advantage of her absentmindedness to snatch the odd mouthful of shrubbery, he said nothing. She became more composed when they cantered along a bridle path alongside a paddy field, and again when he pulled up at a roadside shack in order to get her a quarter of watermelon, but it was apparent only in that she could now gaze at him without embarrassment. It was at this point that she realized her ribbon had come out, and that her hair hung in ungroomed, sweaty strands around her shoulders. But if he noticed that, he didn't show it, either, and merely reached out, as he handed her his handkerchief, in order to push a piece away from her face. She felt the shock of that touch electrify her skin for minutes after.

"You know, Joy, I've had the best time," he said, meditatively, as they walked the horses back toward the yard. "You don't know what it's meant to me, being able to ride."

Joy was conscious that at some point she was going to have to speak, but she felt that if she opened her mouth, she would say something gauche and inappropriate, or, worse, that she would somehow reveal this strange, aching longing that had sprung out of nowhere. If she said nothing, what was the worst he could think of her?

"I don't know many girls who can ride, either. At home, the girls in my village are, shall we say, a little on the beefy side. Village girls. Not the kind I'd normally ride with, anyway. And wherever we dock, the only ones I meet want to go to cocktail parties and be witty, and to be honest I'm not much cop at all that stuff. I had a girl once—and she was a bit like you—but she . . . well. That's all gone. And I haven't met anyone who I could actually relax with for an absolute age."

Oh, but Joy wanted to kiss him. I know, I know, she wanted to shout. I feel that way, too. I feel all the things you feel. But she just smiled and nodded, sneaking glances at him from under her wet hair, simultaneously berating herself for her sudden transformation into the kind of girl she had always despised. She didn't know what she wanted in a man (it had never occurred to her that it was up to her to do the wanting), and now she found herself drawn to him not because of specific qualities, but because of a whole list of negatives: his ability not to make her feel awkward; the fact that he didn't look like a sack of rice on a horse; his tendency not to look at her as though he wished she were someone else. Something swelled and grew in Joy; it was bigger than nausea, but just as incapacitating.

"Thank you. Anyway. Because I've had the best time." he rubbed at his head, so that his hair stood up in front, and looked away from her. "And I know you didn't really want me to come."

Joy stared at him in horror as he said this, but now it was he who looked ahead. She couldn't think of a way of conveying that he had misunderstood, that it was the being-sick thing that she had been running from, not him, without bringing it all back again, and she didn't want him to remember her for that. Oh, where was Stella when she needed her? She always knew how to talk to men. By the time she had decided that a short denial was the best response, it was some-how too late, and they were heading back toward the yard, their horses' heads stretched long and low in front of them, nod-ding wearily as they headed home.

Edward offered to help put the horses away, and Mr. Foghill suggested she might like to refresh herself in the ladies' rest room. On sight of her reflection, she realized that he had been being solicitous. She looked a fright. Her hair was a frizzy, wet tangle, a hair ball in a bathplug. When she tried to run her fingers through it, they halted only inches from her scalp. Her face was both sweaty with humidity and smeared with dust from the trail, and there were green spittle marks on her white shirt, where her horse had attempted to rub his head on her after she had dismounted. She rubbed furiously at her face with a wet hand towel, almost in tears at her inability to remember something as simple as a comb, or spare ribbon. Stella would never have forgotten something like that. But when she walked out, Edward merely greeted her with a broad smile, as if there were nothing remiss in her appearance. It was then that she noticed his own trousers were streaked with sweat and red dirt, clean only from the shin down, where Mr. Foghill had lent him a pair of boots.

"Your carriage awaits," he said, grinning at his own appearance. "You'll need to direct me back. I haven't a clue where we are."

Edward was a little quieter on the way home, and Joy felt her own silence more acutely. She could issue directions, but, despite the ease she felt in his company, could still not muster up anything interesting to say. It would all feel somehow shallow, when what she wanted to convey was that in the space of four short hours he had shifted her very world off its axis. In his eyes she saw other lands, green fields and hunting dogs, eccentric villagers, and a world devoid of cocktail parties. In his voice, she heard a speech free from artifice, and cleverness, continents away from the mannered, mon-eyed language of the Hong Kong expat. In his broad, freckled hands, she saw horses and kindnesses and something else that made her stomach constrict with longing.

"I wish I could have met you sooner," he was saying, his voice carrying away from her in the wind.

"What? What did you say?" Joy put her hand up to her ear.

"I said I wish I could have met you sooner." He slowed the car, so that she could hear better. A car full of naval officers tore past them, honking a lewd greeting. "I—I—oh, I don't know. It's just pretty galling that I leave the day after tomorrow."

A chill ran through Joy's heart. She could feel every vein turn to ice. "What? What do you mean?"

"We sail in two days. I've got one more day of shore leave, and then we've got to head for Korean waters."

Joy could not hide the expression of horror on her face. This was too cruel. To have found someone—to have found him—and for him to leave so soon.

"For how long?" Her voice, when it came out, was small and tremulous. It didn't sound like hers. Edward turned to look at her, caught something in her face, and turned back to the wheel, signaling that he was about to pull over.

"I don't think we're coming back here," he said, gazing back at her. "We do our bit with the Yanks in Korean waters, and then we're headed for New York. We'll be at sea for months." He was gazing right into her eyes, as he said this, seemingly imparting something of the impossibility of connections when one is always on the move.

Joy felt like her head was going to explode. Her hands, she noted, had begun to tremble. It was like being given the key to a prison cell, only to find it was made of rubber. She realized, with dismay, that she was going to cry.

"I can't," she said quietly, biting at her lip.

"What?" Edward had reached over, so that his hand was resting very close to her own.

"I can't just let you go. I can't let you go." She said it loudly, this time, her eyes meeting his full on. Even as she spoke, she couldn't quite believe what she was saying, the sheer inappropriateness, as a young woman of her upbringing, of her own words. But they felt unstoppable, came fully formed out of her mouth like solid, warm pebbles, falling like offerings before him.

There was a long, electrifying pause, during which she thought she might die. Then Edward took her hand. His was warm, dry.

"I didn't think you liked me," he said.

"I've never liked anyone. I mean, I never liked anyone before. I never felt comfortable with anyone before." She was gabbling now, the words tumbling unchecked, but he didn't pull away. "I find it so hard to talk to people. And there aren't people here whom I really want to talk to. Except Stella. My friend, that is. And when you came this morning I was so embarrassed about what happened last night that it was easier to get you to go away than it was to be nice to you. But when you stayed, and we went in the car, and everything, I never felt like that. I never felt like I wasn't being judged. Like I could just sit, and that person would understand."

"I thought you were hungover," he laughed. But she was too intense, too brimful of emotion to laugh with him.

"Everything you've said today I've agreed with. There's nothing you've said that I haven't felt myself. I mean obviously not the hunting and stuff, because I've never been. But all the things you said about cocktail parties and people and liking horses better sometimes and not minding if people think you're a bit odd, well, that's me, too. That's me. It's like listening to my own thoughts. So I can't. I can't let you leave. And if you're horrified by what I've said and you think I'm the most embarrassing, forward creature you've ever met, then I still don't care, because it's the only time I've felt like I was really being true to myself in my entire life."

Two heavy, salty tears had begun a slow pathway down Joy's flushed cheeks, weighted by the emotion behind what was certainly the longest speech of her adult life. She gulped, trying to keep them in check, both appalled and exhilarated by what she had done. She had laid herself prostrate before this man whom she didn't know, in a manner her mother, and probably Stella, too, would have found certifiable. And when she had told him she didn't care, it was not true. If he turned from her now, uttered some polite platitude about what a lovely day he had had and how no doubt she must be feeling exhausted, she would hold herself in until she got home and then find some way of just, well, killing herself. Because there was no way she could bear skating the trite surface of her existence when she had dipped below, and found something cool, and calming, and deep. Say you at least understand what I'm saying then, she willed. Even if you just say you understand, that will be enough for me.

There was a long, painful silence. Another car roared by, accelerating as it passed them.

"I suppose we'd better go back then," he said, placing his hand back on the wheel, and using the other to shift the stiff gear stick.

Joy's face froze, and slowly, imperceptibly, her body shrank back into the passenger seat, her spine so brittle that it was likely to crack. So she had gotten it wrong. Of course she had. Whatever had made her think that an outburst like that could win a man's respect, let alone his heart?

"I'm sorry," she whispered, her head falling toward her chest. "I'm so sorry."

Oh, God, but she was such a fool.

"For what?" said Edward, his hand reaching over and pushing back her damp curtain of hair. "I want to talk to your father."

Joy looked at him blankly. Was he going to tell him that she was a fool?

"Look," he said, cupping her face with his hand. It smelled of sweat. And horse. "I know you'll probably think this is a bit sudden. But, Joy, if you'll have me, I want to ask him about us getting married."

You don't possibly think we're going to say yes, do you?" said her mother, her face illuminated by horror and astonishment that her daughter had managed to elicit such strength of feeling from any man. (Her bad humor had been exacerbated by the fact that they had arrived back before she had had time to put her face on.) "We don't even know him."

She spoke as if he weren't even in the room.

"I'll tell you anything you want to know,

Mrs. Leonard," said Edward, his long, dirty-trousered legs stretched out in front of him.

Joy eyed them with the stunned joy of new possession. She had spent the remainder of the journey in a daze, laughing out loud and half-hysterically at the madness of what they had just done. She didn't know him! He didn't know her! And yet they had grinned at each other with this kind of manic complicity, holding hands awkwardly, and she had willingly launched her life into his grasp. She hadn't expected to find *anyone*. Hadn't even thought of looking. But he seemed to know what he was doing, and he seemed much more likely to know what was right than she was. And he hadn't been remotely fazed by the prospect of putting this insanity to her parents.

Edward took a deep breath, and began reeling off the facts. "My father is a retired judge, and he and my mother have moved to Ireland, where they breed horses. I've got a sister and a brother, both married, both older than I am. I'm twenty-nine years old, I've been in the navy for almost eight years, since I left university, and I have a private trust on top of my naval salary."

The slight wrinkling of her mother's nose at the mention of Ireland had been counterbalanced by the words "private trust." But it was her father's face Joy gazed at, desperately searching for some sign of approval.

"It's awfully sudden. I don't see why you can't wait."

"Do you think you love her?" Her father, leaning back in his chair, his gin and tonic in hand, stared at Edward. Joy flushed. It seemed almost obscene, him saying it out loud like that.

Edward looked at her for a long time, and then took her hand, making her color again. No man had ever even touched her in front of her parents.

"I don't know if either of us could call it love yet," he said slowly, almost addressing Joy. "But I'm not young and foolish; I've met lots of girls, and I know as surely as I know anything that Joy is unlike anyone I've ever met."

"You can say that again," muttered her mother.

"All I can say is I think I can make her happy. If I had longer, I would be able put your mind at rest. But, the fact is, I've got to sail pretty well straightaway."

It didn't occur to Joy to question the speed of his feelings. She was simply fiercely grateful that they appeared to match the strength of her own. Still reeling from the fact that someone had called her unique in a *good* way, it took her some minutes to realize that his hand had started to sweat.

"It's too soon, Graham. Tell them. They don't even know each other."

Joy caught the brightness in her mother's eyes, the agitation behind them. She's jealous, she thought suddenly. She's jealous because she's disappointed in her own life and she can't bear the thought that someone might be about to sweep me out of mine.

Her father stared at Edward for a while longer, as if working something out. Edward held his gaze.

"Well, they do things faster these days," said Graham, motioning to Bei-Lin to fetch some more drinks. "You remember what it was like in the war, Alice."

Joy had to fight to suppress a little thrill of excitement. She squeezed Edward's hand and felt the faintest of returns.

Her father drained his glass. He appeared to be momentarily absorbed in something outside the window.

"So, say I said yes, young man. What would you plan to do about it in thirty-six hours?"

"We want to get married," said Joy, breathlessly. She felt able to speak now that it seemed they were only arguing over timing.

Her father didn't appear to hear her. He was talking to Edward.

"I'll respect your wishes, sir."

"Then I'll say you have my blessing. To get engaged."

Joy's heart leapt. And fell. "You can marry when you're next on shore leave."

There was a stunned silence in the room. Joy, fighting back disappointment, was dimly aware of the shuffling sound of Bei-Lin, behind the door, rushing off to tell the cook. Her mother was staring at her and back at her father. What would people think?

"If you're serious about each other, then it won't hurt to wait. You can buy the ring, make all the announcements, and then get married later." Her father put his glass heavily down on the lacquered table, as if signifying that judgment had been passed.

Joy turned to look at Edward, who was letting out a slow, deep breath. Please disagree, she willed. Tell him you've got to marry me now. Take me away on your big gray ship.

But Edward said nothing.

Gazing at him, Joy experienced the first thrill of disappointment in her new partner, the first microcosmic, bitter recognition that the man in whom she placed her highest hopes, her greatest trust, might not be entirely what she had hoped.

"When will that be?" she said, trying to keep the tremor from her voice. "When do you think you'll be off your ship?"

"Our next proper stop is New York," he said, almost apologetically. "But, that won't be for around nine months. It might even be a year."

Joy sat upright, and glanced around at her mother, who appeared to have relaxed. She was almost smiling, a patronizing smile, the kind of smile that said, Oh, young people—they might think they're in love, but let's see what happens six months down the line. Alice wanted to be proven right, Joy realized, feeling cold. She wanted the affirmation that true love didn't exist, that everyone ended up in marriages as miserable as her own. Well, if they thought this was going to put her off they were wrong.

"Then I'll see you in nine months," she said to the blue eyes of her new fiancé, try-

ing to convey as much certainty into her own
as she knew she felt. "Just—just write."

The door opened.

"God save the Queen!" said Bei-Lin,
entering with a tray of drinks.

Chapter One

October 1997

Kate's windscreen wipers finally gave up just outside Fishguard, sticking, and then sliding resignedly down toward the bonnet, at the exact moment that the rain, which had been satisfied with simply heavy, chose to become torrential.

"Oh, bugger," she said, swerving as she flicked the dashboard switch up and down. "I can't see a thing. Sweetheart, if I pull over at the next lay by, could you reach your arm out and give the screen a wipe?"

Sabine pulled her knees up into her chest

and scowled at her mother. "It's not going to make the slightest difference. We might as well just stop."

Kate pulled the car to a stop and wound down her window, trying to wipe her own half with the end of her velvet scarf. "Well, we can't stop. We're running late. And I can't have you missing the ferry."

Her mother was a generally mild-mannered soul, but Sabine knew that note of steel in Kate's voice, and knew that it said nothing short of a tsunami was going to prevent Sabine getting on that ferry. It was not a huge surprise; it was a note she had come up against many times in the past three weeks, but having to hear yet another reinforcement of her ultimate powerlessness in the face of her mother made Sabine's lower lip jut unconsciously, and her body turn away in mute protest.

Kate, finely tuned to her daughter's mercurial moods, glanced over, noted it, and looked away. "You know, if you weren't so busy being determined to hate this, you might just have a good time."

"How can I have a good time? You're sending me to a place I've been to all of twice in my whole life, to stay in Bog City, with a grandmother you like so much you haven't seen her in bloody years, basically to be some kind of domestic skivvy while my grandfather pops his clogs. Great. Some holiday. I'm just gagging for it."

"Oh, look. They're working again. Let's see if we can make it to the port." Kate wrenched the wheel, and the battered Volkswagen lurched forward onto the wet road, sending tea-colored fans of spray up at each side window. "Look. We don't know that your grandfather is that ill; he's just frail, apparently. And I just think it will be good for you to get away from London for a bit. You've hardly met your granny at all, and it will be nice for you to see a bit of each other before she gets too old, or you go traveling, or whatever."

Sabine stared determinedly out of her side window.

"Granny. You make it sound like Happy Families."

"And I know she's ever so grateful for the help."

Still she refused to look. She knew bloody well why she was being shipped off to Ireland, and her mother knew it, and if she was such a bloody hypocrite that she wasn't going to admit it, then she couldn't expect Sabine to be straight with her, either.

"Left lane," she said, still not turning around.

"What?"

"Left lane. You need to be in the left lane for the ferry terminal. Oh, for God's sake, Mum, why can't you just wear your bloody glasses?"

Kate wrenched the little car into the left lane, ignoring the beeps of protest behind her, and, under Sabine's bad-tempered direction, eased it over to the windswept sign that indicated foot passengers. She drove until she could see a place to park, a gray, windswept tarmac desert, in the shadow of a featureless gray Lubyanka. Why do they make offices look so dispiriting? she thought, absently. As if people weren't already miserable enough when they got there. When the car and its wipers stopped again, the rain obligingly ensured that it was swiftly erased, turning everything outside into an impressionistic blur.

Kate, for whom most things without her glasses were an impressionistic blur, gazed at the outline of her daughter and wished suddenly that they could have the kind of fond farewells that she was sure other mothers and daughters practiced. She wanted to tell her she was bitterly sorry that Geoff was going, and that for the third time in her young life their domestic arrangements were going to be in upheaval. She wanted to tell her that she was sending her to Ireland to protect her, to save her from witnessing the kind of bitter scenes that she and Geoff had barely been suppressing as they ended their six-year relationship; and she wanted to tell her that even though she and her own mother no longer had any kind of relationship, Kate unselfishly wanted her to feel like she had some kind of grandmother, someone other than just her.

But Sabine always made it impossible for her to say anything, was seemingly covered in an ever-growing coat of spikes, like a glamorous, sulky little porcupine. If she told her she loved her she was told off for being so *Little House on the Prairie.* If she reached out to hug her, she felt her child visibly flinch in her arms. How did this come about? she repeatedly asked herself. I was so determined that our relationship would be different, that you would have all the freedoms I was denied. That we would be friends. How did you come to despise me?

Kate had become an expert at hiding her apparently odious feelings from her daughter. Sabine hated it even more if she got needy and emotional; it just made her even more prickly. So instead she reached into her overflowing basket-bag and handed over her tickets, as well as what she considered a generous amount of spending money. Sabine didn't even acknowledge it.

"Now, the crossing will take around three hours. It looks like it might be a bit rough, but I'm afraid I didn't bring anything for seasickness. You'll get into Rosslare at around four-thirty, and your granny will meet you at the information desk. Do you want me to write any of that down?"

"I think I can just about remember 'information desk,'" said Sabine, dryly.

"Well, if anything does go wrong, I've put the phone numbers for the house on the back of the ticket holder. And ring me when you get there. Just so I know you've arrived."

Making sure the coast is clear, thought Sabine, bitterly. Her mother must really think she was stupid. She must really think she didn't know what was going on. There had been so many times in the past few weeks where she had wanted to scream at her, I *know*, you know. I know about why you and Geoff are splitting up. I know about you and Justin bloody Stewartson. And that's why you're shipping me out of the way for a few weeks, so you can carry on your disgusting little affair with both me and Geoff gone.

But, somehow, despite all her anger, she had never quite had the appetite for it. Because her mother had just seemed too sad, too droopily miserable about it all. Still, if she thought she was going to go quietly, she had another thought coming.

They sat in the car for a few minutes. Periodically, the rain would ease, and they would get a glimpse of the unlovely terminal in front of them, but then it would beat down again, turning the picture into a watercolor bleed.

"So, will Geoff be gone when I get back?" Sabine lifted her chin as she said this, so that it sounded more defiant than inquiring.

Kate gazed at her.

"Probably," she said, slowly. "But you can still see him anytime you want."

"Like I could see Jim anytime I wanted."

"You were a lot younger then, darling. And it got complicated because Jim got a new family."

"No, it got complicated because I got one bloody stepfather after another."

Kate's hand stretched out to her daughter's arm. Why did no one tell you that childbirth was the easiest pain?

"I'd better go," muttered Sabine, opening the car door. "I wouldn't want to miss my ferry."

"Let me walk you over to the terminal," said Kate, tears stinging at her eyes.

"Don't bother," said Sabine, and with the hollow slam of the door, Kate was alone.

It was a rough crossing, rough enough for the screaming children to whiz up and down the carpeted walkway on stolen dinner trays, while their parents slid comfortably backward and forward along plastic-covered benches, drinking from cans of Red Stripe and occasionally breaking into noisy explosions of laughter. Others queued, staggering, for overpriced chips at the cafeteria, ignoring the salads wilting under cling film, or played the slot machines that broadcast jangles and sirens alongside the stairs.

Judging by the number of families, and the resolute postponing of hangovers, the Sunday afternoon crossing was popular among weekend trippers.

Sabine sat in a window seat, her personal stereo closeting her from all the irritating people around her. They seemed to be grown from the same stock as the people she saw in motorway services, or supermarkets. People who didn't care that much what they wore; whether their haircuts were so last year; whether the way they sat or spoke was likely to be embarrassing. This is what Ireland is going to be like, she told herself grimly, above the bass-heavy sound of her CD. Backward. Culture-free. An anticool zone.

For the millionth time, she cursed her mother for this exile, this removal from her friends, her manor, her normal life. It was going to be a nightmare. She had nothing in common with these people, her grandparents were virtual strangers, she was leaving Dean Baxter to the evil clutches of Amanda Gallagher just at the point where she thought she was getting somewhere with him, and, worst of all, she wouldn't even have her mobile phone or computer to keep in touch. (Even she had to admit that her computer was too large to transport, while her mother had told her that if she thought she was going to pay to have an "international call" facility on her already overspent mobile, then "she had another thing coming." Why did they say that? If she had told her mother she should thing again, her mother would have started on about how she should have sent her to private school.)

So she was not only to be exiled, but without even the comforts of phone or e-mail. But even as she sat staring grimly at the churning Irish Sea, Sabine allowed herself the smallest sense of relief that she wasn't going to have to be party to the endless tensions of her mother and Geoff slowly and painfully unthreading their domestic web.

She had known it was going to happen before even Geoff had. She had known from the afternoon she came down from her room and heard her mother whispering into the phone. "I know. I want to see you, too. But you know he's impossible at the moment. And I don't want to make things worse."

She had stood, frozen on the stairs, and then coughed loudly, so that her mother put the phone down suddenly and guiltily, and then said, too brightly, when she walked into the living room: "Oh, it's you sweetheart! I didn't hear you out there! I was just thinking, What shall we have for supper?"

Her mother didn't cook supper. She was a useless cook. It was Geoff's job.

And then she had met *him*. Justin Stewartson. Photographer on a left-leaning national newspaper. A man so full of his own sense of self-importance that he had caught the tube rather than travel in her mother's battered car. A man who thought he was *it* because he wore a leather jacket that might have been cool about five years ago, and khaki-colored trousers with desert boots. He had tried too hard to talk to Sabine, throwing in comments about underground bands that he thought she would know, trying to sound both cynical and knowledgeable about the music business. She had given him what she hoped was a withering look. She knew why he was trying to be friendly, and it wouldn't wash. And men over thirty-five could never be cool, not even if they thought they knew about music.

Poor old Geoff. Poor fusty old Geoff. He had sat at home, brow furrowed as he worried night after night about patients whom he couldn't get sectioned, ringing around all the psychiatric units in central London in an effort to stop some other nutter ending up on the streets. He hadn't had a bloody clue. And her mother had merely drifted in and out distantly, pretending to sound as if she cared, until the day that Sabine came downstairs and it was obvious that he knew, because he gave her one of those long searching glances, like, "Did you know? Et tu, Brute?" It was difficult to fool Geoff, because of his psychiatric training. So when she stared back at him, she tried to convey some sense of sympathy, some sense of disapproval at her mother's pathetic actions.

She didn't let either of them know how hard she had cried. Geoff had been irritating, and a bit earnest, and she had never let him think he was a dad of sorts. But he had been kind, and he had cooked, and kept Mum sane, and he had been around since she was a kid. Longer than any of the others, in fact. Besides, the thought of Mum and Justin Stewartson *doing it* made her want to vomit.

The announcement that Rosslare was now a few minutes away came at just after four-thirty. Sabine slid out of her seat and made her way to the foot passengers' disembarkment point, trying to ignore the little flutter of nervousness in her stomach. She had traveled alone only once before, and that had been a disastrous "holiday" flight out to join Jim, her mother's previous live-in partner, in Spain. He had wanted to reassure her that she was still family. Her mother had wanted to reassure her that she still had a father of sorts. The British Airways stewardess had wanted to reassure her that she was obviously a "very big girl" to be traveling alone. But even from the moment Jim had met her at the airport, with his heavily pregnant, wary-eyed new girlfriend trailing in his wake, she had known it was going to be a disaster. She had seen him only once after that, when he had "tried to get her involved" with the new baby. The girlfriend had looked at her like she wanted her to get as uninvolved as possible. She didn't blame her, really. The baby wasn't a blood relative, after all. And she wouldn't have wanted some kid from a previous relationship hanging around like a lost soul.

The doors opened, and Sabine found herself transported along the walkway, hemmed in on all sides by chattering people. She wondered about putting her earphones back on, but she was secretly afraid of missing some vital announcement. The last thing she wanted was to have to ring her mother and tell her she had gotten it wrong.

She glanced around her, wondering what her grandmother was going to look like. The most recent picture she had of her was taken more than ten years earlier, when she had last been to the Irish house. She had only the most distant memories of it, but the picture showed a dark-haired woman, high-boned and handsome, smiling reservedly down at her as she patted a small gray pony.

What if I don't recognize her? she thought, anxiously. Was she likely to be offended? Her birthday and Christmas cards were always short and formal, not the kind of writing to suggest a sense of humor. From the little her mother said it was all too easy to do the wrong thing.

Then she spotted him. Standing, leaning against a desk that may or may not have been the information point, holding up a piece of card with the word "Sabine" on it. He was medium height, wiry-looking, with thick, dark hair cut close against his head. Probably the same age as her mother. He also, she noted as she walked slowly over, had only one arm. The other extended into a semiclawed plastic hand, in the kind of unrelaxed pose more commonly seen on shop display dummies.

She put her hand unconsciously to her hair, checking that it hadn't flattened too much on the journey, and then walked over, trying to muster as much insouciance as she could.

"You've changed, Granny."

He had looked at her quizzically as she approached, as if assessing whether he had the right girl. Now he smiled, and held out his good hand. This involved putting the card on the desk first.

"Sabine. I'm Thom. You're older than I thought. Your grandma said you would be . . ." He shook his head. "Well. She couldn't come because the Duke's got the vet in. So I'm your chauffeur."

"The Duke?" she said.

He had the kind of lilting Irish accent she thought only existed in television series. Her grandmother didn't have an Irish accent at all. She tried not to look at the plastic hand. It had the waxy complexion of something dead.

"The old horse. Her boy. He's got a problem with his leg. And she doesn't like anyone else looking after him. But she said she'll see you at the house."

So her grandmother, whom she hadn't seen for nearly ten years, had chosen not to come and meet her but to look after some mangy horse. Sabine felt her eyes prick unexpectedly with tears. Well, that told her all she needed to know about how her visit was viewed.

"She's a bit odd over him," said Thom, carefully, as he took her bag from her. "I wouldn't read anything into it. I know she's looking forward to seeing you."

"Some way of showing it," muttered Sabine. Then glanced quickly up at Thom to see if he thought her sulky.

She cheered up briefly when they walked outside. Not so much because of the car—a huge, battered Land Rover (although it was obviously cooler than Mum's)—but its cargo, two huge, chocolate-brown Labradors, as silky and sinuous as seals, squirming around each other in their passionate attempts to greet the returning.

"Bella. And Bertie. Mother and son. Go on, get over, you daft animal."

"Bertie?" she couldn't help grimacing, even as she rubbed the two adoring heads, trying to steer the wet noses from her face.

"They're all Bs. Down the line. Like hounds. Except the hounds are all Hs."

Sabine didn't like to ask what he was talking about. She hoisted herself into the front of the car, and strapped herself in. She wondered, with a little concern, how Thom was going to drive without his arm.

Erratically, as it turned out. But as they careered around the gray streets of Rosslare, and then onto the main road toward Kennedy Park, she realized she couldn't be entirely sure whether that was down to his insecure grip on the gear stick. His hand clasped it like an ill-fitting hard hat, rattling quietly against the plastic cover as the car bumped along the rough roads.

As a route home, she decided, it was less than promising. The drizzly, cramped streets of the port town contained no shops she could imagine wanting to hang out in, being stuffed with, as far as she could see, old ladies' stiffly upholstered underwear or car parts, while outside it seemed to be all hedgerow, dotted by modern bungalows bearing a sprinkling of satellite dishes, like some strange fungi sprouting from the brick. It didn't even feel like proper countryside. There was a park dedicated to a dead president, but she couldn't see herself becoming desperate enough for greenery that she needed to use it.

"Is there anything to actually *do* in Wexford?" she had asked Thom, and he had turned briefly toward her and laughed, his mouth curled reluctantly around it, as if it didn't happen too often.

"Our big city girl is bored already, is she?" he said, but it was in a friendly way, so she didn't mind. "Don't worry. By the time you leave here, you'll be wondering what there is to do in the city."

She somehow doubted it.

To take her mind off her nerves, Sabine thought about Thom's arm, which was resting on the hand brake next to her. She had never met anyone with a false limb. Would it actually be attached to him, with some kind of glue? Or would he pull it off at night? Would he put it in a glass of water like her neighbor Margaret put her false teeth? And then there were the practical things—how would he put on his trousers? She had once broken her arm, and found it impossible to do up her fly one-handed. She had had to ask her mother to do it for her. She found herself stealing a look at his fly to see whether there was some sort of Velcro fastening and then glanced away quickly. He might think she was perving at him, and, nice as he was, she had no intention of a bit of one-armed banditry while she was here.

During the rest of the drive, Thom spoke to her only once more, to ask her how her mother was.

Sabine looked at him in surprise.

"How do you know her? You must have been here forever."

"Not quite. But I was around as a lad. And then I left to work in England a couple of years after she did."

"She never mentioned you." She realized as soon as it came out how rude it sounded. But he didn't seem offended. When he spoke, she had noticed, he did so with a kind of permanent time delay, as if measuring the words before he allowed them out.

"I don't know how much she'd remember me. I worked in the yard, and she was never a great one for the horses."

Sabine gazed at him, desperate to ask more questions. It seemed somehow strange to picture her mother here, friends, perhaps, with this one-armed horseman. She could picture her mother only ever in an urban environment: in their house in Hackney, its stripped floors, spider plants, and art-show posters broadcasting their liberal, lower-middle-class credentials. Or eating in one of the ethnic cafés in Kingsland Road, chatting earnestly to her long-earringed, angry female friends, trying to put off the ugly moment when she had to go back to writing her piece. Or arriving home in raptures from some arty film she had seen at the cinema, while Geoff, ever the realist, complained about its diversion from the German school's traditional imagery. Or whatever.

Thinking of Geoff made her stomach clench, and, annoyingly, provoked a renewed fluttering of nerves. She wondered, briefly, if he would try to write to her. Somehow knowing that he and Mum weren't going to be together anymore made it all awkward. She didn't know how to *be* with him anymore. He would probably find some new girlfriend within months, as Jim did, and then Mum would get dumped by Justin Stewartson and end up all bitter and upset and ask why men were "such *aliens*." Well she wasn't going to give her any sympathy. And she was never going to agree to go on holiday with Geoff if he got a new family. That was for sure.

"Here we are," said Thom.

She had no memory of the house at all, apart from its size. From her childhood, she remembered the inside: all dark-wood stairs and corridors that doubled back on themselves, the smells of wood smoke and wax. And she remembered the foxes' faces, mounted and dated according to their demise, jutting from their little shields and snarling impotently from the walls. At the age of six she had found them terrifying, and spent minutes at a time crouched on the stairs, waiting for someone to come past and give her the courage to race past them. From outside she remembered only a mournful donkey, who would bray incessantly when she walked away from its field, so that she felt blackmailed into staying. Her Mum and Jim had thought she was in love with it, and told everyone how sweet it was. She couldn't explain that she felt bullied by it, and was relieved when someone made her go back inside the house.

Now she noticed the exhausted-looking

frontage of the house: the tall Georgian windows peeling their paint, the windowsills chipped and sagging like the mouth of an aging aunt. It had obviously been a grand house once, grander than anybody she knew. But it looked tired, steeped in decay, like someone who had stopped caring and was waiting simply for an excuse to go. It looks like I feel, Sabine thought, and felt an unexpected empathy.

"Hope you've brought your woollies," said Thom, out of the corner of his mouth, as he hauled her bag up the front steps. "It's awful damp in there."

They waited some moments after he rang the bell, and then the door opened, and a tall woman stood before her, dressed in Wellingtons and tweedy trousers, and rubbing bits of hay from her cardigan. She was old, her brow, nose, and chin pushing past dignified pronouncement to the exaggeration of old age. But she stood tall, and lean. When she held out her hand, her fingers were unexpectedly broad and close, like rough sausages.

"Sabine," she said, smiling. As an afterthought, she held out her other hand, too, as if she was expecting a hug. "I'm sorry I didn't meet you at the boat. It's been all go this afternoon."

Sabine didn't know whether to walk forward or not. "Hullo," she replied, unable to say Granny. She rubbed at her hair awkwardly, unsure what to do with her hands. "Nice . . . nice to see you."

Her grandmother withdrew her hands, and stood, her smile looking a little stiffer. "Yes. Yes . . . Did you have a good trip over? That ferry can be awful. Can't bear it myself."

"It was fine." Sabine heard her own voice disappear to a whisper. She felt Thom's presence behind her, waiting, listening to this ridiculous exchange.

"Bit rough. But not bad."

There was a lengthy pause. "Is your horse okay?"

"No. He's not, really. Poor old boy. But we've given him some Bute, so he should have a better night. Hello, Bella, old girl, hello, hello. Yes, I know. Yes, Bella. You're a very good girl. Now, Bertie, don't you dare go upstairs."

Stooping to rub the gleaming coats of her dogs, the old lady turned and walked stiffly into the hall. Sabine stood and stared at Thom. He gestured to her to follow, and then, having dropped her bag on the step, saluted and tripped lightly back down the stairs.

Filled suddenly with a childish urge to ask him not to go, Sabine paused momentarily. Her grandmother, she realized, with some indignation, hadn't even thanked Thom for coming to get her. She hadn't even acknowledged him. Sabine felt the first glimmerings of resentment, carried quietly since she had left London that morning, begin to blossom into something more potent. She walked slowly in, and closed the big door behind her

The scents and sounds of the hall hit her memory squarely with the strength of a demolition ball. Wax polish. Old fabrics. The sound of the dogs' claws clicking on the flagstone floor. Behind her grandmother moving briskly along the corridor, she could hear the weighty tick of the grandfather clock, marking time at the same distant pace that it had done on her last visit, a decade ago. Except her height now allowed her to see above the tables, where the bronze horses stood in rest, or paused in midflight across bronze hedges. On the walls were oil paintings of other horses, mostly referred to by their first names: Sailor, Witch's Fancy, Big Dipper, like half-remembered portraits of family members. Somehow she found them com-forting. I wasn't nervous then, she told her-self. And she's just my grandmother for God's sake. She's probably nervous about having me to stay, about guessing what will make me comfortable.

But she seemed to hide it pretty well. "We've put you in the blue room," she said, upstairs, motioning into a room at the far end of the landing. "The heating's not terribly good, but I've got Mrs. H to lay you a fire. And you'll have to use the downstairs bath-room, because the hot water's given up in here. I couldn't give you the good room because your grandfather's in it. And the downstairs one has got mold on the walls."

Sabine tried not to shiver in the thin cold of neglect and gazed around the room, a curious hybrid of the 1950s and 1970s. The blue chinoiserie wallpaper had at some point been optimistically matched to a more mod-ern, turquoise shag-pile carpet. The cur-tains, threaded with gold brocade, dragged along its surface, as if they had come from a much larger window. An old sink stood on stiff, cast-iron legs in the corner, with a thin, pale-green towel hanging close to the fireplace. A watercolor of a horse and cart sat above the mantelpiece, while a larger, badly done portrait of a young woman who may have been her mother sat on the wall close to the bed. She kept glancing behind her at the door, strangely conscious of her grandfather's silent presence just a few doors away.

"There are a few bits in the wardrobe, but there should be plenty of room for your things. Is that all you brought?" Her grandmother looked down at her bag, and then around her, as if expecting something else.

Sabine paused.

"Do you have a computer?"

"A what?"

"Do you have a computer?" Sabine realized as she spoke that she knew the answer. She should have known it from this room.

"A computer? No, no computers here. What do you need a computer for?" Her voice was brusque, uncomprehending.

"For e-mail. Just to keep in touch with home."

Her grandmother appeared not to hear.

"No," she repeated. "We don't have any computers here. Now, if you unpack your things, we'll have some tea, and then you can go and see your grandfather."

"Is there a television?"

Her grandmother gave her a searching look.

"Yes, there is a television. Your grandfather has it in his room at the moment, because he likes to watch the late news. I'm sure you can borrow it occasionally."

By the time they walked into the drawing room, Sabine had begun to sink under a black cloud of depression. Even the arrival of "Mrs. H," who, short and plump and sweet-smelling as her home-baked bread and scones, could not lift her mood, despite her friendly inquiries about Irish Sea crossings, her mother's state of health, and her own happiness with the bedroom arrangements. There was no escaping it, Thom appeared to be the youngest person there, and he was the same age as her mother. There was no television in her room, no computer, and she hadn't yet worked out where they kept the phone. And Amanda Gallagher was going to steal Dean Baxter before she could make it home. It was what hell must be like.

Her grandmother, when she reemerged into the drawing room, didn't seem to be much happier. She kept looking unseeing around the room as she ate, as if trying to work out some distant problem. Periodically she would stand stiffly up from the easy chair, walk briskly to the door, and shout some instruction at either Mrs. H or some other unidentified person, so that after the fourth time Sabine decided that her grandmother wasn't used to having tea, and felt it something of an imposition to have to sit there with her granddaughter for that long. She didn't ask about her mother. Not once.

"Do you need to see to your horse?" she said eventually, figuring that would give them both an easy exit.

Her grandmother eyed her with relief. "Yes. Yes, you're right. I should check on the old boy. Very good." She stood, and brushed crumbs from her trousers so that the dogs immediately leaped up to check the carpet. Striding to the door, she turned around.

"Do you want to have a look? Come and see the stables?"

Sabine paused. She was desperate to disappear, so that she could indulge her burgeoning misery in private. But she knew it would be considered rude. "All right, then," she said grudgingly. Her Dean Baxter depression could wait another half an hour.

The donkey had long gone ("Laminitis. Poor old boy," said her grandmother, as if she should understand), but the rest of the yard had a strange air of familiarity. It was certainly livelier than inside the house. Along the row of stables, two slight, stooped men moved with bristling brooms and clattering buckets, dividing up a bale of hay into square sections, while behind them horses' hooves scraped on cement floor or thumped against wooden boards in protest. A thin, tinny transistor, balanced on an upturned bucket, spewed fuzzy tunes in the background. Staring at the scene, Sabine suddenly had a vague memory of being lifted up to one of the doors, and of squealing in delighted horror when one of the huge, long faces loomed out of the darkness to see her.

"I assumed you'd be too tired to ride today. But I've hired you a very tidy little gelding from New Ross. He'll do you while you're here."

Sabine's mouth dropped slightly open. Ride?

"I—I haven't ridden for ages," she stuttered. "Not since I was a kid. I mean—Mum didn't tell me—"

"Well, we'll take a look in the boot room

later. What size are you? Four? Five? Your mother's old ones might fit you."

"It's been about five years. I gave up."

"Yes, it's a complete bore trying to ride in London, isn't it? I once went to that stables in Hyde Park. Had to cross a main road even to get to the grass." Her grandmother strode across the yard, and began berating one of the stablehands for the job he had made of the straw bed.

"But, I don't think I really want to."

She appeared not to hear. She had taken a broom from one of the men, and was showing him how to sweep, with short, angry strokes.

"Look, I—I'm not really that fond of riding anymore." Sabine's voice cut across the noise, thin and high-pitched, so that everyone turned at the sound. Her grandmother stopped in her tracks, and wheeled slowly around to face her.

"What?"

"I don't like it. Riding. I—I've sort of grown out of it."

The two stable hands looked at each other, one with a hint of a raised eyebrow. What she had just said had obviously been Wexford code for "I murder babies," or "I wear my knickers inside out to save on washing." Sabine felt herself blushing, and cursed herself for it.

Her grandmother stared at her blankly for a moment, and then turned away, back toward the stables.

"Don't be ridiculous," she muttered. "Dinner's at eight o'clock sharp. Your grandfather will be joining us, so don't be late."

Sabine cried for almost an hour, unheard in her damp and distant room. She cursed her bloody mother for sending her to this stupid place, cursed her stiff, unfriendly grandmother and her stupid bloody horses, and cursed Thom for briefly letting her believe it might not be so bad after all. Then she cursed Amanda Gallagher, who she *just knew* would be getting off with Dean Baxter even as she lay there, the Irish ferry system for not shutting down when the weather was crap, and the turquoise shag pile for being so hideous that if anyone ever found out she had stayed in a room that looked like this she would have to emigrate. Forever. Then she sat up and cursed herself for getting purple and blotchy and snotty when she cried, instead of looking sad in the kind of clear-skinned, big-eyed, melancholy way that men found irresistible. "My whole life is a bloody, bloody mess," she wailed, and then cried some more because it just sounded so much sadder out loud.

Sabine's grandfather was already seated at the dining table when she came slowly down the stairs. She saw his stick before she saw him, jutting underneath the table between his legs. Then as she came around the corner of the dining room, she saw his back, curved as if into a question mark, resting uncomfortably against the tall-backed dining chair, cushioned by a tartan blanket. The table was laid for three, the vast expanse of mahogany glowing between them, but he was just sitting in the candlelight, staring at nothing.

"Ahh," he said slowly, as she moved into his field of view. "You're late. Dinner is at eight. Eight."

A bony finger gestured toward the wall clock, which informed Sabine that she was some seven minutes late. Sabine gazed back at him, unsure whether to apologize.

"Well, sit down, sit down," he said, lowering his hand gently onto his lap.

Sabine looked around her, and then sat opposite him. He was the oldest man she had ever seen. His skin, through which you could almost make out the shape of his skull, was beyond wrinkled; it had divided into hundreds of tiny crevices, like a wetland parched for decades. A thin vein pulsed above his temple, bulging like a worm cast under his skin. Sabine found she could barely look at him; it was somehow too painful.

"So . . ." his voice trailed downward, as if exhausted by its own flight. "You're young Sabine."

It didn't seem to require an answer. Sabine merely looked accepting.

"And how old are you?" Even his questions trailed downward.

"I'm sixteen," she said.

"What?"

"I'm sixteen. Sixteen," she said. Oh, God, he was deaf as well.

"Ahh. Sixteen." He paused. "Good."

Her grandmother suddenly appeared from a side door. "Oh, you're here. Right. I'll bring in the soup." In that "you're here," she also managed to let Sabine know she was considered late. What was wrong with these people? thought Sabine miserably. It wasn't as if they were being timed.

"The dogs have had one of your slippers," her grandmother called, from the next room, but her grandfather didn't appear to hear. Sabine, after some internal struggle, decided not to pass the message on. She didn't want to be responsible for the result.

The soup was vegetable. Real stuff, rather than canned, with lots of visible bits of potato and cabbage. Even though she would have refused it at home, she ate it, because the cold house had made her hungry. It was, she had to admit, rather good.

Feeling the need to make some sociable comment, as the three of them sat in silence, she pushed herself slightly upright and announced it. "The soup is nice."

Her grandfather slowly lifted his face, draining his soup noisily from his spoon. The whites of his eyes, she noticed, were almost completely milky.

"What?"

"The soup," she said, louder. "It's very nice."

Some nine minutes late, the clock in the hall announced that it was eight o'clock. An unseen dog let out a shuddering sigh.

The old man turned his face toward his wife. "Is she talking about the soup?"

Her grandmother didn't even look up.

"She says it's nice," she affirmed loudly.

"Ohhh. What is it?" he said. "I can't taste it."

"Vegetable."

Sabine found herself listening to the clock ticking in the hall. It seemed to be getting louder.

"Vegetable? Did you say vegetable?"

"That's right."

Long pause.

"It doesn't have sweet corn in it, does it?"

Her grandmother looked up and shook her head. She dabbed at her mouth with her linen napkin.

"No, dear. No sweet corn. Mrs. H knows you don't like sweet corn."

He turned back to his bowl, as if examining the contents.

"I don't like sweet corn," he announced slowly to Sabine. "Horrid stuff."

Sabine, by now, was fighting an almost hysterical urge to laugh and cry at the same time. She felt like she was trapped in some terrible third-rate television program, where time froze and no one ever escaped. I've got to go home, she told herself silently. There's no way I can put up with nights and nights of this. I'll wither up and die. They'll find me mummified in a room with turquoise carpet, and they won't be able to work out whether I died from cold or boredom. And I'm missing all the best telly.

"Do you hunt?"

Sabine glanced up at her grandfather, who had finally finished his soup. A thin opaque trail of it was visible at the side of his mouth.

"No," she said quietly.

"What?"

"No. I don't hunt."

"She speaks very quietly," he said loudly to his wife. "She should speak up a bit."

Her grandmother, having gathered the empty plates, walked diplomatically out of the room.

"You speak very quietly," he said. "You should speak up. It's very rude."

"I'm sorry," said Sabine, loudly, and not a little defiantly. Stupid old sod.

"So who do you hunt with?"

Sabine glanced around her, wishing suddenly for the return of her grandmother.

"I don't," she half-shouted. "I live in Hackney. It's in London. There's no hunting."

"No hunting?"

"No."

"Ohhh," he looked rather shocked, as if no hunting were an entirely new concept. "So where do you ride?"

Oh, God, but this was impossible.

"I don't," she said. "There isn't anywhere to ride."

"So, where do you keep your horse?"

"She doesn't keep a horse, dear," said her grandmother, reemerging with a large silver tray, covered by the kind of silver dome Sabine had thought was restricted to comedy butlers. "She and Kate live in London."

"Ohhh. Yes. London, isn't it?"

Oh, Mum, come and get me, Sabine willed. I'm sorry I was so mean about you and Geoff and Justin. Just come and get me. I promise I'll never moan about anything ever again. You can have endless streams of unsuitable boyfriends and I'll never say anything. I'll stay on and do A levels. I'll even stop stealing your perfume.

"Now, Sabine. Do you like it rare or well-done?"

Her grandmother lifted the silver dome, so that the sizzling, brown mound of beef released its aroma into the still air. It was surrounded by a ring of roast potatoes, and squatted in a shallow lake of rich, brown gravy.

"You can have either, dear. I'll carve. Come on, I don't want it to get cold."

Sabine stared at her in horror.

"Mum didn't tell you, did she?" she said, quietly.

"Tell me what?"

"What?" said her grandfather, irritably. "What are you saying? Do speak up."

Sabine shook her head, slowly, wishing she did not have to see her grandmother's taut, exasperated expression.

"I'm a vegetarian."

JOJO MOYES

Chapter Two

It was really quite simple. Apparently. If one took a bath in the downstairs bathroom (as opposed to the upstairs one, which had obviously been installed when the house was built, and last seen hot water some time then, too), then one removed all evidence of one's visit within five minutes of finishing one's ablutions. That meant all damp towels, shampoo bottles, flannels, even toothbrushes and toothpaste. Or one could expect to find them dumped outside one's bedroom less than half an hour afterward.

If one wanted breakfast, then one made sure one was downstairs in the breakfast room by eight-thirty. Not the dining room. Of course. And not at a quarter past nine, by which stage half the day had apparently gone, and Mrs. H had much better things to do than to wait around while everyone had her breakfast, although she was too nice to say so herself. And one had porridge, followed by toast. With honey, or marmalade. Both of which sat in little silver pots. And no, there was no Alpen. Or Pop-Tarts.

And one didn't complain about the cold. One dressed properly, and didn't wander around wearing next to nothing and then wittering on that it was drafty. That meant thick jumpers. And trousers. And if one didn't have enough of them, then one only had to say so because there were lots of spares sitting in the bottom of the big chest of drawers. And only a rude person would comment on how musty they smelled, or the fact that they looked like they had last been worn by Albanian orphans some time before one was born. And that went for footwear, too. One could not expect to wear expensive training shoes around the place and expect to keep them box fresh. One should go to the boot room and find oneself a sturdy pair of Wellingtons. And if one was going to get hysterical about spiders, then one should shake the things out first.

This was all without the rules one should simply not have to be reminded of. Like not letting the dogs upstairs. Or keeping one's boots on in the drawing room. Or turning over the television so that it wasn't on Grandfather's favorite news channel. Or beginning to eat before everyone had been served. Or using the phone without asking first. Or sitting on the Aga to keep warm. Or having a bath in the evening (or of a depth any greater than six inches).

A week into her stay, Sabine found there were so many rules to remember it was as if the house were a person itself, as seemingly persnickety, and set in its ways as her grandparents. At home, she had grown up with almost no rules; her mother had taken a perverse satisfaction in letting her structure her own life, a kind of Montessori existence, so that, faced with these never-ending and seemingly incomprehensible strictures, Sabine found herself increasingly resentful and depressed.

That was until Thom taught her the most important rule, one that did return some small measure of freedom back into her life—never, ever attempt to traverse any distance within the house or grounds at a pace slower than the Kilcarrion walk. This was a brisk, purposeful gait, to be conducted with chin lifted and eyes focused on the middle distance, which, if carried out at correct speed, served to deflect any of the questions such as, "Where are you going?" or, more commonly, "What are you doing? Come on, you can help me muck out this stable," or ". . . fetch the horses in," or ". . . unhook the trailer," or ". . . hose out the dogs' shed."

"It's not just you," said Thom. "She doesn't like to see anyone idle. Gets her anxious. That's why we all do it."

Now that Sabine thought about it, she realized it was true. She had never seen anyone in the house, with the exception of her grandfather, moving at anything less than a rate of knots. And as she had seen the old man only sitting, she couldn't be sure about him.

But it wasn't just the house, and its labyrinthine rules. Sabine, cut off from her friends, with only one brief, unsatisfactory telephone call to her mother, felt isolated and removed from everything she had

known. She was an alien in these surround-
ings, as nonplussed by her elderly relatives
as they apparently were by her. She had left
the house and its grounds just once so far, to
accompany her grandmother to a kind of
hypermarket in the nearest town, where, had
she been inclined, she could have purchased anything from processed cheese to
white plastic garden furniture. There was
that, and a post office, and a tack shop for
horse stuff. No McDonald's, no cinema, no
arcade. No magazines. Seemingly no people under the age of thirty. With the *Daily
Telegraph* and *Irish Times* her only contact
with the outside world, she didn't even know
what was number one in the charts.

Her grandmother, if she noticed Sabine's
steady descent into depression, had evidently decided to ignore it, or treat it as
some kind of teenage foible. She "organized"
Sabine at the beginning of each day, giving
her a succession of tasks, such as dropping
off papers at the office, or fetching vegetables from the kitchen garden for Mrs. H, and
treated her with the same brisk detachment
with which she seemed to treat everyone
around her. Except the dogs, that is. And,
more significant, the Duke.

That had been their worst falling-out so far, worse than her grandmother's insistence that vegetarianism couldn't possibly embrace chicken. It had come two days later, when, swinging on the door as the Duke was led stiffly back into his stable, Sabine had forgotten, as requested, to kick the bottom bolt across, and had subsequently had to watch, aghast, as with a skittishness worthy of a much younger and less lame animal, the old bay horse had worked the top bolt with his teeth, and made his elegant bid for freedom across the yard to the open fields beyond.

It had taken her grandmother and both lads, with the aid of six apples, and a bucket of bran mash, almost two hours to catch him, tramping grimly around the top fields as he came tantalizingly close and veered away again, tail held high like a banner of defiance. When, as it began to get dark, he eventually strolled over, head low with exhaustion and sporting an air of something like embarrassment, he was limping badly. Her grandmother had been furious, had first shouted at her that she was a "stupid, stupid girl" and then, almost tearfully, had focused all her attention on her "boy," alternately rub-

bing at his neck and scolding him in soft
tones as they walked stiffly back toward the
stables. What about me? Sabine, now tearful herself, had wanted to yell at her departing back. I'm your bloody granddaughter
and you've never said so much as a kind
word to me!

That had been the point at which Sabine
had begun plotting her escape. And avoiding
her grandmother, who managed, while never
referring to the incident again, to somehow
make Sabine feel the weight of her disapproval. She had not tried to hug Sabine
again after that. In fact she had apparently
found it hard to say anything much to her for
a day or two; her mood only lifted when the
vet announced that the inflammation in the
Duke's leg was on its way down.

So Sabine spent most of her time with
Thom and the two lads, Liam and John
John, both of whom, like Mrs. H, seemed to
be some kind of distant relatives. Liam was a
libidinous former jump jockey, almost incapable of saying anything that didn't swell into
some kind of double entendre, while John
John, his eighteen-year-old protégé, was
almost silent, his desperation to graduate
into the nearby racing yard etched into his

prematurely weather-beaten skin. Thom, although too quiet, seemed to understand Sabine's frustration and resentment, and would occasionally puncture it with gentle mockery. She had already stopped noticing his arm, which was covered to the wrist by jackets and jumpers. He was someone to talk to.

"So I waited till bloody half past ten until I was sure the old man had finished with the bathroom, and then there was no hot water left at all. Nothing. I was so cold by the time I got out of the bath that my feet were blue. Really. And my teeth were chattering."

Hanging over the stable door, she kicked at a bucket, sending a small wave over its battered edge. Thom, raking down the clean straw that had been piled up along one wall, stopped and raised an eyebrow, and she climbed down, glancing unconsciously over at the Duke as she did so.

"There's no hair dryer, so my hair's gone all flat. And my sheets are damp. Really damp. Like when I get in the bed, you have to peel the top sheet and the bottom sheet apart. And they smell of mold."

"How can you tell?"

"How can I tell what?"

"That they smell of mold. Yesterday you told me that the whole house smelled of mold. The sheets might actually smell quite nice."

"You can see it. Green spots."

Thom guffawed, still raking his straw.

"It's probably the pattern on the sheets. I'll bet you've got eyesight like your mother."

Sabine stared at him, letting go of the door.

"How do you know about my mother's eyesight?"

Thom paused, and then rested his rake against the wall. He bent and removed the bucket from under Sabine's foot, waiting for her to move out of the way before he sluiced the water across the yard.

"You're all blind. Your whole family. Everyone knows. I'm surprised you don't wear glasses."

Thom was like that; she'd think she had the measure of him, talk to him like he was a mate. And then every now and then he'd throw in some piece of information, about her mother, or his own past, and she'd find herself silenced, trying to make this new piece of information fit into the recognizable whole.

The things she knew about him (some gleaned from him, some from Mrs. H, who was a veritable broadcasting network when not in her grandmother's presence) were that he was thirty-five, that he had spent some years in England working for a racing yard, that he had returned under some kind of a cloud, and that he had lost his arm through riding. That had not come from him—easygoing as he was, she didn't yet feel brave enough to quiz him about his amputation—but Mrs. H had told her, "I always thought the horses would be the death of him. He has no fear, you see. No fear. His father was the same." She didn't know the full story, as she didn't like to burden her sister—his poor mother—but it was something to do with when he used to ride over the sticks.

"Sticks?" Sabine had said, picturing some kind of picket fence. Had he impaled himself?

"Fences. He was a jump jockey. It's a damned sight more dangerous than on the flat, I'll tell you that for nothing."

Everything here revolved around horses, thought Sabine grimly. They were all bloody obsessed, to the point where they thought nothing of losing bits of their own bodies.

She had so far managed to put off riding the gray horse in the back field, telling her grandmother that she had a backache. But she knew from her grandmother's impatient expression, the way she had already fished out an old pair of riding boots and a hat and left them pointedly outside her bedroom door, that she was living on borrowed time.

Sabine didn't want to ride. The thought of it made her feel sick. She had managed to persuade her mother that she should give it up years ago, after the weekly drive to the stables had gradually found her becoming nauseous with nerves, morbidly—and usually correctly—convinced that this was the week that she would have to ride one of the "evil" riding school horses, the ones that bolted, and bucked, and chased the others with slicked-back ears and bared teeth, and that this was the week where she would be carried off, out of control, her legs flapping unbalanced against the saddle, her arms hauling back in vain against the reins. It wasn't a challenge, like the other girls seemed to find it. It wasn't even fun. And Kate hadn't even seemed to fight her, when Sabine said she didn't want to do it anymore, as if she had made her daughter do it only out of some uncertain sense of family tradition.

"I don't want to ride," she confided to Thom, as he led one of the tethered horses back into its stable.

"You'll be fine. That little lad's a real gent."

Sabine glanced over at the distant gray.

"I don't care what he is. I don't want to ride. Do you think she'll make me?"

"He's grand. Get on him a couple of times and you'll be fine."

"You're not bloody taking me seriously," she half shouted, so that John John in the next stable stuck his head around the door. "I don't want to ride the horse. I don't want to ride any horse. I don't *like* it."

Thom calmly unhooked the lead rein from the horse, and gave it an appreciative slap on its rump with his good hand. He walked over to her, closing and bolting the door behind him.

"You're frightened, huh?"

"I just don't like it."

"There's nothing wrong with losing your nerve. Most of us have done it at some point."

"Can't you hear me? *God,* you *people.* I just don't like riding."

Thom placed his fake hand on her shoulder. It rested there, stiff and unyielding, curiously at odds with the sentiment it was trying to convey.

"You know, she won't be satisfied until you've at least had a go. It'll make things heaps better. Why don't you come out with me tomorrow morning? I'll make sure you're okay."

Sabine felt like weeping.

"I really don't want to. Oh, God, I can't believe I'm stuck here. My life is just a bloody mess."

"Tomorrow morning. Just you and me. Look, it's better you ride out with me for the first time than with her, isn't it?"

She looked up at him. He grinned.

"You know she'll eat you for breakfast. Most fearless seat in the whole of southern Ireland, that woman. Still rode to hounds until the Duke went lame."

"I'll break my neck. And then you'll all be sorry."

"I certainly will. I can't carry a body all the way back with only one arm."

But the following morning she managed to put Thom off again. This time, however, she had a valid excuse.

"Now. I've got to go out for most of the day, and Mrs. H is going to be very busy, so I'd like you to take care of your grandfather."

Her grandmother had gotten dressed in her "town" clothes. At least Sabine assumed they were her town clothes; it was the first time she had seen her in anything but old tweedy trousers and Wellington boots. She was wearing a dark-blue woolen skirt of uncertain but certainly aged origin, a dark-green cardigan over a round-necked jumper, and her ever-present quilted green jacket over the top. She had placed a string of pearls around her neck, and had brushed her hair back so that it sat, still, in the way old people's hair always seemed to, in waves, rather than its usual electric frizz.

Sabine fought back an urge to ask her if she was going out on the town. Somehow she knew her grandmother wouldn't find it funny.

"Where are you going?" she said, incuriously.

"Enniscorthy. To see a trainer about selling him one of our yearlings."

Sabine sighed in ill-disguised boredom, the information already filtering past her unrecorded.

"Now, your grandfather will want his lunch at one o'clock on the dot. He's asleep in his chair upstairs, so make sure you wake him a good hour beforehand because he will probably want to smarten himself up. Mrs. H will prepare his lunch and leave it in the little kitchen next to the dining room, and one for you so that he doesn't eat by himself. But you'll have to lay the table because she'll be busy this morning, taking the windfalls around to the neighbors. Don't bother Thom in the stables—they've got a lot going on. And don't let the dogs upstairs. Bertie got into your grandfather's room again yesterday and ate his hair brush."

Can't see how it can be of any great loss, thought Sabine. He's got only about two hairs left to brush.

"I'll be back after lunch. Have you gotten everything?"

"Lunch at one. Don't be late. Don't bother Mrs. H. Don't bother Thom. Don't let the dogs upstairs."

Her grandmother stared at her for a moment, with her curiously blank gaze, so that Sabine couldn't tell if she was noting her tone of insurrection or whether it simply filtered past. Then she pulled her head scarf over her head, tied it firmly under her chin, and with a brief, adoring word of farewell to Bella, who had been standing anxiously at her feet, turned and walked briskly out of the front door.

Sabine stood in the hallway for a few minutes until the slam of the door had reverberated into silence, and then gazed around her, wondering what to do. She seemed to spend vast swathes of her day here wondering what to do. All the elements that had effortlessly filled her days at home—MTV, the Internet, hanging on the telephone with her mates, just mooching around the Keir Hardie estate, seeing who was around, what was happening—had been withdrawn, leaving her with this vast, vacuous space to fill. There was only so much time she could spend organizing her room (besides, the blue shag pile made her feel physically sick), and if you didn't like horses, what the hell was there?

She didn't want to go out to the yard, because she knew Thom would just start going on at her about riding that stupid horse. She couldn't watch television because there was nothing on Irish television in the day. And last time she had tried to surreptitiously turn it on in the afternoon, her eardrums had been virtually blasted. "It's so your grandfather can hear the news," shouted Mrs. H, who hurried upstairs to see what the noise was. "You'd best leave it alone." Every night at ten, wherever she was in the house, Sabine could hear the thunderous roar of the news theme tune. Her grandfather would sit, peering at the screen as if he still had trouble hearing, while those around him read their newspapers, politely pretending they weren't being deafened.

Still, she thought, walking slowly upstairs, followed by Bella, her grandmother's absence did confer something of a sense of release. She hadn't realized how anxious the older woman's presence made her until its absence revealed this hitherto unknown sense of calm. A half day of freedom. A half day of boredom. She didn't know which was worse.

Sabine spent the best part of an hour lying on her bed, earphones on loud, reading a 1970s potboiler that Mrs. H had brought her. Mrs. H had evidently decided she understood what young girls needed—romance and more cake—and the way Sabine felt, Mrs. H had gotten it just about right.

It wasn't exactly literature. There was,

however, lots of panting in it. The women were divided into sluts who panted with ill-concealed lust over distracted male heroes, who were just trying to get on with saving the world, or virgins, who panted with restrained longing as the same heroes skillfully seduced them. Only the men actually did anything. The women either got killed off (the sluts) or hitched to the men (the virgins). And despite all the panting, there was relatively little real sex (Sabine flicked first through to see). Perhaps this was what being in a Catholic country was all about. Lots of panting and not much of anything really going on. "Like you, Bella," she said, stroking the dog on her bed.

Panting made her think of Dean Baxter. She had almost kissed him once. It was not like he would have been her first kiss; she had snogged loads of boys, and had done more than snog with some, although less than most of the girls she knew. She had known he was flirting with her, and they had been sitting on the wall of the estate after dark, and he had been sitting really close and joking with her so that she pushed him and he pushed her back, all just an excuse to touch each other really. And she had known that they probably would kiss and felt okay about it because she had liked him for ages and although he was a laugh, he wasn't too pushy, and he wasn't the type to go bragging to his mates afterward. Plus, he didn't think she was weird because her house was full of books and her mum wore second-hand clothes. He had even told some of the girls to back off when they called her "Brainache" and "Spod" for not smoking and taking her exams early. But then he had gotten carried away, and instead of pushing her back, he had picked her up in a fireman's lift, as if he was going to take her somewhere, and she had panicked and shouted at him to put her down, and when he had laughed, she had hit him repeatedly, too hard, across the head. He had dropped her after that, stood back and looked at her, holding his reddened ear, and asked her what was the matter with her. But she couldn't really explain, so she had just laughed, even though she felt like crying, and tried to make a joke of it. But he hadn't laughed, and things had never been quite the same between them, and then a week later she had heard he was hanging around with Amanda Gallagher. Amanda Bloody Gallagher with her long, girlie-girl hair, fabric-conditioned clothes, and cheap perfume. Probably Amanda Bloody Baxter by the time she got home. Perhaps it was time to forget about Dean Baxter. He had bad skin on his back, anyway. His sister had told her.

Sabine shook her head, clearing it of unwelcome thoughts, and thought about Thom instead. She always found it was easier if you thought about someone else. He was the only man around who was remotely good-looking, she had decided. Pretty handsome, in fact. She had never been out with an older man, although her mate Ali had, and she said they "really knew their way around." But she couldn't quite get past the idea of his arm. She worried that if she ever got around to kissing him (or would they just pant, him being Irish?) and they took off their clothes, she might run away in fright when she saw his stump. She liked him too much to upset him like that.

She didn't know whether he fancied her. He always seemed pretty pleased to see her, and always seemed to like her hanging around. Plus, she could tell him anything. But it was hard to imagine him overcome with passion, or staring at her with intense longing. He was too withdrawn, somehow. Too restrained. Maybe he just needed time. Maybe grown-up romance worked differently.

Thinking about grown-up romance made Sabine think of her mother, and she slid off the bed, keen to distract herself.

With Bella padding around after her, she opened her cupboards, breathing in the musty smell of things long undisturbed, and gazing into their dark depths. Her grandparents didn't even have the right sort of junk; other people's bedroom cupboards were filled with cocktail dresses, and old board games, or boxes of letters, or electronic gadgets that no longer worked. Here they had piles of moldering white embroidered linen, tablecloths and the like, a broken lamp shade, and some books, with titles like *A Girl's Guide to Horsemanship* and *Bunty Annual 1967*.

Emboldened by the complicit, silent house, Sabine set off to explore some of the other rooms. Her grandfather's door was closed, but between his and the bathroom was another room that she had not yet been into. Pulling the handle down slowly so that she didn't make a noise, she opened the door and slid in.

It was a man's room, a study of sorts, but without the air of recent activity that characterized the yard office downstairs. That had tables full of letters, and ledgers, and color catalogs full of "stud" horses with names like "Filigree Jumping Jake III—by Filigree Flancake out of Jumping Jemimah," all of whom looked pretty much the same to her, although Thom had said you could count their differences in tens of thousands of guineas. This study held the dusty air of neglect, its half-opened curtains hanging perfectly still, as if they had not been disturbed in years. It smelled of mildewed paper, and unbeaten carpets, and tiny particles of dust glinted, suspended in the air, as she moved. Sabine closed the door softly behind her, and walked into the center of the room, so that Bella paused hopefully and then dropped, groaning, onto the rug.

There were no pictures of horses on the walls in here, apart from a framed cartoon of a shouting huntsman; just a yellowed, framed map of the Far East and a few black-and-white photographs of people in 1950s gear to cover the vast expanse of William Morris-style wallpaper. On built-in shelves by the window sat various-sized boxes, some of which had rolled-up manuscripts on the top, while on the center of the desk stood a large model of a gray battleship, presumably to scale. On a dark wood bookshelf to her right stood lots of hardbacked books, mainly about war and Southeast Asia, punctuated by a couple of humorous cartoon compilations and a paperback on after-dinner speaking. On the top shelf sat a series of decrepit leather-bound books, the gilt almost entirely rubbed off their spines.

It was the other side of the room that caught her eye. Two leather-bound photograph albums, resting on a large box. Judging by their generous icing of dust, they had not been moved for some years.

Sabine crouched down and gently pulled out one of the albums. It was labeled: 1955–. Sitting cross-legged, she pulled it into her lap and opened it, fingering the fine tissue between each of its stiff leaves.

The pictures sat one to a page, and the first was of her grandmother. At least she thought it was her grandmother. It was a posed, studio shot of a young woman on a window seat, wearing a dark, slightly severe suit with a tiny collar, a matching dress, and a string of pearls. Her hair, which was dark brown instead of gray, had been set into waves, and she was wearing the makeup of the age: heavy brows and lashes, and dark, carefully outlined lips. She looked, for all her posing, slightly embarrassed, as if she had been caught doing something suspect. The next photograph was of her with a tall, young man. They stood next to a stand with a plant on it, he beaming with pride; her arm posted uncertainly through his, barely acknowledging him. She looked less embarrassed this time, more sure of herself, curiously dignified. It was something about her bearing, or her tall, slender frame. She didn't slouch over her breasts, looking faintly apologetic, in the way that her own mother did.

Sabine, now engrossed, flicked through the entire album. Toward the end of it, as well as pictures of her grandmother, looking at her most relaxed in a snapshot with another young, incredibly glamorous woman, were pictures of a baby in the kind of elaborate christening robe that you never saw now: all intricate crochet, and tiny, silk-covered buttons. There was no label, so Sabine found herself staring hard at the picture, trying to work out whether this smiling, swaddled baby could possibly be her mother or her uncle Christopher. You couldn't even tell whether it was a boy or a girl—and at that age they seemed to dress babies the same.

But it was in the box that things really started to get interesting: a cardboard-backed picture of her grandmother (it was definitely her, she had decided), arm in arm with the glamorous, shorter girl, both holding little Union Jack pennants, and laughing unrestrainedly. It was odd to think her grandmother had laughed like that once. Behind them was some kind of party, or gathering, with most of the men handsome in white, like Richard Gere in *An Officer and a Gentleman*. There was a tray of tall glasses beside them, which made Sabine wonder if she was drunk, and gilt lettering at the bottom announced that the event had been in honor of Her Majesty Queen Elizabeth II's coronation, in 1953. That was history! Sabine had had to sit still and digest that for a moment; her grandmother had been around to make history.

And then there was the other, smaller photograph. Among the pictures of horses, and unrecognizable, smiling faces on long, thin boats, was a picture of a little girl, around six years old, who was definitely her mother. She had her mother's reddish, curly hair, and, even at that age, her peculiar, lock-kneed way of standing. She was holding hands with a little boy, who may or may not have been Chinese, and smiling broadly from under a straw hat. He seemed a little more awkward, not daring to look the camera straight in the face, but leaning toward the girl, as if for comfort.

So this was how my mother grew up, Sabine thought, fingering the sepia-tinted print. Surrounded by little Chinese boys and girls. She had always known that she spent the first part of her childhood abroad, but until now, looking at her pale cotton dress and hat, she hadn't conceived of her as something exotic. Curious, she began flicking through the other photographs, looking for other pictures of her mother.

Sabine was abruptly roused from her reverie by the sound of a door slamming downstairs and a muffled cry that could have been someone calling her name. Panicked, she leaped toward the door, followed by Bella, opening and swiftly closing it behind her. She glanced down at her watch. It was half past twelve.

She paused for a minute, whispered to the dog not to tell ("Oh, God," she groaned when she realized who she was talking to. "They've got me at it now"), and then walked slowly down the stairs, brushing the dust from her hands as she went.

Mrs. H was in the kitchen, her apron already on. "Ahh. There you are. I'm running late, Sabine," she said, smiling. "I got held up at Annie's. Has your grandfather mentioned what he wants for his lunch?"

"Erm. He hasn't said much, actually."

"Ahh, well. I'll do him poached eggs on toast. He had a good breakfast so he won't want anything too heavy. What'll you want, the same?"

"Yeah. That'll be great." Sabine realized with a lurch that she had not woken her grandfather an hour before his lunch, as instructed. She began to walk back upstairs, shooing away Bella, who tried to accompany her again, wondering whether, if he was really running late, she was going to have to help him get dressed. Please, God, don't let me have to touch him, she prayed, outside his door. Please don't let him mention anything about bed baths or chamber pots or whatever it is old people need to get ready. And please, God, let him have his teeth in so that I don't get hysterical.

"Er—hullo?" she called, through the door. There was no reply.

"Hullo?" She said it louder this time, remembering his deafness. "Grand-Grandfather?"

Oh, God, he was asleep. She was going to have to touch him to wake him up. Sabine stood outside the door and took a deep breath. She didn't want to feel that crepey, translucent skin under her fingers. Old people made her feel funny, even when she looked at them at home. They seemed too vulnerable, too prone to breakage and bruising. Looking at them up close made her toes clench.

She thought of her grandmother's reaction if she didn't do it.

She knocked loudly, paused again, and entered.

The bed, which sat squarely at the far end of the room, was beautiful: a Gothic four-poster, from whose frame ancient bloodred tapestries with glints of Chinese gold thread hung between carved posts of glowing, darkened wood. On the bed itself sat layer upon layer of old silk counterpane, from under which pure white linen sheets could be glimpsed, like teeth in a glossy red mouth. It was the kind of bed one saw in American films, when they were trying to imagine what English stately homes were like. It had the twin, exotic sheen of the Far East, of emperors and opium dens. It was as far removed from her own, creaky iron-framed post as she could imagine.

But it didn't have him in it.

It took Sabine less than ten seconds to realize that not only was he not in it, but that there was nowhere else in the room that he could be. Unless he had climbed into the wardrobe, which she very much doubted (but checked, just to be sure).

He must be in the bathroom. Sabine strode back out of the room and along the corridor. The door was slightly ajar so she called out first, but, hearing no reply, she pushed at it and found that the bathroom, too, had a definite absence of old person.

Sabine's head began to race. Her grand-mother hadn't told her that he was going to go out. She had said he was sleeping. So, where the hell was he? She checked her grandmother's empty room (much more fru-gal, she noted), the downstairs bathroom, and then, feeling increasingly panicked, every single room in the house, from breakfast room to the boot room. He was nowhere to be seen.

It was nearly a quarter to one.

She had to tell someone. She ran to the downstairs kitchen, and confessed to Mrs. H that she had somehow mislaid her grandfather.

"Is he not in his room?"

"No. No. I looked there first."

"Oh, God. Where's Bertie?"

Sabine stared at her, and then behind her at Bella. "I haven't seen him," she said.

"He's gone out with the dog. He's not meant to go out by himself now, especially not with Bertie, because Bertie's young and knocks his stick from under him." She stepped out from behind the table and went to remove her apron. "We'd better go and look for him before Mrs. Ballantyne gets back."

"No. No—you stay here and watch the house. I'll get Thom to help."

Sabine, her chest now tight with fear, ran to the stable yard, peering over stable doors and shouting his name.

Thom, a sandwich held to his mouth, poked his head out of the tack room. Behind him she could hear the radio, and just make out the seated figures of Liam and John John reading the *Racing Post*.

"Where's the fire?"

"It's—it's the old man. I can't find him."

"What do you mean, you can't find him?"

"He was meant to be in his room, sleeping. Mrs. H thinks he may have gone out with Bertie and she says Bertie knocks him over. Will you help me look for him?"

Thom swore under his breath, his eyes already scanning the middle distance.

"Don't touch my lunch, you bastards," he muttered, and then grabbing his coat, walked briskly into the yard.

"I'm really, really sorry. I just don't know what to do. He was meant to be in the house."

"Okay," he said, thinking hard. "You go and check up and down the road, and if he's not there, check the top fields. I'll do the bottom fields and the orchard, and I'll do the barns, too. You're sure you've looked everywhere in the house? I mean, he couldn't just be watching the telly?"

Sabine, now frightened by Thom's expression, felt tears beginning to prick at the corners of her eyes. "Everywhere. And Bertie's gone. He must have taken him out."

"Jesus, what did the old eejit have to go out for? Look, take Bella. And keep calling Bertie—if he's taken a fall, hopefully the dog might take us to him. I'll meet you back here in twenty minutes. And, here, grab a hunting horn, and if you find him, give it a good blow." Handing her a spare, he turned, vaulted over the post-and-rail fencing and began to run toward the fields below them, both of which were surrounded by high hedgerow.

Sabine, with Bella chasing joyfully behind, jogged out of the front gates and up the lane, calling with every second breath. Unsure at which point she should actually turn around, she ran until her chest hurt, past the big farmhouse on the corner, the little church, and a row of smaller cottages. It had begun to drizzle, and the clouds gathered slate gray above her, as if heralding some great doom. Her head filled with unwelcome pictures of the old man in a crumpled heap at the side of the road, Sabine ran harder the other way, until, unable to see a clock, she decided she should go back to check the top fields. "Where are you, you bugger?" she whispered under her breath. "Where are you?"

Then she jumped, her heart briefly stalling, as a huge green tarpaulin half stuck into the hedge moved toward her.

Bella stood stiff legged, a few paces in front of her, her hackles raised. She barked once, in warning. Her heart thumping, eyes wide, Sabine stood still in the center of the road, and then, taking deep breaths, peered closer, lifting a corner.

If she hadn't been so anxious, she would have laughed. Under the huge plastic sheet stood a gray donkey, harnessed to a small cart. It opened its eyes briefly, as if acknowledging her presence, and then turned resignedly back toward the relative shelter of the hedge.

Sabine let the tarpaulin gently drop and began to run again, her eyes scanning from left to right. There was nothing. No sign of him. Above the pounding of her heart and heels, and the thin hiss of the rain in her ears, she could hear no welcoming bark, no impatient upper-class croak, no hunting horn. Sabine, now properly fearful, began to cry.

He was obviously dead. Everyone would blame her, she realized, half stumbling down the grassy hill. He would be found, frozen and damp, probably with his powdery bones broken where Bertie had pulled him over onto the hard concrete, and he would contract pneumonia and his heart would give out and it would all be her fault because she was too busy reading dirty books and being nosy to care. Her grandmother would be angrier even than when she let the Duke out. Thom would never talk to her again. Her mother would refuse to take her back, for effectively murdering her father, so she would be stuck here while the villagers looked on silently and pointed like something out of *Deliverance*, and she became known as The Girl Who Killed Her Own Grandfather.

Sabine had not thought to wear Wellingtons, and down in the boggy pasture, her feet became waterlogged by mud. Viscous and brown, it crept over the tops of her trainers, sucking and releasing each footfall, impregnating her feet with its chilled damp. A week ago she would have been hysterical about the state of her new Reeboks, but she was now so miserable she hardly noticed. Realizing it was now some half an hour since she had set out, she sobbed out loud, wiping her running nose on the back of her hand.

It was at this point that Bella, sodden and

unhappy, began heading back toward the house.

"Don't you leave me as well," Sabine cried, but Bella ignored her, apparently now determined to restore herself to shelter and the comfort of a warm Aga. She didn't know where to look next. She would have to ask Thom. She began to trudge up the hill behind the dog, unsure what she was going to say to Mrs. H, but certain that somehow she would be to blame.

Bella had disappeared by the time she got to the house. Sabine, pushing her wet hair from her eyes, trying to get her sniveling under control, lifted the latch on the back door, and pushed it open, hearing, as she did, footsteps pounding across the gravel behind her.

It was Thom, his hair plastered to his head, and his false arm holding the hunting horn awkwardly to his chest. She was about to apologize when she realized he was looking straight past her.

"You're late," came a voice from down the corridor.

Allowing herself a second to acclimatize to the dark, Sabine stared down the flag-stone passageway, where she could just make out the curved back, the third leg of a walking stick, and two chocolate-colored dogs, grunting happily around each other in greeting. "Lunch was at *one. One.* It's getting cold. I really don't see that I should have to tell you again."

Sabine stood in the doorway, her mouth agape, subsumed by conflicting emotions.

"He got back about five minutes ago," muttered Thom behind her. "We must have crossed paths with him."

"Well, come on, come on. You can't possibly sit down looking like that," scolded her grandfather. "You'll have to change your shoes."

"The old bastard," whispered Sabine, tearfully, and felt Thom's good hand on her shoulder in reply.

Mrs. H, leaning from the kitchen door, mouthed an apology and shrugged helplessly. "Will I get you a dry jumper, Mr. Ballantyne?" she asked, but was waved irritably away. She ducked back inside the kitchen.

Her grandfather turned stiffly toward the stairs, shaking droplets of water from his hat with his free hand. The dogs pushed past him, so that briefly unbalanced, he thrust out a spindly arm to catch hold of the banister.

"I shan't tell you again." He muttered something to himself and shook his head. It was barely visible above the exaggerated curve of his shoulders. "Mrs. H, if you'd be kind enough to bring me my lunch, it seems my granddaughter would rather eat in a corridor."

It had been shortly after tea that Sabine had begun counting up the money her mother had given her, to see if she had enough to get her back to England. Her mother wouldn't like it, but she couldn't see how living with her and the odious Justin could be any worse than staying here. This was impossible. Even when she tried to do the right thing, they acted like she'd deliberately done wrong. They didn't care about her. All they cared about were bloody horses, and their stupid, rigid rules. She could be lying in the kitchen with an ax in her head and they'd tell her off for bringing tools into the house.

She was scanning her ferry ticket for a booking line number when there was a soft knock at the door. It was Mrs. H.

"Why don't you come over to our Annie's with me this evening? Your grandmother says it would be fine, and it'll be nice for you to have some younger people around you." What she meant was, it was probably best if you and your grandparents gave one another a bit of a break. But Sabine didn't mind. Anything was better than spending another evening in with them.

Annie was Mrs. H's only daughter. She lived in the large farmhouse farther up the village, which she ran as a bed-and-breakfast with her husband, Patrick, a much older man who wrote books. ("I've never read one—not my cup of tea," said Mrs. H. "But I'm told they're very good. For intellectual types, you know.") Annie's skills as hostess were less assured—the B-and-B was legendary, according to Thom, for never retaining guests for a second night. She forgot stuff, apparently. Like breakfast. Or even that she had guests at all. And some objected to her habit of walking around the house in the early hours of the morning. But neither Thom nor Mrs. H elaborated on that.

"She's not that much older than you. Twenty-seven. How old are you again? Oh. Well, she's a fair bit older than you. But you'll like her. Everyone does. Just don't mind if she's a bit—well—a bit distracted."

Sabine, walking slowly down the dark, wet

road with Mrs. H, both huddled under a rather tired umbrella, was intrigued, picturing some Maud Gonne type, all wild red hair and floaty skirts, waving away domestic queries with a thin, artistic wrist. Annie's eccentric habits sounded a million miles from those of Kilcarrion House. A woman who forgot to make breakfast wasn't likely to want to hold a formal supper, was she? And a writer husband didn't sound like all he would want to do is talk about horses. She might be able to relax this evening, sparkle, and be witty in admiring company. Perhaps watch proper telly. Annie might even have satellite—lots of Irish houses seemed to. And besides, Mrs. H told her that Thom would pop by later. He often did, apparently, just to see how Annie "was doing."

But the Annie who opened the door was not quite the glamorous eccentric she had envisaged. She was a short woman in a large sweater with straight, shoulder-length brown hair, full lips, and big, sad eyes. They wrinkled into a greeting as she held out her hand—not to shake Sabine's own, but to pull her gently in to the house. She was also, Sabine noted, a little sadly, wearing chain-store jeans.

"Sabine. How are you? Lovely of you to stop by. Hi, Mam. Did you bring the bacon?"

"I did. I'll put it straight in the fridge."

There was no hallway; they walked straight into the living room, almost one side of which was taken up by an old stone fireplace, complete with fiercely burning log fire. Two long, slightly tatty blue sofas sat at right angles to it, while a coffee table sat between them, burdened by huge, precarious piles of magazines and books. Now that she looked properly, books were everywhere. They lined each wall on sagging shelves and sat under stools and tables in irregular heaps. "Those are Patrick's," Annie said, from the kitchen area at the other end of the room. "He's a great one for reading."

"Annie? What have you prepared for the supper?" Mrs. H stood up from the fridge and stared around her, as if expecting to see some pan bubbling on the stove. Annie rubbed at her forehead, frowning.

"Ahh, Mam. I'm sorry. It went clean out of my mind. We can stick something in the microwave."

"We cannot," said Mrs. H, affronted. "I'm not having Sabine going back to the big house saying we never fed her properly."

"I wouldn't say that," said Sabine, who really didn't mind. "I'm not that hungry anyway."

"A skinny girl like you. In fact, look at the both of yous. I've seen more meat on a butcher's dog. Annie—you sit down and talk to Sabine and I'll do us some chops. I put some in the freezer a couple of weeks ago."

"I—I'm not a great meat eater," Sabine ventured.

"Well, then, you can eat the vegetables. And we'll do you a cheese sandwich on the side. How's that?"

Annie grinned at Sabine conspiratorially, and motioned at her to sit down. She didn't talk much, but in that way that prompted confidences, and before long Sabine found herself unburdening herself of the many unhappinesses—and injustices—she was subjected to at Kilcarrion House. She told Annie about the *endless* rules and regulations, and how *completely impossible* it was to remember them all. She told her how *ridiculously difficult* it was to communicate with her grandparents, and how *hopelessly old-fashioned* they were. She told her about how *alien* she felt among all these horse-obsessives, and how she missed her mates, and her telly, and her own home, and all her things, like her CDs and her computer. Annie just listened and nodded understandingly, so that after awhile Sabine suspected she had heard much of this already from Mrs. H. That just fueled her sense of victimhood. For that was what she must be, she mused, if they were talking about her in sympathetic tones.

"And why's your mam not over here, Sabine? Is she working?"

Sabine halted briefly, unsure how much to give away. They were nice people, but she hardly knew them, and she did feel some loyalty to her mother.

"Yes," she lied. "She wanted to come over, but she was too busy."

"What does she do now?" said Mrs. H. "It's so long since I've seen her."

"She writes." She paused. "Not books and stuff. Just features for newspapers. About families."

"Any old families?" Mrs. H shoveled a tray of food into the oven.

"Not really. Family life in general. Problems and stuff."

"That sounds very handy," said Mrs. H.

"You must miss her," said Annie.

"Sorry?"

"Your mam. You must miss her. Her being so far away and all."

"A bit." She hesitated, then said boldly. "We're not that close, actually."

"But she's your mam. You must be close." And suddenly, inexplicably, Annie's eyes appeared to fill with tears.

Sabine stared at her in horror, trying to work out what she could have said to have prompted this. Mrs. H, looking sharply at her daughter, called her over.

"Sabine—I've found a bit of fish in the freezer cabinet. Do you fancy this, if I do it in a butter sauce? Perhaps you could help me defrost it in the microwave. Annie, love, why don't you go and fetch Patrick and tell him we'll be eating in about twenty minutes."

Sabine stood slowly, and, trying not to stare too conspicuously at Annie, walked over to the kitchen.

Annie became very quiet for about half an hour after that. She hardly spoke through supper, and her husband spoke very little, so it was left to Mrs. H and Sabine, who was feeling rather unnerved, to carry the conversation. Patrick was not the writer-type she had imagined: not thin and tortured-looking, but a big man, barrel-chested and slightly

coarse-featured, with lines like plowed fur-
rows along his forehead and down the sides
of his mouth. But he was gentle, and solicitous, and he had that quiet air of intelligence
that made Sabine slightly tongue-tied, and
aware that almost everything she said
sounded trite or stupid.

"Is your dinner all right, Patrick? It was all
a bit of a rush job, I'm afraid."

"It's grand, Mam," he replied. "Lovely bit of
lamb."

Sabine, who found herself staring at
Annie, found it hard to picture the two
together. He was so big and rough-looking,
while she was so small and insubstantial,
as if some melancholy breeze could just
blow her away. And yet he obviously adored
her; although he said little, Sabine noticed
him touch her on the arm twice and once,
gently, rub her back with slow, loving
strokes.

"Have you anyone coming this weekend?"
said Mrs. H, picking up one of her chops with
her knife and fork, and placing it on Patrick's
already overstuffed plate.

Patrick looked at Annie, and then back at
his mother-in-law. "I don't think there's anyone booked. I had a thought Annie and I

might go up to Galway, just for a bit of a change."

"Galway," exclaimed Mrs. H. "Lough Inagh, now there's a beautiful spot. Me and your father used to holiday there every year when you were small, Annie. The weather was always terrible, for some reason, but you used to love it. We bought you these Wellington boots with glitter on, you see, and you just ran up and down in the water all day long."

Annie didn't look up.

Mrs. H, briefly lost in past happinesses, continued: "One night you even insisted on sleeping in them, you loved those boots so much. In the morning your bed was that full of sand I had to shake your sheets out of the window! Ahh, bless. You were only three."

Annie shot a sharp look at her mother, who abruptly shut up. For a few minutes, all that could be heard was the spit and crackle of the fire, and the distant thrum of the rain on the windowsill. Sabine, watching, glanced back at Annie, wondering what Mrs. H had said that was so wrong. But she just looked down again, and pushed her half-full plate toward the center of the table.

Curiously, Mrs. H didn't seem to mind. She just waited until she was sure everyone

had finished and began collecting the plates.
Not in that kind of brisk I'm-doing-this-to-
make-a-point way that her own mother did
when she had been rude to her. She just
seemed genuinely unoffended, as if all she
had to consider was the destination of the
plates themselves.

"It doesn't have to be Galway," said
Patrick, gently, in his wife's ear. "We could go
to Dublin. A city break. It's meant to be a
great craic at the moment."

There was a brief pause.

"Maybe another time, eh?" Annie patted
her husband's arm, stood, and walked without explanation from the room.

Mrs. H pushed her own chair back, and
walked toward the kitchen. "Now, Sabine,
you'll have some pudding, won't you? We've
got some apple pie that I can heat up in the
microwave, or a bit of chocolate ice cream.
I'll bet you'll not say no to some ice cream.
Am I right?"

She didn't give Sabine time to wonder
what was going on. Patrick, with an affectionate kiss on his mother-in-law's cheek,
also left the room, but nodded to a query
about pudding, suggesting he would soon
be back. It was at this perplexing moment

that the door opened and Thom walked in, the wind blowing behind him and his oilcloth coat slick with rain. Sabine almost ran to greet him; she had started to feel a little uncomfortable.

"Have I missed dinner? One of the boxes started letting in water, so I thought I should try and whack a tarpaulin on the roof before I left. It's filthy out there," he said.

"Sit down, love, sit down. Put your coat over by that chair. I've kept yours in the oven. Lamb chops all right for you?" The atmo sphere in the room seemed to immediately relax and expand, so that Sabine sat back in her chair. Thom had that air—he just seemed to defuse tension. Sabine grinned at him and he grinned back.

"Did you get to watch some good telly, then, Sabine?"

Sabine, embarrassed, looked at Mrs. H. "I didn't come just to watch the telly. I wanted to meet—everybody."

"Ahh, was there something you wanted to watch, love? To be honest, what with the dinner and everything I didn't give it a thought. Well, let's have it on while we're having our pudding, shall we? There might be a film on, mightn't there?"

They sat, channel-surfing companionably, as Thom wolfed his way through his food. He ate voraciously, head down, his knife and fork working in tandem to scoop the food into his mouth—the kind of eating employed by siblings of large families, determined not to lose out on second helpings. Mrs. H nodded and smiled with some silent satisfaction. She was evidently fond of her nephew; she looked at him like one would a favored son. Sabine, watching this in the warm room, her own stomach full, and the distant roar of the wind and rain outside, felt a sudden pang that her own grandmother's house couldn't feel enclosed and warm like this one did. She didn't even know these people and already she felt loath to return to Kilcarrion House.

Sabine looked up as Annie walked back in. She was smiling. Patrick was standing behind her, looking slightly anxious.

"Hi, there, Tomcat," Annie said, ruffling Thom's hair. "How's my favorite cousin? You look like a drowned rat."

"You want to try going out some time," said Thom, reaching up and squeezing her hand. "It's called weather."

Still smiling, Annie sat back down at the

table. Patrick sat next to her, gazing at his wife. He didn't touch his pudding.

"Where have you been all week?" Annie said to Thom. "I've hardly seen hide or hair of you."

"I've been around," he said. "Busy time of year. Getting the horses ready for the start of the season. All right there, Patrick?"

"You and your horses. You want to get yourself a girlfriend, have some proper interests. What happened to that girl from the restaurant? She was all right."

Thom didn't look up from his food.

"Not my type."

"And what is your type?"

"Not her."

Mrs. H, wiping down surfaces in the kitchen, burst into a laugh. "You should know by now, Annie. You'll not get Thom to tell you a thing. He could have a wife and six children at home and his own family would know nothing about it. Have you ever met a bloke like him, eh, Sabine?"

Sabine found she was blushing. To her relief, no one seemed to notice.

"Your trouble is you're too picky," said Annie, pushing her melted ice cream around a bowl.

"Probably."

Mrs. H glanced at her daughter a few times, but, apart from that, didn't remark upon her brief absence. She seemed to relax now that Thom was here, and busied herself with the washing up, dismissing Sabine's half-hearted offer to help.

"You sit down. You're the guest."

"Ahh, don't say that, Mam. You'll make her feel like one of the Twoobies."

Sabine glanced at Thom for explanation.

"Twoobies. B-and-Bers," said Patrick. "Our paying guests."

"I thought they were inmates," said Thom. "You're not saying you make them pay as well?"

"You're not a guest," said Annie, ignoring him and placing a hand on Sabine's arm. "You're a Ballantyne, so you're practically family. And you're welcome anytime. I could do with the company." Her smile was genuinely warm.

Mrs. H nodded, as if confirming it. "Would you like a cup of tea, Patrick? I could bring it up to you if you're working?"

"Thanks, Mam. I'm fine with my wine here. Thom, have you got a drink?"

Sabine went to pass him the bottle of wine,

but almost before she could get there, Mrs. H had passed him a glass of orange juice, which he picked up and drained greedily.

"I'll have another drink," said Annie, looking around her. "Where's my glass gone?"

"I washed it up," said Mrs. H.

"Well, you can pass me another one then. I hadn't finished that."

Thom looked up from his food. "How's the book going?"

Patrick shook his head.

"It's a bit sticky at the moment, to tell you the truth."

"I don't know how you do it, sitting up there by yourself day after day," said Mrs. H. "I'd be bored out of my mind. No people, no one to talk to, just those characters in your head. I'm surprised you don't go mad. . . ." She finished washing the pans. "Right, then, I'm done. I'll be off in a minute. Your father's out at his club this evening and I want to be in before he gets home."

"Off to meet your fancy man, eh, Mam?" Patrick stood and held out her coat for her. "Don't worry. We won't say a thing."

"She likes to welcome him home," said Thom, shaking his head in disbelief.

"If I like to welcome my husband home,

then it's no one else's business but our own," she said, pinking slightly.

"And the neighbors," said Patrick, grinning at Thom. "The poor things."

"You're a rogue, Patrick Connolly," she said, now bright pink. "Now, will someone walk Sabine home, all right? I don't want her on that dark road by herself."

"It's only one hundred yards. I'm fine, honest," said Sabine, chafing at the suggestion of her youth.

"Don't worry," said Thom. "We'll chuck her out after closing time."

"Thanks for cooking, Mam," said Annie, walking her to the door and kissing her. She was smiling all the time now, a soft, gentle smile, although it still didn't seem to stretch to her eyes. Right behind her, Patrick kissed his wife tenderly, and then walked slowly back upstairs. She had patted him vaguely in response, as one would a child.

As Sabine watched, Annie closed the door after her mother and then stood still in the center of the room, as if unsure where to put herself. After a few seconds she walked over to the sofa and collapsed on it, tucking her knees under her chin. "Right, Sabine, why don't you find a film or something," she said, looking suddenly, desperately weary. "And you two chat or something. I hope you don't mind, but I'll probably just crash here. I'm all out of talking today."

Your friend Melissa rang, and wanted to know if you were going to go to her party on the fifteenth. I told her I didn't know if you were going to be back or not."

"Oh."

"And O'Malley was sick in your room, but I've put your rug in the dry cleaners and they think it will be no problem."

"Is he all right?"

"He's fine. It's just because I ran out of cat food and he wolfed down a can of tuna."

"You're not meant to give him tuna."

"I know, sweetheart. But the corner shop was shut and I couldn't see him go hungry. He's all right with it when he doesn't eat so quickly."

Sabine had rung her mother the previous day with the intention of begging her for enough money to get her home. She was going to tell her that she loved her, and that she was sorry for being such a cow, and that everything would be better if she could just come home, because she knew, and she knew her mother would understand, that she couldn't stand being stuck here one more minute.

But they had been on the phone some seven minutes now, her mother evidently a bit bemused as to what Sabine had wanted when she left her "urgent" message to call, and yet Sabine just couldn't find the words. She wanted to go back, she really did. But it was somehow slightly less urgent since the previous evening, at Annie's house. And she found that she was still, deep inside somewhere, furious about Geoff and Justin. And it was so *hard* being overly nice to her mother. Kate just got all emotional and said too much back, so that Sabine ended up regretting saying anything and feeling faintly cross, like she had somehow given too much away. Her mother never could just let things be.

"So . . . what have you been up to? Has Granny got you riding yet?"

"No. And I'm not going to."

"So what have you been doing with yourself?"

Sabine thought about the box of photographs that she had revisited this morning, while her grandmother was out at the shop, and the ones she had found of her mother as a young girl with the Chinese boy. She thought of Annie's house, and the way that Annie had just gone to sleep in front of her last night, as abruptly as anything, as if she didn't care what anybody even thought of her doing so. She thought of Thom asking, with just a shade too much awkwardness, what it was her mother did these days.

"Nothing," she said.

Chapter Three

O'Malley the cat sat, like a stone sentry, on the top of the gatepost, his slightly raised fur a textured gauge of the freezing temperatures outside. Across the road, in a woolly hat, Mr. Ogonye worked on his car, as he so often did, thrusting himself determinedly under the bonnet like a circus tamer entering a lion's mouth, and then withdrawing from it, wiping his hands mournfully backward and forward on a piece of cloth, as if plucking up the courage to do it again. Between the dustbins, most of which were still standing by the curb, abandoned since the morning collection, two crisp packets chased each other in gritty circles.

Have you ever wondered whether you and your child are speaking the same language? Well, according to new research from Switzerland, you may not be.

In a report likely to raise murmurs of "I knew it" in households across Europe, social psychologists from the University of Geneva have discovered that what parents say and what children hear are often two different things.

Agnes, wearing a thin blue coat and walking slowly with her new aluminum frame, stopped and spoke to him as she passed, and Mr. Ogonye shook his head sadly, gesturing toward his engine. As they spoke, the cold air solidified into little mushroom clouds in front of them, like speech bubbles waiting to be filled.

"Parents very rarely put themselves into their children's shoes," said Professor Friedrich Ansbulger, who headed the study of 2,000 families. "Yet if they did, they would understand why often their children completely disregard their instructions. It's not necessarily disobedience—it's just that

it doesn't fit their alternative brand of logic."

Kate sighed and made herself look back down at her computer. It had taken her almost an hour to write three paragraphs, and at this rate she was going to be earning an hourly rate that would shock a Bangladeshi sweatshop.

It was not hard for a woman with her imagination to come up with reasons for her inability to work these last days. The house was too silent, for a start. Even though Sabine was rarely in, Kate found their home was curiously deadened by the knowledge that the front door was not about to slam, that she was not going to hear that familiar footfall clumping up the stairs, the closing of her bedroom door, followed by the muffled beat of some inaudible band. And, just occasionally, a muttered hello.

Then there was the central heating, the failure of which had left her swaddled in layers like a bag lady, and at which the plumber had shaken his head with a look of pitied resignation not dissimilar to Mr. Ogonye's own, promising to come back with the right part. That had been three days ago.

Then there was this stupid piece, which just stubbornly refused to write itself. On a good day, Kate could churn out two 800-word features before lunch. Today was not one of those days; contacts failed to return calls, words slid awkwardly around a page; Kate's motivation levels sank underneath her own self-pity.

For this was the first week she had been properly on her own in her adult life. Sabine had always been here; and when she was off on school trips, or away with friends, there had been Geoff, and before him, Jim. She had always known there was going to be someone here at the end of the day, to share a bowl of pasta, a bottle of wine, and mull over the day's events. Now Geoff was gone, Justin was away on a working trip with no discernible deadline, and Sabine was in Ireland, apparently determined to speak to her as little as possible. And it was all her own fault.

She tried, for the umpteenth time, not to think about how Geoff would have gotten the central heating sorted out within hours. He had been the practical one. He had numbers, numbers that summoned reliable workmen whom he had known for years, and who would generally come to them first, as a favor, to be rewarded by a generous "drink," as Geoff always quaintly called it. When he had first urged Kate to give their electrician a drink, she had made him a cup of herbal tea, and the two men had grinned ruefully at each other, then laughed in a backslapping we're-all-blokes-together kind of way. At the time she had hated it, seeing it as evidence of some kind of perceived naïveté on her part. In a freezing house, with the benefit of hindsight, she found it quite endearing. But she couldn't ask Geoff. And Justin, as he had told her regretfully, "didn't do domestic."

In fact, three months into this relationship, there were increasing numbers of things Justin "didn't do." He didn't do phoning every night while he was away. ("Look, sweetheart, it's just not always possible. My mobile is always running out and if we work late, or we're in really dodgy areas, the last thing I can do is go out hunting for a phone box.") He didn't do living together. ("I love what we've got. And I don't want to spoil that. And I would spoil that.") And he didn't do planning for the future. ("You are the most fabulous woman I've ever met. I want to be with you more than anyone I've ever been with. And that's just going to have to do for now.")

Kate, staring unseeing at her computer screen, made herself focus on the things she did do, scolding herself for looking for problems. He loved her, didn't he? He told her all the time.

Glancing up, she could see Agnes, still gamely shoving her frame before her toward the corner of the street, her white fluffy head bobbing on its frail neck like a dandelion in the breeze. She would be on her way to Luis's Café on the High Street, where every day, with relentless regularity, she arrived at twelve-forty-five for her egg, chips, tea, and a solitary chuckle at the tabloids. After that, she would travel, depending on the day, to either the bingo hall, the drop-in center, or the library, returning home only when those institutions closed. It had taken Kate several years of living next door to Agnes to discover that her neighbor's admirably sociable life-style disguised her inability to heat her maisonette properly. Come on, she told herself, chilled by her sudden sense of empathy, finish this piece, or you have to go out.

Perhaps all this solitude would be for the best. Because Geoff was coming for the last of his stuff this evening, and after the disaster that was their first meeting, she couldn't cope with having him and Justin together. It was hard enough seeing Geoff by himself.

Kate sat there, staring at the words in front of her, debating her two mutually unattractive options for the afternoon ahead. Then she swapped her glasses for contact lenses, added an extra layer of clothing, and, with a deep sense of foreboding, headed off to the community center.

Can you push those tables over, the ones by the door? I don't think there are enough for everybody."

Maggie Cheung stood wrapped in her padded coat in the middle of the drafty community hall, directing furniture like a drunken police officer directing traffic. Her brow furrowed in concentration, she would gesticulate emphatically, and then swiftly change her mind, sending Kate or one of the students back across the room with their screeching cargo of Formica tables or molded chairs, as she tried to determine the best way to fit everybody in.

Behind her, in a circle, a group of elderly Chinese women chattered loudly and obliviously in Cantonese, engrossed in a game of

something like dominoes. On opposite sides
of the room, near the old men sipping jas-
mine tea from plastic beakers, two young
women, both silent and miserable as their
children, ignored each other and the solitary
younger man between them.

"There isn't going to be enough room no
matter how you do it," said Ian, the manager,
after a quick burst of mental arithmetic.

"The helpers can eat standing up," said
Maggie.

"It's still going to be tight. It might be better
to do two shifts." Ian's downcast expression
and gray pallor illustrated the difficulties of a
life of publicly funded compromise.

"Better to squeeze everyone in than do
two sittings," observed Maggie. "That way we
stay warmer."

"I'm sorry about the heating," said Ian, for
the fifth time. "It's the budget cuts. We have
to save what we've got for Elderlies and New
Mums on Tuesdays and Fridays."

Kate, now warmed through effort, hauled
her two tables across the room, and slotted
them, under Maggie's instruction, into a circular arrangement close to the kitchen.
Despite the other woman's confidence, she
couldn't see how everyone could eat lunch

at the same time. But Maggie was insistent—this group was meant to forge bonds between the old and the young, the newly arrived and the long-settled—and there was no point at all having an outreach group if all you were going to do was divide them.

"Besides," she said cheerfully, "it's our culture. Everyone eats together."

Kate didn't point out that Maggie's much-referred-to culture was somewhat elastic, taking in trips to McDonald's with her sons, split-shift dining with her doctor husband, who worked erratic hours at the local hospital, and a devotional love of *Coronation Street*. There was never any point arguing with Maggie; like a well-practiced politician she would simply "mishear" anything that didn't fit in to her current worldview, and cheerfully restate her opinions as if they had never been questioned.

"There! All done!" she exclaimed, some minutes later. "And we can keep the tables like this afterward. Did I tell you I've persuaded one of the teachers from Brownleigh School to come and do reading and writing skills? If I see another housing benefit form I think I'm going to die."

"If I don't have some success with Mr.

Yip's form, I think he's going to make sure
I'm the one that dies," said Ian. It was the
closest he came to humor, and Maggie and
Kate smiled obligingly.

"You're not telling me they've sent it back
again."

"Fourth time. I wouldn't mind, but it's me
who fills it in. If I can't do it, after eleven
years working for the council, how the hell
can anybody else be expected to?"

Kate had become a volunteer helper at
the Dalston and Hackney Oriental Outreach
Group almost a year before Geoff left. One
night, when he had briefly emerged, blinking, from the *American Journal of Applied
Psychiatry*, he had bemoaned the shock-
ingly high rates of mental illness in immi-
grants, prompted by the isolation, alienation,
and racism of their inner-city placements,
and had talked of Maggie's work in trying to
combat it. Kate had been surprised at the
extent of Maggie's involvement—despite a
lengthy friendship, Maggie and Kate tended
to restrict their conversations to partner and
kids. But then he had brought it up again
when Maggie and Hamish had come for
supper, and Kate had discovered that Maggie's reticence had only been due to a per-

ceived lack of interest on her own part. She, in turn, had swiftly elicited a feeble promise from Kate to come and help.

"I don't really know what I could do," she said, not sure if she really wanted to. But when Maggie discovered that Kate's early years had been spent in Hong Kong, there was no prospect of escape. "My God, woman. You know Chinese culture!" she had exclaimed. "You are practically Chinese!" And ignored Kate's protestations that from the age of eight her "culture" had consisted of boarding school in Shropshire and village life in southern Ireland. "So what?" she responded. "I've never lived farther east than Theydon Bois."

Even after all these months, Kate was of little practical help. Unlike the other volunteers, she couldn't speak the language, she couldn't cook, and she couldn't find her way around the Kafkaesque requirements of the social security forms. All she could offer was backup help with the reading classes, and her physical presence. But Maggie didn't seem to mind. And Kate had actually enjoyed some of it—watching the volunteer chef from the local take-away cook authentic Chinese dishes in the center's little kitchen, observing the way the older people seemed so much closer and more animated than their European equivalents—had enjoyed her brief immersions into a different world. She liked the way Maggie switched from anglicized to Chinese, the way she gathered these disparate people around her, bringing them together by sheer force of her personality. And in some perverse way, working at the group had helped assuage the guilt she had felt about leaving Geoff, providing an opportunity to buy herself some atonement, once a week, for her sins. Most of the time it worked.

"I didn't think you were coming today," said Maggie, appearing suddenly at her shoulder. Her height meant it was uncommon to view her from any other angle, despite Maggie's fondness for spike heels.

"I nearly didn't," Kate admitted. "Not really in the mood."

"It's always better to get out of the house if you're feeling miserable. Away from gas ovens. Oh, no, you're electric, aren't you? We'll talk at lunch."

"I don't know if I'm really going to stay for lunch."

Maggie didn't appear to hear her.

"Look at them! They should be talking!" she exclaimed, drawing Kate to one side, and pointing at one of the silent young mothers. "Two young girls, two babies. It's absolutely ridiculous having them both sitting there in silence. We must get them talking. Mind you, that one there—we've got to get her to take her baby for inoculations. She's been here nearly six months, but silly girl won't go to the health center."

Four weeks after he had brought her to England, Maggie said, the girl's husband had left, telling her he was going off to earn some money. Apart from an unconfirmed sighting in Nottingham, that had been the last time she had heard of him. She had permission to remain in the country, but no job, a shared bed sit, and not enough money to return home.

"She just needs to get talking to people. Open up a bit. You go and chat to her while I see how lunch is coming on," she instructed, and bustled off.

Working at the center usually put Kate's own problems in perspective. But she had had second thoughts about coming all morning; the mood of despondence prompted by her home's unnatural silence had perversely left her with little appetite for company. Sabine had once told her that they divided girls in her class into "drains and radiators": Radiators being those popular girls who gave out interest and enthusiasm, drawing people around them closer; and drains being . . . well, drains: those who sucked out atmosphere and goodwill like a vacuum. Today, Kate thought, she was a definite drain.

A drain who had to be a radiator. Dragging her feet like a schoolgirl, Kate walked slowly over to the young girl, who sat slumped in her cheap anorak, plastic shoes, and a pervasive stench of misery. She wasn't sure how she could help in the face of such momentous despair. And Maggie knew very well that the girl spoke no English. But with the bossily evangelical air of a Sunday school teacher, she just seemed to expect people to get on with it. Those with a will would find a way.

Kate took a deep breath, stopped a short distance away from the girl, giving her time to realize she was approaching, and then smiled, and gestured toward the baby.

"Hello," she said. "I'm Kate."

The girl, her hair scraped back in a ponytail, and faint bluish shadows denoting more than the young mother's customary lack of sleep, looked blankly at her and then glanced around the room, looking for Maggie, or one of the Chinese helpers.

"Kate," she said, pointing at herself, aware that she was speaking too loud, like an imbecilic colonial expecting that volume alone would help the natives understand.

The girl looked at her wide-eyed and expectant. With a gesture as insubstantial as she looked, she shook her head.

Kate breathed deeply. What on earth was she meant to do? She didn't have that gift for putting people immediately at their ease. Most of the time, she felt too ill at ease herself.

"I'm Kate. I help out here." she said, helplessly. Then: "What's your name?"

The resulting silence was broken by a burst of laughter from the other side of the room, and the rapid gunfire of scattered dominoes hitting a tabletop. The elderly players had concluded their game. Maggie moved among them, exclaiming and congratulating in Chinese, her sleek black hair obscuring her face as she leaned over to examine the board.

Kate turned back to the girl, trying to maintain her smile.

"Boy or girl?" she said, gesturing toward the infant, whose sleeping face was just visible beneath the layers of donated clothing.

"Boy?" She pointed at the man seated nearby, so that he looked at her with a sudden expression of distrust.

"Or girl?" She pointed at herself.

Oh, God, but she sounded like an idiot. Her smile now becoming painful to maintain, she moved closer to the child.

"Your baby is beautiful." It was. They all were, when asleep.

The girl looked at her baby, and then back at Kate, clutching it slightly tighter to her as she did.

I'm going to give up, thought Kate. I'll just point her over toward the food table and let Maggie do it. I'm just not any good at this. She thought, briefly, longingly, of her empty home. Then suddenly, two words flashed into her brain, a mental echo; two words from her childhood, whispered softly from her amah's lips.

"*Hou leng,*" she said, gesturing toward the child. Then louder: "*Hou leng.*"

The girl looked down at the baby and back up again. She frowned slightly, as if unable to believe what was being said.

"Your baby. *Hou leng.*"

Two sweet, soft words: Very beautiful. The international language of flattery.

Kate felt a surge of warmth. She could do this, after all. She racked her brains, trying to remember whether she had achieved the correct tones.

"*Hou leng.* Very beautiful," she said again, smiling with benevolent delight.

Then Maggie appeared behind her.

"What are you doing to the poor girl?" she said. "She doesn't speak Cantonese. She's from the mainland, you daft woman. She speaks Mandarin. She won't have a clue what you're going on about."

Tall, slim, public-school Hamish was an unlikely partner for Maggie. People had been saying so for the eighteen years they had been married. It was not just Maggie's height, the dark, earthy voluptuousness of her, against his insubstantial pallor, or the noisy, Chinese immediacy of her and her children's emotions, set against Hamish's northern European placidity. It was just that she seemed too much for him. Too much for almost anyone Kate could think of, come to that. She was too loud, too upfront. Too sure of herself. Kate was fairly sure she had not changed one iota since adolescence. It was why Hamish adored her.

Kate, on the other hand, had changed with practically every man she had ever been with. It was the changes they had wrought in her that had determined how far she fell for them. With Jim, she had been the young, hip parent, had enjoyed the loose, loving way with which he had treated both her and her daughter, the way that for the first time since Sabine's birth, she had not felt entirely defined by her status as "mummy." He had given her back some of her youth, she had thought at the time, lightened her up, enabled her to stop worrying. Taught her about sex. But then, when things had begun to go wrong, and she had begun to suspect, she had hated the person he made her become. Hated being that paranoid, unhappy wretch, begging for truth, desperately changing her appearance in an attempt to win back his attention from the unseen threat. And when he had finally gone, the sadness had been tinged with relief that she didn't have to be that person anymore.

When Geoff had moved in, she had been an older, wiser lover. She had not given as much to him, conscious of the need, this time, to hold something back. Yet he had given her everything. Everything he had, that is. With Geoff, she had become a grown-up. He had expanded her mind, talked to her about politics, and society, and made her look harder at the injustices of the world around her. If the comfort had outweighed the passion, then that had been fine, she had told herself. She was probably better with someone who kept her steady. With Geoff, she had learned to use her brain, and it had felt like growing up. And he had been so sweet with Sabine, never attempting to push himself on her, or play daddy, but simply providing her with this solid backdrop of love and wisdom.

But then, six years on, had come Justin. Justin, who had made her realize that there was a whole side of her that had lain dormant for years, and now insisted on bursting through to the fore. She was a sexual being, and he made her sexual, and once it had sprung forth, like a geyser, it refused to be subdued. No one had made her glow like he did; no one left her blushing, and walking giddily, like a drunk, at nine o'clock in the morning. No one had surrounded her with a virtual aura of sexuality, a fizzing cloak of pheromones, so that she found herself turning heads, drawing wolf whistles, even when dressed down. And she deserved it, didn't she? She had told herself, desperately trying to rationalize the hurt she was about to cause. She was allowed another chance? Why should she have to give up on romantic love at the age of thirty-five?

"Is this a thin-person conspiracy? While you've been sitting there dreaming, I've eaten nearly all the cheung fun." Maggie, perched against the sink unit of the kitchen, waved her chopsticks vigorously in front of Kate's nose. "Just because you can't tell the difference between Cantonese and Mandarin doesn't mean you're not allowed to eat the food."

"Sorry," said Kate, pushing at her lunch as it congealed in the bowl. She had thought she was hungry, but her appetite, so erratic of late, had chosen again to disappear.

"Oh, God. Not lovesick still. Not the can't-eat-a-thing stage at . . . What is it now? Three months?"

"I don't know what stage I'm at," said Kate, miserably. "Yes, I do. The guilty stage."

Maggie raised a carefully plucked eyebrow. When Kate had revealed she was leaving Geoff for Justin, she had expected that Maggie, who had known Geoff longer, would automatically take sides. But it hadn't happened; Maggie, perhaps fittingly for someone apparently able to hold two conflicting points of view at once, also appeared to have a capacity to retain dual loyalty.

"The guilty stage? Oh, don't be so wet. For God's sake. You're happy, aren't you? Justin's happy? Geoff is, let's be honest, hardly suicidal. Not the type, with all that psychiatric training. Probably giving himself a good therapeutic talking to even as we speak." She honked with laughter, sending a piece of noodle flying across the table.

"It's not Geoff. It's Sabine." Kate paused. "I'm wrecking her life."

Maggie took a last piece of paperwrapped prawn, sighed deeply, and then pushed her bowl toward the overflowing sink.

"I see. So it's adolescent hell, is it? The girl-child giving you a hard time?"

"Not as such. To be honest, she hardly talks to me. But I can see it, written all over her face. She thinks I've ruined her whole life. And she hates me for sending her to stay at my mother's."

"Now, *that* you can't blame her for, if what you have told me is at all true. But as for ruining her life, don't be so melodramatic." She grinned at Kate. "Fine coming from me, I know. But come *on*, she's hardly an abused waif, is she?"

Kate gazed at her, desperate for reassurance.

Maggie held up one hand, and began ticking off her plump fingers.

"One: Is she clothed and fed? Yes. Too bloody well, if you ask me, all that ridiculous label stuff. Two: Have you ever brought anyone cruel into her life? No. All your men—well, both your live-in men—have absolutely adored her, not that the little madam has ever given them much back, bless her. Three: Was Geoff her real daddy? No, as she was at great pains to tell him on any possible occasion. Four: Will she leave home within the next few years and without a backward glance? Absolutely."

"Oh, well, that makes me feel a load better."

"Just being honest, darling. All I'm saying

is that you worry too much. Sabine is about as well adjusted a teenager as you can cultivate around here. And I mean that in a positive way. She's bright, she's bolshie, and she doesn't take shit from anyone. You have no need to worry."

"But she doesn't talk to me anymore. She just stopped talking."

"She's just sixteen, for God's sake. I didn't speak to my parents for about four years, and there were two of them."

"But what if it's because of me? What if she keeps on hating me?"

"You wait till she wants a car. Or a deposit on her first flat. The love will return, believe me. The love will return."

Kate gazed out of the window at the gray frontages of Kingsland Road; the car stereo and hardware shops, the local cafés, grimy billboards and welfare offices that proved that no matter what the estate agents insisted, this "up and coming" area resolutely insisted on going no further. What made her think her daughter was going to be any better off in the cloistered, green acres of Kilcarrion? What good had they ever done her?

She toyed with a plump, pink prawn,

pushing it on a solitary journey around the rim of her plate.

"Do you ever get bored of Hamish?"

She wasn't sure where the question had come from, but once it was out she realized she needed to know the answer. Maggie, her cup raised to her mouth, lowered it slowly and considered with equal levity her answer.

"Bored? Bored . . . I don't know if I get *bored* exactly. I sometimes want to throttle him. Will that do?"

"But what makes you stay together? You can't be happy all the time. Can you?" The last two words came out a little plaintively, so that Kate tried to turn them into a joke.

"Of course we're not happy all the time. No couple is happy all the time, and if anyone tells you they are, she's bloody lying. But you know that." Maggie frowned. "What is this, Kate? Honestly, sometimes you can sound like a fifteen-year-old talking about relationships."

"That's because I feel about as good at them as a fifteen-year-old. But what makes you stay together? What keeps you hanging around at the point at which you want to disappear?" The point, she thought silently, at which I usually disappear?

"What keeps us together? Apart from the cost of a good divorce lawyer and the fact that our house has hardly risen in value in five years? Oh, and those evil trolls masquerading as our children? The truth, Kate? I don't honestly know. . . . Yes, I do. It's that despite being a complete arsehole sometimes, crap with money, frequently drunk, and frankly not a great shag apart from birthdays and special occasions, I genuinely can't imagine being with anyone else but Hamish. Does that help?"

"I've never been in a relationship where I haven't imagined being with someone else," confessed Kate, sadly.

"Oh, I'm not counting fantasizing about Robert Mitchum."

"Nor am I. Oh, God. Robert *Mitchum*?"

"I know," Maggie grinned. "He's my guilty secret. He just looked like he'd have been so *stern*, you know?"

"But I'm not counting sexual fantasies. I have always thought about being with someone else. I have crushes on other people and stuff."

"You *are* fifteen. I knew it."

"Oh, God, what's wrong with me? Why am

I so bloody useless at relationships?" She hadn't actually meant to say it out loud.

Maggie began gathering up the empty bowls piled up on trays around the kitchen.

"Hate to say this, gorgeous, bearing in mind your current squeeze, and all that. But perhaps you just haven't met the right person."

Justin rang at a quarter to seven, shortly before Geoff was due to arrive. Kate was grateful for his call, grateful that over the tinny telephone line the sound of his voice could still flood her with warmth and longing, reassure her that her decision had been the right one. It had been rather unnerving, her conversation with Maggie, even if she had brought it all upon herself with her overly introspective mood. Now Justin, ringing unexpectedly, put it all right.

"I was thinking about you," he said. "And I just wanted to hear your voice."

"Oh, I'm so glad you did," she said, a little breathlessly. "I miss you so much."

His voice sounded a million miles away. "God, I wish you were here. I can't stop thinking about you."

She paused.

"How's everything—?"

"Where are you—?" They both began speaking simultaneously and then broke off, each unwilling to interrupt the other. "You first," said Kate, cursing the telephone system for the awkward time lags.

"Look, I can't talk long. I just wanted to say that I'll probably be back by the weekend. We've only got one more person to see, and then I'm hoping to leave the others here and get out on an early flight."

"Do you want me to meet you at the airport? Just ring when you've got your flight details."

"No, don't bother. I'm not a great fan of all that arrivals reunion stuff."

Kate tried to bite back her disappointment. She had had a sudden vision of them embracing in the middle of Heathrow, he dressed in dusty khaki, lines of exhaustion wiped from his face at the sight of her. For God's sake, she scolded herself. Maggie was right. You really are fifteen.

"I'll cook something nice then. For when you get back."

"You don't need to do that."

"I want to. I miss you."

"I just mean that I'm likely to be knackered, and filthy, and will probably head home first and sleep for twelve hours. I'll see you when I'm clean and rested. We'll go out somewhere fun."

Kate told him she would look forward to it, trying to hide the disappointment she felt at his lack of urgency. She wanted to see him as soon as he touched down; sweaty, exhausted, or whatever, she wanted to smother him in kisses, run him a hot bath, hand him glasses of wine as she listened to his tales of derring-do. Then feed him up with home cooking and watch him doze contentedly on her sofa. But then Justin wasn't really the dozing kind. In fact, she had a strong suspicion that Justin was somewhere not a million miles from hyperactive. He found it difficult to sit still anywhere; he fidgeted and tapped his fingers on his knees, rubbed at his sandy hair, and paced the room. She supposed it was what made him good at his job. Even in his sleep he flinched and murmured as if on some constant nocturnal trail.

Restless, Kate walked slowly up to her room, and stood, staring at herself in the long mirror on the door of the Edwardian wardrobe. What does he see in me? she thought, feeling suddenly vulnerable, at odds with herself. He could have anyone, and yet he picked me: a thirty-five-year-old woman with stretch marks and the definite beginnings of crows'-feet and hair that was, while luxuriant and red, apparently too long for her age, according to her daughter. A woman who, having missed out on her youth, had somehow never gotten to grips with fashion—not knowing where she quite fit in to it all. Sabine told her that the 1950s and 1960s second-hand clothes she got from the shop in Stoke Newington were "a joke"; but Kate had liked them, liked the good fabrics and the feeling of quality that she couldn't afford in a wardrobe of today. She had liked the fact that they separated her from all those thirty-five-year-old mums she saw at Sainsbury's. But now, laid under a sudden cloud of self-doubt, she wondered whether she simply looked odd, out of place. Will he go off me? she thought, peering at her reflection. He was the same age as she was, but his whole lifestyle was so transient, so free of responsibility, that it could have belonged to someone ten years younger.

Would he ultimately want someone who shared that freedom?

Kate closed her wardrobe door, trying to displace the thoughts crowding into her head. She was just no good at being alone; it gave her much too much time to think, too much time to mull over everything. Too much of her happiness was dictated by her love life, that's what Maggie had said. She made herself too vulnerable that way. She had denied it, but had been notably unable to come up with reasons why Maggie was wrong. And Maggie had said what she did without knowing half of it: how Kate had spent a fortune on new bed linens because Justin had once remarked that he slept best on white Egyptian cotton; how she had turned down at least two well-paid commissions because she wasn't sure when he was getting back and didn't want to be working when he arrived; how she found it altogether too much effort to look nice when Justin wasn't here and had spent most of his absence in her black plastic reading glasses, a T-shirt, and a pair of pajama bottoms.

God, but she was no good at being alone. She would get a lodger. Or a dog. Or something. Anything to stop these depressive thoughts. Come on, she scolded herself. Geoff will be here soon. Straighten yourself up.

Glad of a reason to stop thinking, Kate brushed her hair, marveling at the tangles that could be caused by two days' neglect, applied her lipstick, and then, without thinking, applied perfume: Mitsouko, by Guerlain. Then stared in horror at the bottle; Geoff had bought her that perfume. Every Valentine's Day. It was his favorite. He might think she had changed her mind, that she wanted to win him back. Kate stared at her reflection, and then, after a moment's hesitation, took a tissue and rubbed off the lipstick. She did up the top button of her 1950s cream-silk blouse, and removing her contact lenses, put on her unflattering work glasses. Then she wiped at her neck with a handkerchief, trying to remove the scent. She had hurt him enough already; the last thing she wanted to do was unwittingly inflame his passion. With that in mind, a flat, aged, washed-out Kate, the kind she had just spent the last two hours fretting about, was the most thoughtful gift she could offer him.

* * *

He arrived late, which surprised her. Geoff was always punctual. It was one of his "things." She was almost grateful when the doorbell eventually rang; she had found herself seated in silence in the living room, staring as if for the first time at the gaps in the bookshelves and the spaces on the walls where his belongings had been. How would Sabine feel when she saw so many familiar things missing? Had she been attached to any of them? Had she even noticed any of them? How did you know what was going on in the mind of an enigma?

He looked, she noticed, as he walked in past her down the hall, a little better than the last time she had seen him. Less aged by it all. But perhaps that was no surprise; that had been moving day; the weeks since had been an age for both of them.

He stood in the living room, a tall, slightly stooped man of fifty, apparently unsure whether to sit down. Suddenly, perversely glad to see him, Kate smiled nervously at him and gestured toward the sofa.

"Do you want a drink? Your stuff's upstairs but I know you've had a drive, and I don't want you to feel you have to head straight off again."

Geoff rubbed at the back of his salt-and-pepper hair, a gesture she had never seen before, and sat down tentatively.

"Actually, I only came from Islington. I'm headed back there, too."

Kate was sure he had said he was renting a place in Bromley, nearer the psychiatric hospital, but she said nothing. Innocent queries suddenly held the capacity to become loaded. It was none of her business anymore.

"Tea? Coffee? Red wine? There's a bottle open."

"Red would be great. Thanks."

She fussed with the bottle in the kitchen, marveling at how swiftly one's partner could metamorphose into a formal guest. When she handed his glass to him, she felt his eyes search her face, and it made her flush with unwelcome emotion.

"So, how are you?" he said. Which threw her somewhat, because she had expected to ask it of him.

"I'm—I'm fine," she said. "Doing okay."

"Is Sabine still at your mother's?"

"Yes. She didn't like it much to begin with, but she hasn't rung this week. With her I guess that's a good sign."

"No news is good news."

"Something like that."

"Give her my love. When you next speak to her."

She nodded. "Of course I will."

There was a lengthy pause. Kate noticed that the top button of her blouse had come undone, and wondered whether to do it up would look like she was making a point. She pulled her thick cardigan harder around her, hoping that would solve the problem.

"You've not got the heating on?" he said, looking around the room, as if suddenly noticing the cold.

"I've had a few problems with the boiler. The man's coming tomorrow," she lied.

"Is he any good? You don't want to have cowboys messing around—they can wreck the whole thing—electrics, plumbing, the lot."

"Oh, he's very good. Registered and everything."

"Good. Because you only have to let me know, you know. I . . ." he paused, awkwardly "Well. Anyway. I'm glad you've got it sorted."

Kate stared at her wineglass, and felt wretched. It was worse that he was being nice. She found it easier when he was yelling at her. When she had told him about the affair, he had actually screamed that she was a *whore*—a word that had curiously failed to hurt her at the time, in part because it was what she secretly felt herself, but also because it was the only really nasty thing he had ever done, and it gave her an excuse to feel furious with him.

"Actually," he said. "I need to talk to you."

Kate's heart leaped into her mouth. Geoff was gazing at her; his eyes liquid and softened, his face kind. Please don't be in love with me anymore, she begged him, silently. I can't bear the responsibility.

"Shall I get your stuff down first?" she said, briskly. "Then we can talk afterward."

"No."

She stared at him.

"Look, I'd like to talk to you now."

We spend our whole lives trying to get men to talk, she thought. And then when they do we wish we were a million miles away.

At that point, O'Malley padded silently into the room, his black coat bristling and dusted with raindrops. Ignoring her, he walked up to Geoff, and after sniffing with a studied lack of interest at his trouser leg, jumped lightly up beside him on the sofa. Not you, too, thought Kate, desperately.

"This is all very awkward," he began.

"No. No, it's me who should feel awkward. Geoff, I'm so sorry about what happened. I really am. You are such a wonderful man, and I would give anything for things not to have turned out the way they have. I'm so, so sorry. But I've moved on. Moved on, you know?" Here she smiled at him in a way that she hoped conveyed all the love and thanks she had felt about their relationship over the years—and also her determination that there was nothing left to resurrect.

"That's very sweet," he said, looking down at his shoes. They were new, she suddenly noticed. Thick-soled. Expensive looking. Very unlike Geoff. "I'm glad you said that. Because I felt slightly awkward about coming here today."

"You need never feel awkward coming here," Kate said earnestly, half believing that she meant it. "Sabine will always want to see you. And I will always . . ."—here she struggled for the right words—"always care about you. I would hate that we would never see each other again."

"You really feel that?" He was leaning toward her, both hands resting lightly on his knees.

"I do," she said. "Geoff, you have been a huge part of my life."

"But you've moved on."

Kate felt her eyes fill with tears.

"I have."

"I'm glad," he said, and for the first time, his expression seemed to relax. "Because what I need to tell you—well, I was a bit worried, because I didn't know how you were."

Kate stared at him, uncomprehending.

"Look, it just makes it a bit easier for me. Because I've moved on, too. I've—well, I've met someone."

Kate's mind went blank.

Geoff shook his head slightly, as if what he were saying were unbelievable even to himself.

"I've met someone. And it seems pretty serious. And it's made me realize that you were right. You were right to do what you did. Oh, I know I was as hurt as anything at the time. You can't believe how hurt. Which makes it all the more astonishing, really, that this could happen so quickly. Because when did you tell me—what was it, six weeks ago?"

Kate nodded her head dumbly.

"But this person—this woman—has made

me realize that your decision was incredibly brave. Because we were just drifting. We weren't really challenging each other, or making each other happy. And I've got that now. And if you've got it, too, well—God, I can't believe I'm saying this—but I just feel that it's all worked out—somehow—for the best. As long as Sabine is okay, that is."

There was a faint ringing sound in Kate's ears. She shook her head, trying to get rid of it.

"Are you okay?" said Geoff, reaching out a hand.

"I'm fine," she said, softly. "Just a bit—surprised." The shoes, she thought suddenly. This woman had made him buy the shoes. He had been gone three weeks, and already this woman had him buying decent shoes.

"Who is she?" she said, lifting her head. "Is she anyone I know?"

Geoff looked a little uncomfortable.

"That's what I wanted to talk to you about."

He paused.

"It's Soraya."

Kate looked blank. Then: "Soraya? Not Soraya from your work?"

"Yup. That Soraya."

"Soraya, who has come here for dinner? What, five or six times?"

"Yes."

Soraya, Asian queen of psychiatry. Soraya, forty-something, doe-eyed goddess of quality designer labels and expensive shoes. Soraya, inheritor of a vast, immaculately furnished Georgian house in Islington, a private income, and no children. Soraya, witch. Husband-stealer. Bitch. Bitch. Bitch.

"She didn't waste any time, did she?" She couldn't keep the note of bitterness from her voice.

Geoff shrugged and smiled ruefully.

"She was pretty careful to ask whether it was definite. She's very proper, you know. When I told her it was, she told me that if she didn't snap me up, someone else would. She reckons there's a shortage of decent, grown-up men." He had the grace to blush at repeating her compliments, but neither could he quite hide his pride in them.

Kate could not believe this. Geoff, snapped up by the most eligible single woman either of them knew. Geoff, who had suddenly become the glittering prize of the female middle classes. How had this happened? Was she so shortsighted that she had missed some quality in him all along?

"I only told you because you said you were happy with Justin. I would never do anything to hurt you, you know that."

"Oh, don't worry about us. We're fine. Ecstatic." She knew she sounded childish, but somehow couldn't help it.

They sat in silence for some minutes, Kate drinking her wine too fast. Eventually, she spoke again.

"Is it serious?"

"Yes. It is."

"After three weeks?"

"No point hanging around at my age." He tried to make it sound like a joke.

"What, as in living together?" She was incredulous. How could he have a new life already? When she had not even begun to come to terms with the loss of their old one?

"Well, I've got the Bromley place on a three-month lease. But, yes, I spend most of my time in Islington."

"How nice for you."

"You know that stuff has never been important to me."

Kate stared at his shoes. Until now, she thought. Soraya will have you kitted out and turned into one of those designer intellectu-als, all Nicole Fahri jackets and linen shirts, before you know it.

Geoff stroked the cat. Both of them looked too much at ease.

"Did—did anything happen between you before?" The suspicion, which had wormed its way into her mind, had suddenly filled her head like a multiheaded, toxic Medusa.

"What?"

"Well, this all seems terribly convenient, doesn't it? Three weeks after you move out of here you're practically moved in with one of our friends. You've got to admit it's pretty fast work."

Geoff's expression was deadly serious.

"Kate, I can categorically promise you that nothing happened until you told me about your—about Justin. I had thought of Soraya as an attractive woman, but no more than any of our friends. Well, perhaps more attractive, but I'd never thought about her more than anyone else, if you know what I mean."

He was telling the truth. Geoff had always found it impossible to lie. So why did she feel so bitter?

"She says she always liked me, but she

wouldn't have gone near me while I was with someone else. And if she hadn't made a move—well, I would have probably slunk into my rather horrid new flat and licked my wounds for years. You know how I was. You know how I am. I'm just not the type. For infidelity."

And I am, she thought. Although you're too kind to say it. Kate feeling suddenly, inexplicably, left behind, realized she wanted to howl. To shout and scream uninhibitedly, like someone cheated, and cry until her chest heaved and her stomach muscles hurt. And it was all her own fault.

Perhaps, she thought, suddenly, insanely, she would seduce him. Leap on him, claw off his clothes, and make love to him with an animalistic passion that would leave him trembling, no longer smug and secure about the rightness of his new love. She wanted him suddenly insecure, anxious. She wanted to obliterate Soraya and her enigmatic Asian smile. She could do it, she knew she could do it. She knew him better than anyone, after all.

Then she realized that Geoff was staring at her, his expression gentle and concerned. It was the kind of look, she realized, with some horror, he normally reserved for his patients. And that was worse than the near-infidelity. She pulled at her glasses, suddenly remembering with discomfort her pale, unmade appearance.

"Are you okay?"

"Okay? God, I'm great. Just stunned by your wonderful news. I'm so pleased for you." She stood, letting her silk shirt flop open at the collar, shaking her head slightly. "Isn't life grand, eh?"

Geoff, aware that their meeting was being called to an abrupt close, stood also, placing his half-drunk glass of wine on the side table.

"You're sure you don't mind? Believe it or not, it's important to me that you're okay with this."

Kate's eyes glittered.

"Mind? Why should I mind?"

She smoothed at her hair, looking absently around the room.

"Justin will be so amazed when I tell him how everything's worked out. So amazed. And pleased. Yes, we're both very pleased. Now, let's get your stuff, shall we?" she said brightly, and with a broad, fixed smile, walked toward the door.

Chapter Four

That's it. Heels down, sit up straight. There, see? You're doing grand."

"I feel like a sack of potatoes."

"You're doing fine. Just lift your hands up a bit. Just off his neck."

"They're the only thing keeping me on board."

Sabine scowled into her scarf as Thom grinned at her, her breath sending a soft, hot blast back up against her face. Not that she was going to let him know, but she had to admit she was almost enjoying herself. The little gray horse moved obediently under her, its ears flicking backward and forward as

Thom talked, its neck arched like that of a rocking horse. It hadn't tried to buck her off, bite her, kick her, swerve into a hedge, or bolt into the distance, as she had secretly feared. It hadn't even eyed her with that expression of malevolent intent particular to the riding school horses, but instead seemed simply satisfied to be out enjoying the crisp winter morning, accepting its human passenger as a necessary cost.

"I told you your gran was a good judge of horseflesh," Thom said, from the greater height of the big bay horse beside her. He held both reins in his right hand, Western style, while his other arm hung loosely down his left side.

"She wouldn't have put you on anything too lively. She made sure this one here was absolutely bombproof before she'd let them send it over. I heard her on the telephone myself."

Sabine sensed that at this point she was meant to express some kind of gratitude, or admiration. But she couldn't. Her grandmother had barely seemed to notice her the past few days, and when she did it was only to observe some wrongdoing on her part.

Like not washing the mud from her boots before putting them in the boot room. And letting Bertie sleep on her bed in the afternoon. She had even shouted at Mrs. H for putting the wrong sort of butter on Grandfather's scrambled egg, bringing the tray back down herself and going on and on about it as if poor old Mrs. H had tried to poison him or something. Sabine had wanted to shout back at her, but after her grandmother had gone back upstairs to his room with a reloaded tray, Mrs. H had put a hand on her shoulder and said it didn't matter. "She's under a lot of strain. We have to give her a bit of leeway," she said, shaking her head.

"Why does everyone let them get away with it?" she asked Thom, as he dismounted to open a wooden gate.

"Who? Get away with what?"

"Them. My grandparents. Why do you all stay working for them when they're so awful to everybody? I can't believe they pay you a great whack, she's always going on about *economizing*." She spat out the word, as if it tasted bad.

Thom pushed the gate open, tapping his horse on its side so that it pirouetted clumsily around him, and Sabine rode through, her horse's hooves making crude sucking noises in the mud.

"She's all right."

"No, she's not. She never says thank you to you for all the things that you do. And she was rude to Mrs. H yesterday. And yet none of you answers back."

"No point. She doesn't mean it personally."

"That's no excuse."

"I'm not saying it is. But people have their ways, and that's hers. God, it's cold this morning." With a slight grunt, Thom shoved his foot in the stirrup and, pushing up, swung his other leg over the back of the horse. His boots were caked in mud.

"But it's demeaning. She treats you like servants. Like you all lived in the nineteenth century."

Thom patted the bay horse's muscular neck.

"Well, I suppose you could say we are her servants."

"That's ridiculous. You're staff."

Thom was grinning again now. His smile rose up above the scarf wrapped tightly around his neck.

"So, what's the difference?"

"There just is a difference."

"Go on."

Sabine stared at her horse's ears. Back and forth went the right one. Thom could be immensely irritating sometimes.

"It's what she makes it. Them. Both of them. The difference is in how they treat you—as equals, or as . . . as . . . well, without any respect."

She glanced furtively at Thom, wondering if she'd gone too far. She had realized halfway through the conversation that he might legitimately be offended by what she was saying.

But he just shrugged, and pulled a wet leaf from an overhanging branch.

"I don't see it like that. They're good people, your grandparents, but with old-fashioned ways. You've got to remember that they grew up with servants. They grew up in the colonies. They like things done a certain way, and they're just old and easily frustrated if that doesn't happen. Now"—Thom pulled up his horse, and turned to look at her—"if it were just one person they treated badly, or shouted at, or whatever, I think we'd all walk out. There are no mugs in this place, Sabine, whatever you might think. But we understand them. And their ways. And although you might not see it, they respect us, too."

Sabine still didn't agree, but something in Thom's manner meant that she was disinclined to pursue the conversation further.

"And no matter what you might think of her right now, Mrs. H is right. She is under a lot of strain. You should open up to her a bit, Sabine. Talk to her. You might just be surprised."

Sabine shrugged, as if it were beyond her to care. But the strain her grandmother was under, she knew, was down to her grandfather's encroaching ill health. He hadn't come down from his room for five days now, and the doctor, a young locum tenens with an earnest manner, had been a frequent visitor.

Sabine hadn't liked to ask what was wrong. On the one occasion Mrs. H had asked her to take up his lunch tray, he had been asleep, and she had stood, frozen in the doorway, watching appalled and fascinated as, above the vibrant red of the oriental bedspread, the skeletal head painfully drew breath, wheezing and spluttering in fitful slumber. She couldn't have told if he

looked unwell. He was too old to look anything but—well—old.

"Is he going to die?" she asked Thom.

He turned in his saddle and stared at her
briefly, then looked away, as if considering
something.

"We're all going to die, Sabine."

"That's not an answer."

"Well, that's because I can't give you an
answer. C'mon, the weather's closing in.
We'd better get these horses back."

It had all stemmed from the night of the
hounds. Nearly a week ago, Sabine had
woken in the early hours to what sounded
like a pack of wolves outside her window,
their voices raised in a strangled, anguished
chorus. They howled not in a mournful way,
but with a kind of urgent bloodthirstiness, a
bloodcurdling harmony, a song to raise
primeval fears. Chilled, she had climbed
slowly out of her bed, and padded barefoot
to the window, half expecting in her dreamlike state to see a full moon. Instead, in the
dim blue light, she had just been able to
make out below her the thin figure of her
grandmother, her dressing gown pulled
tightly around her, running through the sta-

ble yard, a candlewick apparition. She was shouting at someone to come back. It wasn't the furious, electrified cry of someone chasing a criminal, but brisk, and yet almost pleading. "Come back, darling," she said. "Come back, now. *Please.*"

Sabine had stood, her hand raised at the window as her grandmother disappeared, unsure what to do. She half wanted to help, and yet even watching she had the strong sense that she was intruding on something private.

Then, a few moments later, the howling had stopped. And she had heard footsteps, and then her grandmother's voice again, this time soft and scolding, like it was when she spoke to the Duke. Sabine had pushed back the curtain to see her grandmother slowly walking her grandfather back toward the back door. He stooped and limped, and the wind molded his pajamas around him in the wind, so that his bones seemed to poke right through, like warped coat hangers. "I was just checking on the hounds," he kept saying. "I know that man's not feeding them enough. I was just checking on the hounds."

Sabine and her grandmother had not spoken about this incident. Sabine wasn't even sure if she was supposed to know. But from then on her grandfather had not emerged from his room. And at night, occasionally when she half woke, she could hear the brisk padding of her grandmother's steps along the corridor, as she checked that her husband was still in bed, and had not disappeared on another nocturnal engagement.

Her curiosity awakened, Sabine did, however, ask her grandmother whether she could go and see the hounds. She had wanted Thom to take her, but her grandmother, after giving her one of her looks—as if she couldn't quite believe Sabine might be interested—said she could come up with her later that afternoon. "They're black-and-tans," she told Sabine as they walked briskly through the stable yard. "It's a special breed of hound, we've had in this area for generations." She pronounced it "hind." It was the longest sentence she had said to Sabine in over a week.

"The Ballantynes were always Masters of Foxhounds. That's the leader of the hunt. They started the pack, back at the end of the nineteenth century. And your grandfather has spent the best part of his life making sure it carried on. He was Master until about ten years ago, when he stopped riding. They're a wonderful pack. The last time I went out you should have heard them give tongue." She paused briefly, and smiled, savoring her reminiscences.

Sabine, fighting the urge to giggle at her grandmother's last words, didn't tell her she had ulterior motives. She was convinced the poor dogs would be kept in cruelty; no contented animal could make a noise like those dogs had made. And the thought that they lived in concrete sheds, away from the comforts of warm fires and worn rugs, made her feel almost tearful. What she would do when she saw them, she wasn't quite sure. On her bad days, she resolved to set them free, or contact the local animal-rights people to make a fuss. But that would get all of them in trouble, including Thom. On her better days, she didn't think about the dogs at all.

They were kept a five-minute walk from the house, in a yard surrounded by concrete pens, some of which had high metal gates, or heavy-duty wire in front. It looked like a sort of prison, thought Sabine sourly, as she skipped to keep up with her grandmother. It smelled of disinfectant and dog excrement and something else foul she couldn't identify. How could she look after her Labradors so well, and yet leave these dogs out in this cold?

"How's Horatio doing, Niall?"

"A little better, Mrs. Ballantyne," said the middle-aged man who had emerged from one of the sheds as they approached. He wore a long leather apron, like a blacksmith, and his face centered too closely around his nose, as if someone had squashed it all together. "The dressing should come off that foot fairly soon, and it's all healing up nicely underneath."

"Shall we have a look." It wasn't a question. Her grandmother marched briskly over to a corner pen, and peered into the dark. From behind her, Sabine could just make out a dog, lying in the straw, its bandaged paw tucked protectively under its body.

"What happened to him?" Sabine asked the man. The dog had raised his ears at his arrival, as if expecting something, and drooped a little when he turned away to face her.

"Got run over by a horse. One of the guests at the Equestrian Center didn't hold back, and caught this poor old bugger under the hoof." He shook his head disapprovingly.

"I'll tell you what, Mrs. Ballantyne. They don't give them even the basic rules to follow before they send them out. They just take the money and push them out the gate. Don't even care if they can ride, half the time."

Her grandmother nodded, her gaze still fixed on the dog.

"You're quite right, Niall. You're quite right."

"It's been a lot worse since they turned it into a hotel. At least before it was mainly locals. Now it's all your holidaymakers, businessmen, and the like, and all they care about is going out for a day's hunting. You can't tell them nothing. Old John MacRae at the yard there tells me you'd weep if you'd see the state some of the horses are brought back in."

Her grandmother stared at him. "What, lame are they?"

"Lame'd be the best of it. Some of them keep them going for four, six hours, till they're practically broken winded. He had one bleeding at the nose, the other day. And that little chestnut mare they bought back from Tipperary? You remember the one? Scarred all down here." He pointed at his own side. "Because the stupid woman took it upon herself to wear spurs, and put them on the wrong way up."

Sabine watched as her grandmother winced in sympathy. It was an expression she had never seen before.

"I think I'll have a word with Mitchell Kilhoun," she said, firmly. "I'll tell him he has to look after his animals better or we won't let them out with the hunt."

"You'll have a word with the Master?"

"I certainly will," she said.

"That'd be grand, Mrs. Ballantyne. It breaks my heart to see good animals injured for nothing." He gazed over at the hound, who was licking its good paw in misplaced sympathy. "Poor old bugger could have been shot."

Sabine, who had been gazing absently at the dog, looked sharply up at him.

"Shot?"

Niall looked briefly at her grandmother, then back at Sabine.

"Yes, miss. Shot. Would have been the kindest thing for him."

"To be shot? How do you work that out?"

Niall frowned slightly.

"Well, a hound with three legs isn't no

good to anyone, is he? He'd get left behind. Maybe even bullied. No kindness in that, now, is there?"

"You would really have shot him?" Sabine stared at her grandmother.

"Niall's right, Sabine. An injured hound has no life."

"Well, he has no life if you shoot him." Sabine, enraged, felt suddenly, inexplicably tearful. "How can you be so cruel? How would you like it if I shot Bertie just because he couldn't do his job any more? Don't you have any sense of responsibility?"

Her grandmother took a deep breath. She exchanged a glance with Niall, and then moved as if to steer Sabine back toward the big house.

"They're not pets, dear. They're not like Bertie and Bella. They are hounds, specially bred—"

She was interrupted by the grinding roar of the Land Rover as it swerved into the yard, closely followed by a battered pale-blue trailer. The clattering sound of its approach was met by a cacophany of noise from two of the kennels, and then suddenly the hounds swarmed out into the pens, throwing themselves against the wire in an ecstasy of barking and whining, tumbling on top of one another in an effort to get closer to the outside.

Amid the noise, the driver's door of the Land Rover opened, and Michael jumped lightly out. "Sorry I took so long, Niall. Wasn't no one there to load the bloody thing. Oh, sorry Mrs. Ballantyne, I didn't see you there."

"Come on, Sabine," said her grandmother, suddenly steering her firmly toward the gate. "Let's go back to the house."

But Sabine resisted.

"What's going to happen to the dog with the paw? Horatio? Is he going to be shot?"

Her grandmother glanced briefly at the trailer, the back of which Michael had begun to lower. And began to push, gently, at the small of Sabine's back.

"No. He won't be shot. As Niall said, the vet says he's getting better."

"But, why don't you treat them like the other dogs?"

Niall took the other side of the ramp and, between them, Michael and Niall lowered it to the ground, letting it drop the last six inches with a resounding clang that set the dogs baying even more furiously. They looked, Sabine noted privately, a little scary.

"Sabine, come *on*. We really must get on."

Her grandmother was actually tugging at her now. Sabine stood firmly, staring at her in some amazement. What was the urgency? What was it she didn't want her to see?

A stiff, dark brown leg answered her question. It swung out like an errant clock hand, and stuck rigidly from the back of the trailer at an improbable angle, pointing upward toward the chimneys. On the end of it was a black hoof, still shiny with some kind of decorative unguent. As Sabine watched, Niall casually looped a rope around it and pulled, while Michael, who had run lightly up the ramp, grunted out of sight, in his apparent efforts to propel the thing down.

"What are they doing?" she whispered. She was too shocked to speak properly.

"It's dead, Sabine." Her grandmother's weary tone suggested this had been expected. "It can't feel a thing."

Sabine turned to her grandmother, her eyes filled with tears. Behind her the dogs threw themselves frenziedly against the wire.

"But what are they doing?"

Sabine's grandmother gazed at the corpse of the bay horse, which was sliding, inch by inch, down the ramp.

She paused.

"It's going to the flesh house."

"The flesh house? The flesh house?"

"The hounds have to eat something, dear."

Sabine's eyes grew wide. She stared at the dead horse, and then at the slavering hounds behind her. All she could see was teeth and gums and spittle.

"They'll rip it to shreds." Her voice choked, and both palms flew unconsciously to her face. "Oh, my God, I can't believe you're just going to let them rip it to shreds. Oh, God . . ."

The two men paused, then resumed their pulling, as Sabine bolted through the gate and ran back toward the house.

Mrs. H had made the cup of tea some half an hour ago. But by the time Joy Ballantyne remembered to pick up the mug from the edge of the Aga, a skin had formed on it, so that a pale brown sun sat in the middle of the surface of the liquid.

She should have known it would be a bad idea to take Sabine to the kennels. They were a mucky business at the best of times, and the girl was still covered with the cello-phane sheen of the city. City dwellers found it hard to confront the brutal business of life and death up close, and the city was shot through Sabine like an arrow. And Joy had quite enough to deal with as it was, what with Edward becoming so much worse.

She lifted her head, unconsciously, like a hound, trying to detect any sound of movement from the upper floors. But Mrs. H was out shopping, and the house lay in silence, the only sounds the distant clanking of the hot water system, and the occasional snore and fart of the two dogs, who lay at her feet.

Joy sighed. She had pondered long and hard what to do with this girl, how to tease some enthusiasm, some life out of that tense, watchful little face. But she didn't seem to want to *do* anything, just kept shutting herself away in her room, or trying to make herself disappear in different parts of the house, her dissatisfaction at being at Kilcarrion emanating from her very being like an unpleasant smell. She seemed uncomfortable anywhere: in her room, at supper, if touched by someone when she hadn't been expecting it, even in her own skin.

Had Kate been like this? Perhaps she had. Joy, sipping at her lukewarm tea in the empty kitchen, flicked through memories like

someone trying to locate a page in a book—
Kate's adolescent sulks, her fury at her
parents' inability to understand her own
preoccupations, her later determination not
to ride, so that the bay horse they had spent
months finding for her had stood unridden in
the bottom field, a permanent physical
reminder of the abyss that lay between
them. She was so different from her older
brother, Christopher, who spent every weekend away from Dublin point-to-pointing with
his horses. It was hard to believe they were
of the same blood. But here it was again in
the shape of Kate's daughter.

She had thought this could be rather fun,
Joy conceded sadly, as she finished her tea.
She had wanted to like Sabine. She had
wanted to give her a really fun stay here, full
of fresh air and activity and good food, and
send her back with a glow in those pale
cheeks, and so had spent hours trying to
track down a really nice little horse that
could be her companion. Most of all, she
had wanted the chance to behave like she
had a granddaughter, instead of trying to
shut out the thought of her, like she had had
to since she and Kate had properly fallen
out. When Kate had telephoned out of the

blue and asked if she could send her over to stay, she had mistaken Joy's silence for reticence and immediately, touchily withdrawn her request. But Joy's silence had simply been a reaction of stunned pleasure—never in the past ten years had she imagined she'd have the chance simply to have her granddaughter around.

Now the only times they were both comfortable appeared to be when Sabine disappeared over to Annie's house. Which she seemed to do with increasing frequency. Sabine didn't even seem to like her. And she had to admit that she found the young girl's company made her uncomfortable, even irritable.

Perhaps we're just too old for her, she thought, noting the creaking in her knees as she bent to stroke Bella's soft head. We're too old and too boring and she's used to a city life, the kind of life we couldn't hope to understand. Computers, that was what she wanted, wasn't it? Computers and television? Foolish to think she'd just fit in with us. Foolish to get cross with her, just because she doesn't understand the Duke. Hadn't yet had to exercise any real responsibility. And I should be sorry for her, not frustrated by her,

Joy thought. What a rotten, disjointed little life she's had so far. She can't help who she is. That was really down to Kate.

"Come on, chaps," she said, straightening. "Let's go and find Sabine, shall we?"

Joy's severe exterior contradicted a certain generosity of spirit. Although set in her ways, she was not so rigid that she couldn't flex a little when she was wrong. There were things she could do to make the girl happier, she was sure. Give her a few pounds and ask Annie if she would take her to the cinema. It would do Annie good to get out. She could see if Thom would teach her to drive the Land Rover around the bottom fields. She'd like that. Try to find some common ground.

Joy made her way up the stairs. When she had come up earlier, to bring Edward some fresh water, she had heard sobbing from the blue room, and exasperated and unsure whether any approach would be rebuffed, she had softly made her way back downstairs. She remembered that now with some sense of shame. For God's sake, woman, she scolded herself. She's just a child. You're the one who should be grown-up enough to approach her.

She stood outside the door, listening for

sounds of movement, and then knocked, softly, twice.

There was no answer.

Joy knocked again, and then pushed the door slowly. The bed, although bearing the imprint of a recent inhabitant, was empty. She glanced around, and then feeling some- how conscious of invading Sabine's privacy, she withdrew. She was probably at Annie's. Joy bit back a sudden sense of sadness at the thought that her own granddaughter found it easier to sit in a house full of strangers than with her closest family.

It's not her fault, she told herself. We just haven't tried hard enough to understand her.

She closed the door quietly behind her, as if Sabine were somehow present, and had gone just a few steps down the hall when the door of the study caught her eye. It was slightly ajar.

Joy, irritated, was about to pull it shut, when some instinct told her to look inside. She opened the door and walked in.

It was a room she rarely entered. Edward had given up using it several years ago, and Mrs. H was under his instructions to leave it alone, so it was easy to recognize that things had been disturbed. It would have been easy even if it hadn't been for the two boxes on the floor, and the open photograph album, propped up against one of the rolled rugs.

Joy stared at the photographs, strewn across the floor. There was one of herself, and Stella, laughing at some joke. On coronation day. There was the junk that they had borrowed on Sundays, to visit the beach at Shek O. There was Edward, in his naval whites. And there was Kate, as a young girl. With her little friend. Her little Chinese friend.

Joy felt a sudden welling of fury at the sight of her personal memories strewn carelessly across the rug, as if they were of so little significance. How dare she! How dare she go through these personal things without even asking! She had a sudden sense of her granddaughter as an intruder, as someone surreptitiously ferreting around in her past. Those photographs were *personal*. They were her life, her memories, her private reminders of years past. And then to just leave them carelessly scattered—as if they were of so little consequence.

Choking back a little sob of indignation, Joy stooped, and began throwing the loose photographs back into the box, before replacing its lid, unnecessarily firmly. Then she strode to the door, and marched swiftly down the stairs, so that the dogs, rather than waiting eagerly, scattered at her approach.

It was actually the third time Sabine had seen *Breakfast at Tiffany's*. She knew this bit, where the party woman's hat got set alight and no one noticed. She knew this other bit, where Audrey Hepburn fell asleep in George Peppard's bed (he never tried to do anything to her, not like he would have in real life). And as for the bit where she made him look up his book in the library—well, Sabine could practically recite that bit off by heart. But it didn't matter, because she was much more interested in Annie.

For a woman who seemed to do little other than watch films all day—Annie had subscriptions to all the cable channels, as well as video shops within a twenty-five–mile radius—she rarely seemed to actually watch any of them. Since Sabine had been there, which was almost the whole first hour of *Breakfast at Tiffany's*, she had flicked through two magazines, made marks against a few items of clothing in a thick cat-alog, walked over to look out of the window at least twice, and frequently absented herself altogether, instead staring past the screen into the middle distance. It had gotten to the point where it was more interesting for Sabine to stop watching the film and watch Annie.

But then Annie never seemed to be able to concentrate on anything much. In conversations, as they leaned conspiratorially together over a cup of tea, she would suddenly lose the thread of whatever they were talking about, so that Sabine would have to remind her. Or her face would go all blank, and occasionally she would disappear upstairs for five or ten minutes. Sometimes she would even just drop off to sleep, even in front of guests, as if staying in the present were simply too exhausting. At first, Sabine had found it a bit unnerving, and had wondered whether she were doing something wrong. But then she saw that Annie did it with everyone—with Patrick, with her mother, even with Thom—and she decided it was just Annie's way. As Thom said, everyone had his way, and, provided there was nothing personal, you should just accept it.

"So where were you at this morning, Sabine?" Annie, her feet tucked under her on the big blue sofa, turned away from the television screen. She was wearing a huge fisherman's jumper that seemed to swallow her up. Patrick's probably. "Did you go riding?"

Sabine nodded. She found she had unconsciously mimicked Annie's pose on the opposite sofa, and her bottom leg was getting pins and needles.

"Did Thom take you?"

"Yes." She straightened her leg, observing her socked foot. "Have you ever seen the hounds?"

"Have I seen the hounds? Of course I have. You'll see them up and down this road often enough in the hunting season."

"I mean where they live."

Annie looked at her inquiringly.

"The kennels? Sure. Grisly place, isn't it? Why, did you get a bit of a shock?"

Sabine nodded. She didn't want to tell Annie the whole story. Annie's home was where she got to pretend that life was normal, with television and gossip, and no mad old people, stupid rules, and dead things.

Annie noted Sabine's expression, and then swung her legs around and planted her feet on the floor.

"He shouldn't have taken you. It's not a nice place if you're not used to livestock."

"It wasn't Thom. Do all dead horses go there?"

"It's not just horses. You get cows, sheep, all sorts. They've got to go somewhere. I wouldn't get upset about it. Now, I'm going to put the kettle on. Do you want a cup?"

But of course it took Annie some fifteen minutes to ask Patrick if he wanted tea. By the time she returned to the living room, Audrey Hepburn had gotten together with George Peppard and found her missing cat and Sabine had decided she may have overreacted at the kennels. The animals were dead, as Annie said. And dogs had to eat something. It had just been a bit of a shock to see the rawness of it all. Especially for a vegetarian.

In London, her mother was careful to respect her views on eating meat, making sure that there were always cheese and pasta sauce and tofu in the fridge. And Geoff had often cooked vegetarian for all of them. It made it easier, he said. And it was probably good for them not to eat too much fat. Because it was hard enough trying to keep hold of your beliefs without everyone treating them as if they were some bit of adolescent nonsense. Here, people kept "forgetting" that she didn't eat meat, and serving it up anyway. Or acting as if it were some bizarre foible that she was sure to grow out of. But then there was no life and death at home. Unless you counted what you saw on television. Here it seemed to be everywhere: in the small animals that Bertie worried in the yard; in the horribly named flesh house at the kennels; in her grandfather's creased and craggy face, which no longer seemed to have the energy to even distinguish its various expressions.

"Is my grandfather going to die?" she asked.

Annie paused in the entrance to the kitchen, and then rubbed both hands awkwardly down the hem of her jumper.

"He's not well," she conceded.

"Why won't anyone give me a straight answer? I know he's ill, and I can't ask my grandmother. I just want to know if he's going to die."

Annie began to pour the tea into stripy mugs. She was silent for a bit, and then she turned to Sabine.

"What difference does it make?" she asked.

"It doesn't make any difference. I just want people to be honest with me."

"Honesty, *pah*. You can have too much honesty, believe me."

Sabine, uncomfortably, realized there was a faint note of aggression in Annie's tone.

"If it doesn't make any difference, then it doesn't matter. You should just appreciate him while he's here. Love him, even."

Sabine's eyes widened at this. The idea that love was something one could inflict on that crotchety old man seemed faintly ridiculous.

"He—he's not really a very loving-type person," she ventured, slowly.

"Why? Because he's old? And difficult? Or because you find him uncomfortable to be around?"

Sabine felt increasingly uneasy at the tone of Annie's voice. Annie had been one of the few people she felt understood her, and now she was acting like Sabine had somehow said something wrong.

"I didn't mean to offend you," she said, sulkily.

Annie placed a mug of tea in front of her.

When Sabine looked up again, she was gazing at her, and her eyes were kind.

"You didn't offend me, Sabine. I just think it's important to love people while you have them. However long you have them." Here, her eyes began to fill with tears, and she looked away.

She had done it again. Sabine felt herself chill, conscious that she had somehow again made Annie cry. Why couldn't she get the measure of any of these people? Why did she always feel like she was misreading some crucial signal, like she did when she was hanging around with a crowd she didn't know at home, and couldn't get any of their sayings and in-jokes?

"I do *try* to be nice to everyone," she ventured, quietly, desperate to have Annie think well of her again.

Annie sniffed, and wiped her nose with the back of her sleeve. "I'm sure you do, Sabine. You hardly know them, is all."

"It's just they're not easy people to show feelings to. They're not very—well—feelingly, if you know what I mean."

Annie laughed, and placed her hand on Sabine's. It was cool and soft and dry. Sabine's own were hot with discomfort.

"You're not wrong there. Getting those two to show their feelings . . . well, you'd probably have more luck asking the Duke."

They both laughed, companionably, into the silence. Sabine felt herself relax. They had apparently passed over whatever invisible turbulence she had blundered into.

"But, seriously, Sabine. I mean it. Just because they're not easy with showing it, doesn't mean they don't feel it."

They were interrupted by a sharp rapping on the door. With a quick, quizzical glance at Sabine (Mrs. H and Thom always let themselves in) Annie got out of her chair and walked to the door, pushing her hair behind her ears as she did.

Sabine started to see Joy standing there, tall and rigid in her headscarf, her face taut and her arms, padded in their quilted jacket, fixed awkwardly to her sides.

"I'm so sorry to trouble you, Annie. I was wondering whether I could talk to Sabine."

"Of course, Mrs. Ballantyne." Annie stepped backward, pulling the door farther open. "Come right on in."

"No, I won't come in, thank you very much. Sabine, I'd like you to come home."

Sabine stared at Joy, noting the barely

repressed sense of fury emanating from her grandmother. She quickly ran through a checklist of possible misdemeanors: No, the shampoo bottles were in her room, her boots were clean, her bedroom door was shut to stop Bertie getting in. Yet something in Joy's face left her distinctly unwilling to leave the comfort and safety of Annie's house. She stared at Joy, trying hard to quell her growing sense of unease.

"I was just having a cup of tea," she said. "I'll come along after."

Joy flinched slightly. Something in her eyes turned hard and steely.

"Sabine," she said. "I'd like you to come home *now.*"

Sabine's heart had begun to thump.

"No," she said. "I'm having my tea."

Annie's eyes flickered between the two visitors. "Sabine . . ." she said, and her voice held a warning.

"I'm sure it can't be that urgent," said Sabine, defiantly. She knew she was in uncharted territory now, but something in her rebelled against being marched home to that miserable house, to be railed against for some minor domestic misdemeanor. Sabine had had enough.

"I'll come when I'm ready." she said.

Something in Joy appeared to erupt. She marched past Annie into the room, carrying the chill air of outside around her like a radioactive buzz.

"How *dare* you," she breathed. "How dare you go through my private things. How dare you start ransacking my private photographs without even thinking to ask me. Those were private, you understand? They were not meant for you to look at."

Sabine remembered the photographs with a start, her face pinking with discovery. She had not even thought of putting them away. It seemed unnecessary, as no one ever went into the room. But any sense of guilt was overshadowed by the scale of her grandmother's response. She had never seen her lose her temper before. Her voice crackled, like a dry log in a fire, and her hair seemed suddenly electrified, springing free from its two clips. But as the tirade continued into the charged atmosphere, the adrenaline infected her, and Sabine found herself suddenly shouting in response.

"They're only photographs!" she said, yelling over her grandmother's voice. "All I did was look through a box of bloody photographs! I was hardly going down your underwear drawer, was I?"

"They were not yours to go through! You had no *right*!" Joy's voice lifted on the last word, making her sound curiously adolescent.

"Right? Right?" Sabine stood up, pushing her chair back behind her with a shuddering bump. "I've not had a single bloody right since I came here. There's bloody nothing I can do without your permission, is there? I can't walk around the house, I can't talk to the staff, I can't even have a bloody bath without worrying whether someone's going to come in and stick a ruler in to see whether I'm using too much water."

"Those were my *personal things*!" Joy shouted. "How would you like it if I went through your personal things?"

"You know what? Why don't you go and have a look! Because I haven't got any personal things, have I? I don't get to keep my personal bloody toothbrush in the bathroom. I don't get to watch the programs I want. I can't even use the telephone to make a personal call!" Here Sabine's voice began to break, and she rubbed at her eyes, determined not to let the older woman see her cry.

"Sabine, you could do anything you wanted. But not if you just skulk around the place, refusing to join in. You have to join in."

"To what? Hunting? Feeding dead horses to the dogs? Sorry, *hounds*? Joining the eight million people a day who faff around preparing my grandfather's boiled eggs?" Sabine was dimly aware that Patrick was now standing in the doorway of the kitchen.

"You are a guest in my house," said Joy, speaking as if she were fighting to control her breath. "And while you are a guest, the least I expect is for you not to go rummaging around in things that don't concern you."

"They're just bloody pictures! A few stinking pictures! Apart from the ones with my mum in, they're not even very nice!" Sabine began to cry. "God, I can't believe you are making this into such a big deal. I was bored, okay? I was bored, and fed up, and I wanted to see what my mum looked like when she was my age. If I'd known you were going to throw a bloody wobbly about it I wouldn't have gone anywhere near your stupid pictures. I hate you. I hate you and I wish I was at home." The crying dissolved into deep, ragged sobs. Sabine sank down onto the table and buried her face in her crossed arms.

Annie, who had been standing helplessly, closed the front door, and walked over to the table. She laid a hand on Sabine's shoulder. "Look," she said. "Mrs. Ballantyne, I'm sure Sabine didn't mean any harm."

Patrick walked silently into the middle of the room. "Is everything okay here?" he said.

"You go on up, Patrick. Everything's fine."

"We've got guests. They're wondering what's going on."

"I know, love. Go on up," Annie said. "There'll be no more noise."

Joy shook her head slightly, as if she had forgotten the presence of the other woman. She glanced up and saw Patrick, and looked suddenly abashed at her own outpouring of emotion.

"I'm so sorry, Annie. Patrick," she said eventually. "It's not like me to lose my temper."

He looked at Joy and Sabine warily.

"Really. I'm so, so sorry."

"I'll just be upstairs if you need me," he said to his wife, and walked out.

There was a brief silence, broken only by

the sound of Sabine's shuddering and sniffing. Joy shook her head, as if rousing herself from a reverie. She put both hands to her cheeks, as if feeling their temperature, and then moved stiffly toward the door.

"Annie, I'm so sorry. Please accept my apologies. I—I—yes. Well. I think I had better get back to the house. Sabine, I'll see you later."

Sabine refused to look up from the table.

"I'm sorry," said Joy, opening the door.

"You're all right, Mrs. Ballantyne," said Annie. "It's no problem at all. I'll let Sabine finish her tea and she'll be back with you later."

Joy sat on the edge of her husband's bed. He lay, propped up against a bank of white cushions, gazing across the room at the fire, which Mrs. H had stoked up before she left. It was dark outside, and the only light in the room came from a bedside lamp, and the flames, which flickered in the reflections of the mahogany bedposts, and in the brass handles of the chest of drawers under the window.

"Oh, Edward. I've done an awful thing," she said.

Edward's eyes swiveled rheumily across to Joy's face.

"I completely lost my temper with Sabine. In front of Annie and Patrick. I don't know what came over me."

She rubbed at her eyes with one hand, the other clutching a handkerchief that she had pulled out of her drawer on her return home. It was unlike Joy to cry. She wasn't even sure when she had last done so. But she had been haunted by the thin adolescent figure who had burst into childish tears in front of her, and haunted more by her own violent feelings toward her.

"She got into the study, you see."

Joy took a deep breath, and took Edward's hand. It was bony and dry. Touching it, she could remember when it had been broad and spade-fingered, tanned from working outside.

"She had been rooting through the old Hong Kong pictures. And there was something about seeing them again. . . . I—oh, Edward, I just completely lost my temper."

Edward kept his gaze steady on her face. She thought she could feel the faintest of answering squeezes.

"She's only a child, isn't she? She doesn't

understand. Why shouldn't she look through the photographs? She knows little enough about her family, God knows. Oh, God, Edward, I feel like such an old fool. I wish I could take it all back."

Joy rubbed at her face with the handkerchief. She knew what she had to do, but she wasn't sure how to do it. It was unlike her to turn to Edward for advice. But he seemed to be having a better day. And there wasn't anyone else who could begin to understand. "You were always better with people. Much better than I was. What can I do to make it up to her?"

Joy gazed at her husband, and shifted her weight, so that she could bend better to hear him speak.

Edward's eyes moved away from hers, as if he were deep in thought. After a lengthy pause he shifted his face toward her. Joy stooped lower. She knew he had trouble speaking at the moment.

When his voice emerged, it was hoarse and crackly, like rice paper.

"Are we having sausages tonight?" he said.

Chapter Five

The one advantage to living in a house mathematically bisected by rules and regulations was that it definitely made it easier to sneak around. Sabine had timed her return to Kilcarrion for eight-fifteen, when she knew her grandmother would be eating in the dining room. Even when her grandfather ate upstairs in his room Joy would eat there, at a carefully set table, as if solitarily upholding some grand tradition. And she had worked out a back route, which didn't even involve her passing the dining room; if she came through the back door, and walked silently along the corridor that led to the boot room, she could come up the back stairs, and out onto the main landing without her grandmother even knowing she was there.

Because there was no way she was speaking to her again. The next time she saw her, it would be to say good-bye. She would wait until her grandmother had gone to bed, and then she would tiptoe silently into the living room and call her mother, to tell her she was coming home. Her grandmother didn't have a phone in her room, so she wouldn't hear a thing. And her grandfather never heard anything anyway. As long as the dogs didn't get excited and start barking, she would have it all planned and ready before her grandmother could do anything about it.

The little knot of tension that Sabine had felt for the remainder of her stay at Annie's had not dissipated as she made her plans, but Sabine didn't mind. She was almost grateful. Her sense of fury and injustice helped give her the determination to move on. Yes, she would miss Thom and Annie and Mrs. H, and it was a shame that she had just started, if she had to admit it, to enjoy herself a bit. But there was no way she was staying one more day with that woman. No way. At one point after her grandmother had left, when she had been at the snot-and-shudder stage of crying, she had suggested to Annie that perhaps she could sleep in her spare room. The one next door to Annie and Patrick's room, which never got used by guests. Then she wouldn't have to come back to Kilcarrion at all. But Annie had gone all funny again, and said no, no one was to use that room, and Sabine had decided not to push it. She needed all the friends she could get at the moment.

Sabine pulled out her the holdall from under the bed, and began to throw in her clothes. It was better this way, she told herself. She and her grandmother just didn't get on. She could understand now why her mother never came back to Ireland—imagine growing up with that! Sabine felt a sudden stab of longing for her mother, and comforted herself with the thought that this time the following evening she would be back in the house in Hackney. That was the important thing. She would deal with the Justin thing later.

She moved to the chest of drawers, hauling them open and throwing her clothes in the holdall chaotically, careless of whether they were likely to crease. She was fed up with doing things the so-called right way. From now on she would simply do things her way.

But as she packed, she found she couldn't think too hard about Justin. Or Geoff. Or about the good things at Kilcarrion, like riding with Thom this morning, and the way he put his hand on her shoulder and told her he'd make a horsewoman of her yet. Or the way he kept leaning across to her when they untacked their horses in the yard, and gave Liam a warning glare when he tried to make rude jokes in front of her. Or Mrs. H, and her food, which was loads nicer than she was likely to get at home, with just Mum around. Or Bertie, who followed her around now, and seemed to adore her in a way O'Malley never did, even though she had raised him herself from a kitten. Or even Annie, as weird as she was. Because if she thought too hard about any of these things, Sabine found that what she really wanted was to cry. A lot.

She jumped at the soft knock on the door, then froze. Caught in the act, she thought silently. But then she realized that whatever her grandmother did these days made her feel like that.

Sabine stood still and said nothing, knowing who it was likely to be, but eventually the door opened anyway, slowly and cautiously, making a soft swooshing noise on the blue shag pile.

Her grandmother stood before her, bearing a small wooden tray, on which stood a bowl of tomato soup and some of Mrs. H's buttered soda bread. Sabine stared at her for a minute, tense and still, awaiting the next onslaught.

But Joy merely looked down at the tray.

"I thought you might be hungry," she said, pausing, and then as if having herself waited for some protest, walked slowly over to the dressing table. If she noticed the half-packed bag, she didn't say anything.

She placed the tray gently on the cleared space, and then turned around so that she was facing her granddaughter.

"It's only canned tomato, I'm afraid. I hope that's all right."

Sabine, who stood motionless beside the bed, nodded warily.

There was a lengthy silence. Sabine waited for Joy to move. But she didn't seem to want to.

Instead she clasped her hands together, a

little awkwardly, and half lifted them toward Sabine, forcing her face into a kind of bright smile. Then she thrust them deep into the pockets of her padded waistcoat.

"Thom tells me you rode very well today. Very tidy, he said."

Sabine stared at her.

"Yes. He said you and the little gray got on terribly well. Which is good news. Very good news. He said you had soft hands. And a very nice seat."

Sabine's careful monitoring of her grandmother was briefly diverted by the thought of Thom examining her backside. Was it all riding terminology? Or had he been looking at her for other reasons?

"Anyway. He seemed to think the pair of you would be jumping soon. He's a lovely jumper, that gray. I've seen him out in the field. Brave as a lion, he is. A really generous little soul."

She was beginning to look really uncomfortable, Sabine realized suddenly. She was now twisting her hands together around an old white handkerchief, and she seemed to find it difficult to meet Sabine's eye.

"He'll do a Wexford bank, you know. With no trouble."

Sabine paused, feeling suddenly sad at this old woman's discomfort. It didn't actually make her feel better at all. She lifted her head, and spoke.

"What's that?"

"A Wexford bank? Oh, it's the hardest thing. Not an easy jump at all." Joy was speaking too fast now, as if in relief at Sabine's response. "It's a big old earth bank, probably five or six feet high, with a wide ditch on each side. The horses gallop up to it, then leap onto the top, and the clever ones balance there briefly, as if they were on tiptoes." Here she brought her hands together, facing down, and moved them side by side, like someone adjusting her weight. "Then they leap off again over the other ditch. But they won't all do it, you see. It requires a lot of bravery. And a little wisdom. And some always choose to take the easy route."

"By the gate."

"Yes," said her grandmother, looking at her very seriously. "Some will always take the gate."

The two women stood in silence for a moment. Then her grandmother moved slowly away from the tray, and back toward the door. When she got there, she turned around. She looked very old, and rather sad.

"You know, I thought it would probably be a very good idea if I sorted out that study. I was wondering if you might give me a hand. Perhaps I could even tell you a few bits about where your mother grew up." She paused. "That's if you wouldn't be bored."

There was a long silence, as Sabine stared at her hands. She wasn't quite sure what to do with them.

"You know, I'd really be terribly grateful."

Sabine gazed at her, and then at the tray. Then she glanced over at the holdall on the floor, where her socks hung over the edge, like rude blue tongues.

"All right." she said.

Chapter Six

S.S. Destiny, Indian Ocean, 1954

Mrs. Lipscombe, from under her wide blue hat, was telling them how she had given birth. Again. The midwife had given her brandy, which she had thrown up, not being a drinker ("not then, anyway," she said, and laughed dryly), and the silly woman had bent over, trying to wipe it off her shoes. That, unfortunately, was the point at which Georgina Lipscombe had pulled herself upright, and with a roar, grabbed whatever came to hand, and bore down. Propelled by an almighty final push, the bloodied Rosalind had shot halfway across the room, to be caught like a rugby ball by the vigilant maid who had been waiting nearby.

"Pulled a great handful of that woman's hair out, I did," Mrs. Lipscombe said with some pride. "They said I wouldn't let go of it for the best part of an hour. All poking through my fingers, it was. She was *furious*."

Joy and Stella, seated beside her on sun loungers, exchanged the minutest of grimaces. Georgina Lipscombe's stories were a useful source of entertainment, but once she'd had a couple of gin and tonics, they did tend to get rather gory.

"Was she all right?" said Joy, politely.

"Rosalind? Oh, she was fine. Weren't you, darling?"

Rosalind Lipscombe sat on the edge of the swimming pool, her plump, childish legs half submerged in the cool blue water. As her mother spoke, she lifted her head and stared briefly at the three women before returning to examine her pale feet. Hard as it was to discern any expression, Joy thought she, too, had probably heard this story many times before.

"I don't know why she doesn't swim. It's so hot. Rosie, darling. Why don't you have a swim? You'll burn terribly sitting there."

Rosalind looked up at her mother reclining on the sundeck, and then, silently, withdrew her feet from the water and padded away from the pool and over to the changing rooms.

Georgina Lipscombe raised an eyebrow. "You girls'll find out soon enough. Ugh! The pain! I told Johnnie that was it. That was absolutely it. I was never going through it again." She paused, exhaling a thin plume of smoke into the bright air. "Of course, I had Arthur within the year."

Arthur, unlike his sister, sat by himself in the shallow end, pushing a wooden boat backward and forward across the waves. He was the only other occupant of the pool, despite the heat, owing to the previous evening's ship's variety concert, which, if measured in hangovers, at least, had been quite a success.

The former troop ship, S.S. *Destiny*, had been at sea almost four weeks, and its jaded cargo of naval wives traveling to meet their officers, and officers traveling to new postings, had been desperate for something to divert them from the endless journey, and the now-relentless heat. The days had rolled by, pitching and yawing like the sea itself, punctuated only by the meals, snippets of gossip, and the slow but definite change in climate as they headed away from the port of Bombay toward Egypt. Joy often wondered how the troops would have coped, stuck all the way down below without even windows in their cabins. She would have liked to ask some of the Muslims in the engine room what it was like down in the noisy, oily, thrumming bowels of the ship. But somehow it had been made clear to her that her interest in such matters was not quite the done thing. And desperate for a change from the endless walks around deck, games of cards, or, when the weather was rougher, brandy and ginger ales to combat seasickness, she and the little group to whom she and Stella had found themselves curiously conjoined since their time on board had leaped on the opportunity to do something different.

There had been a lot of drinks. Even more than usual. One of the guests at the Captain's table had started things off with a robust version of "My Blue Heaven," and then, after a few feeble protestations, it seemed to Joy that her fellow travelers had almost fought one another for the chance to sing, tell jokes, or embark upon some ill-advised public revelation. Stella, fueled by three gin and tonics, had stood and sung "Singing in the Rain," making up for her tunelessness by charming everybody with her winsome expression, and she had been followed by Pieter, the burly, sun-kissed Dutchman who did "something in diamonds," who had sung something exclamatory in Dutch, and then tried unsuccessfully and rather physically to persuade Stella to join him in a duet on the piano, clutching at her slim hands as if he could place them on the keyboard himself. Stella's genteel modesty in refusing was much admired at Joy's table, so Joy didn't let slip that the only thing Stella could play was "Chopsticks."

The evening had degenerated after the stewards had brought round a bottle of rather fierce cognac. It degenerated a little further after Pieter accepted a bet to down the remaining third in one fiery gasp. It degenerated properly when Mr. Fairweather and his wife, having already silenced listeners with their reedy rendition of "I Get a Kick out of You," had stood, held hands, and attempted the duet from the *Pearl Fishers*, the painful climax of which had prompted Georgina Lipscombe to snort her drink all over the mauve satin bodice of her dress, and Louis Baxter, one of the traveling officers, to start hurling bread rolls, so that the captain had to intervene and appeal good-naturedly for calm. He got it, eventually, but Mrs. Fairweather, pink with hurt, hadn't spoken to any of them for the rest of the evening, even when she was grabbed and, rigid-faced, forced between two stewards into a chaotic conga line that lurched its way around a circuit of the entire top deck. It was at that point that Joy had noticed Stella had gone missing again.

"You know it's taken me all day just to be able to see straight again," said Georgina, sliding her sunglasses back up her nose. "I don't know how you girls manage to look so hale and hearty. Not being woken up at the crack of dawn by children, I suppose."

"*Ugh.* I look a wreck," said Stella agreeably, smoothing her unruffled hair.

You should do, thought Joy, silently, remembering how Stella had snuck back into the cabin a good hour after dawn had broken.

Now, as they lay on deck in their new two-piece costumes, Joy tried not to think too hard about Stella's increasingly frequent absences. She was pretty sure she loved Dick, the dashing pilot whom she had married shortly after Joy's own wedding ("I wouldn't be sailing halfway across the world to meet him, otherwise, would I?" Stella responded tartly to her tentative inquiries), but there was something about her increasingly flirtatious manner with the other officers, and especially her friendship with Pieter, that left Joy with an unbalanced feeling that could not be wholly ascribed to her lack of sea legs.

She had unwisely confided her concerns to Georgina Lipscombe, with whom they shared a cabin, one night after her children had gone to sleep, and Georgina had raised an eyebrow and suggested that if anything, it was Joy who was being naive.

"Happens on every ship, darling," she had said, lighting up one of her omnipresent cigarettes. "Difficult for some girls to keep the faith when there are lots of lovely officers around. I'd say it was boredom, mostly. What else is there to do on board?"

Georgina's jaded speech, and the casual

way in which she puffed out the last sentence, made Joy wonder if she really was being naive. She hadn't seen Georgina, who was married to a naval engineer, being special friends with anyone, but then there was always a good two hours between when she asked Joy and Stella to leave the cabin so she could read the children a story, and the time when she would actually emerge for dinner. And Joy knew for a fact that it was always the friendly Goanese steward who bathed and read to the two children, because he had told her so. Perhaps Georgina, too, was occasionally diverted by the "lovely officers." Perhaps she was the only woman who wasn't. Joy thought of Louis Baxter, who had been terribly attentive the previous evening, and seemed to be making a point of seating himself next to her. But Louis's presence, agreeable as it was, struck Joy with no such uncertainties. For there was no one on board who could possibly compare to Edward.

As she often did, Joy thought back almost six months to the last time she had seen her husband. Or her husband of two whole days, as he had been then. They had married in Hong Kong, on his forty-eight–hour pass, with just close family in attendance, much to her mother's disappointment, and a reception of coronation chicken and Chablis specially shipped over by one of her father's colleagues, who knew a good man in wine.

Joy had worn a simple, close-fitting white satin dress, cut on the bias ("it'll make you look less lanky," her mother had claimed), and Edward had worn a smile that lasted almost the entire forty-eight hours. Stella had outshone her in a midnight-blue dress with a plunging neckline and feathered hat that caused all the assembled ladies to tut and mutter at one another through the sides of their lipsticked mouths. Her Aunt Marcelle, who had traveled over specially from Australia, had trodden on her train, and then collapsed in an elaborate heap, complaining of the humidity. Her father had drunk too much, and cried, and tipped the French chef in the Peninsula Hotel so much money that her mother had been unable to speak for the last hour of the reception. But Joy didn't care. She was hardly aware of the trappings. She just kept clutching Edward's broad, freckled hand like someone clinging to a life raft, unable to believe that after almost a year of silent doubt (largely prompted by her mother's louder ones), Edward had actually returned to marry her.

It was not that Alice didn't want her to be happy, she had since decided. She was not a malicious woman. She just believed, like an anthropologist studying some strange tribe, that any contact closer than arm's length was bound to end in trouble. "On your wedding night," she had said, gravely one evening, as they carefully packed Joy's trousseau into tissue paper. "You should try . . . well, try to look like you don't mind. Like you're enjoying it." Alice gazed down at the shell-colored silk, trimmed with cream lace, as if struggling with her own memories. "They don't like it if you look like you're not enjoying it," she said, finally. And that was the end of Alice's introduction to married life.

Joy had sat awkwardly beside her, aware that her mother had attempted to impart some kind of important maternal advice. So little had come her way untainted by some implied criticism, that she felt it only right to treat it with some sort of reverence. But, try as she might, she couldn't relate her mother's experience to her own with Edward. Her mother visibly flinched when her father, usually drunk, tried sloppily to embrace her. She swatted at his roaming hands like someone who had accidentally sat on a red ants' nest. Joy spent almost all her waking hours wishing that Edward would touch her.

So when the night had come, it hadn't occurred to her to be frightened. She was simply, by then, desperate to traverse the seemingly invisible divide between those women who *knew* and those, like herself, who didn't. And fueled by a lengthy absence, where she had had little to do but fill that vacuum of knowledge with her own smudged and inaccurate dreams, she had embraced him almost as hungrily as he had her.

It wasn't perfect, of course. She wasn't sure what perfect was even meant to be. But Joy simply relished the closeness of him; let herself be consumed by the simple pleasure of having his skin next to hers; strong, sinewy, male skin, its scent and textures such a welcome departure from the primped and powdered femininity that had guided her life until then. She liked the strangeness of him, the strength of their combined bodies, the way his size meant she didn't feel too big, the way his desire for her didn't make her feel like she was doing anything wrong.

And the following day, joyous and unself-conscious in her newly awakened state, she had met her mother's questioning gaze with a broad, reassuring smile. But Alice, instead of looking relieved, as Joy had intended, had seemed to wince slightly, and then bustled off pretending she had something to see to in the kitchen.

Joy had etched almost every detail of that night onto her memory, to be replayed on the endless, humid nights she spent alone back in the child's bed of her youth. It was just as well that she could, as it was to be five months and fourteen days before she was to see him again, when she would arrive at Tilbury after her six-week voyage on the S.S. *Destiny*.

Stella was also meeting Dick, and both sets of parents had been reassured by the thought that the girls would travel together, although not enough to prevent a deluge of unwarranted advice for the weeks leading up to their departure. Alice was convinced that naval transport ships were "hotbeds of immorality"; Bei-Lin's cousin had worked as a cook on a troop ship during the war, and she had described with some relish an end-less trail of bored naval wives traipsing back-

ward and forward down the narrow stair-
cases that led to the men's quarters. Joy
wasn't sure which her mother was more
shocked by, the idea of extramarital activity,
or the fact that it was with men lower than
officer class. Stella's mother, whose ever-
present "nerves" seemed to jangle like wind
chimes at the best of times, was more concerned about the recent sinking of the
Empire Windrush, which had gone down in a
storm off Malta. But Stella and Joy, free for
the first time from the watchful eyes of their
parents, had determined to make the most
of their adventure.

Except that several weeks in, Stella's idea
of what that meant had turned out to be
somewhat different from Joy's.

"Right. I'm off for a quick stroll," she said,
unfolding her smooth, tanned limbs from the
sun bed and nodding to Georgina Lipscombe.

Georgina gazed up at her. It was impossible to tell what she was thinking from behind
her sunglasses.

"Anywhere nice?" she said.

Stella gestured vaguely toward the bow of
the ship.

"Oh, just need to stretch my legs a bit,"

she said casually. "See what any of the others are up to. Most chaps seem to have stayed in their cabins today."

Joy stared at Stella, conscious of her friend's refusal to meet her eye.

"Have fun," said Georgina. She smiled, her teeth even and white below her sunglasses.

Stella stood, and wrapping her bathing gown around her, walked briskly toward the bar. Joy, feeling suddenly aggrieved, fought the temptation to follow her.

There was a brief silence, during which Georgina accepted another drink from the Goanese waiter who had appeared beside her.

"Your little friend wants to watch herself, darling," she said, still smiling inscrutably from behind her shades. "No faster way to get a name for oneself than to play around on the water."

Joy lay on her bunk, her stockinged feet stretched out in front of her, positioning herself between the window and open door to try to catch a breeze. In these last days of the journey, she spent many afternoons in this manner, unwilling to spend her entire day in the company of the other wives and their fractious, bored children, or the officers, who would congregate in the bars, reminiscing of battles past, and exclaiming over the foibles of mutual acquaintances. When they had set out, Joy had been almost breathless with excitement, desperate to start out on the first real adventure of her life. But since they had begun the long route from Bombay toward Suez, the days seemed to have slowed and stalled as the temperatures rose, their worlds narrowing to the familiar bases of bar, deck, and dining room, so that they had all begun to feel like fixtures on board, rarely even bothering to venture ashore at the ports of call. It gradually became harder to imagine real life existing elsewhere, and, consequently, some chose not to try, letting themselves be carried by the gentle rhythms of life on board, and swayed by the simmering heat, so that their previous pursuits—deck tennis, afternoon walks, swimming—had gradually become too much effort, and even speech itself had become more sparse. Increasingly, now, passengers were sleeping in the afternoon, or watching movies in the evening, only a few singing listlessly as they followed the bouncing ball on the screen. At night, they

would gaze unseeing at unearthly iridescent
sunsets, inured by repetition to their extraordinary beauty. Only those, like Georgina
Lipscombe, who were forced out by the
insistent requirements of their children,
found themselves engaged in any kind of
activity.

Stella became bored, and restless, so
that sometimes Joy actually preferred it
when she disappeared. But it all suited Joy,
who having found the narrow parameters of
ship life a little too close to those she had left
in Hong Kong, found she could indulge her
antisocial nature without remark. She liked
to retire alone to the cabin when she knew
the others would all be out, and gaze at what
she privately thought of as her Edwardian
treasures: his letters, which were fast
becoming grubby and fragile from overhan-
dling, her framed wedding photograph of
them both, and the little Chinese painting, a
blue horse on rice paper, that Edward had
bought her on their first day of married life,
strolling through Hong Kong.

He had roused her early, and she had
opened her eyes wide, briefly uncomprehending in her half-slumber how she could
have ended up in the same bed as this man.

When she remembered, she had reached for him, linking her arms languorously around his freckled neck, squinting against the light. He had pulled her closer, murmuring softly. She could hear nothing but the whispered rustling of the sheets

Afterward, as the sweat cooled on her exposed skin, he had pushed himself up on one elbow and kissed her lightly on the nose. "Let's get up," he whispered. "I want us to have our first morning by ourselves, before the others get up. Let's disappear." Joy had fought a vague feeling of disappointment that he didn't want to stay in their honeymoon bed, and wrap his warm limbs around hers. But, anxious to please, she had raised herself, and climbed into the raw silk dress and short jacket that her mother had had made for her "going away" outfit. They had ordered tea from room service, and drunk it swiftly, gazing shyly at each other across the breakfast table, and then had emerged, blinking, onto the rude, honking streets of the capital, their senses assaulted by the battery of sights, sounds, and less-than-fragrant smells that constituted Kowloon in the early morning. Joy had stared at it all with the stunned incomprehension of a newborn, wondering at how different the world could look in twenty-four hours.

"We'll get the Star Ferry," Edward said, clutching her hand and pulling her toward the terminal. "I want to take you to Cat Street."

Joy had never been to Cat Street market. Her mother, had she dared to suggest it, would have paled, pointing out its history as a haven for criminals and prostitutes (except her mother would have called them "loose women") and remarking on the fact that no one of any *class* ever went there. It was also, based in the Western end of the island, in an area Alice would have described, somewhat perversely, as "too Chinese." But as they sat on the wooden seats of the ferry, cocooned in newly married bliss and oblivious to the chattering voices around them, Edward told her that since the 1949 revolution in China, the area had apparently been flooded with family possessions, many of which were valuable antiques. "I want to buy you something," he said, tracing her palm with his finger. "So you've got something to remember me by until we see each other again. Something special to you and me." He had called her Mrs. Ballantyne then, and Joy had flushed with pleasure. Every time he reminded her of her wifely status, she couldn't help but think of the marital intimacies of the night before.

It was shortly after seven in the morning by the time they arrived, but Cat Street market was already teeming with life; traders cross-legged behind flat cloths, upon which sat old watches, or intricately carved jade on red thread, old men seated on benches next to small fluttering birds in their cages. Ornate gilded trunks. Enameled furniture. All overlaid by the sweet, fried smell of turnip paste, cooked by hawkers who catcalled and shrieked, speaking so fast that even Joy, who knew far too much Cantonese for her parents' comfort, could not hope to understand.

It had felt like the Wild West. But Joy, observing Edward's enthusiasm, had fought the urge to cling to him. He didn't want a clinging wife, he had told her as much the evening before. He liked her strength, her independence. The fact that she didn't "flap and flutter" like the other officers' wives he knew. He had known only one other woman like her, he said quietly, as they had lain, entwined, in the dark. He had loved her, too. But she had died during the war, killed by a bomb in Plymouth, where she had been visiting her sister. Joy had felt her heart clench when he mentioned the word love, despite knowing that this woman could no longer be a threat in the conventional sense. And with that sudden emotion had come the terrifying realization that from now on her happiness was a captive thing, hostage to his unthinking words, almost entirely dependent on the kindness of another.

"Look," he said, pointing at an overcrowded stall. "That's it. What do you think?"

Joy had turned to follow his finger, and seen a small picture, framed in bamboo, propped up against an ornate iron pot. In loose brushstrokes of ink on white paper, it showed a blue horse, twisted as if in the act of breaking free, and yet surrounded by dark lines that suggested some kind of border.

"Do you like it?" he said. His eyes were shining, childlike.

Joy stared at the picture. She didn't, really. Or at least she wouldn't have noticed it, if just she had been looking. But his expression prompted her to try to look at it through his eyes.

"I love it," she said. Her husband. Wanted to buy it. For her, his wife.

"I really love it."

"How much?" he said, motioning to the stallholder, who had been eyeing them, taking in the good clothes, the naval whites. From behind his long, stringy mustache, he shrugged, as if he couldn't understand.

Joy paused, and glanced at Edward.

"*Geido tsin ah?*" she asked.

The stallholder looked at her, and then shrugged again. Joy stared at him, knowing he understood her.

"*Mgoi, lei, Sinsaahn,*" she said, more sweetly. "*Geido tsin ah?*"

The man removed the clay pipe from his lips, as if considering something. Then he named a figure. An exorbitant figure.

Joy looked at him incredulously.

"*Pengh di la!*" she exclaimed, asking him to think again. But the man shook his head.

She turned to Edward, trying to keep the fury from her voice.

"He's being ridiculous," she said, quietly. "He's asking for ten times what it's worth, just because you're wearing your uniform. Let's move on." Edward gazed at Joy, and then at the stallholder.

"No," he said. "Just tell me how much. I don't care what it costs today. You're my wife. I want to buy you a present. This present."

Joy squeezed his hand.

"That's lovely," she said. "But I can't take it. Not at that price."

"Why?"

Joy gazed at him, wondering how to say what she meant. It would ruin it for me, she said silently, because when I looked at it I wouldn't see your love for me, I would see your being conned by an unscrupulous man. And that's not how I want to think of you.

"Look," she murmured into his ear. The smell of him distracted her, making her wish suddenly that they were not in this market at all, but back in their hotel room. "Let's just pretend to walk on. It'll frighten him into thinking he's losing the sale. Then he'll probably offer something reasonable."

But the man just stood and watched as they walked away, so that Edward became increasingly agitated. There was nothing else he liked, he said, as they browsed stall after stall. The picture was perfect. He wanted to buy the picture.

"Let's go into the temple," said Joy, in an attempt to distract him, gesturing at the vibrant red and gold of the Man Mo temple on the corner of Hollywood Road, where incense smoke seethed out, as if only reluctantly offering itself to the gods on its appellants' behalf. But he said distractedly that she should go in alone. He was going to go for a little walk. He shifted a little on his feet, suggesting some bladder discomfort.

Joy turned away from him, feeling wretched, as if she had in some way disappointed him. The morning wasn't turning out how she'd intended.

In the dark confines of the temple, she half wished she'd changed her mind. The group of Chinese people lighting their offerings in the back turned silently to look at her, the *gweilo* invading their sacred space. Not wishing to offend, Joy muttered a greeting in Cantonese, and this seemed to appease them a little, so that they turned away, at least. Joy stared up at the ceiling, from which immense incense spirals dangled, slow burning, and wondered how soon again she could walk out. How soon she could persuade Edward to climb back aboard the Star Ferry so that she could make the most of the last few hours they had to spend together.

Then Edward appeared by her side, beaming.

"I got it," he said.

"Got what?" she asked. But she knew.

"I got it. At a good price." He held out the little painting with both hands, as if making his own offering. "The man dropped his price when you'd gone. Must have not wanted to lose face in front of a lady, eh? I know all this 'face' stuff is very important out here."

Joy gazed at the proud, smiling face of her new husband, and at the little horse on rice paper he held before him. There was a brief pause.

Then: "Aren't you clever," she said, kissing him. "I absolutely love it."

He was so pleased as they walked out, there was really no point her mentioning the fact that she had never actually told him the price to begin with.

Joy, wiggling her toes at the door, stared at the blue horse. Then at her wedding photograph. Then debated whether to treat herself with one of his letters. She was having to ration herself now, conscious that they were beginning to fall apart, but sometimes it was so hard to conjure him up without them. She could get bits of him: the tenor of his voice when he laughed, his broad hands, the way his legs looked in his whites; but it was increasingly difficult to picture him as a whole. The last few weeks before they had boarded the ship she had felt quite panicked, because she had barely been able to do it at all. One week and four days, she told herself, now such an expert at such mental arithmetic that the dates came as naturally to her as her own birthday. Then I will see him again.

"Are you nervous?" Stella had said to her the previous week, as they had discussed what they would wear for the day they actually met their husbands. "I know I will be. Sometimes I wonder if I'll actually recognize him." Stella hadn't seen Dick for almost three months, an absence much shorter than Joy's from Edward.

But Joy wasn't nervous. She just wanted to see him, wanted to feel the solidity of his embrace, to see his face shine, like the sun, down upon her. When she had told the other wives this, during a hairstyling session, Stella had made a fake gagging motion, which Joy had found hurtful, even if she understood why Stella was doing it, and the other wives had exchanged knowing looks. Like her mother's, all those months ago, they suggested that she was still an innocent, a naïf, with a lot to learn about men and married life. Only Mrs. Fairweather had smiled, and nodded as if she understood, but then her husband had never been in the services, and appeared to be joined to her at her well-padded hip. Joy had not said anything public about Edward after that; she had simply kept him to herself, as if guarding some precious secret.

One letter, she told herself, unfolding the most recent, like someone unwrapping a particularly succulent chocolate. One letter a day until I see him again. And then I will pack them away for safekeeping so that I can look at them again when I am an old, old woman, and remember how it was to be separated from the man I love.

The atmosphere subtly altered as they approached the Suez Canal, the faint buzz of potential conflict rousing the passengers from their dreamlike state. The words *Suez* and *government* began to be bandied about at suppers, and the men, conversing in huddles, would look terribly serious, so that Joy, who had no idea what its significance might be, suddenly found herself feeling almost anxious and rather glad of the presence of servicemen. The Brits, according to the First Officer, still occupied the African side of the canal. "But I wouldn't go too near the sides of the decks while we're inside it," he advised, gravely. "You can't trust those Arabs. We've had reports of them galloping up and down the shoreline bearing arms. And it's not unknown for them to use foreign ships for a bit of target practice." All the women had gasped at this, and clutched their necks theatrically, while the men nodded sagely, muttered about the Aswan Dam, and acted as though the women were flapping. Joy hadn't gasped; she found herself electrified. And despite the dire warnings, she found herself unable to sit inside for the entire time that the S.S. *Destiny* passed through the canal, but often sat alone, outside, her head camouflaged by her sun hat, smiling blandly at passing officers' warnings and secretly hoping to see some turbaned assassin on a camel. She knew the officers thought she was a little wild, that the Hindu deck crew were talking about her, but she didn't care. How often was she going to get the chance to take part in a real adventure?

The canal itself turned out to be not the war-torn, concrete-lined canal she had imagined, but a mercurial silver strip of water lined by sand dunes, and punctuated by a near-silent stately procession of ships, gliding along as if strung together. It was hard to believe, in this silent, orderly line, that there could be anything to fear. The only real frisson she felt was that night, when the Captain ordered the lights to be turned out, and they had all sat, temporarily hushed in the darkened dining room, but even then she had found herself perversely grateful for the feeling that something, other than bridge or deck tennis, was actually happening.

It was as the ship headed toward Egypt that the First Officer told them about the fancy dress party. It would be held on the night before they docked at Tilbury, a fitting climax to the voyage, and the Captain had wanted to give them all enough time to prepare their costumes. Joy thought privately that he had probably wanted to distract them all from the journey through Egypt, but she said nothing, as everybody suddenly got very excited, as if mentioning the final night had somehow brought it closer, and they began planning their outfits.

"I want to go as Carmen Miranda. But I don't suppose they'll be able to get me the fruit," said Stella, as they walked back from the dining rooms. Pieter had not appeared at dinner that evening, which had put her in a foul temper, so Joy didn't say what she thought: that Carmen Miranda's outfit might be just a little revealing for a married woman to wear without comment.

"Or I could go as Marilyn Monroe in *How to Marry a Millionaire*. If I could get some new trimming for my pink dress." She paused, gazing at herself in the reflection of a window. "Do you think it would be worth having my hair tinted a few shades lighter? I've been thinking about it for ages."

"What would Dick think?" said Joy, aware as soon as she said it that it was the wrong thing to ask.

"Oh, Dick will take me as he finds me," Stella said dismissively. "He's lucky to have me, after all."

Pieter has said that to her, thought Joy, uncomfortably. It was not something the old Stella would have said. But then it was difficult to know what this new Stella was ever going to say—or, indeed, what it was safe to say to her. From years of feeling able to entrust her with her most painful confidences, Joy now found talking to Stella a little too close to walking on shifting sands. One had to tread carefully, and even then never knew whether one was going to trip and fall.

"Well, if you think Dick would like it . . . I'm sure it would look terribly pretty. But don't you want to look exactly the same as when you left him? So he doesn't feel . . . well, uncomfortable?"

"Oh, Dick, Dick, Dick," said Stella crossly. "Honestly, Joy, you do go on. I told you, Dick would be glad to see me if I turned up looking like an oriental. So why don't you stop harping? It's only a fancy dress, after all."

Stung, Joy said nothing for the rest of their walk to the cabin. At which point, predictably, Stella said she couldn't face listening to those snoring kids and was going for a walk around the decks. By herself.

Her mood had recovered the next morning, and the following few days she became a little more like the old Stella, engrossed as she was in trying to find the right materials to create her outfit. When they got to Port Said, a couple of traders were allowed to come aboard, with trinkets and beads in huge wooden baskets, so that even those women, like Mrs. Fairweather, who would normally have dismissed the Egyptians as beneath their consideration, found themselves fussing and fighting over trimmings and feathers in a manner that was, according to Georgina Lipscombe, frankly undignified.

Joy tried to engage herself in thoughts of costumes and disguise, but as they finally entered the milder waters of the Mediterranean, all she could think of was the fact that within days now, not weeks, she would see Edward again. Sometimes she fancied she could even feel his increasing proximity as a physical presence. Although no doubt Stella would have made gagging motion at that, too.

The night of the party, they were to cross the last lengthy stretch of water and finally enter the English channel. The Bay of Biscay, the old traveling hands warned, was renown for its choppy waters so the girls "should keep ahold of their glasses." "And if they can't keep ahold of their glasses, they can keep a hold of me," Pieter had said, too loudly, so that the women nearest him discreetly shrank away, their smiles calcifying on their faces. But the prospect of the party, or its proximity to home, had gradually infected everyone so that on the last evening, even as the decks became cold and wet with Atlantic spray, whoops of misbehavior could be heard as various exotically costumed passengers ran from one cabin to another.

Mr. and Mrs. Fairweather had dressed as an Indian raja and his wife, wearing genuine costumes that they had acquired during a short and, according to Mrs. Fairweather, rather testing posting to Delhi, and that they appeared to carry with them on sea journeys in case of such events. Mrs. Fairweather had painted her face and arms with cold tea to get just the right shade for an Indian, she assured everyone authoritatively, tugging at her exotic fabrics to disguise the flashing revelation of pale flesh around her middle. Stella, having given up on Marilyn after being told what ship's bleach would do to her hair, had now metamorphosed into Rita Hayworth in *Salome*, sporting an outfit that appeared to have at least two of its seven veils missing. She was slightly peeved to find herself if not outshone then at least equaled by Georgina Lipscombe, who had persuaded one of the naval officers to lend her his whites, and looked rather astoundingly glamorous with her dark hair swept up under its peaked cap. Joy had left it all too late, and subsequently been rather uninspired, so Stella had made her a foil crown and told her to go as the Queen. "We can trim my purple robe with cotton wool to look like ermine. And she doesn't wear a lot of makeup, so you'll be quite comfortable," she said. Despite her passion of less than a year earlier, Stella was no longer interested in Elizabeth. After a brief spell of Margaret ("*much* better dress sense"), she had now moved on to Hollywood.

Joy felt rather silly as Queen Elizabeth, unsure whether it was the presumptuousness of the choice, or the childishness of her outfit that was making her more uncomfortable. But when they finally arrived in the dining hall, and Joy caught sight of some of the other outfits, her mood began to lighten.

Pieter had dressed as an Egyptian trader, his body exposed from the waist up and blacked up with what could have been boot polish so that his muscles glowed and rippled in the dimmed lights. His blond hair was covered with a woolly black cap, crocheted by the elderly Mrs. Tennant, and he carried a basket of beads and wooden carvings. Thoroughly overexcited already, every now and then he would launch himself at one of the women, who would squeal theatrically, and wave him away, laughing and yet looking faintly cross. He never launched himself at Joy.

"Have I gone blotchy?" said Mrs. Fairweather, approaching her as she sat down at the table. "I'm sure the spray has given me spots."

Joy studied her tea-stained complexion.

"It looks fine to me," she said. "But I'll touch it up if you like. I'm sure one of the waiters will do us some cold tea."

Mrs. Fairweather pulled her compact from her handbag and studied her reflection, straightening the jewels in her headdress. "Oh, I'm sure I don't want to bother them. They'll all be terribly busy tonight. It's a special supper, I'm told."

"Hello, Joy. Or should I say Your Majesty?" It was Louis, who bowed low before her and then took her hand and kissed it, making Joy blush. "I must say, you look like you were born to it. Doesn't she, Mrs. Fairweather?"

He was wearing a scruffy tweed skirt and a headscarf, as well as a rather alarming shade of lipstick.

"Oh, definitely," said Mrs. Fairweather. "Positively regal, she looks."

"Oh, please don't," said Joy, laughing, as Louis sat down beside her. "I shall get ideas above my station. May I ask what on earth you have come as?"

"Can't you tell?" Louis looked downcast. "I can't believe you can't tell."

Joy looked at Mrs. Fairweather and back again.

"I'm sorry," she said.

"I'm a land girl." he said, holding up a pitchfork. "Look! I bet you can't believe I got ahold of this!"

"A land girl?"

Mrs. Fairweather began to laugh. "Now I see it," she said. "Can you see it, Philip? Mr. Baxter's come as a land girl. Look, he's even got a bag of potatoes."

"What's a land girl?" said Joy, tentatively.

"Where have you been? Timbuktu?"

Joy looked around her, to see if anyone else shared her lack of knowledge. But Stella was squealing at Pieter, and Georgina Lipscombe was talking to the First Officer, and the only other bystander, a ballet dancer with suspiciously hairy legs, didn't appear to be listening.

"When did you last come to England?" said Louis.

"Oh, Gosh. When I was a child, I think," said Joy. "When Hong Kong was invaded, we were all sent to stay in Australia."

"Fancy that, Philip. Joy didn't know what a land girl was." Mrs. Fairweather nudged her husband, who, from under his turban, was gazing benignly at his gin and tonic.

"Fancy," he said, mildly.

"Did you really never see one?"

Joy began to feel rather awkward. There was always something in gatherings like these, she observed, to make her feel ignorant, or stupid. That was why she loved Edward. He never made her feel that way.

"I don't suppose there was any reason why Joy should know what a land girl was," said Louis, briskly. "I'm sure there are loads of things about Hong Kong that I should never understand. Can I get you a drink, Joy? Mrs. Fairweather?"

Joy smiled at him, grateful for his solicitousness. And the moment passed.

The swell gradually built up as they finished their main courses, so that the waiters had to occasionally clutch at passing bits of furniture to avoid dropping the plates, and the wine in Joy's glass began to tip at alarmingly violent angles

"It's always like this," said Louis, who was seated next to her. His lipstick had rubbed off with his meal, so that she could now look at him without giggling. "First time I came across, I slid right off my bunk in my sleep."

Joy didn't mind. Every huge wave brought her closer to Tilbury. But some of the ladies began to exclaim disapprovingly, as if there should be someone to blame for this meteorological lack of consideration. Their voices rose shrilly, like those of the gulls, above the music, which the captain had ordered to continue, even though as the musicians kept having to steady themselves, it became increasingly disjointed. It was at this point that Stella, making her way unsteadily toward the rest rooms, had almost fallen over, and Pieter had leapt up to help her, sending his chair crashing backward. Joy saw Stella's expression as she thanked him and felt suddenly deeply uneasy.

Louis, watching her, refilled her wineglass, and told her to drink up. "If you drink enough you'll think it's just you swaying, instead of the ship," he said, and his hand accidentally touched hers. Joy, still staring at Stella as she held Pieter's supporting arm just a little too long, had almost not noticed that.

So she had drunk. She had been relatively abstemious up until tonight, but now, like the others, had been infected by a sense of something ending, a recklessness brought on by their isolation, and the thought of the more sober life, a more adult existence ahead. The toasts became louder, and more ridiculous: to the late King; to the old country; to Elizabeth, at which she found herself standing and nodding regally; to the Lone Ranger and Tonto; to the pudding, an elaborate confection of cream, sponge, and alcohol; and to the S.S. *Destiny* itself, as she lurched and swayed her way through the waves.

Joy found herself giggling, and not minding so much when Louis put his arm around her, and stopping noticing quite so much who had disappeared from the table and when. And when the Captain had climbed onto the podium and announced that he was about to award the prize for the best outfit,

Joy had rather rudely heckled him as merci-
lessly as the rest of her table.

"Shhh! Shhh! Ladies and gentlemen!" the
First Officer had insisted, tapping his brandy
glass with the edge of his knife. "Quiet!
Please!"

"You know, Joy, I do think you're absolutely
wonderful."

Joy tore her gaze away from the podium
and stared at Louis, whose brown eyes had
suddenly taken on the liquid longing of a
puppy dog.

"I've been wanting to tell you since Bombay." He placed his hand over hers, and Joy
quickly withdrew it, fearful that someone
might see.

"Now, ladies and gentlemen, steady,
please. C'mon, c'mon." The captain held his
hands, palm down, before him, and then
threw one up sharply as the ship lurched
suddenly to starboard, so that the passengers whooped and catcalled.

"It's an awful long time to be separated
from the one you love, Joy. I know that. I've
got a girl at home, too. But it doesn't stop
you wanting someone else, does it?"

Joy gazed at him, feeling suddenly saddened by the fact that he had had to compli-

cate everything. She liked him. In other circumstances—well, perhaps. But not this . . . Joy shook her head, trying to instill a little sense of regret into that small motion, just to save his feelings.

"Let's not talk like this, Louis."

Louis gazed at her for slightly too long, and then looked down at the table.

"Sorry," he said. "Probably had a bit too much to drink."

"*Shhh!*" said Mrs. Fairweather. "Will you two be quiet! He's trying to speak!"

"Now, I know this is the moment you've all been waiting for, and I'd like to say you've all made a tremendous effort . . . but that wouldn't be true." The captain paused, to the sound of laughter.

"No, no. I'm just joshing. Now, I've deliberated long and hard over these costumes. And over some I've deliberated as long as possible." Here he looked meaningfully at Stella's diaphanous veils. Joy, preoccupied as she was, found herself relieved by the fact that Stella was still at the table. Pieter had been absent for some time. "But the overwhelming decision of myself and my colleagues, has been to award our prize"— he held up a bottle of champagne—"to a man who has proven he is capable of barefaced cheek. Literally."

The assembled passengers paused, briefly silenced.

"Ladies and gentlemen, Pieter Brandt. Or, should I say, our Egyptian trader!"

The dining hall burst into applause, with napkins and half-eaten bread rolls thrown high into the air. Joy, along with the rest of her table, glanced around, trying to locate Pieter among the many elaborately disguised heads. As his woolly black wig failed to reveal itself, the clapping slowly filtered out and a small murmur began to swell, as passengers' heads swiveled around.

Joy looked up at the Captain, who had been briefly silenced by Pieter's nonappearance, and then at Stella, who looked equally nonplussed.

"Perhaps he's off trading," the Captain joked. "I'd better get the cook to go and check on our stores." He stood, and gazed around him, evidently wondering what to do next.

He was interrupted by a sudden whisper at the other end of the dining room. It spread down the line of tables like a soft wind, so that Joy, following its direction, eventually caught sight of its object. All eyes landed on

Georgina Lipscombe, who walked unsteadily through the doors at the end, her hair now loosened from the peaked cap, and hanging in loose curls around her shoulders. She staggered slightly, trying to catch her balance, and reached out to hold the back of an unoccupied chair.

Joy stared at her, trying to take in the significance of what she was seeing, and then looked over at Stella, who had gone quite gray.

For Georgina Lipscombe's immaculate naval whites were now less than pristine. From her epaulets down to somewhere around the middle of her thighs, Mrs. Lipscombe's uniform bore a smudged, but definite imprint of boot polish.

Georgina, apparently oblivious, stared at the faces turned toward her, and then, her head lifted, evidently decided to ignore them. Reaching their table, she sat down, somewhat heavily, in her chair, and lit up a cigarette. There was a brief, loaded silence.

And then: "You absolute tart!" yelled Stella, and flew at her across the table, grabbing her hair, her epaulets, any bit of spare flesh or uniform she could reach before Louis and the First Officer could leap from their own seats to try to pull her off. Joy, stunned and frozen, simply stood, not recognizing this wild-eyed banshee as her friend, her veils tearing and ripping from her costume as she scrambled to get a better hold. "You bloody, bloody tart!" Stella shouted, crying now, her elaborate dancing-girl makeup already streaked around her eyes. Louis managed to grab her arm, forcing her to relinquish her grip on Georgina's hair, but it was some seconds before either man felt quite confident enough to let her go.

"Shhh, now dear," said Mrs. Fairweather, stroking her hair as the men sat her down again. "Come on. Calm down. There's quite enough excitement for one night."

The entire dining hall was silenced. The Captain motioned to the band to start playing again, but there was a long, pregnant pause before they tentatively rediscovered their place in the music. Around them, the other diners stared wide-eyed, laughing in shocked tones or shaking their heads in disapproval, as they slowly returned their attention to their own tables.

Georgina, her hair matted and bunched on one side where Stella had grabbed it, placed a hand to her face, checking for blood. Seeing no evidence of it on her fingers, she gazed around her on the table-cloth, looking for the lit cigarette that had been knocked out of her hand. It was floating, rather forlornly, in Mrs. Fairweather's drink. She calmly removed another from her silver cigarette case, and lit it. Then she lifted her head and gazed back at Stella.

There was a brief silence.

"You silly girl," she said, exhaling a long plume of smoke. "You didn't think you were the only one, did you?"

Joy sat outside on the starboard deck, her arms around the sobbing Stella, wondering how long it would be before she could gently point out the fact that not only were they both soaked, but also her teeth were beginning to chatter.

Stella had cried for more than twenty minutes now, apparently oblivious to the freezing sea spray, and the lurching deck, seemingly conscious only of her own misery as she huddled into Joy's damp and mournful embrace.

"I can't believe he lied to me," she gasped, during a brief interlude from sobbing. "All those things he said . . ."

Joy chose not to dwell on what they might have been. Or what they might have led to.

"She's so awful as well. She's old, for God's sake." Stella gazed at Joy through eyes swollen with tears. Her voice was incredulous. "She's got a hard face, and she wears too much makeup. She's even got *stretch marks.*"

It was not so much that Pieter had cheated on her, Joy was beginning to suspect. It was what Stella saw as his indiscriminate choice of partner.

"Oh, Joy . . . What am I going to do?"

Joy thought back to Pieter Brandt's return to the dining table. He had laughed and made a couple of off-color jokes at first, his inebriation preventing him from picking up on the fact that the table had greeted him in stony silence. Then his laughter had become rather forced, and he had told another funny anecdote, as if trying to restore the mood. But when the Captain came and plonked the bottle of champagne in front of him, curtly announcing "You're the winner" before walking off again, Pieter had apparently, finally, twigged the fact that all was not as it had been when he disappeared some half an hour previously.

"You might need to touch up your boot polish, old boy." Louis had said, staring pointedly at Pieter's pale chest, and then equally pointedly at Georgina's stained frontage.

For obvious reasons it had been impossible to tell whether Pieter had actually gone white, but he had glanced anxiously around at his fellow travelers, and then briefly excused himself, saying that he needed to "stretch his legs." Georgina had looked bored, sucking on her ever-present cigarette and managing to stare into the distance while not actually meeting anyone else's eye. Eventually, apparently peeved by the lack of male attention, she had left the table after him.

But Stella had already gone by then, escorted to the rest room by Mrs. Fairweather, who had wiped vainly at her face with an ill-suited lace handkerchief and appealed to Stella to just stop crying. "You looked so pretty with your makeup," she wittered. "You don't want to let that woman see she's got you all upset." She had looked rather relieved when Joy came in, and had handed Stella over with a touch too much enthusiasm and gratitude. "You two are friends," she said. "You know how to cheer her up. You'll tell her." And then, in a cloud of

Arpège, beads, and translucent fabric, she had disappeared.

"What am I going to do?" said Stella, a half hour later, staring out at the black and frothing sea. "Everything's finished. Maybe I should just . . ."

Joy followed Stella's gaze across the deck and tightened her grip on her friend's arm.

"Don't you dare talk like that," she said, suddenly panicked. "Don't you dare even think like that, Stella Hanniford."

Stella turned to face her, her expression suddenly free from all artifice and guile.

"But what am I going to do, Joy? I've ruined everything, haven't I?"

Joy took Stella's cold hands in her own.

"You've ruined nothing. You just got a little too close to a stupid, stupid man, who, after tomorrow, you will never, ever have to see again."

"But that's the awful thing, Joy. Part of me *wants* to see him again."

Stella looked back at her, her big blue eyes wide with misery. She relinquished one of Joy's hands, and pushed her hair back from her face.

"He was absolutely wonderful. Much bet-

ter than Dick. And that's the worst thing—
how can I go back to Dick and pretend that
everything's okay when I've felt something
so much more?"

Joy felt sick. Part of her wanted to block
her ears, to say to Stella, "Stop! I don't want
to know!" But she was conscious that she
was Stella's only possible confidante. The
only confidante of someone who, while
always a little on the dramatic side, had
gazed out at those waves in a frankly
unnerving manner.

"You've got to forget him," she said eventually. Uselessly. "You've got to make it work
with Dick."

"But what if I shouldn't have married Dick
in the first place? Oh, I was in love with him,
I'll grant you. But what on earth did I know?
I'd only kissed two men before I met him.
How did I know I'd end up liking someone
else better?"

"Dick's a good man," said Joy, thinking of
the handsome, affable pilot. "You were so
happy together. You can be again."

Stella began to cry again. "But I don't feel
like it. I don't want to have to smile at him,
and kiss him, and let him press his horrid old

body against me. I wanted Pieter . . . and now I'm going to be stuck with someone I don't love anymore for the rest of my life."

Joy placed her arms around her friend again, and gazed at the dark sky. There were hardly any stars tonight, the constellations being obscured by the low, mucky clouds.

"It will all be all right," she murmured, into Stella's cold ear. "I promise. It will all look better in the morning."

"How do you know?" said Stella, lifting her head again.

"Because things always are. I always feel better in the daylight."

"No, not that. How do you know that you've made the right choice?"

Joy thought for a minute, not wanting to give the wrong answer. She thought, briefly, of Louis.

"I suppose you don't," she said, eventually. "You just have to hope."

"But *you* do. *You* know."

Joy was briefly silent.

"Yes." she said.

"How?"

"Because I don't feel properly comfortable around anyone else. Being with him . . . it's like being with you . . . except with the love thing added."

She glanced at Stella, who was gazing at her attentively.

"I suppose I feel like he's the male version of me. The better half. When I'm around him, I just want to live up to his version of me. I don't want to disappoint him."

Joy could picture him now, smiling at her, his eyes wrinkled at the corners, his teeth just visible below his upper lip.

"I never really cared what anyone thought of me until he came along," she said. "And now, I can't believe it's me he's chosen. Every morning I wake up and thank God that he did. Every night I go to bed praying that time will go that much faster so that I can be with him again. I think all the time about what he's doing, who he's talking to. Not in a jealous way, or anything. I just want to be closer to him, and if I can imagine what he's doing, then that helps."

He would be asleep now, she thought. Or reading a book. Probably one of his bloodstock books, full of lines of horses stretching back generations, building his dreams on an equine family tree.

"He's more than I ever asked for. More than I ever hoped for," she said, half dreamily. "I just can't imagine ever being with anyone else."

There was a brief pause. Joy realized she had almost forgotten Stella was there.

But Stella was raising herself from their seat near the lifeboats. She had stopped crying, and was pulling her shawl tightly around her against the cold.

Joy pushed herself upright, and wiped the wet hair from her face.

"Yes, well, you're lucky," Stella said, not looking Joy in the eye. "It's been easy for you."

Joy began to stand, too, frowning slightly at her friend's tone.

Stella walked toward the door, and then turned, so that her parting shot blew back at Joy, caught on the night spray. "Yes, much easier for you. No one else ever wanted to be with you, after all."

Chapter Seven

Sabine sat on the floor, in the center of the threadbare Persian rug, staring at the picture of Stella in her evening dress. The muted shades of the tired room she occupied had temporarily receded, replaced by heaving, rain-lashed decks and the shimmering satin and sparkle of seven or so waterlogged sequined veils.

"Did she go back to Dick in the end?" She gazed at the twinkling eyes, the knowing smile, trying unsuccessfully to imagine this girl desolate and abandoned on a wet ship. She looked too sure of herself somehow.

Joy, who had been sorting through a box

of old certificates, peered over Sabine's shoulder.

"Stella? Yes, but not for long."

Sabine turned to face her, waiting for an explanation. Joy put her box down on her knees, and thought for a minute. "He did adore her, but I think her feelings for Pieter Brandt rather shook her up, and after awhile, when no children came along, I think she felt she decided she would rather have a bit of excitement elsewhere."

"So, what happened next?"

Joy rubbed at her hands, to try and dislodge some of the dust. She was glad that she and Sabine were talking again, but it was a little wearing the way Sabine tended to pursue everything. She took a deep breath, as if bracing herself, as Stella had done all those years earlier, to deliver bad news.

"She went through rather a lot of men in the end. Never quite settled with anyone."

"A bit racy," said Sabine, gleefully. She had rather liked the sound of Stella.

"I suppose you could say that. She certainly had a good time when she was younger. It was when she got older that she became a bit sad. Used to drink rather too much."

Joy rubbed at her eye, which had become gritty. "Her last husband died of liver failure, and after she lost him I think it hit home that she didn't really have anyone. She was sixty-two by then, you see. Rather a hard age to be totally by oneself."

Sabine tried to imagine the glowing, glamorous figure before her not just abandoned, but as a lonely old drinker.

"Did she die?"

"Yes. Only a few years ago. In ninety-two I think it was. We had kept in touch, but she moved to a little apartment on the Spanish coast, and we never really saw each other after that. I discovered she'd died only because her niece sent me a rather sweet letter." Joy paused, looking temporarily distracted. "Right. I think I should probably get rid of all these old rosettes. They look a bit moldy. What a pity."

Sabine put the photographs back into the box in front of her, trying to imagine her own mother in the place of Stella Hanniford. She was less glamorous than Stella, but on present form she could easily plow her way through loads of men and end up alone in some Spanish apartment. Sabine had a sudden vision of herself, visiting her, while her mother reclined on a scruffy sofa, clutching a bottle of rioja, reminiscing drunkenly about those she had left behind. "Ahh, Geoff," she would say, her red hair hanging tattily around her shoulders, her lipstick smeared gaily across her mouth. "That was a good year. Geoff. Or was it George? I always get them mixed up."

She brushed the image aside, not sure whether it made her want to laugh or cry, and then glanced surreptitiously at her grandmother, as she poured the old box of rosettes into a black plastic bag, trying instead to reconcile the stiff figure in green corduroy beside her with the perfect picture of young love that had recently taken root in her imagination. Over the past few days, Sabine found herself forced into viewing her grandparents in a new light. This crotchety, stilted old pair had once been a love story to rival anything on the telly. Her grandfather had been handsome. Her grandmother . . . well, she was handsome, too. But what had really struck Sabine was that long wait; all that time apart, and she had still known. All those other officers, and she had kept her faith.

"No one would get engaged after one day

these days," she said, half thinking aloud. "Not if they had to wait a whole year afterward, anyway."

Joy, winding a piece of baling twine around the top of the bag, stopped and looked at her granddaughter.

"No. No. I don't suppose many would."

"Would you do it again? I mean, if you had to do it now?"

Joy put the bag on the floor, and stood in the center of the room, thinking.

"To your grandfather?"

"I don't know. All right, yes. To Grandfather."

Joy gazed out of the window, where the rain beat down in metallic shards. Above the window, a semicircular brown stain marked the place where the guttering had slipped from its place, allowing the water another means to seep enthusiastically into the house.

"Yes," Joy said. "Of course." But she didn't sound convinced.

"Did you ever get nervous? I mean, even before you saw him? After all that time on the ship?"

"I told you, dear. I just felt glad to see him."

Sabine wasn't satisfied.

"But you must have felt something. In those last few moments before you saw him. When you were waiting for the boat to dock, and staring over the edge, trying to locate him. You must have felt a bit sick. I know I would."

"It was a long time ago, Sabine. There were so many meetings. I really can't remember. Now, I must get this rubbish downstairs so that we don't miss the dustbin men when they come around." Suddenly brusque, Joy brushed the dust from her front, and moved toward the door. "Come on, put those away, and we'd better go down and start on lunch. Your grandfather will be hungry."

Sabine, unfolding her limbs and standing, noted her grandmother's rather abrupt manner, but didn't really mind. The last couple of weeks, during which they had spent a couple of hours together most days going through the old photographs and mementos, Joy's starchy demeanor had visibly softened, especially when she would engage upon a long story of her and Edward's early days together. The memories would gradually loosen her abrupt sentences, stretching them into longer, free-flowing stories, infusing them with color, so that Sabine had found herself fascinated, happy to listen as she was briefly allowed a glimpse of a new world of privilege and conformity and bad behavior.

And sex. It was weird to have her grandmother refer to sex. Well, she never actually said *sex* as such, but she had left Sabine in little doubt what it was that had got Stella Hanniford and Georgina Lipscombe into such trouble. Sabine couldn't believe how much they were all doing it in the 1950s. It was hard enough imagining that her mother did it now. Sabine thought of her mother, and wondered, not for the first time, why it was that she couldn't have had a big, romantic love like her grandparents. A real love, she thought wistfully, a love that survived the slings and arrows of fate, that soared, like some kind of 1950s *Romeo and Juliet*, above the petty and the mundane. The kind of love that you read about in books, that inspired songs, that lifted you like a bird and yet stood solid, like a monolith: vast, all-encompassing, enduring.

Joy, standing at the door, turned to face her.

"Come on, Sabine. Do get a move on.

Mrs. H is doing haddock and if we're late taking it upstairs it will be impossible for me to persuade your grandfather to eat it."

So what with her grandmother's defrosting, and getting used to the damp, and actually quite enjoying all the riding (although she still couldn't bring herself to admit it), Sabine's longing for home had, if not disappeared, certainly subsided quite considerably. She didn't miss television as much, anyway. And she hardly ever thought of Dean Baxter. And Mrs. H and her husband had been married for thirty-two years on Sunday, and although that wasn't one of the important ones (it was granite or newsprint or something, rather than gold or diamond), Mrs. H said as far as she was concerned it was good enough to warrant some sort of celebration, and that she, Sabine, along with a good clutch of Mrs. H's family, was invited.

Sabine had felt rather pleased about this; not just because it gave her an excuse to spend the evening out—while she and her grandmother were now friends, dinners at that long expanse of dining table were still something of an ordeal—but because it showed that she was not just becoming part of her own extended family, but part of Thom's and Annie's, too. Having only ever been an only child, and one of a periodic single parent, this was the first real family she had seen up close; a family that seemed endless and sprawling and yet intimate enough for everyone to know everyone else's business; a family where people walked in and out of one another's houses with the surety of possession, simply knowing where they fitted in. But what Sabine liked most was the noise: the endless talking over one another, interruptions, the explosions of laughter, the sharp cracks at one another's expense. Sabine's house had always been quiet. As far back as she could remember it had been necessarily silent, to enable her mother to work, so that it felt gloomy and permanently muffled, as if by a thick blanket. And when she, her mother, and Geoff had sat down to eat, there had been none of this noisy laughter, just Geoff asking her polite questions about her day, treating her somewhat self-consciously like a grown-up, and her mother staring into the distance as she ate, dreaming of who knew what. Probably Justin, thought Sabine, resentfully. For some reason she had started to feel really cross about Justin again.

It was the first time she had been to Mrs. H's house, a bungalow situated on the outskirts of the village. It sat, squat, in the middle of a square plot, surrounded by patio paving and preceded by a series of neatly maintained flower beds. A satellite dish jutted questioningly from the side of it, like an ear trumpet, and there were pale, floral curtains in the windows and window boxes with glowing red and pink cyclamen on every sill.

It sported synthetic stone cladding, which Sabine knew would have made Geoff blanche, and it had been built entirely by Mrs. H's husband, Michael, whom everyone called Mack. In fact the house itself was called Mackellen—which, when Sabine thought about it, was the furthest anyone had gone toward revealing Mrs. H's real name.

"It's a long way from your folks' house, I'll tell you that," said Thom, who had walked Sabine there from the big house.

"Looks less moldy, anyway," Sabine observed, and Thom laughed.

Inside, she saw why Thom was right. As he opened the door, she was hit by the warm breath of central heating full on, and acres of pale, springy carpet underfoot. There were family pictures on the wall, framed photographs, and a couple of embroidered poems, but the dominant popu- lation was of ornaments, ornaments every- where: little glass elephants, laughing, rubber-featured clowns, winsome shep- herdesses with wandering flocks. All shining under the bright lights, all without a speck of dust, bright and cheerful and immaculate. Sabine stared at the battalions of little crea- tures, momentarily dazzled by their sheer numbers.

"Come on in here, Sabine. Shut the door, Thom, you're letting in that damp air. My, but it's a cold one tonight."

Beaming, Mrs. H came toward her to take her coat. Except she looked totally unlike the Mrs. H of everyday; that Mrs. H wore a housecoat of pastel nylon, her hair swept back, and a glowing pink complexion free of makeup. This Mrs. H was wearing a mauve jumper with two gold chains around her neck, one with a cross. Her hair, wavy and shiny, looked somehow bigger, and her face was brightened with makeup, so that she looked suddenly younger, rather sophisti- cated, and not a little intimidating. Sabine felt temporarily unbalanced and realized to her shame that she had never really considered the possibility that Mrs. H might have a life away from the big house, and her roles of cooking and cleaning. Even when she was at Annie's she was buzzing round, engaged in some domestic chore.

"You—you look nice," she said, hesitantly.

"Do I? Aren't you sweet," said Mrs. H, shepherding her through the hallway. "Annie bought me this jumper a couple of years ago and do you know I've hardly worn it. Keep saving it for a special occasion. She tells me off, of course. But it seems too good for everyday."

"Is Annie coming?"

"Annie's already here, love. C'mon, we'll go through. Thom, you make sure you leave those shoes at the door. I've seen enough of that Hoover for one day."

Following Mrs. H, Sabine thought back to the previous day, when, riding past Annie's back garden, she had looked over the wall in the hope that she could see her and wave. Annie had often told her she should call by, so that she could take a look at her on a horse, and Sabine had to admit to being secretly proud of her renewed riding ability.

She had begun jumping, practicing by herself, and was slowly plucking up the courage to attempt small hedges, encouraged by the seeming infallibility of the little horse.

But as she pulled him gently to a halt, and glanced over into the kitchen window, she had caught sight not of a waving Annie, but of Patrick, Annie's husband, sitting at the table, his head buried deep in his hands, and his back slumped, as if under some unwieldy burden. Annie, half hidden by the reflections in the window, was standing across the table from him, simply staring into space.

Sabine had halted the gray horse for a moment, waiting for them to move, but when, after some minutes, neither of them did, she had quickly ridden on, feeling suddenly anxious lest they should see her and think she had been prying. She had since wondered about telling Mrs. H, but couldn't work out how to start the conversation; besides, she had moved briskly, and they were already in the living room.

Mrs. H's family sat around on immaculate, well-stuffed sofas, chatting in small groups and sipping at half-full drinks. To one side, a large, drop-leaf table stood laden with plates and cutlery, decorated with a glittering floral display, and flanked by chairs that sat seemingly within an impossible inch of one another. In the middle of the floor, on a pale blue and cream rug, two young boys played with an electronic racetrack, sending their downscaled vehicles whizzing noisily off the track and into the soft furnishings. The living room was even warmer than the hallway, making Sabine feel uncomfortably sweaty in her thick pullover. She had gotten so used to living in a cold house that she no longer went anywhere with any fewer than four layers, and she couldn't remember without looking quite how presentable the other three were.

Sabine recognized hardly anyone, except for Patrick and Annie, who, she realized with a start, she had never seen out of the confines of their own house. Patrick raised a glass to her in salute. He nudged Annie, who was gazing across the room, and she started slightly, before giving Sabine a broad smile, and motioning to her to come and sit down next to her. Sabine, trying to disengage her vision of them from before, hesitated, then walked over, half propelled by Mrs. H, who had to talk in unusually loud tones to be heard above the chatter and background music.

"This is Sabine, everyone. Sabine, I won't even begin to go around the room with you because you'll never remember all the names. Now, I'm going to start serving in five minutes, so you all come through when you're ready. Thom, you make sure Sabine's got a drink."

Annie was wearing one of her huge jumpers again. Sabine, who was already tugging at her collar, wondered why she didn't look nearly as uncomfortable as Sabine felt.

"How y'doing, Sabine?" said Patrick. "I hear you've been doing well on that little gray horse."

Sabine nodded, privately noting that he looked dreadful. He had dark shadows under his eyes, and at least two days' stubble on his chin. Despite being a big, coarse-looking man, more fitted to farming than writing, Patrick was always clean-shaven and immaculate. He usually smelled of fabric conditioner.

"Will you go out with the hounds next week? See a bit of the Wexford countryside?"

"Of course she will," said Thom, who had sat down on the floor with the boys. "I'll take

her out myself. I'll pop her over a few solid
jumps first, to see whether she'll go the distance, and we'll have a grand day out."

Sabine, staring at him, didn't know
whether to protest about the idea that she
would go foxhunting, or inwardly glow at the
thought that Thom was personally going to
take her. She didn't want to go and kill foxes,
she really didn't. She was a vegetarian, for
God's sake. She had wept over roadkill. But
the thought of spending a whole day with
Thom . . . on their own . . .

"Is your mam with you, Sabine?" It was a
middle-aged woman, with short, aubergine-
colored hair and a pair of heavily padded
shoulders that wrestled for visual command
over her momentous breasts. Sabine looked
at her blankly.

"Sabine, this is Auntie May," said Thom.
"She's Annie's mam's, and my own mam's,
sister. And that's Steven, her husband. They
know your mam from when she lived over
here."

"Can you all sit yourselves at the table?
Mack, take out some serving spoons, will
you?"

"A gorgeous girl, your mother," said the
woman, placing a plump hand on Sabine's

arm. "She used to go to the odd dance with my Sarah. The two of them used to make a right pair. Is she over with you?"

"No. She had to stay at home to work."

"Now that's a shame. A real shame. I would have loved to have seen her. Of course I'd have seen her myself when I went over—what was it, Steven? Two years ago?—but what with my hips and all . . . it's difficult for me to travel much."

Sabine nodded, as she was steered to her chair, unsure what she was meant to contribute.

"Arthritis. A killer, it is. Very little the doctors can do, I'm told. So I'll be in a wheelchair before long. And that'll be the end of me walking. But you tell your mother I said hello, won't you?"

"Sabine, you make sure you just help yourself to everything. This bunch of savages won't wait, so you'll just have to dive in."

"You tell her if she's ever passing she's to drop by. As I said, I may not be able to actually get out much by then, but she'll always find a warm welcome."

"Are your hips worse, May? You never said." This was accompanied by a barely audible chuckle.

"Auntie Ellen? Can I have some juice?"

"The potatoes, Sabine. You won't get fat on politeness around here," said Thom. "If you don't grab your dish while you can, you can bet someone else will."

Throughout this entire exchange, Annie had kept her gaze steady on the curtains opposite, her mind apparently far, far away from the clamor of the overcrowded front room. Patrick, who normally kept up some kind of physical contact with his wife, whether it be stroking her back, or holding her hand, was, unusually, looking away from her and drinking his can of beer with a kind of grim determination.

Oh, God, Sabine thought suddenly, as she gazed at them. It's falling apart. She was an expert at spotting the signs, after all.

"Have some more vegetables, Sabine. You've hardly taken enough to feed a fly."

"You leave her alone there, Mack. She'll have what she wants, won't you Sabine?"

Like a tongue that cannot help but return to worry a loose tooth, Sabine found her attention returning again and again during the meal to the unhappy dynamic between Annie and Patrick. She noticed how Patrick did try, two or three times, to speak to his wife, but how, even when she deigned to answer, she barely seemed to actually see him. Her gaze was always focused on some invisible point just past him. She noticed how Annie drank more than usual, so that her own mother eventually surreptitiously placed a glass of water in front of her. She noticed how Thom, who evidently recognized a little of what was going on, lavished a large amount of his own attention on Annie, trying to make her laugh, colluding with Patrick, drawing her into conversations when she had already seemingly absented herself from the party.

It had been a pity that she had become increasingly anxious watching all this, as Sabine thought she would have probably rather enjoyed herself otherwise. As well as two huge turkeys, there were loads of really nice vegetables, and a piece of salmon just for her, and everyone talked over themselves so much that it didn't matter whether she joined in or sat back and just listened. Thom's family kept teasing him about his solitary nature, and how he was going to end up as a hermit, living in a shed at the bottom of the woods. "I'm sure I saw a little tin-roofed thing down there the last time I walked through," said Steven. "That'd be your first mortgage, would it, Thommo?"

"Nah. That's the home of his girlfriend," said one of the young boys, who both seemed to be called James. "She's out there catching bats to put in her supper."

Mr. and Mrs. H, meanwhile, kept touching each other, and catching each other's eye in a way that, had it been her own parents, Sabine would have found distinctly embarrassing. They were always pawing at each other, and every now and then Mr. H would say something in Mrs. H's ear that would make her blush and exclaim, "Oh, Mack!" and then the rest of the table would catch on and start baying at them to "hold off a wee while," and "can you not wait until we've put the kids to bed?"

Yet, through all this, Annie, while raising the odd smile, was about as animated as one of Mrs. H's ornaments. Except distinctly less cheerful. Sabine watched her, and felt a sense of foreboding. Why was it so hard for Annie just to enjoy herself?

It was halfway through the pudding—a huge confection of chocolate and crushed biscuits, served with ice cream straight from the tub—that Sabine had felt a faint tugging feeling in her womb, a dull, low ache, that suddenly diverted her from table-watching, and caused her to press her legs together in fear.

Oh, God, not here. Not now. The rhythms of her life in Ireland had been so far removed from home that she hadn't even considered it a possibility. But now, silently counting back the weeks as she picked at her chocolate pudding, she suddenly realized that if she hadn't remembered, her body certainly had.

She waited until a particularly raucous exchange, and then slid, surreptitiously out of her chair

"Can you point me to the bathroom?" she whispered to Mrs. H, who was breathless with laughter at something one of her older relatives had said.

"Around the corner, first door on the right," said Mrs. H, laying a hand on her arm. "If that one's busy, try the one by the kitchen."

Sabine locked herself in the bathroom, and with a sigh of dismay, observed the tell-tale sign that she had half suspected, and half feared. She had come completely unprepared. And there was no way she was sitting on Mrs. H's pale upholstery for the rest of the evening unless she had something that could make her feel at ease.

For want of anything else, she wrapped a length of loo roll around her hand, and used that as a kind of temporary protection. And then, opening the various doors as silently as possible, conscious that perhaps it wasn't the done thing to go rooting around in your hosts' bathroom cupboards, she began to root around in her hosts' bathroom cupboards.

Bubble bath, bleach, denture cream (for whom? she thought, trying and failing to picture Mrs. H's teeth), bath salts, spare soaps, and loo rolls. A pair of half-rusty tweezers, cotton wool, a hair net, some long-forgotten prescription medicine, and a bottle of shampoo. No tampons. No sanitary towels. Sabine sighed, and glanced around the bathroom to see if there was anywhere she might have missed.

Having checked underneath the doily dolly, just in case (well, Mrs. H might have been shy), and in the airing cupboard, with the matching pastel-colored towels, Sabine was forced to conclude that Mrs. H was just a little bit too old to provide what she was searching for. The only other person was Annie—she was the right age, after all—but how on earth was she going to be able to get her away from the table to ask her, without drawing attention to herself? They were all so quick to poke fun at one another, and if they knew what she was after and made jokes about it, she would just *die*. She knew she would.

Maybe if I wait here another few minutes, Sabine reasoned, seating herself on the toilet, which was clad in a strange, looped-cloth lid, they will finish pudding and move on to the sofas again. Then it will be easier for me to have a quick word with Annie.

She sat for a while, inhaling the distant smell of synthetic pine, then jumped guiltily at the soft knock on the door. She held her breath for a moment, wondering whether it was one of the men after an empty loo, but then she heard Mrs. H's voice.

"Sabine? Are you okay, love?"

"Fine," said Sabine, trying to make her voice sound as natural as possible. Which meant it immediately rose an octave and wobbled.

"Are you sure? You've been gone an awful long time."

Sabine hesitated, then stood up, and walked to the door, opening it. Mrs. H was standing behind it, slightly stooped, as if she had been listening at the keyhole.

"Are you okay, love?" She said, straightening.

Sabine chewed at her lip.

"Sort of."

"What's the problem? You can tell me."

"I need to ask Annie for a . . . a thing."

"A what?"

Sabine looked away, her need wrestling with the acute awfulness of having to confess her problem.

"Come on, love, don't be shy."

"I'm not shy. Not really."

"What's the matter?"

"Can you get Annie for me?"

Mrs. H frowned slightly, managing to maintain her smile.

"Annie? Why do you want Annie?"

"I need to ask her for something."

"Need to ask her for what?"

Was it really that hard to guess? Sabine found herself feeling suddenly impatient with Mrs. H, for not grasping the nature of her predicament.

"I need to ask her for a pad. Or a tampon,

or something." Even the words sounded embarrassing.

Mrs. H's smile fell away, and she glanced behind her toward the noise emanating from the living room.

"Can you get her?"

"I don't think that would be a good idea, love."

Mrs. H looked suddenly serious, the glow of the past few hours vanishing from her cheeks. "I'll tell you what, you stay in here, and I'll nip next door to Carrie's. My neighbor. She'll have something for you."

And then she was gone.

Sabine sat anxiously in the bathroom until she returned, mulling over the reasons why she wouldn't be allowed to ask Annie for a tampon. Were she and Patrick so poor that it would be an embarrassment? Did they have some weird religious objections to it? A girl in Sabine's school had told her, when they were younger, that Catholic girls didn't use tampons, as they took away their virginity. But Patrick and Annie were married and would have been doing it for years, so surely they couldn't really mind?

Mrs. H, when she returned with her discreet paper bag, did not enlighten her. She just told her to come back when she was ready, and left Sabine alone.

When Sabine returned to the living room they were all still seated around the table, although two of the women were helping Mrs. H to clear the dishes. There was an air of spent mirth, as if they had all shared some gigantic joke. Or perhaps that was just Sabine's acute sensitivity to her recent dilemma; she wasn't entirely sure.

"You didn't want any more pudding, did you Sabine? I left your plate out in case."

Sabine shook her head, glancing over at Annie. She was fiddling absently with her paper napkin, rolling and unrolling it at the corner.

"Now, who's coming for a quick pint?" Mack stood at the far end of the table, and looked toward Patrick.

"I'll join you for a wee while," said Thom.

"You're no good, on bloody orange juice. Who's going to join me in a drink? Steven, you'll come. Good man. Patrick?"

"I'll stay with Annie," he said, looking less than thrilled by the prospect.

"Annie'll come with us, won't you, girl? About time you took a trip down to the Black Hen. You've not been in there in ages."

Annie, glancing at her mother, shook her head. "Thanks, Dad, but I'm not really in the mood."

"C'mon, girl. Your man there wants to have a drink, and he won't go without you, so come and indulge him for the one."

"No. No. You're all right. I'll stay here and help Mam clear up."

"You will not. The dishwasher will take care of this lot. Go on, Annie. Go and have a bit of fun for a change."

There was a warm swell of collusion from the rest of the table. Go on, Annie, they murmured. Go on out. Go and have a drink.

"C'mon, you. I'm sure you owe me a few pints by now, for all those videos I've brought you." Thom stood, and offered her his arm.

"I really don't fancy it. Thanks."

"Ahh, come on. Don't be a spoilsport when your old man wants to take you for a drink."

Annie's face darkened. "Will you all just leave me alone? I do not want to go to the bloody pub. I just want to go home." And having silenced the room, she turned, and half ran out, followed swiftly by Mrs. H.

Sabine stared at the faces around her, shocked by the ferocity of Annie's response.

Thom, catching her eye, tried to give her a reassuring grin. A sort of "women! what'll they do next?" kind of a grin. It wasn't terribly convincing.

"Ellen'll look after her," muttered Mack. "C'mon, lads. We'll head off."

"Yes, you head off," said Auntie May, heaving herself into a standing position, and reaching for a pile of plates. "Go on, Patrick. It'll do you good to let your hair down a bit."

"Y'all right here, Sabine?" Thom lowered his head and raised his eyebrows questioningly.

No, she wanted to answer. But it was obvious no one was going to invite her to the pub, so instead she just nodded in an agreeable manner. "Fine, thanks," she said.

In silence, the men trooped out, just as Mrs. H was coming back in. She and Mack and Patrick exchanged a few quiet words, and then Mrs. H walked briskly into the middle of the room, smiling broadly.

"Annie's gone home for a bit of a lie down. Bit of a headache coming, I think. She says she'll see you all later."

Sabine looked around her, registering that there was no one there who believed in the veracity of what Mrs. H was saying. But no one seemed to want to question her, either; they just busied themselves with the clearing and tidying operation, striking up meaningless conversations about people Sabine had never heard of.

"You go and sit down, Ellen," said Auntie May. "Go and keep Sabine company, and keep an eye on the boys. We'll take care of the kitchen. Go on, it's your anniversary, woman. And you haven't so much as sat down for five minutes since we've been here."

Mrs. H protested until Auntie May held up a jeweled hand to silence her.

"I'm not listening, Ellen. I told you, you keep an eye on those boys. It'll do my hips good to move around a bit, anyway. Stop them seizing up later on."

Mrs. H, still clutching her dishcloth, sat down on the sofa beside Sabine. The boys had turned on the television, and sat, in their socks, staring blankly at the screen. Mrs. H tried, briefly, to talk to them, but it was clear that their attention was elsewhere. Sabine watched her, wondering whether she could ask the unaskable. It was getting to be too much, this feeling of being excluded from some really important secret. It took Sabine back to a recent incident at home, when all the girls in her class had split into exclusive little groups, and those she had thought of as her friends had turned on her and not let her know about a party they were holding, all looking at her with blank, sheeplike faces when she asked, increasingly anxiously, when and where it was. It was not that she really wanted to go (she wasn't actually that keen on parties). It was just the horror of being excluded.

"Is Annie an alcoholic?" she asked Mrs. H.

They had told her in the end, after all. Then it had been Jennifer Laing's turn to be left out.

Mrs. H's face spun around to meet hers. She looked genuinely shocked.

"Annie? Alcoholic? Of course not. Why do you say that?"

Sabine flushed.

"I'm not saying she looks alcoholic, or anything . . . It's just that you all seem nervous of her in company, and no one says anything when she acts a bit odd. I—I just wondered if it was because she drank too much."

Mrs. H reached for her hair and began stroking it down, a nervous habit Sabine had never noticed before.

"No, Sabine. She's not alcoholic."

There was a lengthy silence, during which the boys began to squabble over the remote control.

Sabine, listening to the distant clatter of crockery in the kitchen, began to feel simultaneously embarrassed for having said anything and resentful that, still, no one seemed inclined to give her a reason for Annie's odd behavior. It had become more odd, recently, as well. She seemed to have forgotten how to tidy up, so that every time Sabine stopped by, the living room, which had always leaned toward the vaguely messy, had started to appear somewhat chaotic. She fell asleep more often, and when awake, often didn't even seem to hear what you were saying. Perhaps it was drugs, Sabine thought suddenly. It wasn't exactly the inner cities, but she was sure she had seen something on the news about drug use in rural areas. Perhaps Annie was on drugs.

Mrs. H had been gazing at her hands. Then she stood, and motioned to Sabine to do the same, glancing behind her at the kitchen.

"C'mon," she said. "Let's you and me have a little chat."

Mrs. H's bedroom was as immaculately tidy as the rest of her house, and possibly even warmer. Her bed was headed by a raspberry-pink padded board, from which spread a huge, embroidered quilt. The pink of the quilt was matched by the velour curtains, and picked up by the trimmings of the cushions on the easy chair in the corner. A running frieze around the ceiling picked out carefully washed-out pastel images of bunches of grapes, interwoven with green stems and leaves. It was the kind of room that normally she and her mother would exchange mischievous grins at—they both knew it was poor taste to have everything matching—and yet Sabine didn't feel either as confident in her beliefs, or as malicious. At the moment the cozy, warm uniformity of Mrs. H's house seemed far more inviting than anything her own family had to offer.

The far end of the room contained an array of fitted cupboards, some of which contained mirrored panels. It was from one of these, as Sabine watched herself duplicated, that Mrs. H opened a door, and then, slowly pulled out the drawer behind it.

She motioned to Sabine to sit down, and then, walking back, sat heavily beside her, handing her its contents: a silver framed picture of a little girl, beaming into the sun, sitting aside a bright blue tricycle.

"That's Niamh," she said.

And then, as Sabine frowned, staring at the broad toothy grin, the blonde hair: "That's Annie's daughter. Was Annie's daughter."

She paused.

"She died two and a half years ago. A car hit her as she ran out of the gates. Annie hasn't really been the same since."

Sabine stared back at the little girl, feeling her heart thump with shock and her own eyes prick suddenly with tears.

"Three, she was. Just had her third birthday. It's been a bit difficult for Annie and Patrick, as they haven't been able to have another child. They've tried, but it's not happened. And that's been an extra burden for Annie to bear. That's why I didn't want you asking her for . . . well. You can see. It's just an added reminder, every month."

Mrs. H's voice was quite cool, measured, as if this were her way of containing the raw, explosive emotion behind what she was saying. Sabine could feel it, like a huge shelf rising up to her esophagus, filling her chest, and making her want to cry out loud.

"We hope she'll come through eventually," Mrs. H continued quietly. "It's been an awful few years. But some people seem to take longer than others."

"I'm really sorry," Sabine whispered. An alcoholic. How crass Mrs. H must think she was.

"You weren't to know," she said, patting her hand. "We don't talk about Niamh because it seems to make things worse. Annie doesn't like to have pictures of her around, so I keep this in my drawer. It's a pity though." She traced the outline of the little girl with her soft finger. "I would have liked to have a few pictures around. Just to remind me, y'know?"

Sabine nodded, still transfixed by this little girl. Downstairs, she could hear Auntie May and the others laughing.

"Is that her room? In Annie's house?"

"Next to Annie and Patrick's? Yes, that was hers. Annie doesn't like people to go in." She sighed. "I keep telling her it's time to clear it out, but she won't listen. And I can't force her."

Sabine thought for a minute.

"Has . . . has she seen a doctor?"

"Oh, she was offered counselling. And the priest tried to help. But I think she and

Patrick thought they could get through it alone. Now, I think Patrick may be regretting that decision, but it's a bit late. She won't see anyone now. Not even a doctor. You've probably noticed, she doesn't really like going out of the house."

They sat in silence, both reminded of Annie's abrupt departure that evening. Sabine gazed over at the picture of the little girl. She was wearing red Wellingtons and a T-shirt with a penguin on the front. Sabine didn't think she had ever seen a picture of a dead child up close before. Staring into her eyes, she almost fancied she could see something prescient there, some foreshadowing of her own death in that gappy smile.

"Do you miss her?"

Mrs. H shook her head, and, standing, placed the photograph carefully back into the drawer. When she closed it, she stood for a second, facing into the cupboard, so that Sabine could no longer see her face.

"I miss both of them, Sabine. I miss both of them."

Much as she loved Annie and her family, Sabine had been quite glad to spend a couple of days alone with her grandparents. She had needed the time to come to terms with what Mrs. H had told her, to resite Annie in her imagination from "eccentric and difficult" to "tragic young mother." She didn't really know what to say to a tragic young mother, and had not yet decided what this was going to mean for their friendship. Before they had felt like equals of sorts: Annie's being married kind of balanced out by her hopeless lack of practicality; Sabine's youth balanced by her superior knowledge of what was in and out (or that's how Sabine saw it, anyway). Now, everything had shifted. And Sabine wasn't sure how she was meant to behave. Mrs. H, seeming to sense this reticence, had been a decidedly unobtrusive presence in her life, while simultaneously letting Sabine know that it had been a pleasure having her to supper, and that everyone had enjoyed meeting her very much. She was nice like that; the whole family were.

But then even her grandmother was being nice at the moment; she had served up vegetable pie for the previous night's supper, and now kedgeree, a weird concoction of rice and egg and fish and sultanas, which somehow combined to taste better than its parts. "It's a hunting breakfast, really," she had said, as Sabine had stared goggle-eyed at her plate. "But it makes a good light supper, too."

Sabine decided she was in a good mood because her grandfather had "perked up" as the doctor called it. Glad as she was for everybody, Sabine wouldn't have quite called it perky. What it meant was that he had been able to walk downstairs, shooing the dogs away from him with his stick, and having eaten a miniscule amount, was now sitting in the drawing room in one of the high-backed chairs beside the fire.

After she had helped her grandmother clear the table (this spirit of cooperation could work both ways, after all) Sabine was about to escape up to her room, when her grandmother called her back.

"I've got to go out and check on the horses," she said, putting her quilted coat on, and tying an old woolen scarf at her neck. "I want to put a poultice on the Duke's leg, so I may be a little while. Would you mind keeping your grandfather company?"

Sabine, her heart sinking, tried not to betray how much she did mind. Keeping her grandfather company appeared to be a contradiction in terms. He had hardly spoken over supper, except to remark "poor sheep," apparently in relation to some observation he had made a good few hours previously about the state of the neighboring farm's pasture. And he had barely seemed to notice she was there. He had certainly not noticed Bertie was there, and had managed to tread on him twice, eliciting bloodcurdling yelps, as he both sat down and raised himself from the table. The thought of having to make polite conversation with him for the whole hour before the ten o'clock news made Sabine want to run for the door.

"Sure," she said, and walked slowly into the dining room.

He had his eyes closed, so Sabine picked a copy of *Country Life* from the pile on the coffee table, and walked silently over to the overstuffed chair opposite. She would have quite liked to lay on the sofa, but the room was so cold and damp that a place near the fire was a prerequisite for any kind of inactive stay.

She flicked through the magazine for some minutes, wondering which of the exotic homes in the Maldives belonged to various pop stars, and then snorting at the blonde, vacant-eyed debs. But there was nothing very interesting, unless you were interested in old churches of East Anglia, or organic butchers, and so before long she found herself staring at her grandfather instead.

He had more lines on his face than anyone she had ever seen; they didn't sweep down in long, etched lines, like Geoff's had when he got worried about his patients. Or faint delicate ones, little whispers from the future, like those she could see on her mother. No, her grandfather's crisscrossed one another in an almost regular pattern, almost like the markings of an old map, except more parched-looking. In places the skin was so thin that she could see blue veins running underneath it like B-roads, half camouflaged by large brown liver spots, and where it joined his scalp, odd, stray gray hairs stuck out like lone travelers in the desert.

It was hard to imagine ever being that old. Sabine looked down at her own hands, her own skin, through which only the faintest of mauve lines could be detected, plumped up by youth and good living. His were so bony that they looked almost clawlike, the nails thickened and yellowed, like horn.

She started slightly as he opened his

eyes. She knew it was rude to stare, and he would no doubt remind her of it. He gazed at her from under reptilian lids, then his gaze slid left and then right, assessing that they were alone in the room. In the silence, the logs spluttered and crackled, sending small sparks flying out, like lemmings, over the grate.

He opened his mouth slightly, paused, and then spoke.

"I'm afraid I don't *do* much anymore," he said, slowly, enunciating each word with some care.

Sabine stared at him. His face looked suddenly animated, as if concentrating hard on the message it was trying to get across.

"I tend . . . to just *be*."

He closed his mouth slowly, as if the effort of speaking had exhausted it, but maintained his steady gaze.

Sabine, gazing back, felt the faintest flicker of understanding. And some sympathy, aware that she had just received some kind of apology. She nodded, the faintest of movements, an acknowledgment of her own, and then turned to face the fire.

"Good," he said, finally. And closed his eyes.

Chapter Eight

The morning of the hunt, Kilcarrion remembered what it was for. It was as if the house itself had awoken from a deep slumber, and began creaking into action like the cogs of a rarely used machine, bent on pursuing its purpose. Sabine awoke to find her clothes laid out at the end of her bed, a cup of hot tea thrust into her hands by Mrs. H, and a level of activity downstairs and outside that made the Kilcarrion walk look like a sedate stroll. The dogs, infected by it, barked and scrabbled in the hall; the telephone rang periodically, like some kind of alarm, heralding the minute changing of arrangements.

Even the boiler, whose distant rumblings would often wake Sabine in the middle of the night, seemed to clank and shudder more determinedly.

Mrs. H fussed around, lighting her fire, straightening her things, and telling her who was going to be "out" today, while her grandmother kept popping her head around the door, and urging Sabine to "do come *on*," except she said it like she was excited, rather than angry. Sabine could hear her downstairs in the yard, barking instructions at the lads, as, slowly, and with shaky fingers, she tried to get herself dressed.

While obviously revolting, immoral, and the height of cruelty, it had to be said that foxhunting was a pretty glamorous sport. She could tell from the clothes she had been lent by Joy: silk-lined and made to measure, the navy-blue coat, and cream jodhpurs made her look like a character out of a period drama (her grandmother had smiled broadly as she finished her off—the first time she had done so widely and unselfconsciously); she could tell by the way her horse and Thom's horse were both plaited and quartered, their coats burnished to a conkery sheen by a good hour's heavy-duty grooming; she could tell by the way her grandmother had fussed and flapped in a distinctly ungrandmotherly way about tying Sabine's stock, how to safely attach her own gold pin, and whether her boots were shiny enough. . . . All of which was why, some two hours later, when she and the horses were eventually unloaded at the meet, it was patently clear to Sabine that they had some-how ended up in the wrong place.

They were not in the grounds of some stately home, surrounded by pink-coats (they were never called red, her grand-mother had said), and drinking champagne or whatever it was from a silver stirrup cup. Under driving rain, they had been unloaded at a crossroads seemingly in the middle of nowhere, and as the horses' hooves came crashing down the wooden ramp onto the tarmac, all Sabine could see were a motley array of muddy ponies bearing children in plastic mackintoshes and sweatshirts, a couple of large, clumsy horses and tweedy farmers, and an array of rather scruffy horses and footfollowers of all different sizes and colors, flanked by people in waterproofs and carrying umbrellas, their hair wet and windswept, or woolen hats pulled firmly over their heads. There were even a couple of young men in camouflage jackets, seated on quad bikes. And there was mud everywhere: on the verges, churned into brown soup by the wheeling, impatient hooves of the horses; on the boots of the riders; and halfway up the legs of the hounds, who milled about between them all, letting out the occasional bark or yelp. There were only about three people wearing pink coats, and one of those, disappointingly, as he had a thread-veined face and a bulbous, pockmarked nose, Thom had pointed out as the Master.

It was not like the pictures, not like the placemats on her grandparents' tables, which depicted a herd of spindle-thin Thoroughbreds and pink-coated men of privilege. It was not like the oil paintings she had viewed on their walls. It wasn't even like the news reports on television, where dreadlocked hunt saboteurs chanted and blew whistles, waging a class war against the minor members of royalty on horseback. It was like a kind of equine picket line, but with dogs and bikes added. And possibly more dirt.

Sabine felt vaguely disappointed; although she still had ambivalent feelings about coming on a hunt, she had persuaded herself that it was important to see something up close before condemning it, and, more pertinently, had secretly looked forward to Thom seeing her not as the baby of the family, milling around in layers of jumpers and Wellington boots, but having to view her afresh, a vision of navy blue and polished leather, the dashing lady rider in her glamorous environment. Albeit a dashing lady rider whose nerves had left her with a frequent desire to go to the loo.

"Here, take your Mars Bars," said Thom, stuffing a couple of chocolate bars into her hand. "You'll need them later." He had rammed his hat onto his head, and was trying to control the wheeling Birdie, a young Thoroughbred overexcited by his second trip out on the hunting field. The wind lifted the young horse's tail and flared his nostrils, and he skipped sideways and backward as leaves flicked up to meet him.

"Bloody Liam's been winding them up," he said, as Joy expressed some concern. "Thought it would be a laugh to start blowing a hunting horn before we'd even loaded them. Now this lad doesn't know whether he's coming or going."

The effect of a hunting horn on the horses of Kilcarrion had astonished Sabine. Thom had blown one once, several weeks ago, when he had been trying to persuade Sabine that horses actually enjoyed it. The Duke had rushed to his stable door and thrust his huge head over, glancing left and right, and then promptly relieved himself with excitement.

"How do you know it's not just fear making them do that?" Sabine had challenged. "I'd probably come and have a look and poo myself if I was frightened of a noise."

"You know when these lads are frightened," said Thom. "They'll lay their ears flat against their heads, and kick out. You'll see the whites of their eyes. You still don't believe me? Okay. If I was to open this door now, Dukey boy would go over and stand by the horse box, ready to go."

Just to prove a point, he did, and he had.

Sabine had almost laughed out loud at the sight of the old horse, walking determinedly over, and then waiting patiently by the ramp. And, as Thom had given him a Polo mint, and led him slowly back to his stable, she had to admit that even if she didn't like hunting, in this yard of quadrupeds at least, she was in a minority.

Now, as Thom gave her a leg up onto the gray, Sabine found herself feeling sick with nerves. Picking up on the tension, the normally well-behaved horse stamped, and champed at his bit impatiently, his ears flicking backward and forward like gear levers.

"Whatever you do, don't overtake the Master." A head-scarfed Joy, straightening Sabine's stirrup leathers, was repeating the instructions she had already given her twice on the journey over. "Keep your horse out of the way of the hounds, and don't go barging your way over the jumps. If someone is lined up, then you hold back and wait for them to go. Don't gallop through the middle of fields. And don't wear that little man out," she said, stroking the horse's nose with a damp hand. "Let him go until he's tired, and then we'll come and meet you with the horse box. I don't want you pushing him till dark, just because you get carried away."

Sabine, whose stomach was now turning over with fear, thought she was probably the least likely person to get carried away that she could see. Unless they meant in a coffin.

Everyone else seemed to be grinning, exchanging greetings, and admiring horses. Was she the only one convinced that she was going to die?

"Don't you worry, Mrs. Ballantyne," said Thom, swinging his leg over the saddle. "I'll take good care of her."

"Don't let her get too far to the front of the field, Thom," Joy said, anxiously. "It's very wet going and there's a bit of a badly behaved crowd going to be up behind the Master."

Sabine followed her gaze to a group of young men, who, laughing, were tickling one another's horses with their whips, making them shy and buck.

"Idiots," said Thom, but smiling. "Don't worry, Mrs. Ballantyne. I'll hold back."

And then, suddenly, with a few blasts on the horn, they were all off, the hundred or so shod hooves clattering along the wet road.

"Smile!" said Thom, grinning down at her. "You'll have a grand time."

Sabine didn't feel she could tell him what she thought: that she was more likely to kill herself under one of these insane animals' hooves, that she didn't feel able to jump off a curb, let alone over a five-barred gate, and that she felt so nauseous that it was quite likely she was going to have to throw up off the side of her horse.

"I don't want to see anything killed," she said, her head down against the wind. "I don't want to be anywhere near. And if they try and do that blood thing on my face, I'll probably kill them all. Master or not."

"I can't hear you," said Thom, pointing his whip ahead. "C'mon, stay with me. We're headed into that next field."

From then on, the day seemed to pass by in a kind of blur. As soon as the horses felt the spring of wet turf beneath them, they bolted, racing up the side of the pitted, boggy hill, and Sabine, caught in their midst, found her initial lurch of fear displaced by a sense of mounting excitement, as the various grinning, mud-splattered faces cantered past her. When they had reached the top, Sabine had found that she too was grinning, and forgot to remove it when Thom arrived next to her.

"You okay?" he said, raising his eyebrows.

"Fine," she said, breathlessly.

"We'll get some color in those cheeks today," he said, and then they were off again.

The first part of the hunt flashed by at

almost breakneck speed; boxed in to the ragtag assortment of horses and riders, Sabine found herself placing her trust in the little gray horse, frequently closing her eyes and clutching hold of his mane as they approached the stiles and hedges that they flew over in a moving population, like liquid. She didn't have time to stay frightened; and, soon, noticing the numbers of tiny children on ponies and reckless estate kids on scruffy skewbalds, she realized there was little that they were going to face that she, on the bigger, braver horse, couldn't, too.

Sabine had no idea where she was headed. Or what she was meant to be doing. Her eyes stung, her mouth was filled with the taste of mud, kicked back by those in front, but she found her heart thumping with excitement, so that she often urged her horse to go faster, trying to make her way farther forward in the field. Thom tried to stick with her as much as possible, but often they would become separated, either when one had to wait to jump into the next field, or simply because the hunt divided, and there would be a period of standing around and blowing of horns until everyone was reunited.

There was an awful lot of standing around in hunting, Sabine discovered. Usually just when you had got used to galloping along. It seemed to take place simply so that people could chat to one another, remarking upon their and their horses' performances, or gossiping about who had disappeared with whom, seemingly ignorant of the fact that the rain pelted down around them, sending channels of water down their waxed jackets and clamping the horses' tails unhappily to their quarters. The fact that Sabine knew no one except Thom did not seem to have excluded her from this: A plump, middle-aged woman had told her she was "doing grand" and remarked that she knew her mother; a very thin man with a beaky nose had told her that he knew her horse; and one of the scruffy children had asked if he could have a bite of her Mars Bar. She had given him the whole thing. But then she had been preoccupied, for it was as they stood around like this that a young girl with long blonde curly hair tied back in a hair net would frequently approach Thom, and chat and laugh, and elegantly wipe the dirt from her nose, or, smiling, ask him to do it for her. She fancied him; it was *so* obvious. She was practically gagging for him. But when Sabine said this to Thom as they waited for one of the older men to climb back aboard his recently vacated saddle, he looked blank, and shook his head as if he hadn't even noticed.

Annoyingly, he seemed determined to baby her today, too. Twice he jumped off, and said he wanted to check her horse's girth, thrusting her leg and the saddle flap out of the way as he heaved the buckles up a further notch. But it wasn't done with any flirting, or unnecessary touching of her thigh, and when Sabine had rather recklessly tried to wipe the mud from his white hunting stock, he had laughed, and wheeled his horse away, in order to do it himself.

"You worry about yourself, now," he said, tapping inexplicably at his head. "There's a lot worse that can happen out here than a bit of mud on your gear."

They had been out almost three hours when Sabine realized she hadn't actually seen a fox. She was ashamed to think that she had completely forgotten that chasing and killing one had been the aim of the day, but then she was no longer anywhere near the hounds, and her horse, along with three or four others, had somehow taken a different turning from the main body of the hunt, and were all walking in a sedate manner, "giving the horses a breather," as the ruddy-faced farmer at the front put it.

Sabine had lost Thom in a forest, when he had dismounted to help one of the horses, who had gotten a leg caught in barbed wire. There were four people standing around the animal, one of whom had produced wire cutters from his jacket, and Thom had held the stricken horse's head while the delicate operation to free him took place. "You go on," he had called to Sabine. "We may be a while here. I'll catch you up." He had apparently stopped worrying about her, a misplaced emotion, as it turned out, as some ten minutes later, the gray had skidded on a timber table and she had pitched over his head.

"Are you all right?" said one of the younger men, who had immediately jumped down to help her, while someone else caught the horse.

"I'm fine," she said, heaving herself up from the squelching earth. "Just a bit muddy."

That was an understatement, she realized, a little sorrowfully. Her creamy white jodhpurs were now brown over one leg, like a cut-price jester, while Joy's beautiful navy jacket was plastered in mud.

The man pulled a rather grubby handkerchief from his pocket and handed it to her. "For your face," he said. "There's a fair bit around your eye."

When she raised it to the wrong eye, he initially corrected her, then, taking it from her, wiped at her face himself. It was at this point that she noticed him: brown eyes, pale skin, a broad smile. Young.

"You're not from here, then," he said, helping her over to the gray horse, who had been checked over and found sound. "Not with that accent. London, is it?"

"Yup." It sounded too bald. "I'm staying with my grandparents."

"Where?"

"Kilcarrion. It's in a village called Ballymalnaugh."

"I know it. Who are your folks?"

"They're called Ballantyne."

He reached down for her boot, offering to give her a leg up.

"I know them. The old couple. English. Didn't realize they had any rellies."

She looked down at him, grinning.

"Oh. And you know everyone's business, do you?"

He grinned back. He was quite good-looking, really.

"Listen, London girl. Round here, everybody knows everyone's business."

He had stuck with her after that, chatting, and now, as they walked in their little group down the wet lanes, he was still chatting. He lived in a village about four miles away from hers, was hoping to go to Durham University in England, like his brother, and spent his spare time "mucking around" on his parents' farm. He called himself Robert, everyone else called him Bobby, and Sabine didn't think she had ever met anyone who talked quite as much.

"So, d'you go out much, Sabine?"

"What, in London?"

"No, here. I'm sure a pretty girl like yourself has no shortage of offers in London."

Sabine narrowed her eyes at him. Bobby had a way of saying charming things that hinted just gently that he was also taking the mickey. Sabine was very conscious of the possibility that people were taking the mickey.

"I go out a bit." she said.

"The pub and stuff?" he said, pulling his horse back slightly so that they were alongside each other.

"Stuff like that," she said, a little disingenuously. Sabine had not been to a pub since she had gotten there. Her grandparents were not really pub people, and Thom had never shown the slightest inclination to invite her.

"You want to go out sometime?"

Sabine flushed. He was asking her out! She stared at her hands, berating herself for the flood of color to her face. God, she could be uncool sometimes.

"If you want," she muttered.

"Well you don't have to," he said. "I won't twist your arm or anything." He was still grinning.

Sabine smiled back. She could make up her mind how she felt about him when she got home. And how on earth she would explain any potential date to her grandparents.

"Okay, then."

"Good. Now, hold on tight, I think we're going to take the shortcut back to the others."

Before she had had a chance to reflect upon Bobby McAndrew, Sabine found herself galloping across a field, close on the heels of his bay horse. It was just beginning to get dark, and as they raced toward the far end, Sabine realized she had begun to ache all over and could no longer feel her toes. Her eyes focused on the mud-spattered hindquarters in front of her, she felt a sudden longing for a long, hot bath, and hoped that they weren't too far from home. She had no idea where she was going to meet Thom, and if she couldn't find him, she didn't know where she was meant to meet her grandmother. She hadn't really been listening this morning.

She was so busy worrying about finding her way back that it took some seconds before she realized Bobby was shouting at her. She strained her ears against the whistling wind to hear what he was saying, shaking her head, so that in the end he pulled back a little, and yelled toward her face.

"There's a Wexford bank ahead," he said. "It's a bit of a tough one. Dig your heels down deep and grab hold of his mane."

Sabine, her eyes widening, glanced at where he was pointing. Ahead of them, she could make out two horses, who seemed to be taking near-vertical leaps onto the top of the bank, and then, in a scrabble of mud and hooves, flying off again. Sabine's heart stopped.

"I can't do that!" she shouted.

"You'll have to," yelled Bobby. "The only other way out of this field is back the way we came." And she saw him gathering up his reins, ready to make the leap himself.

Sabine decided that a long trek by herself had to be preferable to a broken neck, and made to pull up. But the gray was having none of it. Determined to remain with his fellows, his neck thrust forward, as inflexible as a ramrod, and he plowed toward the bank, heedless to her tuggings and pleadings. Sabine had no time to think; either she baled out now, onto the wet turf beneath her, or she trusted this animal, and just did her best to stay on. The bank, which loomed before her, looked impossibly big, the shadowy ditch before it as dark as a grave. She saw Bobby's horse check himself, and then thrust forward, making the leap, skidding a little at the top, and, with his accompanying shout, disappear from sight.

And then she let go of the reins, thrust her feet deep in the stirrups, and shut her eyes. I'm going to die, she thought. I love you,

Mum, and then suddenly the horse swept forward and up under her, so that she whiplashed backward, lurching backward on the saddle and, as she briefly opened her eyes, they were on top, and his neck was bowed, checking the correct position for his feet, and then, as she closed her eyes and squealed, they were leaping down again, an impossible distance, so that she collapsed on his neck as he landed, her feet free from her stirrups and her arms clasped chaotically around his neck.

"Here. Here." shouted Bobby, pushing one of the loose reins into her hand and laughing. "You made it. Good for you."

Sabine, pushing herself upright, found her mouth bubbling wide with laughter, and her hands patting the little horse beneath her, unable to believe what they had just achieved. "Good boy, good boy," she sang joyously. "You clever, clever boy." Her blood infused with adrenaline, she wanted to shout and exclaim, and jump the bloody thing again.

"I didn't think I'd make that one myself. You did grand just staying on."

She turned to Bobby, her face illuminated by a wide, unmasked smile. And spoke the words whose significance would be entirely lost on a farmer's son from four miles away. "I didn't take the gate!"

It didn't feel somehow fair that someone who had just jumped the biggest bank in the whole entire world should have to spend quite this much time washing mud from horses' legs, cleaning tack, and polishing one's boots, even when one was really, really aching and one's bum bones felt like they had been hit by an iron bar and one was so cold that one's fingers kept being all weak and bendy and useless like raw chipolatas, but Joy was quite clear: "Your horse comes first. He's served you very well today, so the least you can do is give him a jolly good rubdown."

By the time Sabine had gotten every last bit of mud off—and Irish mud seemed to have this infuriating ability to get *everywhere*—she had almost come down from her posthunting high, and was beginning to feel pretty chilled and stiff and that it was she who was in need of a rubdown and a hot bran and molasses mash (it had in fact smelled so good that she had tried it herself—disappointingly, it tasted like carpet underlay). Unfortunately, it was at that point that Joy had come down the stairs to the boot room and informed Sabine, with the closest thing to an apology that she had ever seen, that because of some problem with the hot water, there wasn't going to be enough for her to have a bath.

"You are joking," Sabine had said, feeling suddenly as if she were going to cry. The thought of simply peeling out of these damp clothes in that damp room and putting on some other chilly ensemble was too depressing.

"No, I'm not." She paused. "But I have had a word with Annie and she says they've no guests tonight and you're more than welcome to have a bath over there."

Joy half smiled at her as she went to close the door.

"You didn't really think I'd let you do a day's hunting without a hot bath at the end of it, did you? It's practically the best bit."

Sabine had grinned back, wondering privately at her grandmother's weird sense of humor, and then run upstairs to get her towel and shampoo. A bath at Annie's! Limitless hot water! Soap that didn't have deep gray fissures running through it! No freezing, shivering sprint from the bathroom to her bedroom! Sabine found herself practically running across the road, the proximity of such warmth and luxury infecting her with a renewed energy.

It was clear, however, when she opened the door, that there was something of a chill in the air at Annie's house. She had burst into the living room, desperate to tell Annie about her day, and Bobby asking her out, and thank her for the bathing experience ahead, but as she had caught sight of them both, staring away from each other from the opposite ends of the room, the words had frozen on her lips.

"I—I—hi, there," she had said, halting in the doorway. It was unnaturally quiet in there; even the ever-present television was turned off. It was the wrong kind of silence: weighty, burdened by words that had come before.

"Sabine," said Patrick, straightening up slightly.

Annie, the neck of her oversized jumper pulled up under her chin, just looked at her as if she hadn't seen her. Sabine stood for a moment, shifting her weight from leg to leg, unsure whether she should back out.

"I—is it still all right if I have my bath?"

Patrick had nodded, but Annie had slowly lifted her head, uncomprehending.

"Bath?"

"I thought—my grandmother—"

"You just said she could have a bath. You told Joy on the phone. I *heard* you." Patrick sounded exasperated, as if this were merely the latest in a long line of such exchanges.

Annie shrugged.

"Sure you can have a bath. Anytime."

Sabine stared at her, anxiously.

"Now? My grandmother said it would be okay to come now."

There was a short pause.

Patrick, unable to watch Sabine's indecision, couldn't bear it.

"Of course it's fine, Sabine. We've been waiting for you. You go on up now, and give us a shout if you need anything. Take as long as you want."

Sabine began to walk slowly through the living room toward the stairs.

"I've brought my own towels," she said softly, as if that might help lift Annie's mood.

But it was Patrick who spoke.

"You're fine, Sabine. Have a nice one."

Sabine lay in the bath for some time, but it was not out of relish. She had found herself lying perfectly still in the water as it cooled, listening for the acoustic hints of argument: the too-lengthy pauses, the staccato voices, the low hum of exasperation that characterized adult rows. They were obviously having one of sorts; but it looked kind of one-sided, as if Annie had refused to engage in battle and left Patrick to do it all himself. Annie being her friend, normally Sabine would have mentally leaped to her defense: How could he be horrible to a woman who had lost her daughter? How could he pick arguments with someone who still had not come to terms with her grief? And yet there was something about Patrick, when she looked at him closely, that seemed to suggest he was the one suffering more.

She didn't really want to go back downstairs. She didn't want to have to walk back through that battle zone, smiling and making polite conversation with Annie and Patrick just so she could go and lie on her bed and feel wretched. If I wanted to enter a war zone I could have stayed at home, she thought, and smiled grimly at her own wit. But it wasn't really a smiling matter. She didn't want Patrick and Annie to split up. Patrick obviously loved Annie, and Annie obviously loved their daughter, and they should be supporting each other so that they could get through it, not pulling apart. Sometimes it seemed so simple to Sabine that she could hardly believe that adults could get it so wrong.

But then they seemed to complicate things for the hell of it; her mother was always questioning things, even when they were going well. She could never just accept anything. And Sabine knew exactly what would happen once Justin moved in (if he hadn't already): He and Sabine would eventually fall out, and Kate, having spent however many months trying to act like they were all one big happy family, would begin weeping over the kitchen table about how she had ruined everyone's lives and did Sabine think they would be happier on their own? Because she wanted to give her some say in the matter, she really did. . . . Sabine knew exactly what she would say to this— she was quite fond of rehearsing arguments with her mother, and sometimes amazed herself when they ran true to predicted form—she would say, "Oh. So now I get a say in our life, do I? How come I never got a say when Geoff was leaving? How come I

never got a say when Jim was going? Huh?"
And her mother would be all crushed and
apologetic and realize that she should have
been much more like her own mother all
along.

Sabine lay silently and soaked up the
injustices of being sixteen and powerless.
Finally, conscious that her fingers had shriv-
eled like prunes, and that the temperature of
the water was no longer on the warm side of
comfortable, she climbed out and began
toweling herself dry.

There was no one there when she came
back through the living room. She didn't
know whether to be relieved. But as she ran
back down the wet road toward Kilcarrion,
something made her look back. Annie, silhouetted against the light, stood at the side
window, looking out over the garden. She
didn't see Sabine. She didn't seem to see
anything. Over her too-thick jumper, both
hands held her stomach.

A special supper for you tonight, Sabine."

Her grandmother placed the steaming pot
in the middle of the shining table, and lifted
the lid with a distinctly un-Joy-like flourish.

"Mrs. H made it for you specially. Roasted

vegetable casserole, with vegetarian herb and cheese dumplings. Good warming food after a day's hunting."

Sabine breathed in the rich smell, feeling her stomach constrict with hunger. She had regretted giving that boy her Mars Bar for most of the afternoon, only the pinch of extreme cold taking her mind from the griping of her stomach.

"I thought I'd have it, too, to keep you company."

"It looks lovely," said Sabine, wondering whether it would be rude to reach in now and serve herself.

"I always think you need a good stew, or casserole, to warm you up after a day on the field," said Joy, rummaging around in the dresser for napkins. "I used to get so hungry . . . and I'd always find that even if I packed sandwiches, they would always end up falling out of my pockets, and getting trodden on by a horse."

Please hurry up, willed Sabine. According to the rules, she couldn't start eating until Joy had sat back down. Her stomach, responding to the scent of the food, let out a rumble loud enough to make Bertie's head turn inquiringly.

"Now, where did I put those napkin rings? I'm sure they were in this drawer. Perhaps Mrs. H has put them in the kitchen."

"Can I—can—?" The rich, aromatic smell of the sauce was making her dizzy.

"I think I'll just go and have a look. You don't mind waiting for a minute, do you?"

"Actually, I—"

They were interrupted by a distant clunk and thump outside the dining room. Both dogs leaped up from their places underneath the table, and ran to the door, whining and scrabbling to be let out.

Joy, turning from her task, walked briskly over and opened it.

"Edward! What are you doing?"

She stepped backward, and Sabine watched as the old man made his unsteady way into the room, shuffling and wheezing, bent low on two sticks like some prehistoric quadruped.

"What do you think I'm doing?" he growled, not looking up from the floor as he edged his way forward. "I'm coming for my supper."

Joy cast an anxious look in Sabine's direction, and Sabine, out of deference to her feelings, looked away. For it was not

Edward's unheralded presence at the dining table that had alarmed her grandmother, but his unconventional mode of dress. On his bottoms he wore a pair of thick cotton pajamas, overlaid with a rich red paisley pattern, teamed with his slippers, from which Sabine could just make out his purple, painfully swollen ankles. On his upper half, over his pajama top, he wore a crisp white jacket, cut with a mandarin collar, sporting epaulets and emanating a faint but definite scent of mothballs. Some kind of naval uniform, Sabine guessed. Round his neck, like some kind of subzero dandy, sat Joy's cashmere scarf, mauve with blue flowers.

As Sabine stared at her plate, he made his way to the table, and sat down, gingerly, in his chair. Settled, he laid down his sticks, sighed, leaned forward, and peered closely at the polished table in front of him.

"I haven't got a plate," he announced.

Joy stood by the door, her brow furrowed.

"I wasn't expecting you down this evening. You told me you weren't hungry."

"Well . . . I am hungry."

There was a short delay, as if they were speaking on an international telephone line. Joy, wiping pointlessly at her trousers, waited until she was sure his mind was made up. Then she moved toward the kitchen, shooing the dogs bad-temperedly before her as she went.

"I'll set you a place."

Satisfied, her grandfather sat back in his chair, and gazed around him, as if trying to locate something. When he caught sight of Sabine, he stopped and laid a hand heavily down on the table.

"Ahh. There you are."

Sabine smiled uncertainly.

"Now." He paused, inhaling wheezily. "I understand you've been out hunting."

It was said with some satisfaction.

Before Sabine could speak, Joy re-emerged with crockery and cutlery, which she laid briskly and precisely in front of her husband.

"Yes. She's had a jolly good day out."

Edward peered slowly upward at his wife, his face blank, but his voice thick with irritation.

"I want to speak to my granddaughter. I would rather you didn't interrupt."

Joy raised an eyebrow, but ignored him. She returned to her place, and began dishing out the vegetable casserole.

"Now . . . ," he said carefully, eyeing Sabine with something that she almost swore was mischief. "Was it a good day?"

Apart from quite enjoying the spectacle of seeing her grandmother told off, Sabine, relishing the taste of the first mouthful, hardly wanted to be interrupted by speech.

"Yes," she said, nodding vigorously so that he wouldn't ask her to repeat herself.

"Good, good . . ." He sat back again, smiling. "What horse was it you rode? Was it the Duke?"

"No, Edward. The Duke is lame. You know the Duke is lame."

"What?"

"The Duke. Is Lame." Joy poured Sabine a small glass of red wine and pushed it toward her.

"Ohhh. Lame, is he?" Her grandfather paused and looked at his food. "Oh, dear . . . What's this?"

"It's vegetable casserole," said Joy, loudly. "It's Sabine's favorite."

"What meat is it?" he prodded unsteadily at it with his fork. "I haven't got any meat in mine."

"It doesn't have meat. It's all vegetables."

He looked up suspiciously.

"But where's the meat?"

Joy looked briefly exasperated.

"I didn't give you any," she said, finally. "There was none left." She glanced swiftly at Sabine, acknowledging her lie, but daring her granddaughter to do the same.

Edward stared at his plate.

"Ohhh . . . Does it have sweet corn in it?"

"Yes," said Joy, picking at her own food. "It does. You'll have to pick it out."

"I don't like sweet corn."

"Sabine jumped a Wexford bank today," Joy said determinedly, her voice lifting. "Thom told me."

"You jumped a bank? Jolly well done." The corners of her grandfather's mouth lifted into a smile. Sabine found that her own met it. She still found herself swelling with pride when she thought about it.

"Jolly tricky, those banks."

"The horse did it all, really," Sabine said modestly. "I just hung on."

"Sometimes the best thing you can do is leave it to the horse," said Joy, wiping her mouth. "Yours is a clever enough chap, anyway."

Sabine, gazing around her at her grandparents as they ate, had a sudden sense of being part of a wider family, of how pleasant it could be to bask in their approval. She didn't think she had ever had a sense of pride like this; there had been passing her exams in the summer, but that had all been tinged with the Geoff-and-Justin thing; although she had felt privately pleased, to join in her mother's pleasure at her achievement would have meant some kind of collusion, and Sabine had spent those months feeling far too angry with her for that. Somehow, with her grandparents, it was less complicated. I don't really mind being here, she thought suddenly. I might even like it.

"So . . . how many times did you draw?"

Sabine looked up at her grandfather, and over at her grandmother's place, which had been suddenly vacated. She had no idea what he was talking about.

"Sorry?" she said weakly, listening for the sound of her grandmother's imminent return from the kitchen.

Her grandfather looked briefly impatient, apparently tried by the effort of having to repeat things that were patently easy to hear.

"I said, how many times did you *draw*?"

She couldn't have said exactly why, but Sabine didn't want to admit that she didn't know what he was talking about. She had so enjoyed their unaccustomed and tacit approval; it would have felt like breaking a spell. Her grandfather would be disappointed, as if she were some kind of imposter. Her grandmother would wear that blank, yet faintly exasperated expression that until so recently had characterized their every exchange. She would be Sabine, the townie outsider, again.

"Six."

"What?"

"Six." It sounded like a good, middling sort of a number.

"Six times?" Her grandfather's eyes widened.

Her grandmother walked back in, bearing a loaded bread board.

"Did you hear that, Joy? Sabine's hunt today. Drew *six times*."

Joy shot a sharp look at Sabine. Sabine, already aware that she had said the wrong thing, tried very hard to convey some kind of explanation in her return look.

"That's astonishing," he said, shaking his head at his plate. "Last time I heard of a hunt drawing six times must have been . . . was it nineteen sixty-seven, Joy? That winter we had the Pettigrews over. That was five or six times, wasn't it?"

"I don't remember," said Joy, shortly.

"I might have got it wrong," said Sabine, desperately.

"Six times," said her grandfather, shaking his head again. "Well, well . . . Still, jolly good season, sixty-seven. Good horses that year, too. Do you remember that little colt we bought in Tipperary, Joy? What was his name?"

"Master Ridley."

"Master Ridley. That's the one. All the way to Tipperary, and we spent so much money on the horse we didn't have any money over for the hotel. Had to stay in a caravan. Didn't we, darling?"

"We did."

"Yes. Stayed in a caravan. Freezing it was. Full of holes."

"It certainly was."

"Jolly good fun, that. Yes." He smiled slowly to himself, his creased old face taut wih the effort and Sabine, glancing over at Joy, noted that she had allowed her own expression to soften slightly. "Yes." she said. "Jolly good fun."

"Sounds a laugh," Sabine mumbled, taking the opportunity to help herself to another dumpling.

"Six times . . . D'you know, there's nothing like hound music," he said, lifting his head, as if sampling some distant tune. "No sound like it."

He paused, and then looked directly at Sabine, as if really seeing her for the first time.

"Not like your mother at all, are you?" he said.

And then collapsed, face first, into his casserole.

For a brief, dreadful second, Sabine stared at him, wondering absently if this was some kind of joke. Then Joy, with a shout of horror, leaped from her seat and ran over, lifting her husband's head from the plate, and cradling it to her shoulder. "Get the doctor!" she yelled at Sabine.

Sabine, jolted from her frozen state, pushed her chair back and bolted from the room. As she rummaged through the numbers on the telephone table, dialing the number with shaking hands, the terrible vision of her grandfather swam in front of her. It was an image that, she already knew, would haunt her long after its origins had been restored to normality. His eyes had been half closed, his mouth half open. Streams of hot, tomato-colored liquid ran in rivulets down the crags of his face. They had dripped off the flowery scarf and onto his immaculate white shoulders, like pale, thinned blood.

Kate sat down on the sofa next to Justin, and considered whether she should lean against him, and perhaps gently run her fingers through his hair. Or reach for his hand. Or even rest her fingers on his thigh, in a relaxed yet proprietorial manner. She paused, gazing surreptitiously at his face, trying to gauge which would be the most appropriate. These were not concerns she might have worried over at such length two months ago, but two months ago she had still felt uninhibited with him, confident that her every move upon him would be met by a return gesture.

Because Justin-of-today did not share Justin-of-two-months-ago's constant desire to touch, hold, or stroke her. Most nights he didn't even seem that bothered about whether he even sat next to her. And Kate, desperate to bridge this apparent distance between them, found herself acutely self-conscious, trying to manufacture a warmth that no longer existed without her efforts.

She settled for a seat right up close to him, and a leg casually resting next to his.

"Do you want more wine?"

He didn't take his eyes from the television.

"Yeah. Lovely."

"I love Fleurie. It's my special treat to myself."

He snorted slightly at something on screen. Then glanced next to him, where she was filling his glass.

"Very nice."

"I don't think I know your favorite wine." She wanted them to talk to each other again, to really, really focus on each other, spilling secrets they hadn't known they held, desperate to pour themselves out in front of each other; here, this is all that I am, take me. When she and Justin had first gotten together, she had been struck by the idea of herself again as someone with potential; he had seemed to see endless possibilities in her, had made her believe she could be bigger than she was, that they could be bigger together. Now, when he came around, he sat himself, remote control in hand, in front of the television. Then asked what they were having for supper.

"It's called being settled," he had said, when she had gently broached the subject one night. "It shows I'm comfortable with you. You can't expect high passion to last forever."

But then why did I leave Geoff for you? she wanted to shout back at him. At least with him I didn't get to do the cooking and all the washing up. At least Geoff wanted to talk to me in the evenings. At least Geoff occasionally wanted to make love.

"So what is your favorite wine?"

"Sorry?"

"Your favorite wine. What is it?" She could hear new threads of steel in her voice.

"Wine? *Erm* . . . never really thought about it." He paused, as if trying to engage half his brain on the task, aware that some kind of response was going to be necessary. "Some of the Chilean ones are nice."

It was as if once the specter of Geoff and the threat of discovery were gone, there was no longer enough excitement to fuel his desire for her. And Kate had found herself fighting a resentfulness, a suspicion that she had slowly and unwittingly taken on another role, becoming a kind of mother substitute to him, providing meals, domesticity, and a safe haven for someone whose real passion was out on a distant road, seen through a lens shutter.

"It's a pretty nice arrangement for him," Maggie had observed the previous week, eyeing Justin's bags of camera equipment in the hall.

"What is?"

"Nice house, place to stay, with food and sex all thrown in. Useful place to store cameras. And no responsibility. No commitments. No bills." She raised an eyebrow, and walked briskly into the kitchen, where Kate had been making the tea.

"Why should he pay bills if he doesn't live here?" Kate had felt irritated by Maggie's tone. But she was also acutely conscious of Justin's proliferating bags of equipment; she had a feeling Sabine was not going to be quite as amenable to their presence as she was.

"No reason at all. I just thought that after all this time he would want to come and live here."

"Look, Maggie. Not everyone wants to be like you and Hamish. Justin's a free spirit.

More important, I've just come out of a very messy breakup. You know how messy. And the last thing I want is someone else diving in here, cluttering up my life, before I've even had a chance to enjoy it on my own."

She had almost convinced herself.

"Ahh. I didn't realize you had split up with Geoff to be *on your own*. Sorry, darling. I thought you had said you wanted to be with *Justin*. So forgetful! Must be my Alzheimer's coming on." And Maggie, with a sly sideways look, had effectively closed the conversation.

She was right, of course. But Kate was not about to admit that she had made a mistake. Because that would mean that all this pain, all this mess, the deeper fracturing of her already precarious relationship with her daughter, had all been for nothing. And it would mean that once again, despite being thirty-five and a veteran of God knows how many relationships, and someone who thought she knew exactly what she was doing, Kate had gotten it wrong about men. Again.

She thought, uncomfortably, of Sabine, whom she had last spoken to more than a week ago. Her daughter had been relatively pleasant, had unusually failed to berate her for any apparent shortcomings, had even failed to rise to the bait when Kate accidentally mentioned Justin. But when Kate had gently tried to suggest it might be a good time for her to start thinking about coming home, Sabine had politely but definitely changed the subject. Even more disturbing than the apparent refusal was its manner. Sabine had never expressed concern about her mother's feelings; most of the time she had gone out of her way to be unpleasant to her. This new, adult Sabine, was not just gently telling her she disapproved of her mother's life, but apparently creating her own, as far away as possible.

Kate fought the sudden lump in her throat. I'll just have to try harder, she thought, gazing at Justin's legs in their moleskin trousers, stretched out in front of her. I'll give Sabine a little space. Then remind her of all the things she loved about London. I won't be clingy and desperate; I'll just sit tight until she's ready to come back to me. And I won't read too much into Justin's behavior. He's a good man and he loves me; we've just fallen into boring domesticity a little too quickly. I just need to shake things up a little.

Kate took a deep breath, and ran her hand through her hair, mussing it up a little.

"So," she said, placing a hand on his leg. "Did you enjoy supper?"

She had cooked tuna steaks, his favorite. She was actually getting quite good at cooking.

"It was great. I told you."

"So . . ." She let her hand move slowly up his thigh, and murmured into his ear. "I wondered if you fancied a dessert. . . ."

Oh, God, she sounded like some substandard porn film. But she had to keep going. Self-consciousness would kill it.

"Great," he said, turning from the television to face her. "What have we got?"

She paused, trying to maintain her seductive smile.

"Well, it's not exactly a conventional dessert I had in mind."

He looked blank.

"But it could be sweet . . . I guess . . ."

Are you really that dense? she wanted to yell. But instead, determined to pursue her chosen path, she slowly let her hand suggest what she had in mind.

There was a lengthy silence.

Justin looked at her, then down at her hand, then back at her face. He smiled, and then raised his eyebrows.

"That . . . that's a really nice thought. But to be honest, Kate, you haven't half made me feel peckish for a bit of pudding. Is there anything sweet in the house?" He paused. "A bit of chocolate maybe? Or ice cream?"

Kate's hand stilled. She stared at him.

"Well, you put the thought in my mind," he said, a little defensively. "I didn't want anything sweet until you started talking about desserts. Now I really want something."

For a brief, insane moment, Kate fought the urge to go and check the freezer compartment. Then she thought she might hit him. Then she thought she should probably leave the room until she had decided which of the many seething emotions she was prepared to act on. But, perhaps luckily for Justin, she was interrupted by the shrill ring of the telephone.

He made as if to pick it up, and then, catching something in her expression, sank back against the sofa cushions.

"Hello?" she said, aware that he was staring at her, as if bemused by her response.

"Kate?"

"Yes?"

"It's your mother."

It's Sabine, Kate thought wildly. She's had an accident.

"What's happened?" There was no reason her mother would ring her otherwise. It had been years since she had last done so.

"I thought I should let you know. Your father . . . has been taken rather unwell. He collapsed this evening. He—he's in the hospital." She faltered, her voice strained, as if waiting for some response. When none came, she paused, then let out a deep breath. "As I said. I just thought I should let you know." And she rang off.

Kate gently replaced the handset, aware that as well as shock, she was still consumed by an overriding sense of relief that it wasn't Sabine who had been hurt. She had been so relieved that her daughter was safe that she hadn't quite been able to take in the significance of what Joy had actually said.

"It's my dad," she said eventually, to Justin's inquiring face. "I think he's dying. She wouldn't have rung me otherwise." Her voice was surprisingly steady.

"You'd better go," he said, placing his hand on her shoulder. "Poor you. D'you want me to book you a flight?"

It was about an hour after he'd gone, as she phoned around the various airlines, and discovered with equal amounts of frustration and relief that thanks to a combination of arts festivals and medical conferences, and her own finally deceased car, that unless she wanted to pay a small ransom it was likely to be at least two days before she would be airborne to Waterford Airport, that Kate realized: Not once, despite his sympathetic demeanor, had Justin offered to come with her.

Chapter Nine

Christopher Ballantyne and his wife, Julia, looked so alike that according to Mrs. H, had they married thirty years earlier there would have been "serious talk" in the village. He had dark, wavy hair, matched exactly in shade by his wife's own, and set springily atop a broad head, like the ill-fitting top of a sponge cake. Both had the same slightly beaky noses, the same lean physiques, similar strong views on most topics, especially hygiene and politics, and both talked in the same, explosive, braying tones, as if every sentence had been pumped out of them by bellows.

And both, Sabine noted, somewhat resentfully, treated her with that same air of indulgent detachment that they would any houseguest. Except in her case, she felt it was a deliberate attempt to let her know that she was not, despite her blood ties, a *true* part of the family. Not like they were. And that would be Kate's fault, of course.

Christopher had marched into the place like he owned it on the night that her grandfather had fallen into the casserole, telling Joy, somewhat pointlessly, as far as Sabine could see, that "she would be fine now." He and Julia had been at a hunt ball in Kilkenny, which had been "a stroke of luck" as he rather tactlessly put it, and they had immediately driven down and moved their things into the good guest room next to her grandmother. It had never occurred to Sabine up until then to question why she had not been given the good guest room, which had a far nicer carpet, and a big glowing chest of drawers of walnut veneer, but when she mentioned this to Mrs. H, Mrs. H had said that Christopher "liked to have a room of his own" to come home to. And that he and Julia "did come and visit a lot." Not like me and my mum, in other words, thought Sabine. But she said nothing.

If Joy had noticed any of the resentment Sabine felt, she didn't comment. But then she seemed awfully distracted, not having Edward in the house to look after. Wexford General Hospital had decided to keep him in for observation and while Sabine had not liked to ask her what exactly was the matter with him (there didn't seem much left of him to observe), it was obvious that it was serious, not just because her grandmother looked pale and strained and seemed unnaturally quiet, but because Sabine had noticed that whenever she wasn't in the room, Christopher would check the backs of furniture, and underneath the rugs for little handwritten stickers, to see if there had been any changes in the spoils that Joy had some months ago already begun to divide between her two children for after her and Edward's deaths.

"Very sensible idea, Mother," he had said to her. "Saves any confusion in the long run." But Sabine had heard him mutter to Julia that he didn't think it was right that the grandfather clock in the hall, or the gilt-framed oil painting in the breakfast room had "Katherine" stickers on them. "Since when has she shown any interest in this place, anyway?" he had said, and Sabine had slunk silently back into the shadows and resolved to monitor every sticky label in the place, to make sure Christopher didn't start swapping them around.

Julia, meanwhile, had insisted on "helping" around the house. So determinedly had she helped that Mrs. H's normally amenable expression steadily became more and more fixed, as if it had been set in aspic. Julia had already "organized" the kitchen, so that she could help prepare everybody's food, and been through the fridge, questioning whether it was really necessary to keep some of these old leftovers, and whether it wouldn't be easier for Julia to buy some "nice shop-bought" bread instead of Mrs. H making that dense old soda bread every day. When she left the room, Sabine told Mrs. H more than once that she thought Julia was an interfering old cow, but Mrs. H would only respond, "She means well," and observe, like someone repeating a mantra, that it wouldn't be long before they would return to Dublin.

Considering they were the only aunt and uncle she had, Sabine should perhaps have been more surprised that she had met

Christopher and Julia only a handful of times
before. Once had been at their wedding, in
Parsons-Green, when Sabine had been very
small. All she remembered about that occasion was that she had been invited to be a
flower girl, but her mother had somehow got
her dress slightly different from the other
girls', possibly as a result of a miscut pattern, and that she had spent the day in a
quiet frenzy of humiliation at her puff
sleeves, while the little blonde flower god-
desses around her, sensing a misfit, froze
her out. The most recent occasion had been
several years earlier, before they moved
from London to Dublin, when they had held
a "little do" and, in a spirit of reconciliation,
invited Sabine, Geoff, and her mother to
come along. It had been full of city people
and lawyers, and Sabine had soon snuck off
to watch television in their bedroom with
Julia's cats, trying to ignore the pubescent
boy in the corner who had snogged his
thirteen-year-old girlfriend for almost the
whole of *The Railway Children,* and wondering when they could go home. As if heard by
some deity, she had been rescued by Geoff
and her mother little more than an hour after
they had arrived, and Geoff had spent the

whole journey home ranting about capitalists, while Kate sat silently, interjecting the odd "Yes, well, they are my family, you know," but not sounding like she was really offering any kind of defense.

It was partly because of the the sheer awfulness of being around Christopher and Julia that Sabine quietly took over some of the duties of looking after her grandfather when, two days later, frail, blanket-bound, and seemingly welded to a wheelchair, he came home. Out of respect for Joy's feelings, her son and daughter-in-law tended to leave him to her sole care (that was their excuse, anyway, Sabine told Mrs. H, but she knew it was because they wanted to go out riding), but Joy seemed to quite like it when Sabine came and sat with him, or read to him from the letters page of the *Horse and Hound.* Much of the time, he didn't seem to notice her, but Sabine was privately convinced that he bore an expression of deep irritation whenever the brisk young nurse, whom Christopher had paid to come for most of the day, helped him cheerfully upright and announced that it was time for him to go "to the little boys' room." And occasionally, when Sabine chatted to him about what she had done with the gray, or passed on some snippet that Thom had said in the yard, she was sure she could see his eyes flicker and a shadow of interest pass, like a distant cloud, across his face.

Joy, meanwhile, simply responded to her husband's return by becoming busier than ever. There was apparently more to do in the yard, the house was a disaster, and if Liam and John John didn't clean some of that tack, then it was, of course, going to fall to bits. She never mentioned what the doctors had said, or discussed why her grandfather no longer seemed to eat anything at all, or why there was now a frightening array of bleeping medical equipment stationed around his bed, as if placed on high alert for some forthcoming disaster. She just told Sabine in a rather vague manner that she was doing "a grand job," popped her head around the door occasionally as if to reassure herself that he was still alive, and then spent even more hours, if it were possible, ministering to her tired old horse in the yard.

"It's all right," said Sabine after the nurse had disappeared, as she sat down in the chair beside her grandfather's bed, once again grateful to escape the maelstrom of activity downstairs. "You can relax. We've gotten rid of them all again."

She pulled his covers up higher around his concave chest, noting that his frailty no longer made her want to squirm. She was just grateful that he looked peaceful, and alive, and not covered in tomato juice.

"Now don't you worry about me being bored or anything," she said, whispering close to his ear, as she prepared to read to him from this old Rudyard Kipling book she had found in the library, about horses playing polo in India. She knew he could hear her, even if the nurse raised her eyebrows, like she was doing something stupid. "I meant to tell you the other day," she said, softly, as she began. "Sometimes I just like to sit and be, too."

For her eighteenth birthday, Kate Ballantyne had received three gifts of significance. One, from her parents, was a top-of-the-range, general-purpose, dark-brown pigskin saddle, which was opened by her with despair, as she had specifically asked for a brassiere and a new pair of trousers. Another, also from her parents, was an invitation to a sitting with a local portrait artist, in order that

she could mark the occasion of her adult-
hood. This also prompted a less than grateful response; they had chosen the very artist
who had just completed a large oil painting
of her mother's new gelding, Lancelot. The
third gift . . . well, the third gift had come
about as an indirect result of the second.
And that had come much later.

Sixteen and a half years later, Kate
thought of these as she sat in the back of the
taxi, breathing in the pungent smell of in-car
air freshener as she headed from Waterford
Airport to Kilcarrion. She had been to her
family home precisely three times since she
had left home shortly after that eighteenth
birthday; once to show them the newborn
Sabine, twice with Jim, when she had
thought that her being part of a "family"
might soften their attitudes toward her, and
now, some ten years on. Why does it always
rain here? she thought, distractedly, wiping
at the steam on the window. I can hardly
remember a time when it didn't rain.

It had taken her almost two days to get a
flight to Waterford, and Kate knew already
that her delayed return would be used, like a
riding whip, against her, even though her
mother had been at pains to ring and tell her

when he "stabilized." She didn't care enough to come straight away, that would be the muttered refrain. Even though her own father was at death's door. Too busy gallivanting with the latest fancy man, probably. She sighed to herself, thinking of the irony of her last conversation with Justin. He had seemed less shocked and disturbed by her abrupt ending of their relationship than by her insistence that he remove his bags from her house before she left for Ireland.

She wasn't even really sure why she was coming; apart from her desperate need to see her daughter again, she had no real emotional ties to the place. Her father hadn't spoken to her with any warmth or civility since she was eighteen, her brother and his wife would simply patronize her and drop loaded comments that staked their greater claim to the family house, and her mother had long been more comfortable talking to her dogs. I came because my father is dying, she said to herself, trying out the words, to see if, even after all this time, they could elicit some awful sense of occasion, of potential loss. But all she really felt was dread at the prospect of being in that household again, tempered with relief at the thought of seeing her daughter.

I'll stay a couple of days, she told herself, as the cab paused on the edges of Ballymalnaugh. I'm an adult. I can leave whenever I like. It's always possible to cope with a couple of days. And then perhaps I can persuade Sabine to come home with me.

"Have you come far?" The driver evidently felt a need, now that he had neared his destination, to secure his tip.

"London."

His eyes, two beetles under bushes, met hers in the rearview mirror.

"London. I've got family in Willesden." He paused. "It's all right, love, I won't ask you if you know them."

Kate smiled thinly, gazing out of the window at the familiar landmarks: There was Mrs. H's house, the Church of Blessed Peter, the forty-acre field that her parents had sold to a farmer the first time they had run out of money.

"You been here before, then? Not an area that usually gets many tourists. Usually I take them up north. Or to the west. You wouldn't believe the numbers that go to the west, now."

Kate paused, gazing at the stone wall that fenced Kilcarrion House.

"No. Never," she said.

"Just visiting friends, then?"

"Something like that."

Just think of it as picking up Sabine, she told herself. That will make it all bearable.

Except it wasn't Sabine who met her at the door. It was Julia, dressed in jodhpurs, a huge, scarlet fleecy body-warmer, and matching socks, who, after a great flurry of kisses and exclamation, said rather pointedly that she had "absolutely no idea" where Sabine was. "She seems to spend most of her time either hiding in the yard, or closeted away with Edward," she said. Julia always spoke in a way that expressed bemusement at other people's actions.

Kate, trying to hide her irritation at the too-intimate way in which Julia referred to her father, decided she must have gotten it wrong. Sabine would not want to hang around the horses. And she was even less likely to be "closeted away" with her father.

"But what am I doing?" Julia exclaimed, taking one of Kate's bags. "Do come in! Where are my manners?"

They've been bulldozed by your acquisitive instincts, Kate thought bitterly. And then told herself she had no right, as it was not as if, for the past sixteen years, she had cared whether the house was hers, or indeed razed to make way for a McDonald's drive thru. She adjusted her glasses on the bridge of her nose (she had, of course, forgotten her contact lenses), trying to take in the home that was no longer hers.

"We've put you in the Italian room," Julia trilled, as she "showed" Kate upstairs. "I don't think it's leaking at the moment."

In the decade since her last visit, it was as if the house had aged in dog years, Kate thought, looking around. It had always been cold, and damp, but she couldn't remember these brown water stains spreading down the walls, like sepia-tinted maps of far-off continents; nor could she remember everything looking this shabby and threadbare: the Persian rugs worn down to a patchy network of grayed cotton threads, the furnishings scuffed and chipped, evidently long past their deadline for repainting. She didn't recall the smell; the ever-present distant hum of dog and horse now mingling with those of mildew and neglect. And she hadn't remembered this chill; not a dry cold, like her house had seen when her boiler had broken, but a damp, seeping, long-standing cold that had permeated her bones within minutes of her arrival. Kate stared at the back of Julia's dense fleece with new eyes. It certainly looked warmer than anything she had brought.

"We've actually managed to warm up the place a bit," said Julia, throwing open the door of Kate's room. "You wouldn't believe how cold they had let it get. I told Christopher, it's no wonder Edward got ill."

"I thought it was a stroke," said Kate, coolly.

"Yes, it was a stroke, but he is old, and terribly frail. And the elderly do need their comforts, don't they? I've told Christopher we should take him back to Dublin with us, back to a bit of proper central heating. We've got a room all ready. But your mother won't have it. She wants to keep him here."

The tone of her last words left Kate in little doubt as to Julia's opinion of this course of action. By keeping her husband in Kilcarrion, she was effectively resigning him to an early grave, it said. But Kate felt a sudden communion with her mother. Her father would always rather be here, cold and damp, rather than smothered to death in Julia's pastel-colored, centrally heated embrace.

"Between you and me, Katie, I can't wait to get back to our house," Julia said, pulling out one of the drawers, to check that it was empty. She was prone to offering such fake "confidences," words that meant nothing but suggested some intimacy on the speaker's behalf. "I do find this place depressing, even if Christopher loves it so. And our neighbor is looking after the cats and I know they'll be simply miserable by now, poor things. They hate it when we go away."

"Oh. Your cats," said Kate politely, suddenly remembering Julia's passion for the two insolent-looking felines. "Are they still the same ones?"

Julia placed a hand on her arm. "You know, Katie, it's very sweet of you to ask, but they're not. Well, Armand is still with us, but Mam'selle sadly passed away last spring." Kate noted, with some fear, that Julia's eyes had suddenly filled with tears.

"Still, she had a good life . . . ," she mused, distantly. "And you know we've got the sweetest little girl to keep Armand company. Poubelle, we call her," she laughed delightedly, her good humor suddenly restored. "Because she's never out of our kitchen bin, the little madam."

Kate tried to smile, wondering how quickly she could escape Julia's freesia-scented hold, and try to locate her daughter.

"You must be desperate to unpack. I'll leave you to it," Julia said. "But don't forget, tea is at four-thirty prompt. We've persuaded Joy to have it in the breakfast room now, because it's that little bit easier to heat. I'll see you down there."

With a parting flutter of her fingers, she was gone.

Kate sat heavily on her bed, and gazed around her at the room she had not seen for ten years. This had not been her own room; Julia had told her that Sabine was occupying that, while Julia and Christopher occupied the room that had always been his. The other "dry" guest room was apparently occupied by her mother. It didn't surprise Kate; she had suspected they often kept separate rooms even when she lived at home—her father's snoring, her mother had explained, unconvincingly. But she found it hard to reconcile anything in this room with her childhood or teenage self; it was as if the house had aged faster than anyone else, ironing out any badges or markings of familiarity as it went, and it felt, genuinely, like it had nothing to do with her.

Why should I care? thought Kate, briskly. My life hasn't been here since Sabine was born. My life is back in London.

But still she found herself gazing around at the pictures on the walls, peering into the cupboards, as if waiting for some jolt of recognition, even some pang of melancholy, for an earlier, less complicated life.

She was making her way down the stairs when she first caught sight of Sabine. She had her back to her, and was crouching by the dogs, pulling her riding boots off, and exclaiming to Bella and Bertie fondly as they pushed their noses at her face that they were both "dopey, dopey animals." Bertie, becoming overexcited, jumped up on her, sending her collapsing gently backward onto the hall carpet, and Sabine laughed, pushing him away, trying to wipe her face as he slobbered over her.

It didn't even look like her daughter. Kate stood and stared, feeling a simultaneous joy at this uninhibited display of affection, and a distant ache that somehow this place, this

frozen wasteland of emotion, had suc-
ceeded where she had failed in eliciting it.

Sabine, sensing a presence, turned
around, and jumped slightly as she saw her
mother on the stairs.

"Sabine," said Kate impulsively, and thrust
out her arms. She had not been prepared for
the sheer emotional pull her daughter's
presence could have on her. It had been
weeks.

Sabine stood, some kind of indecision
flickering across her face.

"Oh . . . er, hi, Mum," she said, and, with a
small step forward, allowed herself to be
hugged, and then pulled very gently backward when it felt like it was going on too long.

"Look at you!" exclaimed Kate, shaking
her head. "You look . . . you look . . . well,
you look great." You look like you belong
here, she wanted to say. But that phrase
held so many dangerous implications that it
had frozen on her lips.

"I look like shit," said Sabine, staring down
at her muddy jeans, and her oversized
jumper, pincushioned with pieces of straw.
Her head dipped, and her thin hand ran
through her hair, and immediately she had
returned to the old Sabine, self-conscious,

hypercritical, and desperately wary of any kind of compliment.

"You've got your glasses on," she said. She made it sound accusatory.

"I know. In all the commotion, I stupidly forgot my lenses."

Sabine stared at her face.

"You should get some new frames," she said, and turned back to the dogs.

There was a brief silence, as Sabine bent to pick up her boots.

"So . . . ," said Kate, aware that her voice sounded too high, too eager. "Have you been out riding?"

Sabine nodded, placing them behind the door.

"I never thought your granny would have you riding. Do you like it? Has she gotten you a horse?"

"Yeah. She's borrowed one."

"Great . . . great. It's nice to rediscover old interests, isn't it? And what else have you been doing?"

Sabine looked at her, irritably.

"Not much."

"What, just riding?" The door of the breakfast room was open. Kate noted with some relief that no one was in there yet.

"No. Helping out. Doing stuff around here." Sabine paused, to shoo the dogs into the breakfast room, and then with an action seemingly born of long habit, placed one of her socked feet up against one of the oil heaters.

"And . . . you're happy? Everything's been going okay? I—I've hardly heard from you lately. I was wondering if you were all right."

"I'm fine."

There was a prolonged silence, during which Sabine stared determinedly out of the window, eyeing the darkening sky.

"We don't normally have tea in here," she said, eventually. "We normally have it in the living room. But *Julia* . . ."—she pronounced it lengthily, and with some scorn—"thinks that the log fire doesn't get the room warm enough. So now we're having it in here."

Kate sat tentatively in one of the chairs, desperately trying not to show how wounded she felt by Sabine's apparent indifference. "We normally," she had said. "We normally," like she had lived here all her life. Like she felt proprietorial about the place.

"So," she said, brightly. "Do you want to hear about O'Malley?"

Sabine, switching feet, looked at her.

"He's all right, isn't he?"

"Yes, he's fine. I just thought you might be interested in what he's been up to."

"He's a *cat*," said Sabine dismissively. "What is there to tell?"

My God, thought Kate. Whatever lessons it is they give to teenage girls in how to cut people down to size, Sabine evidently got my share.

"Don't you want to ask me anything about home? How my work's going? How the house is?"

Sabine frowned at her mother, trying to work out what exactly it was that she was asking her to say. She seemed desperate to try and provoke some response from her, as if she had expected her to be all over her, bombarding her with demands for news from home, jumping up and down like some television reunion. And perhaps, a week or two earlier, she might have done it. But she felt different about this place now, and seeing her mother so suddenly . . . well, it had put her on edge. That desperate need for her had evaporated with her arrival. It was like boys, when you spent all week thinking about them, desperate to see them, and then when you did you felt all complicated, like you didn't know whether you wanted to see them after all. Like they were somehow better in your imagination than in real life.

She eyed her mother surreptitiously as she gazed around the room, looking a bit lost and pathetic. For the last two months all she had thought about was the good stuff: Kate being supportive, and kind, and being able to tell her anything. And now—when she looked at her—her overriding emotion was—well, what? Irritation? The faintest feeling of being invaded? Looking at her reminded Sabine of the whole Justin and Geoff thing. Listening to her reminded her that her mother could never just relax and let her be; she was always pushing for more than Sabine felt comfortable giving. Why couldn't you have just been cool? she wanted to say to her. Why couldn't you have just said hi, and let me come to you? Why do you always have to push me so hard that I end up pushing you away? But she just stood, warming her frozen feet against the oil heater, swallowing her emotions.

"Ahh. Katherine," said Christopher, striding into the room. "Julia said you were here." He placed a hand on her shoulder, and inflicted a distant kiss. "Good journey over, was it? Did you come by ferry in the end?"

"No. I flew. Couldn't get an earlier flight," said Kate, aware that she was already sounding defensive.

"Oh. Yes. Yes. I heard. Never mind, looks like the old man's improved a bit."

No, he hasn't, thought Sabine. I've spent nearly every day with him, and he's not improved at all. But she said nothing.

"So, how long are you staying?"

He sat down on her father's chair, and glanced around, as if waiting for Julia or Mrs. H to enter bearing the tea tray. Kate didn't know how to answer. Until he dies, she wanted to say. I thought that's what we were all here for.

"Not sure yet," she said.

"We'll probably have to head back tomorrow," Christopher announced. "Work is getting antsy about me returning, and to be honest, now that he's looking better, there doesn't seem to be the same sort of urgency as there was a few days ago."

While I wasn't there, thought Kate.

"I'll probably pop down on weekends, though," he continued. "Just to make sure they're doing okay. Keep an eye on them.

Make sure they're keeping him warm enough, that sort of thing."

"He's got his fire going all the time," Sabine interjected. She couldn't help herself.

Christopher hardly seemed to see her. "Yes, yes, but this old house is terribly damp. Can't be doing him any good. Now, where's Julia? And where's Mother? I thought we were having tea at four-thirty prompt."

As if in answer, Joy suddenly appeared at the doorway. Her hair, which was rarely compliant, had sprung out of whatever loose arrangement had held it, like an overused scouring pad. Her navy-blue jumper was patched at the elbows, and her socks, visible beneath worn corduroy trousers, were less ill-matched than of polarized origins altogether.

"Katherine. Yes. How are you?" she moved forward, and then, hesitantly, kissed her daughter's cheek. Kate, reeling from the familiar scents of faded lavender and horse, noted with some shock how far her mother had aged since they had last met. Her skin, previously weather-beaten, now looked like it had been battered and scorched by the elements, sunshine and cold air leaving it pale, thread-veined and leathery, and scored by deep lines. Her hair, once a dark gray, was now pale silver. But it was her eyes that suggested the greatest trials of age; where once they had been steely and focused, they now appeared slightly sunken and distracted. She looked smaller, somehow, less robust. Less frightening.

"Did you have a good journey? I'm sorry, I didn't know you were here. I was out in the yard."

"It's okay," said Kate. "Julia saw me to my room."

"And you've found Sabine. Good. Good. . . . Sabine, did your grandfather want tea?"

"No, he's sleeping." Sabine was sitting on the floor, flanked by the dogs. "I might try him again in half an hour."

"Yes. Good job. Now. Where is Mrs. H with the tea things?" And Joy turned and disappeared from the room. Kate stared at the space where she had stood. That was it? she thought. Ten years we haven't seen each other, my father is dying, and that was it?

"She's been a bit—well, not all here, since Dad took ill," said Christopher, after she left.

"Definitely not herself," said Julia, who had

come in behind her. "Almost like it's all made her ill herself."

"She's all right," said Sabine, defensively. "She's just a bit distracted."

"She's a bit forgetful." Julia shook her head. "I've had to tell her twice that we'll be back on Saturday."

"I think we should have someone in to look after them. Both of them." Christopher stood, and peered out into the passage, as if checking for eavesdroppers. "I don't think they're managing by themselves."

"And it's terribly difficult doing anything for them," said Julia. "They are so set in their ways."

"Mrs. H looks after them. And you got that nurse in. They hate having her around as it is. They wouldn't want anyone else."

Kate stared at her daughter, astonished at this defense of her grandparents' way of life. Christopher stared at Sabine and then looked over at Kate, as if blaming her for this unforeseen piece of impudence. But Kate, between the two of them, didn't feel qualified even to venture into the argument.

Sabine's voice was rising. "They don't *like* people mucking in from outside. Mrs. H does everything, and she's said that she'll do extra when it's needed. I don't see why you can't just let them be."

"Yes, well, Sabine, that's a lovely thought, but you've known your grandparents all of five minutes. Julia and I have been helping out here for years. I think we know what my parents do and don't need."

"No, you don't," said Sabine, furiously. "You've never even asked them. You just came in here and took over. You never asked Grandmother if she wanted a nurse—you just stuck her in here. And Grandfather hates her. He makes this groaning noise when she comes in the room."

"Your grandfather is very ill, Sabine," said Julia, gently. "He needs professional care."

"He doesn't need someone bossing him about for not going to the loo properly. He doesn't need someone telling him to eat his vegetables like he's a baby and then talking about him like he's not even there."

Christopher's patience finally drained away.

"Sabine, you know absolutely nothing of what my parents do and don't need. You and Kate have had virtually nothing to do with this family for years, and you are quite wrong if you think you can just march in here and dictate how this house is run." His face had gone quite pink. "Now, this is a very difficult time for all of us and I'd appreciate it if you kept out of matters that don't concern you."

"I'll go," said Sabine, loudly, "when they want me to go. Not when you want me to go. And we all know you're only interested in their precious antiques anyway. I've seen you checking the furniture—don't think I haven't." Scrabbling up from the floor, her face flushed and tearful, she ran from the room, shouting, as she slammed the door on the way out: "They're not bloody dead yet, you know."

Joy, reemerging with the tea tray, jumped at her granddaughter's abrupt exit. "Where's Sabine gone?"

"Oh, off on some teenage sulk," said Christopher, dismissively. He looked, Kate noted, even more flushed than her daughter had. Whatever Sabine had said about furniture had evidently held some truth.

"Oh." Joy looked briefly at the door, as if considering whether to follow her, but then glanced around the room and decided reluctantly that her place was probably there in the breakfast room.

"Perhaps she'll come back," she said hopefully. She leaned over, fussing with the teapot, and setting cups on saucers. "I do like having her around." She glanced up at Kate almost shyly as she said this. Kate, witnessing this unheard-of display of emotion— the Kilcarrion equivalent to a normal person ripping off all their clothes and declaring undying love through a loudspeaker—felt suddenly, and inexplicably, chilled.

Tea was not a comfortable affair, Sabine's absence leaving an unavoidable hole in the proceedings, like a head hastily cut out of a family photograph. Joy kept fretting about what she was doing, wondering repeatedly whether it was worth saving her some fruit-cake, while Christopher sulked, and Julia talked too loudly about nothing of any consequence, trying to maintain the semblance of a happy atmosphere. Kate, who had already decided that this visit constituted a nightmare even worse than she could have envisaged, said almost nothing, responding to tactful queries about her work, and acknowledging the pointed lack of reference to her love life, while fighting a desperate urge to go and see if her daughter was okay. She would have gone, she wanted to, but something told her that Sabine would simply push her away, or tell her that she didn't understand, and she didn't know if she could take that much rejection in one day.

But it wasn't to be the end of it. When Joy finally left, announcing to her half-drunk cup of tea that she was going to check on Edward, Christopher, apparently still stung from Sabine's previous remarks, had asked Kate pointedly "when she was going to teach her daughter some manners."

"Chris, please don't," said Kate, wearily. "I'm tired, and I'm not in the mood."

"Well, she's going to have to learn them from somewhere, isn't she? And she plainly isn't getting them from you."

"Meaning?"

"What I say. That you're not exactly bending over backward to make sure she knows how to behave in company."

Kate stared at him, her blood already ringing in her ears. He had started. She had been here all of two hours and he had started, as if the last sixteen years hadn't even happened, and they were just brother and sister, sitting in the family home, with him picking on her yet again for her inability to behave properly.

"Oh, for God's sake, Chris. I've just gotten here. Give it a rest."

"Let's not, darling." Julia, who allegedly came out in hives at the merest hint of a family row, had stood, as if to leave the room.

"Why should I give it a rest? She's come back here, now that the old man's on his way out. Having made sure that her daughter's wheedled her way around Mother first. I think it's only fair that she hears a few home truths in return."

"What did you say?" Kate, primed as she was for her brother's crabbiness, could hardly believe what she was hearing.

"You heard. It's patently obvious what you've been doing, Katherine. And I'm telling you, I think it's despicable."

"You think I wanted to come back here? You think Sabine wants to be here? My God, I always knew you had a low opinion of me, but this takes the biscuit."

Her brother thrust his hands deep in his pockets, and turned mulishly away from her, toward the fire.

"Well, it's a bit convenient for you, isn't it? Not remotely interested in either of them for bloody years, and now that he's on his way out both you and your daughter are over here like carrion crows."

Kate stood. "How *dare* you," she said furiously. "How dare you suggest that I give a bloody fig for Mummy and Daddy's money. If you care to look past your own bloody paranoia, you'll remember that I've done pretty well without any of it up to now. Unlike some I could mention."

"That money was a *loan*."

"Yes. A loan that you still haven't paid back, what is it, eleven years later? Even though your own parents are shivering in an uncentrally heated house that looks like it's falling to bits. That's really bloody generous, that is."

"Oh, please don't," said Julia. "Please . . ." Turning from one to the other, and apparently concluding that no one was going to take any notice of her, she exited the room.

"And who do you think is paying for what they do have?" Christopher had come closer now, his greater height allowing him to loom over her as he shouted. "Who do you think is paying for the bloody nurse at four hundred pounds a week? Who do you think is paying for her to keep her old horses going, just so she can pretend that her life is what it always was? Who do you think puts money in their account every month and tells them it's from their investments, knowing full well they wouldn't bloody take it otherwise? Look around you, Katherine. Open your eyes. If you'd cared to come back more than once every ten years, you'd have seen our parents are completely bloody broke."

Kate stared at him.

"But then you never were particularly interested in anything that went on beyond your own nose, were you? Or should I say beyond your own lower half. I suppose you'll be looking up Alexander Fowler while you're here, now that you've gotten rid of the latest bloke, won't you? I'm sure he'll still be up for a quickie—only riding you ever really liked, if I remember."

Kate's arm ripped out and she slapped him hard on the side of his face.

The atmosphere around them seemed to suddenly disappear. She stood, breathing hard, shocked at her own action, staring at her hand as it stung with the violence of the impact. He stared back at her, one hand half raised to his cheek.

"So," he said, eventually. His voice was low and poisonous. "Does she know, yet? Does your daughter know her esteemed origins?" He paused, scanning her face for a reaction. "Has she met her father? Or perhaps you could arrange for her to sit for him, too. What a lovely family portrait that would be."

"Rot in hell," said Kate, and pushed past him, out of the door.

The summerhouse had never been the kind of summerhouse more generally conjured up by those delightful words. It had never looked summery, for a start; its windows had always been grimy and double-glazed with moss, rather than gleaming and radiant in sunshine; its interior was not full of cheerfully painted wrought-iron furniture, but old packing cases, dried-up pots of paint and varnish that had long since welded themselves shut, and creatures that scuttled behind unidentified cuts of wood. It had never held a summer party, or a buffet table, or provided the decorative focus of what stragglingly remained of Kilcarrion's formal gardens. But then that had never been the summerhouse's purpose, as far as Kate had been concerned. In her childhood, it had served as a den, somewhere to escape and dream of the rightful family who would, of course, soon be coming to claim her. In her teenage years, it had provided a safe place to practice smoking, and listen to music on her radio, and dream about the boys who never fancied her because she lived in the big house and never knew the right things to wear. Sometime later, when there had been a boy, it had been a place to meet secretly, away from the appalled eyes of her family.

Now, it was a place to unleash her true feelings about her visit.

"Bugger buggery buggering bugger bugger bugger it," she sobbed, smacking the wall in impotent fury, making the aged electric light shake and flicker. "Bugger them. Bugger them. Bugger buggering everybody. Bugger bloody Christopher. Bugger Justin. *Bugger. It.*"

She was sixteen again: unable to do right in the eyes of her family, helpless against their combined certainties, their shared worldview. Her professional self, her status as a mother, her self-esteem had all been swiftly and effectively stripped away, leaving her as powerless, faced with the wrath of her elder brother, as she had been three decades ago, when he would sit on her, pinning her arms down with his knees, and drop small insects on her face.

"I'm thirty-bloody-five years old," she said out loud, to the spiders, and the old cartons of weed killer. "How can they make me feel like this? How do they bloody do it? How do they make me feel like a child?" She paused, aware of how daft she sounded, and this made her more furious. "How come—how come I'm here two hours and I end up swearing my head off at a bloody wall?"

"Glad to be back, then?"

Kate spun around, blanching at the unheralded visitor. And then stood very still, her mouth hanging slightly open, like a half-hearted imbecile.

"T-Thom?" she said, haltingly.

"How are you doing?"

He took a step farther into the summer-house, so that his face was visible under the bald, electric light. He was clutching two fertilizer bags under one arm, and held an old crate in the other hand.

"I didn't mean to give you a fright," he said, his eyes not leaving her. "I was in the stores shed and saw the light. Thought I might have left it on."

His face had broadened. Back when she had lived here, it had always been narrow, gaunt almost. But then he had been in training for his jockey's license, and preoccupied with keeping his weight down. Now, his shoulders were wide, and under his thick jumper his body looked sturdy, solid. It was a man's body. But then when they had last met, he had really been a boy.

"You—you look well," she said.

"You look grand yourself." He smiled, a slow, amused smile. "You don't *sound* quite as sweet as you used to."

Kate flushed, her hand lifting unconsciously to her unflattering glasses. "Oh, God. I'm sorry. It's—well, you know what my family is like. They don't exactly bring out the best in me."

He nodded. He was still gazing at her. Kate felt the pink of her cheeks slowly spreading to her neck.

"God." she said. Then. "I—I really didn't expect to see you."

He just stood there.

"I didn't think you worked here anymore."

"I didn't. Came back a few years ago."

"Where were you?" She paused. "I mean, I know you went to England after I did. I just wasn't sure what you did."

"Went to Lambourn. Worked at a racing yard for a while. Moved to another one in Newmarket. Screwed up, and decided to come home."

"Did you become a jockey? I'm sorry, I

never read the racing papers, so I never knew."

"I did for a while. Not a great one, to be honest. Had an accident, so I ended up working in the yard."

It was then, as he slightly lifted his arm, that she saw his hand. She flinched, as she suddenly realized that its lack of animation had nothing to do with Thom's own stillness. He watched her eyes meet it, and looked down, the faintest hint of discomfort making him shift on his feet. Kate realized she had prompted this, and felt ashamed.

There was a long silence.

"What happened?"

He looked up at her, more comfortable with her directness.

"Got tangled up with a horse in a starting gate. By the time they got me out it wasn't worth saving." He lifted it, as if examining it himself. "It's all right. Doesn't bother me anymore. I get along okay."

Kate didn't know what to say. She felt suddenly overwhelmed by grief that Thom, Thom of all people, with his energy and easy grace, his joyous physical ability, should be crippled.

"I'm sorry," she said.

"Don't be." His voice had hardened. He evidently didn't want her sympathy.

They stood in silence for a few moments, Kate glancing down at her feet, Thom still gazing at her. When she finally looked back at him again, he looked embarrassed, as if caught doing something he shouldn't have been.

"I'd better be off," he said, eventually. "Got to finish the horses."

"Yes." She found she had removed her glasses, and was fiddling with them, in one hand.

"I'll see you around."

"Yes. I—I'll probably be here a few days at least."

"If the family don't drive you nuts, eh?"

She laughed, a short, humorless laugh.

He turned to leave, ducking slightly as he walked through the door frame. "Your daughter, Sabine," he said, turning suddenly to face her. "She's great. Really. You did a grand job."

Kate felt her face break into a wide smile, probably the first since she had arrived there.

"Thanks," she said. "Thanks a lot."

And then he was gone, a pale figure disappearing into the darkness.

Chapter Ten

It is never easy to return to the place where one grew up. Especially when one's mother is apparently uncomfortable with the mere fact that one had grown up. But then Joy, who expected little in life to be straightforward, had never anticipated a reunion between her and her mother to be either warm or easy.

For one thing, it had been six years since Joy had last been in Hong Kong; six years in which she had followed Edward around the world on his various postings, six years during which she had become, she was sure, if not a different person, then surely one whose confidence and expectations would have eclipsed those of the old Joy by far; six years during which her father had died, and her mother had steadily become more closed off and bitter about her life still remaining.

Joy had heard about her father's heart attack by telegram, while they had been staying in naval quarters in Portsmouth. She had grieved silently, from under a weight of guilt that she had not been there when he died, and a suspicion, that had she allowed herself, she might have wished her mother to have been the one to go first. "Oh, well, I suppose she's got what she wants," she had said, to Edward, so that he raised his eyebrows at her sharp tone. "She can go off and marry someone else now. Someone who meets requirements."

But far from being released by his death, Alice had made the late Graham Leonard the renewed focus of her life, becoming, if it were possible, even crosser with him than she had while he was alive. "It's too late for me now," she would write, in her increasingly scrawled dispatches, the unspoken lines of which suggested quietly that she wouldn't have been left in this mess had he had the decency to go earlier, before her waist had thickened, her skin had sagged, and gray had become the dominant color of her hair, rather than an apologetic hint of things to come. Before Duncan Alleyne, frightened off by her suddenly available state, turned his attention to the more youthful Penelope Standish, whose husband, while frequently absent, was very much alive. In those letters, she had also managed to suggest in a somewhat martyred tone that she both resented Joy's absence and chafed at any suggestion that Joy should come back to be with her. "You have your own life now," was a particularly recurrent phrase, when Joy reluctantly offered the spare room in wherever she was posted at the time. It fell off the page in Alice's sarcastic tones. "You do not want to be burdened with an old woman." (If Joy had used the words "old woman" five years previously, she mused, Alice's tongue would have whipped so sharply it could have torn paper.)

"Dear Mother," she would write blandly in reply. "As I have told you, Edward and I would be delighted to have you stay with us at any time." It was quite safe, she knew; Alice would never substitute her house in

Robinson Road, with its parquet floors and good views (her husband's death may have been untimely, but it had been well insured) for what she believed were the cramped and "immoral" conditions where naval couples lived so close together. But in every letter, Joy made sure she dropped in at least one reference to either infestation, bad behavior among the servants, or screaming children next door, just as a kind of insurance.

Because Joy did not want to return to Hong Kong. In her six years as a naval wife, she felt she had left the old Joy, with her lack of freedom, her awkwardnesses, and her unhappinesses behind, and instead of feeling the pressure to be like someone else, had increasingly enjoyed the freedom to just be. Her desperate urge to discover a world outside had been sated by their frequent moves around the globe, from Hong Kong to Tilbury, on to Singapore, briefly to Bermuda, and finally to Portsmouth; Edward once remarked that his was the only naval wife he knew who greeted the reappearance of the packing cases with an eager smile, rather than a resigned sigh. But Joy, unencumbered by children (they had agreed that they would probably rather wait) or a desire to settle down, had relished every new place she had been sent; whether the gray, salty skies of southern England, or the baking sands of the tropics. It was all somewhere new; it all helped widen her view, like a camera lens offering suddenly panoramic vision, and it all lessened her fears of being hemmed in, restricted, tied to a more formal, rigid life.

Most important, it had all meant being with Edward, who, while becoming a less God-like figure in her presence, had been, in his affection and attention, so much more than she had ever expected that it had taken her more than three years to stop uttering her daily silent prayer of thanks. She was happy; she had tested out these words on herself numerous times, as if saying them could provide some kind of superstitious barrier to their disappearing. She liked the feeling that they were a team, two people working in tandem, unlike her parents' or many of the other marriages she had watched while growing up, bent and bowed under the weights of disappointment, obligation, and vanished dreams. Joy had not had to relinquish her dreams; she had only just begun to allow herself to have them.

However, she had to learn certain accommodations: how to run a household (and here, Joy had found a certain unforeseen sympathy with her mother when faced with the problems of "difficult" staff, cranky boiler systems, and the relentless, mind-numbing question of what to provide at mealtimes). Having always been a rather solitary person, someone who was perhaps happiest in her own company—and thus well able to cope with his lengthy absences—she had also had to get used to the fact that Edward was a man who needed a lot of attention; so much so that in the first years of their marriage she would have to fight feelings of claustrophobia when, on his return, he would frequently follow her around from room to room, like a dog begging for scraps. She also had to learn to be more sociable. Edward's position required him to entertain a lot; his new colleagues, his business associates, his opposite numbers on visiting ships. And it was Joy's job to organize the dinner parties, devise the menu, instruct the help, and ensure that he always had enough uniforms (whites for the days, "bumfreezer" short jackets and mess dress for the evenings) to look as he should.

She didn't mind; parties were somehow different as Edward's wife, free of the endless introductions to potential partners, the simmering undercurrent of matchmakers' wishes ill-met. She rarely embarrassed him these days, even when she ran out of things to say; he always said he'd rather have her company than theirs anyway. Sometimes the other men, with slightly fixed smiles, told him off for being too attentive to his own wife. It wasn't really the done thing, apparently, to show that much interest.

So she and Edward had developed a code. A rub of the nose if someone was being particularly boring, a repeated smoothing of the hair to denote pomposity, a pulling of the left ear if one was desperate to be rescued. And Edward always rescued her; arriving at her side with a drink, a joke, ready to steer off the offending party. There was another code; one to suggest a certain impatience to be on their own. That always made Joy blush. Edward was very keen for them to be on their own.

But it would be different in Hong Kong. She was sure of it. She would become Awkward Joy again, badgered by her mother, renown as someone a little "difficult" in company, no great beauty. Good old Graham's daughter. (Wasn't it a shame? And him so young and all.) Lucky to have married at all. But an awful long time married with no children. (What would people think?)

They had arrived back in the colony on one of the wettest weeks on record, when the new, high-rise naval quarters on the Peak were permanently shrouded in gray mist, and the high humidity levels left Joy's hair springy and unmaneagable and meant that she had to change her clothes at least three times a day, just to stay presentable. But the block was newly built, and Joy, overseeing the Chinese help as they brought her furniture into the spacious, third-floor apartment, had been thrilled to note that not only did it have a huge, light living room overlooking Aberdeen harbor, and a separate dining room, and no less than three bedrooms, but that it held one of the ultramodern dehumidifiers, which, although noisy, helped combat the ever-present threat of mold that existed through the rainy season.

Because fighting mold was a neverceasing battle among the women of the colony, and they set about it with the same joyless determination with which their husbands had faced the Japanese. It wasn't out of choice; if one didn't install little electric heaters in one's wardrobe, or relentlessly wipe one's leather shoes, the closed, warm, dank confines of the apartments would ensure that two weeks later one's best alligator shoes were likely to have become green felt, and one's best clothes been newly lined with little filigree patterns of green. One's box of cigarettes (even if you didn't smoke, Joy had discovered, it was important to have a box to offer) had to be especially well looked after—there was nothing more embarrassing than watching a guest try to light a damp cigarette. And all the while, the smell hung in the air, musty and unpleasant, warning of invisible spores all around. Joy had set the dehumidifier going even before her belongings were all in, and she and the three Chinese boys stood, and nodded in approval, as with a low rumble, the machine visibly began to draw the moisture from the air.

They had been lucky to get the apartment, one of the other wives told her, as she advised Joy on the best way to lower a basket on a rope when the postman whistled, in order to pick up one's post (it was such a bore to walk all the way down); since the communists took over in China, there had been a huge influx of Chinese escaping into Hong Kong, causing the most frightful accommodation problems. And it all looked somehow more chaotic, and crowded, with the shanty towns springing up on the hills, and every inch of the harbor filled with boat people on their little sampans. Plus, the colony had become an even more important commercial center, and there were all sorts moving in, grabbing the best houses, and pushing up rents.

There were some welcome developments: the Dairy Farm food shops meant that while it was easiest to get one's amahs to do the shopping for fresh food, it was now possible to buy special treats for entertaining, like oysters, which were flown up from Sydney. There were more shops, selling a greater variety of things; it was easier to get hold of magazines, and books; and the influx of young nurses and teachers meant that it was an awful lot easier to make up the numbers at dinner. They were rather jolly, most of the nurses, Joy discovered, toughened, but humorous about their experiences with the troops, and tended to be terribly popular with the young officers (more so than the teachers, who tended to be less lively and, more important, significant older). They were also often bold enough to accompany the men to the burgeoning neon nightlife of Wan Chai, where clubs like Smokey Joe's and the Pink Pussycat were springing up, capitalizing on the desperate need among both visiting troops and lonely traders for after-hours entertainment. Joy was rather curious about these clubs, and would have quite liked to have discovered what it was that was quite so scandalous about some of them, but Edward didn't seem interested, and it wasn't the kind of place where a reputable woman went alone, especially after dark.

Joy's mother, meanwhile, complained bitterly about the never-ending racket from the construction work, and the fact that all the good views were disappearing, obscured by the upstart blocks from farther down toward the waterfront. She could no longer see the sea from her west-facing windows, she remarked, due to the office blocks springing up around Central and Des Voeux Road, while getting on a tram had become a most unpleasant business. Which meant she was quite impressed by Joy's car, a white Morris

10, which Joy would drive cautiously down to the harbor every day, in order to meet her husband from work.

"I'll drive you to Stanley Market, if you like," said Joy, observing her mother's astonished face as she backed the car out of the garage. Alice found her daughter's independence astonishing. *Unusual*, was the word she used to Joy. "A bit mannish for my tastes," was what she said to Stella's mother. She could afford to admit this to Mrs. Hanniford, as everyone knew that Stella had walked out on her pilot husband, and her family was therefore in no position to judge.

"I wouldn't want to put you to any trouble," said Alice, clutching her clasp bag tightly to her stomach with both hands, as if holding in her innards.

"Look, Mummy, it's really no trouble. I need to get a new table linen and you can help me choose it. Come on, it'll be a nice day out."

Alice paused. "I'll think about it."

While Joy's predictions of social awkwardness, and of her own regression to a teenage state, had failed to materialize with their return, those regarding her difficulties with her mother had proven wearingly accurate. While she suffered little maternal inter-ference (if anything, she found she had to push Alice into accompanying her any-where), there was still this purse-mouthed sense of disapproval, this crushing air of dis-appointment, but now potently teamed with a new air of martyrdom, and a sharp tinge of jealousy. If, when Edward arrived home from the dockyard, he attempted anything more affectionate than the most distant peck on the cheek, Alice's head would swivel, as if on castors, to pointedly look away from them both. If he invited Alice to supper (he was amazingly patient, thought Joy, gratefully, but that was because both knew Alice could have little impact on his life), she would reluctantly accept, but only after repeated claims that she "didn't want to intrude." If he suggested he and Joy go riding in the New Territories, just the two of them, Alice's eye-brows would shoot up like he had suggested they indulge in some public sexual deviance before the hors d'oeuvres.

Joy tried to understand, but, as she told Edward privately, it was rather galling to have to play down one's personal happiness in order to keep one's mother in a good humor.

"I know," she said to Alice shortly after her unaccompanied visit to Stanley, as her mother fingered the newly purchased table linen with a barely concealed look of disapproval. "Perhaps you could help me find an amah."

"What kind of amah?"

"I don't know," said Joy, who was frankly exhausted. "Just someone to help out a bit. Do some washing. I hadn't realized how many shirts Edward would get through in the humidity."

"But who does your cooking?"

"I have been," said Joy, almost apologetically. "When we're not entertaining, that is. I quite like cooking for him."

"You'll need a wash-amah and a number-one amah for cooking," said Alice, firmly, her confidence boosted by Joy's apparent deficiencies on the domestic front. "And then number-one amah can look after the children when they come."

She didn't seem to notice Joy's sharp glance in her direction.

"Now," she said, leafing through her little leather-bound address book, "there's a wash-amah called Mary in Causeway Bay who is looking for work. I took the liberty of taking her number last week, because Bei-Lin was being absolutely impossible, and I thought she should know that she's not irreplaceable, no matter how long she's been with me. She's not been the same since your father passed on, you know. Definitely more sullen, she is. And I'm sure Judy Beresford said she knew of a number-one amah whose family was heading overseas. I'll ring her and find out if she's still available. She'll be very good for you." She paused, glancing at Joy, her brows briefly lowering suspiciously. "That's if I'm not interfering," she said.

Good news about the shirts," said Edward, as they ate supper. "You have many strengths, my darling, but laundry is not one of them. I was beginning to think I was going to have to do them myself. But what on earth do we need another hired help for? It's not as if we have children."

Joy looked up from her food.

Edward met her gaze. Then stared, for a long time, at the table in front of her.

"How come you're not drinking?" he said.

Kate stood just behind the door, watching from the hallway as her mother and daughter sat, heads almost touching, discussing one of the sepia-tinted photographs in Joy's calloused hands. Sabine, bent over, was exclaiming that the old white car was "*so* cool," while Joy laughed about how fearful she was of driving it on Hong Kong's already crowded roads. "I had only just learned to drive," she was saying. "Your grandfather taught me, as the instructors were so expensive, but he did have to grit his teeth rather. And we always had to stop afterward for a brandy dry."

She had come up to try to find Sabine, who seemed to be permanently closeted with either one of her grandparents, reading to her grandfather, riding her horse, or bombarding her grandmother with questions about life "in the olden days," as she put it, even now that the threat of Christopher and Julia had receded as far as Dublin. It meant that for the past few days of her stay, Kate, at something of a loose end, had found herself trailing sadly around the house and its grounds, asking somewhat pathetically if anyone had seen her daughter, grateful for any time Sabine chose to spend in her company.

But then Sabine seemed to be choosing

to spend as little time as possible in her company. And Kate told herself she did not feel so much rejected (Sabine hadn't wanted to spend much time with her since she turned thirteen) as completely bemused by this apparent passion for all things Irish. She seemed to have embraced her grandparents with an unself-conscious affection, discovered an unlikely love for the little gray horse in the back field, and, most surprising of all, relinquished her urban need to be "cool" in all circumstances. She didn't even care that her trainers were covered in mud. But she also failed to disguise her evident irritation at Kate's attempts to help, whether it be an offer to carry up her father's lunch tray, or to give Sabine a break by reading to him. "She's quite proprietorial about him these days," said Mrs. H, with some affection. "You'd never have guessed it from the way she was when she came."

Mrs. H had been the one voice of sanity in the house, providing the warmest of the various welcomes (they were welcomes, Kate thought bitterly, only in the loosest sense of the word), and reassuring her that her daughter's evident happiness at Kilcarrion had been a relatively recent development.

But then Kate saw the way Sabine spoke to Mrs. H, and that made her feel excluded and inadequate, too.

There had been one brief thawing in their relationship, when Kate had visited Sabine's room one night and volunteered the information that she and Justin were no longer together. She thought she had a responsibility to let Sabine know, and had told her gently, fearful of the possibility that this would be interpreted as further upheaval in her daughter's life (and also of making herself cry if she allowed herself to describe it as anything less than briefly and clinically). But Sabine had merely gone very still, as if listening for something that she had long expected to hear, and then satisfied, told her that it was "hardly a surprise."

"So you don't mind?"

"Why should I mind? He was a prat."

Kate tried not to flinch at Sabine's blunt assessment. She had forgotten her daughter's delicate way with words.

"So you think I've done the right thing?"

"Why should I care what you've done? It's your life." Sabine had turned away, as if keen to read her book, signifying the conversation was closed. She paused. "I was half expecting it anyway," she muttered, staring unseeing at the page in front of her.

Kate sat, her eyes fixed on her daughter's face.

"Well, you've never stuck at anything, have you? None of your relationships lasts. Not like Grandmother and Grandfather."

The words were quietly said, but held the powerful kickback of a firearm, and Kate, wounded, had backed out of the room. Since then Sabine had been slightly warmer to her, as if aware that she had perhaps been too harsh, but she still seemed more comfortable around almost anyone else at the house.

And now, this morning, she hadn't been able to find her at all, and the study had provided the answer.

Yet seeing them sit there, close, relaxed, more comfortable with each other's company than either of them ever was in hers, Kate felt a huge lump rise to her throat, and a childish sensation of being left out. She turned, and closing the door softly behind her, made her way back down the stairs.

Had Sabine been aware of the tears that her mother shed in her absence, she might have felt some measure of guilt, or a desire to comfort her—she was not, after all, a malicious girl. But she was sixteen, and as such, had more important things to think about— like whether or not to go out with Bobby McAndrew. He had rung two days after the hunt (keen, but not toe-clenchingly keen, she had noted approvingly) and suggested they go out—to the pub, or the pictures, or whatever she fancied. Joy, who had initially answered the telephone, had seemed too distracted to take very much notice, merely handing the receiver over to the paling Sabine with the remark that "one of her little friends" was calling. Bobby, who had overheard, had laughed, stating: "It's your little friend Bobby here," and that had sort of broken the ice, so that Sabine didn't feel quite so weirded out by the idea of going on a date with an Irish boy.

But now, with Saturday a matter of days away, she found herself wavering in her determination to go. It would be easy to get out of the house (no one seemed to take too much notice of what she was doing at the moment) but she wasn't entirely sure that she wanted to spend an evening with Bobby after all. She couldn't remember if she fancied him, for a start; his face had sort of become blurry and indistinct, and all she really remembered was that he didn't have dark brown hair or olive skin, which was, she had recently decided with the aid of one of Mrs. H's women's magazines, "her type." And he would probably want to jump her bones at the end of the evening, especially if they went to the cinema, and even if she liked him, she hadn't worked out whether that would be a bit like being unfaithful. Because even if Thom had not yet shown any proper signs of wanting to jump her bones, she didn't want to close off that particular avenue just yet. He might be being shy.

Annie was no help, either. True, she had listened to Sabine's predicament, but it was in that Annie-esque way that seemed to involve looking out of the window, rubbing lengthily at her hands, flicking on the television once or twice, and then walking around the room aimlessly, as if looking for something she had lost (if she could only remember what it was).

"You should go," she said, vaguely. "It's good for you to make friends."

"I don't need any more friends."

"Well, then it will be good for you to get out

of that house. That's an awful lot of time you've been spending with your grandfather."

"But what if he wants to be more than friends?"

"Well, then you've got yourself a boy-friend."

"But what if I don't know if I want a boyfriend?"

Annie had looked rather exhausted at this point, and told Sabine She Really Didn't Know, and She Was Terribly Tired, and then, eventually, Would She Mind Coming Back Later, Because She Thought She Might Take A Little Nap. Which, frustratingly, was roughly what most conversations with Annie seemed to consist of these days. Sabine would have liked to ask her mother, and maybe even ask her if she would buy her something new to wear. But her mother would either flap embarrassingly about Sabine's "date" as she would call it, and insist on driving her there so that she could say hello, or get all hurt and silent about the fact that she was making a life for herself in Ireland. She knew it bugged her mother, the fact that she liked it here. But that's not my fault, she wanted to yell at her, when she saw her slinking around the house with a face like a wet weekend, as Mrs. H would have put it. *You were the one who turned our lives upside down. You made me come here.*

She had been quite pleased about the Justin thing, even if she hadn't let Kate know. But it was so obvious that he had dumped her mother, and not the other way around, and somehow that made it even harder for Sabine to have any respect for her.

She told her grandfather in the end. It was quite easy to talk to him these days, now that he didn't yell at her to speak up all the time, or get cross about mealtimes. He just liked her to sit with him and chat away; she could tell because his face would sort of relax, like melting butter, and occasionally, when she held his hand (it was actually sort of papery and soft—not creepy, like she had expected), he would squeeze it ever so faintly when she finished talking, like he understood.

"You'd probably like him," she told him, her socked feet up on the bed beside him. "Because he's into hunting, and he's quite a good rider. He doesn't hold the mane or anything when he goes over jumps. You might even know his family. They're called McAndrew."

(Here she was sure she felt a soft increase in pressure.)

"But it's not a serious date or anything. I mean I'm not going to marry him and have his babies. It's just good for me to make some friends."

A thin, clear trail of saliva had somehow leaked out of the side of his mouth, like a tiny river making its way down a mountainside. Sabine took the handkerchief from the bedside table and wiped at it gently.

"I once did that on a tube," she said, grinning. "I had been out really, really late the night before, although Mum doesn't know this, because I was staying at my mate's house, and I just fell asleep on this man next to me. And when I woke up there was this little damp patch on his shoulder where I'd dribbled on him. I wanted to *die*."

She paused, and gazed at him.

"Well, I was really embarrassed, anyway. I suppose it's not a bad trick though. If I decide I don't like this Bobby McAndrew, then I can always just dribble on him in the cinema. That should see him off."

Sabine jumped off the bed, conscious that it was nearly time for the nurse to return from her lunch break.

"I'll let you know what happens," she said, cheerily, planting a kiss on his forehead. "Stay cool."

Behind her, buried under the layers of quilt, and surrounded by his bleeping sentries, Sabine's grandfather closed his mouth.

Kate had written four options on pieces of paper: GO BACK TO LONDON; GO BACK TO LONDON IN A WEEK; GO AND STAY AT A HOTEL AND BUGGER THE COST; AND DON'T LET THE BASTARDS GRIND YOU DOWN. According to Maggie, you were meant to fold them up, throw them in the air and grab one, and fate would decide which instruction you should follow (or perhaps it was Freud, Kate could never remember). As a method for action, it never failed to provide the wrong answer. While every cell in Kate's body urged her toward the ferry back to Fishguard, the paper method suggested number three, which, sensibly, she couldn't really afford and knew that it was the least likely to provide any kind of solution anyway.

But this is what a week in the parental home had reduced her to, she mused, as she strode furiously through the mud-locked fields that ran alongside the river. Schoolgirl tricks and superstitions. A sulky resentment of her parents. An inability to speak without saying the wrong thing. An emotional age of fifteen.

This was not how she had planned her return; she had wanted to sweep back in, serene and gracious, a successful writer, perhaps with a couple of books to her name; a handsome, intelligent partner, a happy, loving daughter; possessor of a natural self-confidence that would have forced them all to acknowledge that she had been right—that there had been other ways to live than theirs. That's why they're being nice to you, she had wanted to shout at her daughter. Because you're doing it all their way. It's easy for them to be nice to you when you're doing what they want. It's when you do what *you* want that it all gets complicated.

But of course life didn't work like that. She had returned as—if not the family black sheep, then something definitely downtrodden, apparently stupid, and ready for the chop. She was just the misfit again—the one who didn't ride, who looked eccentric, who couldn't hold down a proper job, a decent relationship—a view so pervasive that now even her own daughter was viewing her through those same unrosy spectacles. And because she didn't have that well-paying job, or that decent man, she couldn't even take herself off for a drive, or disappear to the pub, or perhaps to watch a film, like any normal adult might, but was left impotently tramping through wet fields as her only real option to escape the horrors of the family home.

Ballymalnaugh didn't even have particularly attractive countryside. Just row upon row of featureless, hillocky fields, their supposedly emerald green turned brown under the ceaseless gray skies, lined by scrubby hedges and punctuated by bleak, windswept crossroads. It didn't have the undulating charm of the Sussex Downs, or the wild, untamed beauty of the Peaks. What it did have, she thought sourly, was wet sheep. And skeletal, dripping trees. And mud.

Of course, it had begun to rain. Because her whole life was part of some big cosmic joke. And of course, being a stupid townie, she hadn't thought to bring either a waterproof or an umbrella. As water began to seep determinedly down the back of her collar, Kate glanced up at the glowering sky, darkening as the evening began to close in, and thought longingly of option number one. Just go, she thought. Go back to London. Daddy seems stable enough; he could go on for months yet. She couldn't really be expected to put her whole life on hold until something happened, could she? But then there was the matter of Sabine; Kate had the unsettling suspicion that if she were to disappear to London, any chances of bringing Sabine home would disappear with her.

As if echoing her mood, the rain suddenly came down harder, turning the gently permeating misty shower into near-solid, glassy sheets. Kate, pushing forward toward a copse, realized she could hardly see, the gray, wintry scenery around her becoming blurred and indistinct. Why don't they make windscreen wipers for glasses? she thought crossly, shivering in her near-sodden wool jacket, as she made for the slight cover of the trees.

It was then that she heard the sound: a muffled, thumping sound, irregular in beat, punctuated by a distant jingling. Squinting, Kate glanced through the trees in the direction of the noise. She could see almost nothing through her blurred lenses, but gradually, through the rain, was able to make out the shape of a horse, coming toward her through the woodland. Huge and gray, snorting fearfully, and surrounded by the shifting steam of its own body, it looked like that of a medieval knight, returning from some awful battle. Kate shrank back into the trees.

But the beast had apparently seen her. It slowed, and walked closer, its head lowering to confirm what it, in turn, thought it had seen. It was then that she saw him. Astride the horse, half hidden under a huge brown waterproof and a wide-brimmed hat, was Thom. He glanced over twice, as if making sure it was her, and then pulled up.

"You all right?"

Kate had to fight the paralysis that his sudden appearance had provoked. Her voice, when it came, was glib and urban, determinedly distanced from her true feelings.

"Nothing that an umbrella, a complete change of clothes, and a new life wouldn't cure." She pushed her hair back from her face. "I'm just waiting for the rain to die down, so I can head back."

"You look soaked." He paused. "Do you want to get up? This boy's good as gold. It'll get you back an awful lot faster."

Kate eyed the huge gray horse, its huge,

plate-sized hooves moving restlessly too close to her feet, its massive head shaking up and down with impatience to get out of the rain. Its eyes swiveled, flashing hints of white, while its breath came in shots of hot steam, like a dragon's.

"Thanks. I think I'll wait."

Thom sat, very still. She could feel his eyes upon her, and felt suddenly disadvantaged, being so far beneath him. She rubbed at her glasses.

"I'm fine, honest."

"You can't hang around here. This rain's not going, it's settling in. You could be waiting all night."

"Thom, please . . ."

But he had leaned forward, and swinging his leg over the back of the saddle, dismounted. Holding the horse's reins in one hand, he walked over to her, his boots squelching in the wet earth, and pulled the brown hat from his head.

"Here," he said. "Take this." He rubbed his hand through his short, dark hair. Where his hand was wet, the hair stood up in short, sleek spikes.

"And this." He had removed his waterproof, and thrust it at her. She took it wordlessly, gazing at him in his thick jumper, already dusted with the first drops to force their way through the sparse canopy above. It was impossible to tell about his arm, she noted, unless you looked at that hand.

"Go on, put it on," he said. "I'll walk you back."

"But you'll get soaked."

"But not for long. If you stay here in that thing," he pointed dismissively at her jacket, warm enough for the worst that London could throw at it, "you'll catch pneumonia. C'mon, it's sheltering rain."

"I feel . . . I feel . . ." she hesitated.

"Cold. Wet. Go on. The quicker you do, the quicker we can get back."

She put the coat on. Cut to cover the saddle as well as its passenger, it reached down almost to her ankles and swished around her shins. He grinned as she placed the hat on her head.

"Why don't you trot back," she said, pleadingly. "Then you won't get so wet. I'm fine with this lot on."

"I'll walk you back," he said, firmly, and she decided not to argue any more.

They followed the stream, their silence punctuated by the slop-clop of the horse's hooves, and the occasional metallic jangle of the bit against its teeth. Beyond the hedge, the mist had come down so that where one could usually make out Kilcarrion's distant chimneys, only a silent gray nothingness remained. Kate, despite herself, found she had begun to shiver.

"Is there a reason why you're out on your own?" They were having to speak unnaturally loudly, shout almost, to be heard above the thrumming of the rain.

"As opposed to being on a horse?"

He laughed. "You know what I mean." Kate stared at her boots. Her footfall trudged sludgily, out of rhythm.

"It's not very easy," she said eventually. "Coming back, I mean."

"That's for sure."

"So, why did you?" She stopped, and looked at him. "Why did you come back?"

Thom, who had also been watching his feet, glanced up at her, and then looked away.

"Ahh. Too long a story."

"We've got at least half an hour. Unless a taxi comes past."

"True. But you first."

"Well, I came back because my father is

dying. Or at least I think he's dying. But you probably know more about that than I do." She paused, and stared at him, but he shrugged slightly, as if in contradiction. His jumper, she noted guiltily, had started to hang lower from the extra weight of the water.

"And I wanted to see Sabine. But something seems to have happened while she's been here, and she . . ." Kate lifted her head, trying to keep the choke from her voice. "She doesn't seem to want to come back."

There. She had acknowledged it. She glanced at him, waiting for some response, some suggestion of judgment on his part, but he just kept walking, staring down at his feet.

Kate sighed.

"I can't say I blame her. There's been . . . well, there's been a lot of upheaval at home. I left my partner for someone else, and then he turned out . . . well, he turned out to be not what I'd expected. And so in the end I ended up on my own." She tripped slightly, and glanced up at him, trying to smile. "Probably no great surprise to you."

But Thom kept walking. She paused again, fighting the swelling urge to cry.

"Still, I thought she'd be pleased. I thought she'd want to come back, and just be the two of us. Because she's never really liked anyone I've been with. And I thought she'd hate it here, with all the rules and stupid deadlines for meals, and hunting, hunting, hunting. I always wanted her to grow up free of all that, you see. None of that rigidity. None of that formality. None of that constant sense of things being either right or wrong. I just wanted her to be happy, to be my friend. But . . ." Here she pulled up her spectacles and rubbed at her eyes, grateful that under the broad brim of the hat, it would probably just look like she was struggling with the rain. "She seems to have liked it. In fact, she seems to prefer it to living with me. So, the reason I'm out here in the rain is, frankly, that I feel a bit of a spare part. I don't know what to do with myself. And I don't think anyone here really knows what to do with me."

She let out a long shuddering breath, glancing over at Thom. "Bit of a mess, really," she said, apologetically.

Thom, one arm now thrown over the low-hung neck of his horse, didn't look at her. He appeared to be deep in thought, oblivious to the rivulets of water running from his hair down the lines of his jaw and dripping onto his collar.

They walked on in silence until they reached a five-barred gate, which, solicitously, he opened, holding his horse back and away from her until she'd gone through.

"Stupid, really," she said, feeling a desperate need to fill the silence. She didn't think the countryside could be this quiet. "There's me, thirty-five years old, and still not able to sort my life out. You'd think I would have worked it out by now. My brother has. Most of my friends have. Sometimes I think I'm the only person who has not been given the set of rules . . . you know, the ones that show you how to grow up."

Her voice, she realized, had begun to rise. She had begun to babble.

"Are you not going to say anything?" she said, once he'd shut the gate behind them.

He looked at her. His eyes, outlined by black, wet lashes, were surprisingly blue. Or perhaps it was just that everything around them seemed so gray.

"What do you want me to say?" he said. It sounded, peculiarly, like a genuine question.

*　*　*

A quarter of a mile away, in a room only slightly less damp, Sabine and Joy were going through some of the album photographs. It had been at Joy's suggestion, which had surprised Sabine, but then lots of things about Joy's behavior surprised her these days: the fact that she had accepted Sabine's plans to go out with a boy without a murmur; the fact that she had suddenly started letting the dogs, to their apparent relish, sleep nights on her bed; the fact that she seemed to want to do almost anything rather than sit in the same room as her husband.

Whom she adored.

Sabine stared at the formal photograph of the couple on their sixth wedding anniversary. She was seated on a stool, dressed in a dark, button-down dress with a wide, striped collar and full skirt, and her smile suggested some repressed sense of mirth. He, again in whites, stood behind her, one hand on her shoulder, the other clasping hers with a kind of loose affection. He was looking down at the top of her head, and also appeared to be trying not to laugh.

"He was the most awful photographer," said Joy, fondly, wiping nonexistent dust from the page. "He was a lovely Chinese fellow, but with the most terrible English expressions that the troops had evidently told him meant something quite different. He thought he was telling you to sit closer together, but he'd say some awful piece of slang, like . . ." Joy paused, and glanced at Sabine. "Anyway, your grandfather and I had terrible trouble keeping a straight face. If I remember rightly, we absolutely howled afterward."

Sabine stared at the picture, reanimating it in her imagination into the two laughing lovers, conspiring in their mirth, erupting in some joint emotion as they emerged, blinking into the sunlight. It was as if they had some invisible shield around them, as if their happiness left no room for anyone else to get in. I want a man to look at me like that, Sabine thought. I want to feel that loved.

"Did you and Grandfather never argue?"

Joy paused, folding the tissue paper back over the page.

"Of course we did. Well, not argue as such, more disagreements."

She looked up, and out of the window.

"I think it was a bit easier for our generation, Sabine. We knew what our roles were. There wasn't all this fussing and fighting over who did what that you seem to get today."

"Plus, you had servants. No moaning over who did the washing up."

"No. That did help."

"But he must have upset you sometimes. You must have hated each other's guts sometimes. No one's perfect."

"I never hated his guts, as you so charmingly put it."

"But you must have rowed. Everyone rows." Please don't let it just be my mother, she said, silently.

Joy compressed her mouth, as if considering her words carefully. "There was a day, one day, in which your grandfather upset me very much."

Sabine waited for an explanation of this dreadful deed, but none appeared to be forthcoming.

Joy drew breath, and continued. "I was very, very unhappy afterward, and I thought: Why on earth should I stay? Why should I stick this out? It's too difficult. And then this ridiculous phrase came to me . . . from the coronation ceremony. You know we were rather obsessed by the coronation when we were your age. And as I understood it at the time, it was about the need to stick with something, in order to get your reward. It was about duty. And honor. And I thought of how excited everyone had been at this young woman giving up her life, and her life with her dashing new husband, in order to fulfill her duty—to rule over her "temporal kingdom," as they put it. And I realized it wasn't just about oneself, about one's own happiness. It was about not letting everyone else down, about keeping other people's dreams alive."

She paused, gazing out of the window, into the distance, held briefly captive by her own memories.

"So I stuck with it. And all those people who would have been disappointed if I hadn't . . . well, I think they were happier as a result."

But what about *you*? Sabine wanted to say. But her grandmother suddenly became rather brusque. "Good gracious, look at that rain," she said. "I had no idea. Come on, we've got to get those horses out of the bottom field. You can help me before you go out."

JOJO MOYES

Chapter Eleven

Thomas Keneally had left Ireland aged nineteen, without money or job prospects, bound for Lambourn, in England, where, he was assured by his fellow jockeys, a man with his light hands and, more important, bollocks of steel, would find work as a jump jockey. He left behind him a good job, at least two offers of work from reputable Irish trainers, and his distraught parents, who while acknowledging that teenage sons grew up and moved away, had always assumed it would be his elder brother, Kieron, who went first. Thom's father had hoped it would be; Kieron had crashed his car twice now, and never, unlike

Thom, gave his mother a portion of his wages toward housekeeping. Both parents declined to ask their younger son why he was leaving, but had been discreetly informed by his aunt, Ellen, who worked at the big house, that it "might have something to do with the daughter." For this reason, Thom's mother, until she died almost nine years later, bore a weighty, if silent, grudge against Kate Ballantyne, despite the fact that Thom had never so much as mentioned her, she had met her all of twice, and Kate herself had left Ballymalnaugh under a cloud some months before Thom's departure. There was the baby, of course, but Thom, unusually, had nearly bitten her head off when she had asked whether it was anything to do with him. He wasn't the kind of lad you pushed for answers, even then.

He had, as predicted, found work fairly easily, in the forty-strong yard of a well-known woman trainer, who managed to combine a twinkling ability to flirt with even her animals, with the stamina (and build) of a cart horse, and a temper that could sear third-degree burns on raw skin. She liked Thom; he was straightforward, good with the horses, and, most of all, was not afraid of her. There was some resentful gossip among the existing lads that she liked him for better reasons than that, but Thom was so fiercely ambitious, and so hardworking, that it was hard for anyone who spent any time with either rider or trainer to take them seriously.

He was not, as the racing crowd put it, one of the boys. He neither disappeared with his colleagues to the local pub on a Friday night to dissolve his meager wages in beer nor brought local girls back for raucous after-hours drinks to the side-by-side cramped and badly heated mobile homes that passed for their accommodations, nor sat with mugs of artificially sweetened black coffee after morning stables, complaining about the poor pay and backbreaking hours that are the trainee jockey's lot. He worked, studied form books, rode out at every opportunity, and sent what little money he had leftover back to his parents. It was, even he had to admit afterward, pretty nauseating behavior.

Which was why, when, four years later, a bad-tempered four-year-old by the name of Never on Sunday panicked in the stalls, and went over, crushing his arm so badly that it was left hanging by two tendons and a shattered bone, the only person who really grieved for him was the lady trainer (she was also grieving for herself; she hadn't had anyone work as hard as he had the whole time she'd been in business) and the bookies, who had long noted Thom's uncanny yet gratifyingly predictable ability to bring a horse home in second place. The other lads, while sympathetic (it could have been one of them, after all) harbored a silent sense of schadenfreude, and told one another reassuringly in hushed tones that being "teacher's pet" evidently got you nowhere.

Thom, meanwhile, spent a large part of the following year in hospital, first fighting off an infection that had resulted from the amputation, and, later, having his first false limb fitted. He did not, it is fair to say, adjust well to his new handicap at first, despite the efforts of the lady trainer, who, showing an unlikely loss of her customary hardheadedness (one that led even Thom to question whether he had been wrong in his assessment of her feelings toward him), told him he could have a job for life working in her yard.

That offer became slightly less fervent after Thom started drinking. It was withdrawn completely after, following twelve pints of Australian lager and a brief, messy interlude with a barmaid who claimed she could tell certain things about him from his shoe size, that he drove the lady trainer's Range Rover into a ditch in the early hours of the morning, writing it off in the process. He then walked home, ignoring the wound to his head, and the fact that the vehicle's alarm was heralding a new dawn for half of Berkshire, and was still asleep on his blood-sodden sheets when the lady trainer broke into his mobile home and asked him (except she didn't exactly ask) to pack his bags.

He worked at a number of yards after that, less reputable yards that cared less about his increasing reputation for drinking and womanizing, and thought they could capital-ize on his earlier shrinking reputation for hard work and effectiveness with horses. He usually managed to disappoint them with-in six months; he was always good with horses, but difficult with the other lads, mer-curial in temper, and, worst of all, frequently rude to owners. The last lad to crack a joke about his false arm found himself hanging upside down from a bridle-cleaning hook with a hoof pick parked somewhere that swiftly became the stuff of local legend.

This downward spiral culminated in his last posting, working for a trainer also from Ireland, whose methods and company had raised eyebrows in the kind of horse racing circles that Thom had once been used to. Now, handicapped more by his reputation than by his arm, and determined to ignore his parents' requests to come home, he found himself accepting J. C. Kermode's offer of a position with what passed these days for alacrity.

J. C. was a short, wiry former jockey with a brain as sharp as the metal teeth of a curry comb, and a patter as smooth as hoof oil. It did not take long for Thom to realize that these two gifts, essential in any trainer, could be less admirable when joined by an ability to bend the truth like Uri Geller with an old spoon.

J. C.'s greatest gift was not training horses (in fact, his record was dismal), but the ability to persuade gullible new owners not only to park their horses with him, but also to buy more, and then to ignore the ever-mounting yard bills that he managed to ratchet up as part of their "special training routine." The climactic example of these were Dean and Dolores, a socially climbing couple of divorcées from Solihull, who J. C. sat next to on a plane from Dublin, and by the time the plane had landed, had persuaded that not only would they have "the best laugh" accompanying him racing at Uttoxeter, but that also, if they liked it, he had just the filly for them. Dean, the oversized and unlovely managing director of a kitchen utensil company, had rarely had anyone work so hard to convince him of his wonderful company. His new wife, Dolores, was still in shock from her divorce-related expulsion from Solihull's social crème de la crème, as she put it, and was deeply taken with J. C.'s flirtatious manner and vocal admiration of Dean's business acumen. Before the air hostesses had asked them to fasten their seat belts for landing, the pair had already pictured themselves in the winners' enclosure at Ascot (in Dolores's case, having smiled a glamorous smile to the television cameras, and hence to all those Solihull bitches who stuck by her ex-husband), and J. C. was on his way to the sale of a particularly problematic three-year-old called Charlie's Darling, with a ewe neck and a vicious and unpredictable buck.

If Dean and Dolores were J. C.'s "cash cow," as he frequently described them to

Thom, they were also to be his downfall. Although initially seduced by the racing scene, and by the idea of themselves as owners (a view aided by Charlie's Darling's completely unforeseen win in the three-thirty seller at Doncaster and J. C.'s tendency to bring Thom along; Dolores liked Thom). Dean and Dolores were left with something more than indigestion after their "fun days out" at the track when gradually the huge bills accumulated from their string of four horses. He was sure, he confided to a disbelieving Dolores, that J. C. was "up to something." Dolores, whose racing day wardrobe now accurately reflected in exact hues her "jockeys' colors," told him he was being ridiculous. But when Thom bored of flirting with her (it made him feel like an idiot, he mulishly told an exasperated J. C.), she, too, began to question the beneficence of their great new friend J. C.

Then J. C.'s old friend from Ireland, Kenny Hanlon, appeared. He had gotten to hear about his old mate's financial good luck with these gullible British owners, and decided he'd quite like a slice of that particular pie. Best known for his rather controversial fruit-machine rental firm (it was said that on nearly all his machines one of his plums was missing), he began turning up at race meetings; with a jovial greeting to J. C., he would slide into the seat so recently vacated by Thom and shower compliments on the increasingly insecure Dolores, ignoring J. C.'s silent fury on the other side of the table (for a man with two cauliflower ears, it was said, he had an astonishingly winning way with the fair sex). It was only a matter of weeks before he was dropping Iago-like hints into her own, multiply pierced ear: Was she entirely sure that J. C. wasn't adding a little something to the bill? He was renowned for it, she should know. Was she sure he was getting her the best horses, and not just the old nags? They hadn't had many winners lately, after all. Might she be interested in moving the horses somewhere else? He knew just the place—and he could guarantee that Dean's feed and vets' bills would drop by at least a third. And did she know quite how delicious she looked in that shade of mauve?

Thom and J. C. woke one morning to discover a horse box in the process of removing the four horses from their stables, to go to another yard in Newmarket. Newly opened it was, the implacable driver said, as J.C. went purple with rage. Some fellow called Kenny Hanlon. It was at that point that things had gotten a bit out of control. J.C. had punctured the horse box's tires with a pitchfork, so that the driver had called the police. There was a succession of nighttime raids between the two yards, lifting saddles, rugs, even a microwave oven, supposedly "in lieu of payments" on both sides. But when Kenny Hanlon was suddenly fingered by the tax authorities for supposed nonpayment of tax on his fruit machine operations—a charge that resulted in a prison sentence of some four years, and the subsequent burning down by suspected arsonists of J.C.'s yard—Thom decided he had had enough of the racing scene. He quit drinking and came home.

He had told Kate this story—minus the bit about his late mother's feelings toward her—on the slow wet walk back to Kilcarrion, a walk that had become even slower when, shortly before they reached the gateway to the house, he suggested they pause for a few moments in a deserted bus shelter. There, seated on the benches as the big gray horse dozed, and periodically accepted Polo mints from Thom's hand, he had filled in, in somewhat less emotional terms than Kate had, the last sixteen years or so of his life.

He had, after she commented that it was strange, them both ending up here again, also stared for a disconcertingly long time into Kate's eyes, so that she blushed and felt temporarily unbalanced. But then she had been unbalanced by lots of her reactions to Thom: by the fact that, increasingly, when she bumped into him around the house and its grounds, she found herself becoming more tongue-tied rather than less, and, worse, that at least twice she had blushed; by the fact that his habit of staring at her very directly when he spoke left her unable to concentrate on what it was he was actually saying; by the fact that the last few nights in the inaccurately named Italian room (unless they meant Venice, she thought, eyeing the latest spreading damp patch) it had been Thom's, rather than Justin's, face that she had found herself picturing.

Had he always been this attractive? Or had the weathering of pain and suffering cast compelling new shadows on his face? (Maggie had often accused her of being unhealthily attracted to those she termed "walking wounded.") Had he always been this good at listening? Gazed at her so attentively? She couldn't say; the Thom she had known at nineteen had been such a different, less confident character. And the Kate she had been had been so much more confident, so determinedly impulsive. So sure that there were bigger and better things awaiting her.

You fool, she had told herself, one afternoon, as she lay on her bed like a teenager, contemplating such questions. You're bloody incapable of existing anywhere without imagining some kind of flirtation. This is exactly what got you into so much trouble last time. This is exactly what Maggie has been criticizing you for.

So she had decided to avoid Thom; had busied herself in her room, working on long-standing writing projects that she had brought with her; had borrowed her mother's car and taken herself off to explore some of the nearby sights, and, most important, had avoided the summerhouse, the back fields, the yard—anywhere, in fact, where she thought the slightest possibility existed that she might run into him.

He had seemed not to notice at first, and

then, catching her scuttling across the drive to the car one morning, had said, close into her ear so that she jumped: "Are you avoiding me?"

She had denied it, had stuttered that of course she wasn't, that she was busy, had to pop into town, had an awful lot of work on. But he had just nodded slightly, and raised an eyebrow, and she had known that he knew. And she had decided even more furiously that she should stay away from him. Away from trouble.

And had said yes when he asked if she'd like to go out for dinner.

Annie's door was unlocked, as was normal, but somewhat warily, Joy knocked on it twice before entering. She was not entirely sure, given recent events, what to expect. When there was no response, she gently pushed it and walked in, stopping on the threshold to give her eyes time to adjust to the dim light. The living room looked both neglected and as if some whirlwind had recently passed through, scattering books and papers over every available surface as it went. The curtains, which had not been opened, shrouded the room in gloom, the few thin slivers of light to slice through catching the particles of dust suspended by Joy's arrival. It looked like the scene of some great crime, resting quietly on its turbulent secrets.

"Annie?" she said, clutching the tin of shortbread to her chest.

She didn't often venture out into the village these days, there being so much to do around the house, especially now that Sabine was helping her sort out all those old papers. More important, privately, she suspected that it would be tempting fate to venture too far away. She had left her with Edward, flicking through some of the old souvenirs that he used to bring her when he returned home. Edward seemed to like spending time with Sabine. Sabine could sit in; Joy could manage everything outside; it made things so much simpler.

"Are you there?"

There was an answering rustle from the kitchen.

"Annie?"

"Hello?" came a male voice. A head shot out from the doorway, that of a sharp-featured man, probably in his forties, with short, businesslike hair. "I couldn't find anyone," he said apologetically. "So I thought I'd help myself to breakfast. I hope that's okay."

"Oh," said Joy, glancing around. "I'm sure that's fine. You're a guest, are you?"

"Anthony Fleming," he said, thrusting out a hand. He was wearing a Windcheater and quite the tightest pair of shorts Joy had ever seen. Brightly colored, and made of some kind of shining nylon, they molded themselves around him, outlining the finer points of the man's anatomy in a manner that, had Joy been the type to blush, would have provoked a color of damsonesque hues. Instead, she just blinked rather hard, and looked away.

"Joy Ballantyne," she said, extending her own, a little less forcefully. "I live across the road. Is Annie around?"

"I haven't seen her since last night," said the man, who had returned to his bowl of cereal. "She let me in, and found a place for my bike—I'm cycling around Ireland—but then there was no sign of her this morning. I'm a bit fed up, to be honest, as I've been hanging around for ages. And cornflakes and slightly off milk are not exactly my idea of bed-and-breakfast."

"Oh," said Joy, unsure what she could offer this man in return. "I'm afraid I can't help you there."

There was a short pause.

"Annie . . . ," she said, slowly. "Annie's had a bit of bad luck lately. She's normally a little better organized." She was aware of how weak these words sounded, faced with the chaos and grime around her.

"That may be," said Anthony Fleming, rinsing his bowl under the tap, and adjusting his cycling shoes. "But I can't say I'll exactly be rushing back. Not my idea of Irish hospitality. Not like the last place I stayed, in Enniscorthy. The White Horse. Or House, I can't remember. Do you know it?"

Joy didn't, but the man, apparently placated by simply being able to state his dissatisfactions to somebody, collected his bicycle from one of the outhouses and departed, after rather gallantly leaving with Joy the full amount due for his overnight stop.

After she had watched him cycle off down the road, she turned to the kitchen, seeing it properly for the first time. It was not a happy sight: dishes piled up in the sink, half submerged in rank, greasy water. A stale, half-eaten loaf sat upside down on a plastic chopping board. A selection of cardboard wrappers from ready-made meals formed rickety, multistory towers on the surfaces that weren't littered with chocolate wrappers, stale crumbs, or out-of-date pints of milk, the organic indicators of a disintegrating life.

It wasn't a huge surprise, although she had been surprised that Mrs. H hadn't seen it. It was she who had confided unhappily that Annie's husband, Patrick, had finally tired of a wife who no longer even seemed to notice he was there; a wife who neither wanted to share anything with him, talk to him, nor even argue with him, and had left. "He's a good man," she had said, as Joy stood by, a little uncomfortable with Mrs. H's unbidden confidences. "But I can't blame him. Lately she'd try the patience of a saint, floating around like she's in another world. She won't talk about Niamh, won't admit that this is what's causing it. She won't open up to him at all. Half the time she won't even talk to me."

It was Mrs. H's uncharacteristic and public grief that had prompted Joy's visit; Annie had gotten so bad the last week or so that she would not let her in, she said, so when Joy suggested that she pop around with a tin of biscuits, Mrs. H had accepted gratefully. "She won't expect you," she said. "She'd probably just open the door to you."

But what on earth do I tell her about this? Joy thought, gazing around her. She didn't want to interfere; she wasn't the type. People should generally be left alone to sort themselves out, if that's what they wanted.

But this . . .

"Annie?" she said, letting herself out the back door into the kitchen garden. The vegetable patch, from which Annie had once prided herself on conjuring up ripe, green produce, now looked bare and infertile. The grassed area spilled messily over into the borders, where the browned, brittle remains of the summer's plant life wound itself sadly through the earth.

She backed into the house, closing the door behind her. The utility room, once competently stocked with toilet rolls, kitchen rolls, and sacks of potatoes, was cold and almost empty. The dining room bore a thin sheen of dust.

"Annie?" she called up the stairs. "Are you there?"

Niamh's room was the last that Joy entered. Anyone who knew Annie felt unwilling to enter that place, not because of any superstition about the little girl who had once lived there, but because of an awareness of the depth and fragility of Annie's grief. Someone who had lost a child, according to village wisdom, should be allowed to grieve in whichever way she chose; the awfulness was so unimaginable that unlike other life events—weddings, christenings, disappearing spouses—no one felt qualified to suggest a right or wrong way of dealing with it.

"Annie?" she said.

Annie was sitting on the carefully made child's bed, her back to the door, and a plastic doll in her right hand. She didn't immediately turn around when Joy called her name, but continued to stare out of the window at the brown fields beyond, as if she hadn't heard.

Joy stood in the doorway, taking in the children's toys, the brightly colored curtains, the curling wall posters, unsure whether to venture farther in. She already felt like she was intruding.

"Are you all right?" she asked, tentatively.

Annie's head moved slightly to the right, as if she were examining the doll. She lifted it slowly, and ran her finger over its face.

"I keep meaning to do some dusting," she said. "It's a bit of a mess in here."

She turned her head so that she could see Joy, smiling a strange, bleak smile. "Housework, eh? It always gets away from you."

Annie looked pale and tired, her hair lank over her face, and her movements slow and precise, as if the very act of moving at all exhausted her. She sat awkwardly, swaddled in her usual layers, bound up as if in an attempt to further remove the world outside. Joy, who had hardly seen her recently, apart from the interlude when she had argued with Sabine, wondered with a heavy heart at how grief could transform someone from the bright, sparky young mother of three years previously, to this seemingly drugged automaton. It made her think of Edward, too, and she swatted the thought away.

"I—I've brought you some biscuits."

It sounded so ridiculous somehow. But Annie didn't seem remotely surprised.

"Shortbread. How lovely."

"I wasn't sure how you were. We've not seen much of you around lately."

There was a long pause, during which Annie seemed to be examining the doll's face, very carefully, as if for damage.

"I wondered if you needed any help with anything. Shopping, perhaps. Or . . ."—she didn't like to say cleaning, with its implications—". . . a bit of company. Sabine always loves to see you. Perhaps I could send her over later."

She paused, remembering the money in her hand.

"Oh. And a Mr. Fleming, your guest, left this for you." She held out her hand, and then, meeting no response, stepped forward and placed it quietly on the dresser.

"How's Mr. Ballantyne?" Annie said, suddenly.

Joy took a deep breath.

"He's fine, thank you. A little better."

"That's grand." She placed the doll carefully on the bed and turned toward the window again.

Joy stood, unsure whether she was being dismissed. Eventually, she stepped forward, thrust the tin of shortbread onto the bed, and began to back out. The poor girl's thoughts were evidently elsewhere. There was little that Joy could do. She would tell Mrs. H that Annie definitely needed some help, perhaps even to be taken to her parents' home for a while. Perhaps she should have some—

what was it they all had these days?—some counseling.

Quietly, her footfall muffled by the thick carpet, Joy left the room.

"Patrick's left me, you know," came the voice.

Joy turned around. Annie still faced the window. It was impossible to see her expression.

"I just thought you should know," she said.

There were two dates leaving Kilcarrion House on Saturday night, although both parties would have been at pains not to let them be described as such. Sabine had decided she would go out with Bobby McAndrew, had accepted his offer of a trip to the pictures, helped choose the film from the local paper, and then spent the following days worrying about whether he would try to seat her in the back row and stick his hand down her top. She wasn't entirely sure, but she thought she might have gone off him again.

"I'm going to wear my black jumper, the polo-neck one, so that he doesn't get any ideas," she had told her grandfather. "And my jeans, so that I don't look like I've tried or anything."

Her grandfather's eyes had swiveled across to her. Behind him, the technology, encased in its plastic surround, bleeped a regular pulse. "Don't look at me like that," she said, scoldingly. "It's perfectly smart for nowadays. Just because you lot used to wear suits and stuff to go out."

Her grandfather had looked away again. Sabine had grinned at him, and placed his hand back on the bedspread.

"Besides. If he's a right pug, then I want to make myself look as horrible as I can."

But Bobby McAndrew hadn't looked terribly puggy. He had worn a pair of dark green trousers, dark brown, heavy-soled boots, and his own black woolen polo neck, which had made her want to giggle. Perhaps he was terrified that she was going to jump on him. He had also driven his own car, which was quite impressive; it was only a little Vauxhall, but it was a nice color. And Sabine, who had never been on a date with anyone who drove before (she hadn't actually been on that many dates full stop), quite enjoyed the feeling of maturity conveyed by a boyfriend with wheels. She also liked the chivalrous way that Bobby reminded her to do up her seat belt (as opposed to when her mother reminded her, in which case she was simply being a nag). She leaned forward and turned on the stereo, and the voice of a famous female singer had flooded the car, warbling on about lost love and sleepless nights. Listening, Sabine had realized with a start that it was well over a month since she had heard any kind of pop music. The woman's voice, once one of her favorites, sounded almost alien, a bit self-indulgent, and silly. She had leaned forward again and turned it off.

"You don't like music?" said Bobby, glancing over at her. He smelled of aftershave. It wasn't too awful.

"Not really in the mood for it," she had replied, and gazed coolly out of the window, quietly pleased with the way that sounded.

The showing had been on early, the film had been funny enough to make her laugh out loud without thinking, and Bobby had failed to embarrass himself or her by clammy-handing her in the dark (she had spent much of the first half on the edge of her seat, primed to retaliate), so when he asked if she fancied a pizza, Sabine said yes. No one had told her what time she had to be back, and at Kilcarrion such opportunities were to be relished. She also, she admitted, didn't mind spending a bit more time with Bobby; it was good after all this time to hang out with someone her own age. Even if she had forgotten quite how irritating teenage boys could be.

"Vegetarian, are you?" said Bobby, eyeing her choice of pizza over his menu.

"Yes. So?"

"And you hunt?"

She sighed. Gazed around her at the bustling restaurant. The waitress had looked at her as if she were too young to be there.

"I went once. To see what it was like. And we didn't catch anything, did we?"

"Do you wear leather shoes?" He leaned down, as if to peer under the table.

"Yes, I do. Until they make decent rubber ones I don't have much choice."

"Do you eat wine gums? You know they're made out of bits of cows. It's the gelatin in them."

Sabine grimaced, wishing Bobby would change the subject. He had done this nonstop since they left the cinema; this conversation-as-battle thing, joking and trying to score points off her. It had made her laugh at first; now it was becoming exhausting.

"Do you ever stop going on?" she said, with a smile, to try to take the sting out of her words.

"Going on?"

"I just don't eat meat. I don't want a fight about it."

"Point taken."

He had looked up at her from under his lashes, the faintest flicker of embarrassment showing on his face. From behind him, the waitress, who had stacked shoes and too much makeup, dropped a glass of coke heavily onto the table.

"So how's the old man? I hear he's on his last legs."

"He's all right." Sabine felt strangely defensive. "How come you're so interested in my family, anyway?"

"I told you, London girl. Here, we like to know everything about everyone's business."

"Nosy."

"No, just efficient gatherers of information. Knowledge is power, you know."

"I'd rather have money."

He paused, rubbing his hand through this hair. "Actually, I asked because I wanted to know when you'd be going back to England."

Sabine paused, her fork halfway to her mouth.

"Well, common sense says that if he— well, if you're here to help look after him, and he—well . . . I heard you'd probably be heading off soon."

Why should you care? Sabine wanted to ask him. But it seemed too forward.

"He's not dying, if that's what you're saying."

"So you'll be around awhile. I mean, your mam's not dragging you home with her."

"My mum doesn't have any say over what I do," said Sabine, pertly, skewering a piece of mushroom on her fork. "I could stay here forever if I wanted."

"You don't miss London too much, then?"

Sabine thought for a moment.

"Actually, apart from a couple of my mates, I don't really miss it at all."

It got easier after that. Bobby's manic conversational dueling eased off, and he seemed to relax, so that talking to him became more like talking to one of her friends. He still mugged at her, and did too many silly voices, and was a bit what Mrs. H would call "excitable," but he looked at her in a nice way, and she decided, as they drove home, that if he tried to stick his tongue in her mouth she probably wouldn't hit him or anything. Not too hard, anyway.

"So, where's your dad?" he said. They had been singing to one of his tapes, which had just paused, while it turned itself over.

"My real dad? I don't see him."

"What? Not at all?"

"Nope."

"Did he and your mam have a falling out, or what?"

"Not really." Sabine traced her finger around the steam on her window, writing her initials in curly lettering. "I don't think they were together very long before I came along. And I think he didn't really want to be a dad, and she didn't really want him involved anyway. Plus, she wanted to live in England." This was the official version, the version her mum had told her back during her early teens, when she had been briefly fascinated by her origins.

"You don't mind?" Bobby looked incredulous.

"Why should I mind? I've never met him. If someone didn't want to be my dad, I'm hardly going to go chasing after him, am I?"

"Do you know who he is?"

"I don't know his name. I think my mum did tell me, but I've forgotten. I think he was an artist, though."

Sabine wasn't being purposefuly vague; her paternity, to her, genuinely wasn't a big deal. In London, there were loads of people her age who didn't have any contact with their real dads. The only times it had bothered her had been when she was much younger, and had wondered why her family wasn't like the ones in her books. She had thought about him a bit, since coming to Ireland; it was inevitable when you knew that he lived somewhere nearby. But it was like she said: She had far too much pride to go chasing after someone who had never been particularly interested in her. Besides, she knew such reunions didn't often work out: She had seen the talk shows.

But she didn't tell him the other bit. The bit her mum had told her when she was a bit tipsy; that they had gotten together when she had been his artist's model. The only other boy she'd confided that to had gotten all unnecessary and started going on about topless shots, and whether her mum was "a bit of a goer." Sabine didn't think Bobby would do that, but she didn't know him quite well enough to be sure.

Bobby was silent for a minute, checking the mirrors as he indicated and headed toward Ballymalnaugh. It was nearly a quarter to eleven, according to the clock on his dashboard. She hoped no one was going to get funny about it when she got home.

"Dads are a right bore, anyhow," he said, looking straight ahead. "You're probably better off without one. Mine's always on my case about stuff. Too much aggro, you know?"

Sabine nodded as if she did. She knew he was being kind because he felt bad for her. But that was okay.

The other date was not going quite so smoothly. In fact, it would not have been entirely inaccurate to say it was not going at all. Kate, having stood in front of her reflection in her room for some three quarters of an hour, had decided that she could not go out to dinner with Thom. There was Christopher, for a start; he was due back this evening and, the moment he discovered her plans for the evening, would be proffering barbed comments and declaiming indiscreetly to Julia that it was only to be expected of her. There was her mother, whose discovery of Kate "going below stairs" as she would no doubt see it, could make their already cool relationship only frostier. She hadn't liked it when she had gone out with Thom as a teenager; she was unlikely to like it any better now. It was probably not the done thing to go out with men, anyway, when your father was supposedly dying. She should really be sitting by his bedside looking pained. But that would displace Sabine, who already spent most of her time up there and seemed to get irritated whenever she offered to help. And Kate had to admit to being secretly relieved that no one seemed to want her to spend any time with him; they had hardly spoken since she left home, and he had made it clear that that was not likely to change.

But it wasn't just that this date was inappropriate, in so many ways. More important, it would just reaffirm all the worst beliefs that she increasingly harbored about herself: that she was incapable of functioning without a man, that she seemed to seek out the unsuitable, that she allowed herself to be so much flotsam and jetsam on the great, turbulent sea of romance. It's time I took charge, Kate told herself, eyeing her complexion, which had begun to dry out in the cold. It's time I learned to live on my own. To put my daughter first. To be a responsible adult, whatever that means.

What would Maggie do, she had wondered (a question she had increasingly asked herself, and one that had prompted the premature ending of her relationship with Justin—not that he had seemed unduly devastated by it). She would have canceled, she concluded, refusing to acknowledge the tiny sting of disappointment that Virtual Maggie's verdict invoked. She would definitely have canceled. In fact there was no way that you could look at it, no single approach, and not end up with Maggie canceling. She knew; she'd tried. Kate took a deep breath, pulled another jumper over her head, and went out into the yard to find Thom.

"I can't come." It was a little balder than she had intended.

Thom was stringing up a hay net in one of the stables, under the watery light of a flickering electric bulb. Behind him, the big gray horse that she had seen that wet day in the copse ran an inquiring, rubbery muzzle around the remains of his feed bucket.

Thom didn't look round. "Why?"

"Because . . . it's a bit difficult. I've got to look after Sabine."

"Sabine's out on a date."

He finished tying a knot in the hay net, twisted it a couple of times, and then, with a slap of the horse's rump, walked out of the stable, bolting the two locks behind him. The yard, which was now dark and almost empty, echoed under his footsteps.

Kate stood, her mouth very slightly ajar.

"You didn't know? She's gone out with one of the McAndrew brothers. He's a good lad. You don't need to worry."

Hurt, fury, and humiliation impacted themselves upon Kate like a car crash, mangling her confidence and self-possession. Sabine hadn't even mentioned this boy to her, yet the whole house evidently knew she was going out with him. How did it make her look, to be her mother, and yet the last person to know? What had she done to Sabine to make her want to wound her so?

Worse, she had shown her up to be a liar.

Thom walked on to the next stable, so that

despite her wrong-footedness, she was forced to follow him. He opened the next stable, peered in, and then pulled out a half-empty water bucket.

"So why else can't you come?" he said, using his good arm to sluice the remaining water down the drain.

Kate looked at him, trying to determine whether there was any anger in his tone. There didn't seem to be.

"It's just too complicated," she said, briskly.

Thom picked up the bucket and placed it back inside the stable, shutting the door behind him. He stopped for a moment, leaning against the metal covering that ran along the top.

"Because . . . ?"

His eyes were soft, hinting at amusement. His short, dark hair was sprinkled with hayseeds, like the pelt of an animal. Confined in her pockets, her hands itched silently to rub at it. Don't make me do this, Kate pleaded silently. Don't make me start going through the reasons.

"Thom . . ."

"Look. It's not a big deal. It was just a bite to eat. I thought you were looking fed up, and

I know your family isn't the easiest lot. It was just meant to give you a bit of a break. Don't worry about it."

He turned, and walked on to the next stable, leaving her behind him in the yard.

"Another time, eh?" he shouted over his shoulder. Cheerfully.

Kate stood, overwhelmed by a feeling of stupidity. She had misread it; he had just been offering a friendly couple of hours away from her family. Like her brother said, why did she assume the world revolved around her? She shifted her weight on her feet, aware of a growing numbness in her toes, yet unwilling to disappear into the house.

Go on, a silent voice urged her.

Don't you dare, said Virtual Maggie.

"Thom?"

"Yup?" He was in the tack room now, stuck his head out as she drew nearer. His expression was blank, friendly.

"I could murder a drink, though."

He paused, and again she felt that same disorientated sensation as his gaze settled on her face.

"Fine."

"So, you'll come? We can just have a drink?"

"I'll meet you at the Black Hen. You remember where it is?"

He was laughing at her. It was the only pub in the village.

"At about . . ."—he checked his watch—"seven-thirty, then. See you up there."

Kate walked up the unlit road toward the pub, playing with her glasses in her pocket, placing them back on her nose, and then just as swiftly removing them and placing them back in her pocket. It was a less stationary repeat of her performance an hour earlier, when she had sat in front of her dressing table, trying to tame her hair, alternately putting on and rubbing off her makeup, and wondering whether, in some immensely subtle way, she had just been out maneuvered. He had seemed genuinely unbothered whether they went out or not, which meant that this was obviously not a *date* date. But it still wouldn't have looked good on paper: RECENTLY SEPARATED MOTHER ARRIVES HOME, FATHER ON DEATHBED, GOES OUT WITH GOOD-LOOKING MAN WITHIN TEN DAYS OF ARRIVAL. Everyone else would assume it was a date.

And even if she knew it wasn't, she really

didn't like the thought of having to go out with her unflattering glasses on.

Off, she had decided. Even if it wasn't a date, there was no reason why she shouldn't look attractive. After the Justin debacle, her self-esteem needed all the padding it could get. On, she thought, as she found herself walking gently into a hedge. Off, she decided, as she reached the door of the Black Hen. And pushed the wrong side of it for some moments before it was opened from the inside by someone making his way out.

Because her eyesight was so inept, Kate's hearing was finely tuned to pick up the subtle, but distinct lull in conversation as she walked into the warm, fuggy atmosphere of the pub. But the other advantage to not being able to see properly was that it made one remarkably impervious to what other people thought. Kate, unable to make out the interested expressions on the faces of those around her, often culminating in the odd murmur of recognition, moved more confidently through the smoke-logged bar than most women walking into such an establishment on their own (and in the Black Hen, there was not much in the way of competition).

There were disadvantages, however: namely, that one tended to trip over unmarked steps, career into those drinkers precariously transferring their rounds from the bar, and find it near impossible to locate in the dim light the person one was seeking. And one was left with the thorny question of whether to admit defeat and pull out one's glasses (thereby publicly admitting one's vanity) or carry on regardless, squinting as one tried to negotiate the blurry boundaries of table and body.

"I'm sorry," she said, clutching at a man's elbow, after she had knocked most of his pint over his shoes. "Please let me get you another one."

"No, let me," said a voice, and through the dim light and cigarette haze, Kate gratefully made out the shape of Thom's face.

"I'm over here," he said, steering her through the tables toward his own. "Sit down and I'll get you a drink."

Kate sat, trying to determine whether to pull her glasses from her pocket. In this darkened pub, her usual struggles to see what was around her were made even harder. But those glasses were *so* unflattering. She was still haunted by Sabine's expression of derision when she had seen her wearing them.

Thom placed the glass of white wine on the table in front of her.

"I can't vouch for its quality," he said, lifting his orange juice to his lips. "They keep only the one bottle in here, and that has a screw top. I'll get you something else if it's like vinegar."

"What are you having?"

"Oh, this. Orange."

She looked at him inquiringly.

"Haven't drunk really since my racing days. I worked out I'm one of those people— what do you call them?—who can't have one without having ten."

"Addictive personalities."

"Something like that."

"You don't seem the type," she said. "Too careful."

She could just make out his smile.

"Ahh, Kate Ballantyne. That's because you haven't seen me for almost half my life."

The wine did taste like vinegar. It made her pull in her cheeks, as if sucking on rhubarb. He laughed, and bought her a pint of Guinness. "It's meant to be different here," she said, feeling an irrational need to keep the conversation neutral. "But not being a Guinness drinker at home, I couldn't tell."

His hand was resting on the table in front of her. It didn't fidget, like Justin's had, restlessly moving from car keys to cigarette packet, thrumming out irregular rhythms on the tabletop. It just rested, broad and spade fingered, its darker hues beaten out by the weather. She wondered if it felt rough, from working outside all the time, and fought the urge to touch it.

"So, have you sorted things out with Sabine yet?"

Kate felt the familiar stab of pain.

"Not really," she said. "I mean, she doesn't get so angry with me as she did in London, but she just seems to act as if I'm a bit of an irritant. Even a bit irrelevant."

"She seems happier," he said.

Kate's head shot up.

"Than what?"

"Than when she came."

Kate stiffened.

He paused, raised an eyebrow. "I didn't mean anything by it."

"I'm sorry. I guess I'm a bit oversensitive about it all."

She took a swig of the Guinness. It tasted dark, reassuringly iron-y.

"I told you, I like her. I think she's great."

"She likes you. I think she tells you more than she does me."

"Is this you feeling sorry for yourself?"

She smiled, feeling her face relax for the first time. Her shoulders, she realized, had risen up around her ears with tension. "I guess I'm just jealous. Of you. Of my mother. Of anyone who can get Sabine to be relaxed, and happy. Things that I don't seem to be able to do."

"She's a teenager. She'll come around."

They sat in silence, listening to their thoughts above the gentle clamor of the people around them.

"She looks like you," he said.

Kate looked up, wishing suddenly she could see the expression on his face.

Suddenly, from her right: "Is it Kate? Kate Ballantyne?"

She swiveled around, to see the face of a young woman, stooping slightly from her standing position to greet her.

"It's Geraldine. Geraldine Leach. We used to go out riding together."

Kate summoned up a vague picture of a plump girl with plaits so tight that they left red welts above her ears. Nothing else. Disconcertingly, she couldn't make out the girl's face now.

"Hi . . . ," she said, holding out a hand. "Nice to see you."

"And you, and you. Are you back for good, or just visiting?"

"Oh, just visiting."

"You live in London, don't you? Oh, I'd love to live in London. I live over at Roscarney. It's about four miles away. You should stop by if you've got time."

Kate nodded, trying to look both grateful and noncommittal.

"It's a bit chaotic. I've got three kids now. And Ryan, that's my husband over there. The biggest kid of the lot. But you'd be more than welcome. It'd be good to catch up. I haven't seen you in—what is it? Must be twenty years. God . . . doesn't that make you feel old?"

Kate nodded and smiled, not wanting to feel quite that old.

"You look just the same, you know. All that lovely red hair. I would have killed for your hair when I was younger, you know? In fact,

I still would. Look at this gray coming through! Do you have kids yourself?"

"Just one," said Kate, who was aware of Thom's silence, on the other side of her.

"Ahh. Grand. What did you have, boy or girl?"

"Girl."

Geraldine seemed to show no inclination to move on.

"I'd love a girl. What is it they say? You keep a boy till marriage, but a girl you get for life. I'd kill you for your girl. Mind you, my boys will be with me till they're thirty, the home comforts they get. My own fault, I never trained their father properly."

She bent low, so that Kate caught a whiff of scent.

"He's a miserable so-and-so if he doesn't get things how he likes them. I always say he was born two drinks behind, you know what I mean? No coincidence he ended up working for the tax . . ."

Kate's smile was becoming fixed.

"Well, I won't keep you," said Geraldine, eyeing Thom. "Sure you've got lots to catch up on. You make sure you come over, now. It's fifteen Black Common Drive. You can find me in the phone book. We'll have a grand time."

"Thanks," said Kate, as she left. "That's very kind."

She took a long draft of her drink, trying not to look around to check that Geraldine Leach had definitely returned to her spot behind the bar.

"I could leave now," said Thom, grinning.

She raised her eyes to his.

"Don't you dare."

They both laughed.

"Where were we?"

Kate looked down at her glass.

"I think we were talking about Sabine."

"So, let's talk about you."

Kate looked up. There was something about the way he looked at her that made her feel transparent. "I don't think I want to. I'm not very interesting at the moment."

Thom said nothing.

"Whenever I tell people anything about my life, I feel like I'm just repeating the same old chain of disasters. I bore myself, just talking about it."

"Are you happy?"

"Happy?" It sounded like an extraordinary thing to ask. She thought for a minute. "Sometimes, I suppose. When Sabine's happy. When I feel like . . . oh, I don't know.

When does anyone feel happy? Are you happy?"

Thom paused.

"Happier than I was. I guess I'm content."

"Even being back here?"

"Especially being back here." He smiled at her again; she could tell by the white of his teeth. "Believe it or not, Kate, this place was the saving of me."

"My mother, the guardian angel." Kate laughed, bitterly.

"Your mother's all right. You two just see the world through different eyes, that's all."

"Easy for you to say," she said.

"Sabine managed it. And she and your mam were at each other's throats to begin with."

There was so much she didn't know about her own daughter's life, sometimes it felt overwhelming. Kate mourned her little girl, who would rush from school into her arms, stumbling over her words in her frantic attempt to tell what she'd done, who she'd seen. She could still feel the weight of her, snuggled under her arm as they sat on the sofa, watching children's programs, exclaiming over the day's events.

"Can we not talk about my family? I thought

you were taking me out to cheer me up."
Don't let them spoil this, she thought. Don't
let them intrude on every part of my life. She
wanted, she realized, to have him entirely to
herself.

He held up his glass, as if considering
whether he could make it last until she had
finished her Guinness. "Okay. We can't talk
about you. We can't talk about your family.
How about religion? That's always one to get
the blood going. Or, what's changed in Ballymalnaugh since you left? That should be
good for—well, some minutes."

She laughed, grateful for his neutralizing
of her darkening mood. There was something about Thom that invariably made
things seem better.

"Kate?"

She turned on her stool, to where a
middle-aged man was leaning heavily
toward her, clutching a pint.

"Stephen Spillane. I don't know if you'd
remember me. I used to work at the big
house. Y'all right there, Thom?"

"Fine, Stevie."

Kate squinted, trying to distinguish the
features in this huge, ruddy face.

"I saw you from over there, on the other

side of the bar, and I says to myself, 'That looks like Joy Ballantyne's girl.' Well, I didn't know if I was right or not till I got up close—it's been, what is it? Ten years?"

"Nearly seventeen," interjected Thom.

"Nearly seventeen years. Well, now, and here you are again. And are you here for long?"

"No, I—"

"Is that young Kate Ballantyne?" Another man, one Sabine didn't recognize, had arrived at her shoulder. "I thought I knew that face. Well, if that isn't a turn up. A long time since we've seen you here."

"Now, Kate. You remember the priest, Father Andrew."

Kate smiled and dipped her head, as if she did.

"Not that you were a great one for the Sunday service, now."

"The young people have other things to think about these days, Father."

"And not just the young people, Stevie, eh?"

"Did you move to London?" Stephen Spillane had now pulled up a chair next to her. He smelled of rolling tobacco and, peculiarly, bleach. "Are you anywhere near Finsbury Park? You remember my boy Dylan? He's living in Finsbury Park. I should give you his number."

"I'll bet there's a lot changed around here since you last came home, eh Kate?"

"I'm sure Dylan would be glad to take you out. He's a great one for the pretty girls. Are you married now?"

"Oh, look, here's Jackie. Jackie—do you remember Kate Ballantyne? Edward Ballantyne's girl. Over from England. Jackie—get us a drink there, will you?"

Whether it was being frequently interrupted, or unable to properly make out the faces of those she was talking to (or, perhaps, the fact that she really wanted to be alone with Thom), Kate found maintaining what passed for polite conversation exhausting. No, she said, she was not here for long. Yes, it was lovely to come back again. Yes, she would pass on his good wishes for her father's speedy recovery. Yes, she was sure the old hunt hadn't been the same since he'd stopped as Master. And, worst, yes, it would be lovely to say hello to some of those people she hadn't seen for sixteen years, who remembered her as a teenager.

Oh, so there they were, on the other side of the bar. Of course it would be great if they came over to the table. What else could she say?

"Except we've got to get back, Kate," said Thom, suddenly. "Remember, your mam wanted you home early this evening, to help out."

Kate frowned at him.

"You did promise her we'd be back by eight-thirty."

Belatedly, she caught on.

"Oh. Yes. I'd forgotten." She stared around her at the well-meaning, indistinct faces. "I'm sorry. Perhaps we could catch up the next time I come in? That would be lovely," she said, smiling broadly. Scenting escape, she could afford to be gracious.

"Ahh, that's a terrible shame. And us only just gotten started."

"She looks grand, though. Doesn't she? Big city living suits you, girl."

"But Thom has obviously got other things on his mind, eh? We wouldn't want to get in the way of Thom's plans." Kate was not so blind that she couldn't make out Stephen Spillane's exaggerated wink.

"So, what do we do now?" she said, under her breath, after their various good-byes, as Thom steered her toward the door.

"You wait outside," said Thom. "I'll be two secs."

He emerged, moments later, with a couple cans of Guinness and two of orange juice tucked under his false arm. (Even she could tell his limbs apart; it was a mild night, and with his jumper pushed up, the plastic forearm shone under the light of the pub windows.)

"It just so happens I know a great watering hole, not far from here," he said. "And you don't get bothered by the locals."

The electric light in the summerhouse could not be seen from any room in the big house. Unusually, the little building's two windows, although generous, faced away from the greater one, casting their dim glow over a patch of wilderness on one side, and the overgrown remains of a patio garden on the other. Growing up, Kate had often wondered who had built it, and whether they had designed it specifically so that there would be no curious, intruding voices from the house. Now, she wondered whether the bare lightbulb cast harsh shadows on her face, and whether the benefits of moving back out of it were outweighed by the fact that if she did she would hardly be able to see.

"Not exactly the Ritz, I'm afraid," said Thom, cracking open a can and handing it to her.

"But then I've always found the Ritz somewhat lacking in old cans of varnish," she said, seating herself on the horse blanket that he had laid over the old crates.

"Not forgetting animal life." He reached up, catching a spider's web with his hand, and clearing it from above her head. Wiping his hand on his trousers, he sat down on another crate, some feet away from her, and opened his own can of orange juice.

She found she noticed the distance. They had linked arms when they half-ran from the pub, and she had giggled manically, like a schoolgirl, filled with a delicious feeling of escape. She could still feel the peculiar sensation of his unyielding arm next to hers.

"We could have stayed in the pub," he said apologetically. "But you know what they're all like—they wouldn't have left you alone for the rest of the night."

"I was struggling."

"I thought it would be easier to talk somewhere else."

"We could have just gone back to yours," she said, unthinking.

"And if I'd suggested it, you would have gone home."

Kate caught his smile, and found her own drifting slowly from her face. He was right. She would have thought it too intimate, too risky. And yet what could be more intimate than this? The two of them hiding out, in their old haunt, redolent with memories, its very timbers suffused with the bittersweet scent of years past?

Kate gazed around her at the neglected old summerhouse and felt suddenly awkward, as if caught somewhere she shouldn't have been. She thought, unexpectedly, of Justin. And then Geoff. What am I doing, sitting here, with this man? she thought. This is ridiculous. Virtual Maggie loomed before her, her mouth pursed in mock disapproval, wagging a virtual finger.

"You know what? I should go," she said, weakly. She was suddenly grateful that she couldn't see his face properly.

He put his drink down, before standing up. It made it somehow harder for her to move.

"I should really go."

"What are you frightened of?"

There was a brief silence. She looked up, trying to find his face. But he had stepped out of the light, and she could see nothing except the harsh glare of the light on an upturned paint tin. Squinting vainly, she heard him, his feet depressing the boards. She was aware of him as an almost mono-chrome shadow, looming toward her. Then she caught the subtle scents of him: soap, mixed with the faint, earthy smell of horse, overlaid with the more recent layers of smoke and beer.

Immobilized, she took a sharp breath as she felt his hand gently dip into her pocket. Slowly, he removed her glasses, gently opening them and placing them carefully on her face. The plastic of his false hand was briefly cold against her cheek.

He squatted down, so that their faces were level. "What are you frightened of?" he said again, softly.

She paused. She could make out every eyelash.

"You."

"No."

She looked at him, seeing clearly for the

first time the way his eyes curled up in the corners, the way his lips closed when he breathed out. The small, pale scar under his eyebrow. I don't want to see you this clearly, she thought. You were easier blurry.

"No." He looked serious. "You've no reason to be frightened of me. I'd never do you harm."

She kept staring at him.

"Then I'm frightened of me."

He reached forward and took ahold of her hand. His felt dry, weathered. But gentle. She wondered, absently, what the other one felt like.

"I ruin everything, Thom. I get everything wrong. I'll do it with you, too."

"No," he said, again.

His eyes stayed on hers. She felt liquefied, had to remind herself to keep breathing. Tears had sprung, unaccountably, to her eyes.

"I can't let this happen. You don't know me anymore, Thom. You don't know what I'm like. I can't trust what I feel, you see? I'm not reliable like that. I think I'm in love with people and then a few months down the line I find out I wasn't after all. And then everyone gets hurt. I get hurt. Sabine gets hurt."

She was acutely conscious of the pressure of his hand. She wanted to rip her own from his grasp. She wanted to move it, to be swallowed up into it, to press her mouth into it, feel it against her skin.

Thom's eyes kept burning into her. She looked away, out of the window, talking into the air.

"Can't you see? This is happening at all only because I'm here, and alone, and needy, because I've just broken up with someone. I know exactly what's happening. I'm not self-sufficient, you see. I'm not like you, and Sabine, good with your own company. I need closeness, and attention. And because I can't get it from them, I'm looking for it from you."

She was speaking too fast now, her voice lifting.

"Look, if I were a horse, you'd have me down as having bad form. That's what I have. Bad form. For God's sake, Thom. Don't you remember? Don't you remember what I did to you sixteen years ago? Don't you care how much I hurt you?"

He looked down, studying her hand. And then lifted his eyes to hers.

"If you were a horse," he said. "I'd say you had been in the wrong hands."

Kate stared at him. He was now so close that she could feel the warmth of his breath on her skin.

"It would be a disaster," she said, beginning to cry, great salty tears sliding their way down her skin. "It would be a bloody disaster." And then, as Thom gently took her wet face in his two mismatched hands, she leaned forward and placed her mouth against his.

Chapter Twelve

The Duke stood facing into the corner of his stable, his head low, and his tail tucked tightly into his rump, as if awaiting a blow. His hipbones jutted upward, like pieces of planed furniture, and his coat, which once shone with the prismatic gloss of rude health, was dull and roughened, the texture of an old piece of cheap carpet. Above his eyes sat two sunken hollows, while his lids sat halfway down, like a curtain preparing to drop.

The vet, a tall, thin man with an academic air, ran a hand down his neck, patted him, and then moved through the thick bed of straw toward Joy, who was waiting by the door.

"I'm afraid he's not a well lad, Mrs. Ballantyne."

Joy blinked a few times, and looked down, as if digesting something she had nevertheless long expected to hear.

"What is it?"

"It's mainly the osteoarthritis. That and the painkillers we've been giving him."

He paused. "The bute doesn't appear to be working anymore. In fact, I think it's doing him more harm than good. I think he may have developed an ulcer, which is common in horses that have been living off bute for a while, but he's also got diarrhea and weight loss, which is not great in a horse his age. I'll take these blood samples with me, but I'd put money on him having hypoproteinaemia—that's low blood protein." He paused. "He's also tired, his heart is struggling a bit, and I think everything is just winding down, poor old boy."

Joy's face was very still and very stern, its features rigid. Only the most careful of observers would have noticed the faint tremor, the sole clue to what she was keeping in check.

"Is the ulcer my fault?" she said. "Have I been giving him too much?"

"No. It's not remotely your fault. It's a common toxicity reaction in horses who have had to take the drug for some time. It's partly why some places don't really like us using it anymore. But in a horse his age, there was very little else we could do. And he's done very well on it for an awful long time. How old is he now, twenty-seven? Twenty-eight?"

"Can we give him something else? Change the drugs?" Joy held her hands low in front of her, as if in supplication.

The vet squatted down, placing his instruments back inside his case, and closed it with a determined snap. Outside, the sky was bright and blameless, at odds with the atmosphere of foreboding inside.

"I'm sorry, Mrs. Ballantyne. He's had a good innings. But I don't think we can really spin things out for much longer. Not if we want to be fair."

He said the last sentence with a sideways look at Joy. He knew how much the horse meant to the old lady, but really they had been prolonging the inevitable for months.

Joy walked up to the horse's head and pulled gently at his ears, an affectionate, unthinking gesture. She looked at him, pushed up his forelock, as if examining his face, and then rubbed at his nose. The horse pushed his huge head toward her, and then his eyes half closed, and he rested his chin on her quilted shoulder, so that her knees gave slightly under the weight. The vet stood at the door and waited. He knew his customer well enough not to hurry her.

"I want you to come tomorrow," she said, eventually, her voice low and firm. "Tomorrow morning, if that's convenient."

The vet nodded.

"In the meantime, I want to ask you a favor."

He looked up.

"I want you to give him something. Something for the pain. Something that won't upset his stomach." She paused, lifting her head a little imperiously. "I know you must have something."

The vet raised his eyebrows and shifted his feet.

"To be honest, Mrs. Ballantyne, there's not much—"

"Anything," she interrupted. "There must be something."

The vet took a deep breath, and expelled

it slowly, with outblown cheeks. He stared at the straw-strewn floor, thinking.

"There is something," he said, finally.

Joy nodded, expectant.

"It's an experimental drug. It's not something I'd normally prescribe for a horse like yours. I'm certainly not meant to. But, yes, it will kill his pain. To the legs and the stomach."

"I want you to give it to him."

"I really shouldn't. It could lose me my license."

"It's only for a day," said Joy. "I'll pay. Whatever you like."

"That's really not necessary."

He rubbed at his head. He looked up at the sky. He let out another long breath. "If I do, I'd appreciate it if you didn't let on. To anyone."

Joy turned back to her horse and muttered something gentle. Her face had softened, as if anticipating the prospect of her own relief.

"You'll bring it today," she said, not looking at the vet. She was rubbing the horse's nose again, fussing with him, running her broad old hands over his bones, movements borne of a lengthy familiarity.

The vet shook his head slightly, and turned toward the door. He was too soft. His partner would be furious if he knew.

"I've got one more job this morning. Then I'll bring it over." He turned. "How's Mr. Ballantyne, by the way?"

Joy didn't look up. "Fine, thank you," she said.

Several miles away, Kate sat in the Land Rover, gazing through the windscreen at the Hook Head lighthouse, a monochrome monolith silhouetted against the shimmering blue of Waterford Harbor. It was the first clear day for weeks, and the huge lighthouse and the little houses surrounding it sat, weathered and bleached by the watery winter sunlight, as the waves churned and foamed restlessly over the ancient limestone.

Her lungs still acclimatized to the sootier, city atmosphere, she breathed in the salty air, carried on sharp winds from the seafront below them, like a connoisseur savoring a fine wine, listening to the newborns' cries of the gulls and guillemots suspended on invisible channels above. She was wearing her glasses, and even at this distance they were periodically hit by tiny flecks of spray, glinting like diamond chips in the bare light.

"You don't ask much, do you?" she said, not looking at Thom, beside her.

"I mean, about what happened to me. About Justin—my last partner. Or Geoff."

Thom turned to face her.

"Why, do you want me to?"

The clouds skidded across the distant horizon, buffeted by unseen winds.

"I just thought you'd want to know. Most men do. Want to know about your history."

"I know all the history I need to know." He turned his head back to face the sea, taking a sip from a plastic cup of coffee. "You can ask too many questions, sometimes."

"But you don't question any of it. You don't even want to know what I think about all of this. Whether it's a good thing."

"As I said, you can ask too many questions sometimes." He raised an eyebrow. "Especially with someone like you."

They had sat there for almost half an hour, peacefully relishing the brief escape from Kilcarrion, and its attendant complications. For almost half of that, they had lain in each other's arms, exchanging lazy kisses, gazing at each other intoxicated and brimful of unspoken anticipation. It wouldn't be today; that was understood. But it didn't matter. It was good enough just to be with each other, to be held, to be alone.

It had been several days since they had been together in the summerhouse, and Kate's feelings of panic and guilt had stealthily been overridden by a desperate need to be near Thom, to see him smile, to have him to herself. She had woken the day after in a raw panic, any warm feelings from the night before subsumed by her terror at having "gotten involved" again, and had sought him out in the yard, cornering him and telling him firmly (although with a slightly hysterical edge to her voice) that it had all been a terrific mistake, and that she was sorry if she had led him on, but she should really just be on her own right now. Thom had nodded, said he understood, and remained just as impassive when on three other occasions that day she had located him, and in hushed and urgent tones, explained again why it was impossible, how she had thought it over and realized that they were totally unsuited, and that she liked him much too much to wreck his life.

Kate had then gone upstairs to her room and wept, furious with herself, and suddenly bereft, so when Thom, unusually, had come into the breakfast room the following morning in order to inform Joy that he was going into town to pick up some bits from the tack shop, Kate had wondered, seemingly casually, whether he could give her a lift while doing so. There were a few things she needed in town. Christopher—with his bloodhound ability to scent any indiscretion on her part—had left on Sunday evening, Sabine was out, and Joy had not noticed anything odd; she noticed little at the moment, apart from the fading health of her old horse, and the seemingly endless tasks that had suddenly acquired an urgency around the house and yard, and so they had snuck off, careering away in the Land Rover, as secretly gleeful as truanting children. Kate, by now unable to suppress her frantic need to touch him, had reached for his hand, and then had to stop herself from shrinking away when she came into contact with hard plastic instead of yielding flesh.

"You get used to it," he said, apparently amused. "I used to make myself jump, rubbing my nose in my sleep. Or worse."

He had glanced sideways at her as he spoke, a sly smile playing about his lips.

Kate had glowed with something that could have been embarrassment, but undoubtedly contained something more pleasurable. Neither had spoken for some minutes after that, both silenced by the vision Thom's words had provoked.

"So what about you, then?"

Thom finished his coffee, and placed the cup on the dashboard, next to the old woolen gloves, baling twine, and a yellowing copy of the *Racing Post*.

"What about me?"

"Well, there must have been someone. It was more than sixteen years, after all."

Thom looked down, and shrugged.

"I wasn't a saint. But there was no one special."

Kate was incredulous.

"In sixteen years?" Her voice held the faintest tinge of fear, hijacked by the less enticing specter of unhealthy obsession on his part. "There must have been someone. Did you never want to get married? Never live with someone?"

"There were a couple of girls I was fond of." He turned to face her again, reaching for her hand with his own. "But we're different. I don't find it that easy to get involved. I'd rather be on my own than with someone who isn't . . ." His voice tailed off.

Kate silently filled in the gaps. Suitable?

Perfect? The one? The prospect of the latter made her break out in a sweat—it was too soon for him to be talking like this; she wasn't entirely sure she had made the right decision getting involved as far as she had. But there was also another unwelcome prospect: that of an implied criticism in what he'd said. We're different. I'd rather be on my own than . . . than be like her? Was he suggesting she was indiscriminate?

She took a sip of her own coffee, formulating and rejecting various responses. But she didn't ask him what he'd meant. As he said, you could ask too many questions sometimes.

Two men, tiny figures, like insects, busied themselves around a small boat, one pointing and gesticulating. A third trudged backward and forward along the seafront, collecting objects unknown.

"Were you angry with me?" she said, eventually.

"At first."

His blue eyes reflected the unusually clear skies. They stayed fixed on some distant point, perhaps lost in history. "It's hard to stay angry with someone for long. Someone you care about, anyway."

Kate bit her lip.

"I'm sorry."

"Don't be. We were young. We were bound to screw things up one way or another."

"But I screwed it up."

"You just got there before me."

"You're terribly Zen these days."

He smiled. "Zen? Is that what they call it? Nah . . ." He grinned, a long, slow smile that spread across his face. "I've just learned not to get wound up about things I can't change."

Kate hesitated. Couldn't help herself.

"Like your arm?"

"Yeah." He looked down at his left hand, resting lightly on his thigh. "I guess that was a pretty good introduction. You can't argue with a missing limb. . . . You can't argue with anything missing."

They sat in silence, watching the gulls wheel and hover over the bay. The little boat was pushed out to sea, one little figure waving off the two who had climbed within it. It leaped the first few waves like a salmon fighting its way upstream.

Kate pondered the possible interpretations of things missing. There were things she wanted to hear from him that she knew she would shy away from, things that were both necessary and impossible to hear. Still contradictory, said Virtual Maggie. Still obsessed by romance and its possibilities. Still not standing on your own two feet. Oh, bog off, Kate told her.

"There was one thing that troubled me," he said, his gaze still fixed away from her.

Kate had been tracing the palm of his hand with her finger. She looked up.

"It's going to sound a bit strange. But it bothered me for a long time. . . . I wanted to ask you . . . why him?"

She hadn't expected that. She blinked, hard.

"I mean, you hardly knew him. I know we weren't together that long, or anything, but I didn't understand why you would give him something that special. I didn't understand why . . . well, why not me?"

For the first time, he looked troubled, unsure of himself. He closed and opened his mouth a few times, as if struggling with unfamiliar emotions. "I keep looking at Sabine," he said, eventually. "And I'm so conscious . . . that she could have been mine."

Kate thought of Alexander Fowler, of the

birthday portrait, of the furious and perverse determination behind her unsolicited unzipping of her old-fashioned velvet dress, and of the twin emotions of amazement and opportunism that had run riot across that man's face, confronted with her newly naked teenage body. It had been hot in there, she remembered; suffused with the smells of turpentine and oil paint, flanked all around by half-finished images of people she didn't know. She remembered dressing, afterward, as he disappeared into his house on a hunt for cigarettes, and feeling like they now knew her rather better.

"If it had been you, it would have meant something," she said slowly. "And I suppose I didn't want it to mean that much." A gift horse, that had been the expression that he used. It had made her cringe at the time.

Thom stared at her, his own expression blank, still uncomprehending. Behind him a solitary gull wheeled and cried.

"If it had been you, Thom," she said, tightening her hold on his hand, "you would have made me stay."

Sabine, sitting by the upstairs window, watched as the Land Rover turned into the drive and discharged her mother onto the gravel outside the house. She was holding a newspaper and something unidentified in a brown paper bag; nothing she couldn't have gotten in town with her grandmother later, Sabine observed. She was also running her hand repeatedly through her hair—a dead giveaway that you fancied someone; Sabine had read it in a magazine. No doubt if she looked closely enough, her mother's pupils would be dilated, too.

She turned away from the window, toward the bed where her grandfather was sleeping, letting the heavy curtain fall. Too busy fancying men to spend time with her own father, she thought bitterly. You could count the number of times she'd been up to see him on one hand. Grandfather didn't even seem to realize his own daughter was staying here, that was how involved she had gotten. Then again, apart from the nurse, Sabine seemed to be the only one to get involved these days. Her grandmother was always too busy. Or fussing over the Duke, who, John John told her with apparent relish, was headed for the great cat-food factory in the sky.

Sabine sat lightly on the edge of the bed,

careful not to disturb him. He seemed more comfortable sleeping, these days. When he was awake, he often got agitated, and his breathing came in hoarse, labored gasps that made Sabine's own chest feel tight and anxious. She would hold his hand then, trying not to feel panicked when his grip sporadically tightened, like it was practicing for rigor mortis.

"He off again?" said Lynda, the nurse, walking briskly into the room with a jug of fresh water. "Oh, well. Best thing for him."

Lynda (she had inserted the "y" herself, she told Sabine) was going to leave full-time nursing for a career in aromatherapy once this job was over. She never said at what point she would consider it over, but they both knew when that was.

"Just gone," said Sabine.

"Why don't you go off? Go and enjoy yourself? I know, I would. You spend too much time up here." Sabine waited for her to add that it "wasn't healthy," another Lynda favorite, but it didn't come.

"Go on. I'm going to sit and watch my soaps for half an hour, so you might as well go. And, yes, you don't have to say it, I'll have the volume down."

Sabine went, disappearing into the study in order to reexamine the piece of paper that had become a long-term resident in her pocket. It was now two days since she had received the letter from Geoff informing her that he was going to get married to that Indian woman, and she still didn't know quite what to do about it. She had initially assumed that her mother had been sent the same news, but nothing in her demeanor since appeared to justify that belief. If anything, she had been more cheerful.

It wasn't just the news that Geoff, like Jim, had found a new family that bothered her. It was what it said about her own family. Why hadn't Geoff ever asked her mother? They had been together six years, and he had seemed a committed kind of bloke. He had even tentatively mentioned being a "surrogate father." Kate, Sabine had been forced to conclude, was evidently not the kind of girl men married. Not like her grandmother, who had managed to get herself asked after just one day. She was the kind of girl who allowed herself to be used and dumped again and again and again. It was hopeless, her lack of self-respect. That permanently eager expression she wore around men, like she would be grateful for whatever emotional scraps they threw out. Sabine stared at the now-familiar phrases of the letter, with its slightly earnest desire "to keep her in the picture," its promises that he would "always be there for her." It was not that she had wanted her mother to marry Geoff; just that the fact that he had never asked her somehow made her even more irritated with her mother than she had been already. It felt like another failure.

She looked down at the photographs that she and her grandmother had not yet gotten around to sorting: the baby pictures of Christopher and Kate (he looked pompous even then, she decided) in burgundy, gilt-embossed borders, and the photographs of Kate and the little Chinese boy. Sabine would have really liked to know more about the Chinese boy, but Joy had been too busy to finish them off, she had said the last time they had sat there, reverting to her brusque, matter-of-fact voice. There were too many other things that needed doing right now. Sabine should just do with them what she wanted.

He seems to have been the only bloke who ever stuck around by you, thought

Sabine, fingering the photograph of the two of them grinning toothily from under their hats. Whatever you had, Mum, you definitely lost it somewhere.

"Sabine?"

Sabine jumped. Kate stood in the doorway.

"I wondered if you wanted some lunch. Your granny said she's not hungry, and your grandfather's asleep, so I was wondering if you wanted to grab a bite with me."

"I hope you didn't wake him up," said Sabine, shoving the letter back into her back pocket.

"No, darling, he's asleep. The nurse told me."

"And I suppose you didn't think to check."

Kate forced herself to maintain her smile. Nothing was going to spoil today—neither her mother's blunt dismissal of Kate's offer to cook (Mrs. H was off visiting a doctor in Wexford Town to see if he had any advice about Annie), nor her daughter's apparent irritation at any attempt to help. She shifted her weight slightly, so that she moved farther into the room.

"I thought I'd just do some soup. And bread and butter. Mrs. H was kind enough to leave us a loaf."

"Fine. Whatever."

Sabine turned away from her, back to the photographs.

But Kate didn't go away.

"What are you doing?"

What do you *think*? thought Sabine. "Just sorting through some old photographs," she said, noncommittally. "Grandmother said I could."

Kate's gaze had landed on the top of the box.

"Is that me?" She walked over and bent down, picking up the photograph of herself and the Chinese boy. "My God," she said, adjusting her glasses. "I haven't seen these for years."

Sabine said nothing.

"It's Tung-Li," she said. "My amah's son. We used to play together . . . until—" She broke off. "He was a sweetheart. Terribly shy. He was probably my first childhood friend. There were only a few months between us."

Sabine, despite herself, looked over.

"There was a pool at the back of the apartments where we lived. In Hong Kong. And when none of the other families were around, he and I used to play water dragons in there. Or ride my red bicycle around the edge. We fell in a couple of times, if I remember. My amah was furious." She laughed. "She had a hell of a job drying off anything in the wet season, so having one's best shoes in the swimming pool was really a no-no."

"How old are you there?"

Kate frowned. "I think we moved to the swimming pool place when I was about four, so . . . probably about five? Or six?"

"What happened to him?"

Kate's expression changed. She looked suddenly less animated.

"Well, I sort of had to stop playing with him."

"Why?"

Kate paused.

"It's just the way things were then. Your— your granny had very firm ideas about what was proper. And apparently playing with Tung-Li wasn't proper. Not for a girl like me."

"What, even though you'd been friends for all that time?"

"Yes." Kate thought back, her face now closing off with remembered injustice.

Sabine stared at the photograph.

"It doesn't sound like Grandmother," she said.

Kate's head shot up. She couldn't help herself.

"You don't think so, do you?"

"She's always been all right with me."

"Well, darling, one day you'll find out that Granny is not always the sweet old lady that you now think. She can be as hard as nails, too."

Sabine looked at her mother, simultaneously shocked by her unusually hard tone, and perversely feeling the need to contradict it.

"You think it's fair to separate two children, just because of the color of their skin?"

"No," said Sabine, conscious of the feeling of being backed into a corner. "But things were different then, weren't they? People didn't see things the same way. It was the way they were brought up."

"So you'd have thought it was fine if I'd made you eat meat back home—because that was the way I was brought up? Because it was, you know. If I'd refused to eat meat here I would have been told to live off potatoes or nothing."

"No, of course not."

"So, Sabine, how come everything Granny does is somehow okay, somehow excusable? And yet how come everything I do, no matter how well intended, is thrown back in my face?"

Kate didn't know where this had come from, yet somehow the sight of that picture had brought the ancient sense of injustice back to the surface, and made her infuriated again. She was tired of taking the rap for all the wrongs of the world, tired of taking Sabine's sharp cracks with equanimity, of being burdened both by the guilty acknowledgment that she had ruined everyone's lives and by having to keep moving on, nodding and smiling, from underneath it.

"Sometimes, Sabine, believe it or not, your mum is the wronged party. Occasionally, just occasionally, she is in the right."

She had reckoned, however, without her daughter's inbuilt mulishness. And the capacity of the sixteen-year-old for self-righteous self-belief.

"I can't believe you think you're always in the right," Sabine said, furiously. "Not after the way you've behaved."

"What?"

"Fair enough. So, Grandmother made you have other friends when you were living out in the tropics. She was probably only trying to do what was right for you. You would have probably gotten people talking about you and stuff, the way things were then."

Kate began to shake her head, slowly, disbelievingly.

"She's told me lots about it, you know. About all the rules and things. About how people got talked about if they didn't do things the right way. And even if you were right, it's not as if you've gotten it right since, is it? It's not like you ever put other people first. I mean you can't even be bothered to spend time with your own dad, even though you came here because you thought he was dying. You're too busy flirting with anyone who comes your way. So that you can add another bloody failed relationship to your list."

"Sabine!"

"Well, it's true." Sabine was aware she was overstepping a mark, but felt too infuriated to care. Who was her mother to judge other people? "You get through men like Grandfather gets through handkerchiefs. You don't seem to care how it looks. You could have been more like Grandmother and Grandfather and hung on till you found the right person. Had some commitment. Really stuck with something. You know, real, true

love. But you just go from man to man without even caring. I mean, look at Justin! How
long did he last? And Geoff? God, you don't
even care about him getting married."

Kate, about to launch into an equally
heated response, froze.

There was a brief silence.

"What did you say?"

Sabine paused.

"Geoff. He's getting married."

She took a deep breath, suddenly aware
that her mother might not have gotten a letter after all. "I thought you knew."

Kate looked down at her feet, stuck a
hand out to a shelf, to steady herself.

"No," she said carefully. "I didn't know.
When did he tell you?"

Silently, Sabine pulled the crumpled letter
from her back pocket and handed it to her
mother. Kate, now leaning against a desk,
read the contents without speaking.

"Well, that didn't take him long, did it?"

Oh, God, thought Sabine suddenly. Her
eyes have gone all watery.

"I thought you knew," she said again.

"No, I didn't. It's quite possible he wrote to
me at home, but I wouldn't have gotten it,
being here."

There was a lengthy silence. Outside, someone dropped a water bucket, sending a distant crash reverberating through the yard and a male voice yelled at a horse to stand still. Kate didn't even jump; she stood up, like someone sleepwalking, and made her way slowly to the door.

"Well. I'll do some soup then," she said, rubbing her hair from her face. "And some bread."

Sabine sat on the floor, feeling like she might cry.

"I'm sorry, Mum," she said.

Kate smiled at her, a slow, sad smile.

"Not your fault, darling," she said. "Not your fault."

They had eaten lunch in near silence; Sabine, unusually, trying to make conversation, consumed with guilt over her unwitting bombshell. Kate had nodded, and smiled, grateful for her daughter's rare attempts to spare her feelings, but both had been relieved when it was finally over and they could go somewhere where their recent conversation didn't loom over them, like a rain cloud threatening further showers. In Sabine's case, this meant riding the gray over to Manor Farm, where they had said she was free to use the cross-country course on their land to practice her jumping skills. In Kate's, it meant spending the first proper time since she had arrived at Kilcarrion sitting with her father.

She had sat for best part of an hour in the chair next to his bed, while Lynda periodically appeared to check monitors, bedpans, and offer cups of tea. Although every attempt had been made to make his room cheerful, sitting in the near silence, staring at the once animated face, the father who had once swung her in his arms, and reduced her to putty by tickling, Kate had felt consumed by the gloom, saddened by the fact that she had been unable to live up to what he wanted of her, and the fact that he was going to die without them being able to bridge the abyss between them. I do try to get it right, she told him. I do try to make things work, to put other people first. But you and Mum are a hard double act to live up to; I wish you'd understand that. I wish you'd tell Sabine that.

He didn't respond; she didn't expect him to. She just sat there, willing her silent thoughts across to him, and thumbing unseeing through the books that Sabine had placed on his bedside table.

It was nearly dark when she sought Thom out, and asked him to meet her in the summerhouse. He had looked carefully at her expression, noted her inability to look him in the eye, and said nothing.

When he arrived, whistling his way through the overgrown gardens, he didn't kiss her, just leaned against the doorframe in an overly casual manner, and smiled.

She was sitting on the crates where he had placed the blanket, her arms placed protectively around her knees like a child, her hair half covering her face.

"It has to stop. Here."

Thom ducked his head in order to try and catch her eye. His tone was light, humorous.

"Till you change your mind again?" He paused. "Shall I give you half an hour?"

Kate looked up. Her eyes, behind her glasses, were red-rimmed, sore.

"No. I'm not going to change my mind. I'm going home."

"I don't understand."

"I don't expect you to."

"What's that supposed to mean?"

"What I say. I'm going home. To London."

"What?"

It was the first time he had sounded angry. Kate glanced up at him, and saw the hurt and incomprehension on his face.

"Look, Kate, I know you. I know you change your mind like the wind changes direction. But what the hell is this all about?"

Kate looked away from him, not wanting to see.

"I'm doing this for all of us," she said, quietly.

"What is this?"

"Like I said, it's best for everybody."

"Bullshit."

"You—you don't understand."

"So tell me."

Kate pressed her eyes tightly shut, wishing she could be anywhere but here. "It was just something I heard, today. Something Sabine told me. And it made me realize that whatever I might think about you, however we might feel right now, that I'm just back on track to make the same mistakes I always have."

She paused, wiping her nose on the back of her sleeve.

"I didn't give this enough thought, Thom. I

didn't think about whether it had a chance of going anywhere. I didn't think about the people it would hurt if it all fell apart. And it will fall apart, you see? You and I have absolutely nothing in common. We live in different countries. We don't know anything about each other apart from the fact that we still find each other physically attractive.

"So, it's a pretty sure thing that I'll manage to screw this up somehow. And the thing is, every time I screw something up, I lose another little bit of my daughter's respect. Worse, I lose a bit of my own."

She sat, trying not to sniff, her face now buried in her crossed arms, so that her voice emerged muffled.

"Anyway. I thought about all this today, and I decided it's best for everyone if I just go back home. I'm going to get the ferry tomorrow. Daddy won't miss me—he hasn't even realized I'm here. And my mother has done her best to ignore me since I arrived. Sabine . . ." Here, she let out a long, shuddering sigh. "Sabine, I've decided should stay here. She's much happier over here than she ever was in London. Even you noticed it, and you've only known her a couple of months. She can come home if and when she feels like it. Or to start university. I'm not going to force her to do anything. But I just thought I should let you know."

She stared through her arms at her feet. They had bits of straw sticking to them, from earlier, when she had walked around the yard, trying to locate her mother.

"So, that's it, is it?"

She looked up. Thom was breathing hard, rubbing at the back of his head with his good hand.

"Bye-bye, Thom, again. Sorry if I led you on, but I've decided what's best for everyone and you're just going to have to lump it."

Kate stared at him.

"Well, bullshit, Kate. Bullshit. I'm not going to let you do this again. You don't dictate single-handedly what happens in any relationship, and you don't presume to act on my behalf."

He turned and began pacing up and down the cramped floorspace, seemingly oblivious to the tins that he kicked as he moved. The air crackled, electrified with his anger.

"I've sat here for days listening to you tell me what's right and what's wrong with us getting together. And I know you, so I figured the best thing was to sit tight, just let you get it all out of your system. But just because you decide something is wrong, doesn't mean that it is, okay? Just because you've suddenly decided you've dipped your toe too far into the water, doesn't mean you can pull the bloody plug out."

He shook his head to himself, trying to calm his breathing, and sat down heavily on an upturned bucket.

"Look. Kate. I've been in love with you a long time. An awful long time. And I've been out with all sorts of girls since—lovely girls, with big smiles and bigger hearts. Girls, believe it or not, even lovelier than you. And the more I went out with, the more I realized that if something's missing at the core of it, if you don't feel that—that—that bloody thing, the thing that is just incontrovertibly right— then there's no point. Right? And then you come back, which I never expected, and I knew straightaway. I knew from the first time I saw you in here, swearing at the walls and crying like a bloody adolescent, and something in here"—he thumped at his chest— "something just went '*Ahh*. So *there* it is.' And I knew."

She gazed at him, troubled, her bottom lip pushed out. She had never seen him angry before; she had never known him to say so many things at the same time before. She almost flinched as he moved off his bucket, and sat down next to her on the crates.

"Look, even if you don't know yet, Kate, I do. And I don't care about all the other eejits you've been out with, and I don't care about the fact that we live in different places. Or that we don't even like the same things. Because it's just details, okay? It's just details."

He took her hand, and held it between his own two. "And I know I'm not perfect. I'm too used to being on my own, and I get crabby about stupid things, and . . . and I've got a bloody arm gone. I know I'm not the man I was."

She shook her head, not wanting him to mention it, not wanting him to suggest it as a factor.

He shook his head back at her, his voice suddenly quieting. "But I tell you, Kate, I'll tell you this—if you go now, you're wrong. Really wrong. And it'll be because you're the one who's crippled, not me."

He paused, then seemingly out of nowhere, lifted her hand and pressed her palm to his mouth. He kept it there, his eyes closed, apparently silenced by his own action. Kate, heedless of the tears now rolling down her cheeks, reached out her other hand and stroked the side of his face.

"But how do we know, Thom?" she said, tearfully. "How do I know?"

"Because I know," he said, opening his eyes. "And just for once, you're going to have to trust me on that."

They walked out of the summerhouse together like wary travelers venturing out after a great storm, for once not thinking about the possibility of being seen. Thom said he had to check on the horses, and Kate said she would accompany him, hoping to locate Sabine. She wanted Sabine not to be anxious, to know that she was fine about Geoff, even if she didn't yet feel ready to tell her why.

Liam was sitting outside the tack room on a bale of hay, polishing a bridle with a soft cloth, and whistling through his teeth to a tune on the radio. He gave them a knowing look as they approached, but said nothing.

"Are the horses in from the bottom field?" said Thom, checking the bottom bolts on a stable door.

"Yup."

"Is Sabine back?"

"Just taken the gray into the stable. We've moved him into the far one, as the roof's started leaking on that middle one again."

Thom swore quietly under his breath, glancing up at the missing tiles. "I'll have to throw another tarpaulin over it. We don't have any of those tiles left just to wedge in, do we?"

"Used them up months ago," said Liam. "Been anywhere nice?" He looked Kate slowly up and down, so that she was conscious of her flushed cheeks, her tingling skin.

"Just sorting out a bit of paperwork," said Thom. "I thought you said all the horses were in."

Liam turned to face him, and then followed his gaze down past the barn to the bottom fields.

"They are."

"So who's that?"

Liam stood, and squinted into the peach-colored evening sunlight, holding a hand up to his brow.

"Looks like the Duke," he said, frowning.

"But he's been lame for months. That horse isn't lame."

Thom was silent, his face unmoving.

Liam adjusted his hand, trying to see better. "And who's that on him? Someone's on him."

"What is it?" said Sabine, who had just approached, carrying her saddle. She glanced at her mother, wondering what she was doing in the yard.

"I can't see," said Kate. "I can't see anything that far."

"That's Mrs. Ballan—"

Liam stopped, as Thom placed a hand on his arm.

"C'mon," he said, quietly. "We'll leave them to it."

"What?" said Sabine. "Is that my grandmother riding? Who is she riding?"

"Bloody hell. She's not ridden in years." Liam shook his head in astonishment.

"C'mon," said Thom, steering them away toward the house. "Let's go inside."

He glanced over his shoulder as they walked away, leaving the distant, regal figures of the old woman and the stiff old horse outlined against the setting sun; his once-

proud head held high, his ears flicking backward and forward to the sound of her voice,
as they wove their way slowly down to the
woods.

Chapter Thirteen

Joy stayed in her room for two days after the
Duke was put down; the first time, said Mrs.
H, that she could remember her succumb-
ing to anything, let alone grief. She had
risen at dawn, and spent the first two hours
of the morning in the old horse's box,
grooming him and talking to him, so that
when the vet finally arrived, he found not a
sorrowful, condemned animal, but an apparently buoyant one, his battered old coat burnished by sheer effort into a pseudohealthy
gloss. She had then stood with him unflinch-
ing, one hand on his face, his chin resting
comfortably on her shoulder, as the vet

raised the humane killer. So relaxed was the Duke in this position that when he fell, his weight almost pulled her down underneath him; it was only Thom, waiting behind her, who had managed to drag her away in time. They had all stood for some minutes, unspeaking, looking at the still body on the thickly cushioned floor. And then, with a polite thank-you to the vet, she had walked resolutely out of the stable toward the house, her arms stiffly by her sides, her chin raised. And not looked back.

She was funny like that, mused Mrs. H. Wanting to send the old horse off proud. Spending all that time on him. Not like her own husband, thought Sabine, knowing it was what everybody was thinking.

Because it was during the second day that Joy had locked herself in her room, refusing food and asking visitors, somewhat formally, to please leave her alone, that Edward's breathing worsened, and Lynda took it upon herself to call the doctor, out of fear that if she didn't, he might not be around by the time his wife deigned to reemerge.

Sabine, white-faced and watchful, had sat holding her grandfather's hand as the doctor took his pulse, pressed his stethoscope to his bony old chest, and conferred in hushed whispers with Lynda.

"It's all right," she said irritably. "You can tell me. I am his granddaughter."

"Where's Mrs. Ballantyne?" he said, ignoring her.

"She's not coming out of her room today. So you'll have to talk to me."

The doctor and Lynda exchanged looks.

"Her horse died," said Lynda, with a raised eyebrow. And seemed vaguely disappointed when the doctor nodded, as if he understood.

"Is Christopher around?"

"He's away."

"Is your mother still here?" he said.

"Yes, but she doesn't have anything to do with my grandfather." Sabine spoke slowly and carefully, as if she were talking to idiots.

"It's that kind of family," said Lynda. She was becoming rather free with her opinions these days.

"Look, why don't you just talk to me? I'll tell my grandmother when she comes out."

The doctor nodded, as if contemplating this response. But then he looked at Sabine, and compressed his mouth into a thin line.

"I don't think we can wait that long."

Shortly afterward Kate, flushed with the new confidence of the well-loved, decided to take matters into her own hands. She had marched along the corridor, rapped sharply on her mother's door, and, ignoring Joy's croaking protestations, had walked into the sparsely furnished little room, and told her that the doctor urgently needed to talk to her.

"I can't come right now," said Joy, not looking at her. She was lying on her single bed, her back turned to the door, her long, thin legs, in their battered corduroy trousers, curled up in a near-fetal position. "Tell him I'll call him later."

Kate, who had never seen her mother look vulnerable (she wasn't even aware that she had ever assumed a horizontal position in daylight before), tried to keep her voice firm. To sound determined.

"I'm afraid he wants to speak to you now. Daddy's really not well."

Joy lay still on the bed. Kate stood there for a long minute, waiting for some kind of response.

"I'm sorry about the Duke, Mummy. But you are going to have to get up. You are needed downstairs."

Outside, she could hear Sabine padding

softly down the corridor to her own room, sniffing mournfully. When she had finally gauged the seriousness of her grandfather's condition, she had, somewhat out of character, burst into noisy tears; a helpless, childish burst of crying where her fists screwed like balls into her eyes, and rivers of snot and dribble fought for channels down her chin. It had been Kate's shock at this uncharacteristic display of emotion that had fueled her decision to act. At some point, her mother was going to have to talk to her. It was all very well her leaving everything to Sabine, but at times like this she had to remember that her granddaughter was only sixteen years old.

"Mummy—"

"Please go away," said Joy, lifting her head slightly, so that Kate could just make out the red-rimmed eyes, the flattened, matted gray hair. "I just want to be left alone."

Outside, in the corridor, Kate heard the sound of Sabine's door closing. She lowered her voice.

"You know what? It would be really nice if you listened to me. Just once."

Joy looked away, through the window.

"Look, whatever you think of me, Mummy,

I'm still Daddy's daughter. And I'm here. Christopher's not. And it's not fair for Sabine to have to cope with all this on her own. Someone has to decide whether Daddy is going to go into hospital, and, if not, what we are going to do." She paused, rubbed at a mark on her trouser leg.

"Right. If you're not downstairs in five minutes, then I shall decide with the doctor what's the best thing to do with Daddy." With a deep sigh, Kate turned and walked out of the little room, closing the door firmly behind her.

Joy arrived in the drawing room just as the doctor was finishing his cup of tea, her hair smoothed back, and her eyes almost obscured by puffy folds of skin.

"So sorry to have kept you waiting," she told him.

Kate, seated opposite in one of the easy chairs beside the fire, didn't know whether to laugh or cry.

It's like she would do almost anything rather than talk to me," she said afterward, absently fingering an unidentified leather strap, as she sat with Thom in the tack room.

She was sunk into an old armchair, her legs stretched out near the three-bar electric heater that, while glowing brightly, seemed to do little to dispel the cold. The air, stark and clear outside, condensed into little clouds of steam as she spoke. "I mean, at a time like this a family is meant to pull together. Even a family like ours. And yet she just marches around, making herself busier and busier, staying away from Dad, and yet refusing to talk to me about what we should do about him. Christopher's stuck in Geneva at some conference, and Sabine is too young to have to make those sorts of decisions, so it's not like she's got anyone else to talk to, is it?"

Thom sat, rubbing the dirt from a bridle with a piece of wet sponge, deftly unpicking buckles and stripping it apart with his right hand.

"Am I really that useless? Is it so inconceivable that I might be able to help her?"

He shook his head.

"It's not about you. It's about her."

"What do you mean?"

"It's easier for her to grieve for her horse than for her husband. She's so knotted up, your mother, so used to keeping it all inside. I don't suppose she knows how to deal with what's going on."

Kate thought for a minute.

"I don't agree. She's always found it easy enough to get cross. I think it's about me. She just doesn't want to let me feel that anything I do could possibly be of any use to her." She stood, facing the door. "She's never been proud of anything I did. I've always gotten it wrong in her eyes. She just doesn't want to let that change."

"You're awful hard on her."

"She's been awfully hard on me. Look, Thom, who was it who said I couldn't live at home when I got pregnant with Sabine? Huh? How much do you think that hurt me? I was eighteen years old, for God's sake." Kate was now pacing the little room, running her hand along the saddle racks that lined one side.

"I thought you didn't want to stay."

"I didn't. But that was partly because they were so bloody awful to me."

Thom paused, lifted the bridle to the light, searching for patches of inbuilt grime, and then lowered it onto his knee.

"That was a long time ago. You should move on. We've moved on."

Kate turned to him, her mouth set in an obstinate scowl that, had she seen it, her late grandmother Alice would doubtless have remarked was exactly like her mother's.

"I can't move on, Thom. Not till she stops judging me for everything I do. Not till she can start accepting me for who I am."

She had folded her arms, and stood there, glaring at him, her hair falling over her face. He put the bridle down, and stood upright, placing his arms tightly around her, so that her body, inevitably, became fluid, and relaxed within them.

"Let it go."

"I can't."

"For now. We'll do something to take your mind off it." His voice was soft, tender. Kate lifted her finger and traced his lips. The bottom one was very faintly blistered, from the cold.

"So, what did you have in mind?" she murmured. "You know the house is full of people."

He grinned, his eyes lifting mischievously.

"I think it's about time you came riding."

Kate stared, and then pulled back, away from him.

"Ohhh, no," she said. "You might have gotten Sabine. You are not getting me. I've spent the last twenty years thanking God that I didn't have to get on another bloody horse. No way."

Thom walked slowly toward her. He was still smiling.

"We could go for miles. It's a beautiful day."

"No. No way."

"We could just walk, slowly, and head down to the forest." He paused. "Where no one can see us."

Kate shook her head, her mouth firmly closed, in the manner of someone trying to stave off an unwelcome kiss.

"I don't ride, Thom. Horses scare me. I'll be quite happy if I never ride another one in my whole life."

His good hand crept behind her neck, pulling her gently toward him. He smelled of soap, and of the sweet, musty scent of meadow hay.

"You don't have to ride one. You can get on with me. I'll have my arm around you the whole time."

Kate felt dizzy, intoxicated by the nearness of him. She placed her arms around his collar, wanting to sink into him, wanting to feel him sink into her. Her eyes closed, and she let her head fall to one side, feeling his warm breath on her exposed neck.

"I want to be on my own with you," he whispered, and the vibrations of his voice made the hairs on the back of her neck stiffen exquisitely.

Then she jumped back, as she heard the sound of a stable door slamming shut.

There was the sound of approaching footfall, and then Liam appeared at the door, his thin, weathered face dark against the bright light outside. He stood, a blanket under his arm, his gaze flickering from Thom, who was seated, cleaning tack, to Kate, who stood, casually resting against one of the saddles.

"Gorgeous day," he said. It was directed at Thom, but his eyes rested on Kate. "I thought I'd probably leave the blankets off the bay colt, for now. He's not as thin-skinned as we thought."

Thom nodded. "Good move. I was thinking we should probably turn him out, now that the weather's improving," he said. Then looked up, inquiringly, only the briefest of glances directed at Kate.

"So, you going to be around all day, Liam?"

Sabine walked down to the stable yard, her hands thrust deep in the pockets of her jeans, her chin buried in the polo neck of her jumper, so that only her eyes and nose, both of which were pink and slightly raw-looking, emerged. Her grandfather was dying, that was basically what the doctor had said, even if he had dressed it up in all sorts of "problematics" and "prognoses." Her grandfather was going to die, her grandmother had gone all strange because her horse had died, Annie hadn't answered her calls for ages, and the whole thing was falling apart. The only proper family she had ever had was falling apart.

Bertie at her feet, Sabine sat down on the wooden bench by the paddock, and wiped at her nose with her sleeve. She was increasingly having to fight a suspicion, stupid as it sounded, that it had something to do with her. The two families she'd had at home, Jim and Geoff, they had fallen apart. Now her Irish family, whose numbers had all been perfectly well and normal when she arrived—well, maybe not normal, exactly, she conceded—that was all disintegrating, fracturing, and fading around her. Nothing was as it had been when she came. Nothing. And if it didn't have anything to do with her, then what was it?

Sabine let out a long, shuddering sigh, so that Bertie looked up questioningly, before resettling his nose between his paws. Bobby had told her she was being ridiculous when she told him her theory on the telephone. "Old people die. Old horses die," he had said. "That's what happens. You just haven't been up close to it before." He had been nice. Not made any jokes about it all, as if understanding that she really needed to talk to someone. She would have talked to Thom, she thought bitterly, but even he was never around these days. He hadn't offered to take her out riding for ages, and when it was just the two of them in the yard, he was just pleasant and jokey with her, like he was talking to John John, or even some stranger.

Sabine stood, suddenly conscious of the cold, rubbed at her elbows, and walked over to the stables, poking her head over the top of each door to see who was in and who wasn't. She had toyed with speaking to her mother. They had gotten on okay for a couple of days, since the Geoff letter. But sympathetic as Kate might have been, any conversation with her about Kilcarrion was going to be too difficult, clouded by Kate's inability to get on with Joy, and muddied by the fact that both knew that she wanted to leave Ireland as soon as possible, and Sabine didn't.

Because that was the crux of it: Even if her grandfather died, she didn't want to go. She had gotten used to it here: its rhythms and structures, the way you knew what was going to happen. Most of the time. She liked the horses. The big house. The people. She couldn't imagine spending hours aimlessly hanging around the housing project, where all that mattered was who was wearing what and whether people fancied one another. If she tried to talk to them about riding, or hunting, they would take the mickey out of her, make out she had turned posh. They would make her feel different, more different than she already felt. Somehow, home didn't feel like home anymore. And hearing that, Sabine thought guiltily, was going to break her mother's heart again.

She pushed open the stable door, trod softly inside, and put her arms around the gray, who, engrossed in a hay net, ignored her. After some minutes, she walked out, closed the door carefully, and made for the tack room. A ride would blow the black clouds away. That was what her grand-mother always said.

Liam was alone in there, swiping at a horse blanket with a brush that seemed more clogged with hairs than the fabric it was trying to clean.

"Thought I'd take the gray out," she said, reaching for his bridle.

"Nice day for it," said Liam, grinning. "Mind you, it's always a nice day for it."

"Har-har," said Sabine, trying not to smile. She didn't feel Liam should be encouraged.

"You going out by yourself?"

"Yes? So?"

"Nothing."

"Go on."

Liam shrugged. "Thought you'd rather have company. Thought you liked to ride out with Thom."

Sabine struggled to lift the saddle off the rack, determined not to blush.

"Well, I don't know where he is. And there's no one about today. Not really."

"Well, now, you might just be surprised."

Sabine looked at him.

"I think Thom's headed over to the forest. On the big horse." He dropped the brush in a box on the floor and gave the blanket a shake. "I can't remember whether he had anyone with him or not."

He turned to the next blanket on his pile, a peculiar smile playing about his lips. "Have a good one," he said.

Sabine frowned at Liam, and then walked out of the yard, her reins dragging on the floor behind her. Liam could be really odd, sometimes.

Deep Boar Forest, as it was known locally, neither was particularly deep, nor, to anyone's knowledge, did it contain any boars. It ran, about a quarter of a mile wide, along the course of a small river, which backed two local country estates and provided trout fishing in season, and opportunities for local teenagers to lose themselves, unspied upon by their elders, in summer. It was, however, long; pursuing the winding river for almost a mile and a half, so that those who wanted to convince themselves that they were far from civilization could do so, protected by the shelter and the near silence of the trees and shrubbery around them.

It was halfway down this river path that Thom pulled the big bay hunter gently to a halt, and, swinging his right leg over the back of the saddle, sprang lightly onto the soft, peat-cushioned earth. Looping the reins over his left arm, he reached up to help Kate down. Rather less gracefully, she slithered down the horse's shoulder, then made her way slowly to the recumbent tree trunk, and seated herself gingerly on its mossy surface.

"I'm not going to be able to move tomorrow," she said, rubbing at her backside and wincing.

"It's the day after that will really get you."

"You don't have to sound so pleased about it."

Thom stroked the horse's nose, and then led him over to another tree. He untied the lead rope around the horse's neck and clipped it onto his bit, securing him to a branch with a loose knot. Then he walked slowly over to the trunk and sat down beside her, pushing back her hair and kissing her nose.

"Was it really so bad?"

She grinned ruefully. Looked down as if she could see the emerging bruises through her clothes.

"I wouldn't have done that for anyone else."

"I hope not. If we'd have sat any closer

we'd have been flouting public decency laws."

"Oh, I didn't get the feeling that you minded too much."

They leaned together and kissed for a long time, Kate breathing in the damp, mysterious scents of woodland, the musty smells of rotting leaves and sharp tang of new growth mingling with the subtler ones of the man beside her. She was, she realized, unequivocally happy.

"I love you, you know," he said, when they pulled apart.

"I know. I love you, too."

It hadn't required any effort at all. No soul-searching. No trauma.

Above them, the bright sunlight cast spindly rays through the green canopy, illuminating the earth around them in winking, moving spotlights. The breeze gently rustled the undergrowth beneath them, an invisible hand running lightly across its surface. They kissed again, his hands now entwined in her hair, forcing her gently back onto the wide bed of the tree trunk, so that she could feel his weight upon her. It made her weak with longing, and she clutched at him in return, trying to bring him closer, closer.

Time stilled, dissolved in the feeling of him against her, of their mingled breathing, of the feel of his lips against her skin.

"Oh, Thom," she murmured into his ear. "I want you."

She felt his cheek, rough against her, and his stillness as he paused. Then he pushed himself up on his good hand, his eyes fixed on hers. "I want you," he said, and stooped to bestow a kiss, like a blessing, on her face.

She reached up, feeling there was too great a distance between them, pulling him down toward her. But halfway down, he stopped, his strength holding the gap between their bodies.

"No," he said.

"What?" She squinted, as a shaft of sunlight broke the shady cover above them, briefly unable to see his face. Oh, God, she thought suddenly, it's the glasses. I shouldn't have worn the glasses.

"I don't want to do it here. Like this." He pushed himself fully upright, his breathing still irregular. "I don't want it to be . . . sleazy."

"How could this be sleazy?" Kate, also struggling upright, fought to keep the impatience from her voice.

"Not *sleazy,* then. The wrong word." He

rubbed at the back of his head, reached for her hand, turned it over.

"I just want it to be perfect. It . . . I don't know . . . I waited so long . . . it's you, you mean too much."

Kate stared at her palm, aware of the slow dissipation of the heat within her body. Replaced by a different kind of tenderness. A different power.

"It won't be perfect, Thom."

He glanced up at her, two perfect blue irises in black borders.

"You can't expect it to be perfect. If you build this up too much, we'll disappoint each other. Believe me." I know, she added silently.

He looked down, still studying her hand.

"Just because it's been such a long time coming, doesn't mean we should make it more significant than it is. It'll probably be a bit awkward, at first. I mean, we've got to get used to each other."

Unconsciously, he glanced at his arm. Kate shook her head.

"We've both changed, Thom. We both have to start from scratch. I think it will be perfect, but eventually. And I think it's more important that we just start from some-where." She smiled, looked around her.

"Even if it's not here. Or for the next couple of days. Because frankly, I don't think I'm going to be able to move my legs."

The mood eased, expanded. He looked back at her, breathed out, a short, half-laughing breath. And then he lifted her hand and, his eyes still fixed intently on hers, took hold of the inside of her wrist lightly with his teeth. At the touch of his mouth on her skin, Kate's spine became molten, her vision, even from behind her glasses, blurred. She swallowed hard.

"You're right," he said into her wrist, his eyes still burning into hers. "We shouldn't make it the be-all and end-all."

He let go, and placed her hand gently back on her lap. Smiled.

"But you're wrong, too, you know. It will be perfect."

Sabine turned toward home, lifting her left leg forward with a newly practiced ease, and loosening the buckles on the horse's girth, so that he could relax a bit, too. She had ridden him hard this afternoon, determined to focus only on the physical sensations of his sinewy frame pounding rhythmically across the turf beneath her, the glorious, all-absorbing feeling of him lifting and stretching over the jumps, keen to blank out the complications that lay ahead.

She wasn't going to go home. She was just going to have to tell her mother. She would visit her, she would explain, and she would ring her every week, but she was going to live here. Where Grandmother needed her. Where she felt happiest. Maybe she wouldn't say that last bit, she thought, lengthening her reins, so that the gray's head drooped gratefully. It sounded a bit cruel. Even for Mum.

The lowering sun glowed red, casting a silent, Scandinavian glow over the empty fields, and tinting the top fields, still tipped with frost, with pink hues. Behind her, exhausted, Bertie trotted listlessly at a safe distance from the rear hooves, his paws clicking lightly on the tarmac. She could always go back every other weekend, if her mother was really desperate. She knew she didn't like being on her own. But she would have to understand that it was partly her own fault; that it was she who had sent Sabine here after all. And it wasn't her fault if she got on with Grandmother and Grandfather so much better than she did.

"Perhaps they'll even let me keep you,"

she said to the horse, so that his ears pricked forward. "One more horse wouldn't make any difference, would it?"

But it wasn't just a selfish thing. If she was here, she could help her grandmother with Grandfather. She was always too busy doing other things, and they could save money if they let Lynda go. Plus, Mrs. H might have to spend more time with Annie, if she needed counseling, so they would need someone to make lunch. As long as Mrs. H still made the bread, Sabine thought she could probably cope with that.

And in the meantime, she could ride every day. And help cheer everyone up a bit. And keep an eye on Christopher and Julia. And perhaps keep seeing Bobby. She definitely wanted him as a friend, even if she wasn't sure about the other thing.

She was just rounding the corner behind the Church of Blessed Peter, when the gray stopped, his head lifting abruptly, his ears pricking forward. His nostrils widened, as if scenting something, and he let out a long, low snicker of greeting. Bertie, moving up in front of him, looked up, too.

Sabine, jolted from her reverie, glanced around to see if there was another donkey in the hedge. But, following the animals' line of vision, she spied in the distance the big horse from the yard, making his way slowly along the hedge by the forty-acre field. He was facing her, so at first, from that distance, she thought she could just about make out Thom astride him, and Sabine wondered whether to shout a greeting. Then the horse turned slightly to his left, and Sabine realized that there were actually two people on the horse. One was Thom. The other, behind him, was her mother. She could make out the red of her hair, glowing against the plowed dull brown of the field. She had her arms around his waist, and was resting her head on the back of his shoulder.

Sabine blinked hard, at first unable to believe what she was seeing, and then, when it was confirmed, frozen by its ramifications.

Her mother was terrified of horses. There would be only one possible reason why she would be up there.

She thought, suddenly, of what Liam had said.

She waited until they had passed, ignoring the restless stomping of the gray, her own gaze gradually becoming as cold as her stilled limbs. And then, only when she was sure she was out of view, she let her horse walk on toward home.

Kate lay in the bath, the bubbles up to her chin, and her toes emerging from the steaming water at the other end, little pink sausages, lined up underneath the lime-scaled taps. Her body was already beginning to ache—she had known it would—but it was filled with such a pleasant sensation of ease and release that she no longer cared. Thom loved her. He really loved her. Everything else was detail.

Closing her eyes, she thought of how he had felt, his breath upon hers, his arms around her, how he had felt on the horse, the quietly erotic sensation of his body pressed tight against her, their silence against the muffled lift and fall of the horse's hooves below. She thought of how, after they had talked on the old tree stump, he had, at her urging, peeled off his jumper and opened his shirt, to reveal to her the mechanics of his arm. He had been a bit uncomfortable at first, she could tell, and then, perhaps to hide this, almost defiantly relaxed about showing her and talking about it, his eyes

flashing up to test her reactions at each revelation. But it wasn't that it would have made
any difference, she had wanted to tell him.
She just needed to know. It was a part of him
she couldn't imagine, and now that they had
seemingly crossed a barrier, she needed to
know it all.

The hand, he explained, was silicone. It
had a slight gripping facility, but not much.
(He could have had a claw arrangement,
which would have given him a greater ability
to grip, "but it made me feel like Captain
Hook. I couldn't ever forget about it, seeing it
sticking out like that.") It extended into a
plastic covered wrist, and then became a
brief arrangement of metal cables and near-
cylindrical tubing before welding itself, in a
tight web of harness, around his shoulders.
"Couldn't you have gotten one of those fancy
electronic ones?" said Kate, running her finger along it. "The ones that respond to your
nerves, or whatever? Don't they look more
realistic?"

"Not if I wanted to keep doing this job," he
said. "This old thing doesn't mind the wet, or
the dust from the hay. It doesn't have too
many bits to jam. And besides, I can get by
fine with my right hand most of the time."

A lot of people who lost arms, he said, didn't even bother. Too much hassle, and they could be uncomfortable at first. He had persevered because he didn't like being stared at. And people did stare; they couldn't help themselves.

She had lifted the silicone hand then, and kissed it, and Thom had pulled her closer to him, kissing her hair in return. She hadn't really thought about it after that; it had been not knowing what lay under the jumper that had made it compelling. She just thought about what life might be like with Thom; what it would be like to wake up to those irides-cent blue eyes, to casually snuggle up against that broad, work-hardened chest. How did you know? She had once asked her mother, back in the days when they could talk about things like love. You just do, she had said, almost matter-of-factly, a response Kate had found deeply unsatisfactory at the time. But perhaps she was right, she thought wonderingly. Perhaps, just perhaps, this was it. It didn't feel like before; the kind of anx-ious, hiccupy love she thought she had felt for Justin; the grateful, reserved love she had felt for Geoff. This had passion, yes, but it felt simply solid; immovable, like there was nothing she could do to alter it, even if she had tried. Inevitable. Smiling to herself, she bent her knees and submerged her face slowly under the water, allowing its warmth to flood over her.

Because Kate spent so much time alone in her house, she had gradually lost the habit of locking the bathroom door; it was an irrelevance when there was no risk of anybody walking in. So it was something of a shock, as she opened her eyes to find Sabine standing there.

"Sabine?" she spluttered, wiping the bubbles from her face. "Are you all right? What do you want?"

"Couldn't you leave it alone?" Sabine spat, her hands on her hips, her face contorted with fury. "Couldn't you have just managed without a bloke for five minutes?"

Kate fought her way upright, fighting the urge to cover her nakedness under the harsh gaze of her daughter.

"Wha—?"

"You're disgusting! Do you know that? You disgust me! You're like a bloody whore!"

"Now, hold on . . ." Kate fumbled for the

towel at the other end of the bath, sending a small tidal wave of water crashing onto the bathroom floor. "Just wait—"

"I even felt sorry for you! D'you know that?" Sabine was shaking her head now. Her hair, which had been flattened by her riding hat, stuck up at unlikely angles. "I felt sorry for you about Geoff! I felt really bad about saying anything. And all the time you—you were just. . . ."—she struggled with the words—"you were just shagging Thom. Throwing yourself at him. God, you make me *sick*!"

"I haven't slept with Thom," Kate stood up, hanging onto the radiator as she climbed out of the bath. "I haven't slept with anybody."

"I *saw* you! I saw you riding with him! With my own eyes!"

Kate shook her head, dumbly, crushed by the raw hatred in her daughter's face.

"Sabine, it's not like you think—"

"What, you're telling me you're not involved with him?"

She paused, breathed out.

"No, I'm not saying that."

"Don't lie to me, then. Don't try and cover it up. God, Mum, when I came here, I really felt for you, d'you know that? I really felt for you having to grow up here. I thought they were impossible."

She was now crying, her breath coming in short, ragged gasps, her eyes screwed tight to try and stop the flow of tears.

"And now, now, I just wish—I just wish I could have grown up with them and not you. People who love each other, properly, even if they don't always show it. People who stick by each other. People who don't go off jumping into bed with any old bloody bloke that comes along. Why couldn't you have been more like them, huh? Why do you have to be such a . . . such a *slag*?" The last word cut through the steamy air between them like a cold blade

"I haven't slept with him," said Kate quietly, clutching her towel, tears now running down her own cheeks. But Sabine was already gone.

She had fled the house without any real idea of what she was going to do next, her mind a jumble of conflicting thoughts, like the shards of a mirror, reflecting back upon one another, yet making no sense. She had ended up in the stable yard almost by instinct, sure somehow that the uncomplicated company of horses and dogs was safer than the human variety inside the house. How could she? she thought, her arms locked around the gray's impassive neck, her cheeks wet against his coat. How could her mother throw herself at Thom, of all people? The one person, since she had come here, who she had felt really understood her? Did she have no self-control at all? Why did she have to spoil everything?

Sabine relinquished her hold and sank onto the floor in the corner of the stable, trying to think back to what her mother had actually said. She had claimed that she hadn't actually slept with him. But it was obvious that she was going to; if Sabine shut her eyes she could still make out that image of her, pressed up against Thom's back, as he slowly steered the horse toward home. Even from that distance, Sabine had been able to discern her expression: smug, pleased with herself. Reveling in their intimacy. The same sort of expression she used to wear when she looked at Justin, and thought Sabine wasn't looking. She rubbed at her eyes in the darkening stable, trying to dispel the image of them together. Why did she have to end up with a mother like that? Once, she had felt close to her, had understood that Geoff was difficult, but that her mother was trying to maintain some kind of a family, even if it wasn't the conventional kind. Now she didn't know who she was; since Justin, she just seemed to be a different person. Someone who didn't seem to have any limits. It didn't just make Sabine angry, it made her feel a bit wobbly, as if she were standing on shifting sands.

She stood up, and plunged her hands into the gray's water bucket, placing them, blue-cold and wet, over her face to try and cool her feverish thoughts. The water felt icy, comforting. It was as she stood there, her palms pressed to her face, that she heard him, gently chiding the horse in the next stable, the muffled slap of a hand on a muscular rump. There was a metallic rattle, and then the hollow thump of a horse, clumsily backing into the wall. And for several minutes, Sabine stood very still. As if she were thinking.

Except she wasn't thinking.

Sabine pushed her hair back, wiped her eyes, and loosened the collar of her shirt. As an afterthought, she removed her jumper,

wrestling it over her head and laying it carefully over the stable door. Then she walked
out of the gray's stable, and quietly into the
next one along, closing the door behind her.

Thom, his back pincushioned with straw,
was facing the wall. He glanced behind him,
his face temporarily illuminated by the yellow
light of the lightbulb.

"Hiya," he said, hoisting the hay net high
onto the ring, and pulling a knot into it to
secure it there. "Come to give me a hand?"

Sabine leaned back against the wall of
the stable, her eyes fixed upon him.

"I pulled a stone the size of an egg out of
this fella's hoof earlier," he said, still tugging
at the hay net. "You'd have had to see it to
believe it. No wonder he was trotting up lame
yesterday."

Sabine slid along the wall, inching closer
to him.

"My own fault for not noticing," he muttered, giving the hay net a final twist.
"Wouldn't believe you could make a mistake
like that after twenty years, would you? So,
where have you been?" He finally turned
toward her. And then had to shift round and
step back slightly, when she was closer than
he had expected.

"I took the gray out," she said, lifting one knee and bending it slightly underneath her. "Nowhere special."

"He's going really well for you now," said Thom, smiling. "You get on well with him."

Sabine looked up at him from under her lashes.

"And you?"

"Oh, he's too small for me. But yes, he's my type. Brave, straightforward little fellow. No side to him."

"I wasn't talking about the horse."

Thom stopped, his head tilting to one side.

"Do we get on? You and me?"

Her voice was low, mellifluous. The stable seemed to grow very quiet, the rude chomping of the horse magnified in the near silence.

"We get on fine." He frowned, staring at her, trying to work out where this was headed.

Sabine stared back at him.

"So you like me?"

"Of course I like you. I liked you the first day I met you."

Sabine took a step toward him. Her heart was beating so hard, she was sure he must be able to hear it.

"I liked you, too," she whispered. "I still like you."

The tip of her tongue ran around her lips, moistening them.

Thom, still frowning slightly, turned away from her, reaching for the broom, which was propped up against the manger in the corner. He stopped. Then he rubbed at the back of his head, as if considering something, and turned around, stooping to pick up the near-empty water bucket as he did so.

It fell to the ground with a clatter that made the horse jump.

Sabine stood, a few feet away from him, her shirt open to the waist.

She was wearing nothing underneath it.

"Sabine . . ." He stepped forward, as if to cover her up, and paused. But she pre-empted him, moved toward him, placing her right hand gently on his chest, her slim frame laying itself against him, a delicate pressure.

His right hand she picked up and, looking briefly down, placed, slowly but firmly, on her bare left breast.

"Shhh," she said, her eyes wide, lost in his.

Under his hand, her skin trembled.

Thom stared at her, his own eyes widened, his breath short with shock.

"Sabine . . . ," he said again, shaking his head. But she reached up, and, pulling his head down, lifted her lips to his.

There was a brief, terrible silence. And then Thom broke away, pushing himself backward, stammering and shaking his head.

"Sabine. No. No, I'm sorry—I'm sorry—but . . ." He turned toward the door, holding on to it. Then he picked up the bucket with his silicone hand, his good one wiping at his eyes, at his face, as if to dispel his own vision. A light flickered on in the tack room, its fluorescent strip reflected in the cobbles of the yard. Outside in the yard, Bertie began to bark.

"Sabine. I can't—you're lovely, really, but . . ."

Sabine had begun to shake. She stood before him in the near dark, suddenly pulling her shirt awkwardly around her, her bottom lip trembling. She looked very fragile, and very young.

Thom, his face suddenly filled with concern, took a step back toward her.

"Oh, God, Sabine, come here. . . ."

But she pushed past him, and with a muffled sob, fled into the darkness.

* * *

Kate found Joy in the study, a chaotic knot of gray hair visible atop a stiffly upright green quilted back. She was seated at the desk where Kate's father had once sat, sifting through a box of paperwork, some of which she placed in a neat pile before her, but most of which was thrown into the metal wastebasket beside her feet. There was no meditative consideration of each piece, just a brisk glance and then a firm referral, to either front or below. To her left sat the box of photographs that Kate had found Sabine leafing through two days previously, seemingly next in line for systematic and apparently ruthless rationalization.

Kate, who had half-run up the stairs, took a deep breath, and knocked on the door, despite the fact that she was already inside the room.

Joy turned around in her seat. She looked mildly surprised to see her daughter standing there, and glanced behind her, as if expecting someone else.

"Well. You'll be pleased to know you got what you wanted."

Kate walked into the room, running her finger along the shelf, her voice, low and even.

Joy frowned.

"Honestly, Mummy, I knew you disapproved of me, but the fact that it's taken you just—what is it—two and a half months? Well, that was impressive. Even by your standards."

Joy shook her head, turned fully around.

"I'm sorry. I don't quite understand—"

"Sabine. It's taken you a matter of weeks. But she now despises me as much as you do."

Mother and daughter stood, staring at each other in the dusty old room. It was their longest contact since Kate's arrival.

Joy lifted herself from the chair; her movements were slower than Kate remembered, they seemed to cost her more.

"Katherine—whatever has happened between you and Sabine has absolutely nothing to do with me."

She moved around to face her daughter, one hand still clamped on the back of the chair.

"I have no idea what you're talking about. Now, if you'll excuse me, I've got things to see to downstairs."

"Oh, *there's* a surprise."

Joy's head shot up.

"Well. There's always something to do downstairs, isn't there? Always something to do rather than talk to me, your own daughter."

"You're getting hysterical." Joy refused to look at Kate, who was now standing in her path.

"No, Mummy. I'm not hysterical. I'm perfectly calm. I just think it's about time you and I had a chat. I am *tired*"—here she couldn't avoid the lift in her voice—"of having you politely ignore me, like I was some kind of bad smell. I want to talk to you, and I'd like to do it now."

Joy looked at the door, and then around her at the floor, which had been largely cleared of the boxes that had laid there for years. There were dark squares on the old carpets, dusty stencils of where they had stood.

"Well, let's try and make it fairly swift. I don't like to leave your father for too long."

Kate felt the fury rise up in her throat, like bile.

"What have you said to Sabine about me?"

"I beg your pardon."

"What have you said? She was fine, when she left London. Fine. And now she despises everything I do. Everything I am. And do you know what, Mummy? Some of the things she says—well, they could have come straight from your mouth."

Joy stood stiffly, bracing herself.

"I have no idea what you're talking about. I have not spoken to Sabine about you."

Kate laughed, a hollow, humorless laugh.

"Oh, you might not have said anything specific. But I know you, Mummy. I know how you are. How the things that you don't say can be as poisonous as anything you do. And believe me, something has happened. Because my own daughter now holds you up as a bloody template for true love. And everything I do is now bloody well deficient."

"That is nothing to do with me." Joy's face was rigid. "And I really don't have time for this. Really."

But Kate would not be stopped.

"You know what? I'm sorry I couldn't be like you and Daddy, okay? I'm sorry I never did the whole white-wedding thing. I'm sorry I'm not still with my childhood sweetheart. But you know what? Times change, believe it or not, and not many bloody people my age are with their childhood sweethearts."

Joy stood, gripping the chair even more tightly.

"I can't live up to you, okay? I can't live up to you and Daddy and your bloody love story to end all love stories, okay? But it doesn't make me a bad person. It doesn't mean you can judge me for every little thing I do."

"I have never judged you."

"Oh, come *on*, Mother. You've found me wanting on every little thing I ever did. You judged me for Sabine, for Jim. You made it plain you didn't approve of Geoff, even though he was a bloody doctor."

"I didn't judge you. I just wanted you to be happy."

"Oh, rubbish! Rubbish! You couldn't even let me have the friends I wanted when I was a child! Look!" She reached over, and pulled the photograph of herself and Tung-Li from the pile. "Remember him? I bet you don't."

Joy glanced at the picture, and looked away.

"I remember very well who that is, thank you."

"Yes. Tung-Li. My best friend. My best friend who I wasn't allowed to play with because you didn't think a girl of my class should be playing with her amah's son."

Joy looked suddenly weary. She stepped backward, onto the chair.

"That's not it, Katherine. You've got it quite wrong."

"Oh, have I? I seem to remember you were pretty unequivocal about it at the time. In fact, I think you told me. Not appropriate, that was the phrase you used. Do you remember that? Because I still bloody remember, Mother. That was how much it hurt me. Not Appropriate."

"That's not how it was." Joy's voice was quiet now.

"He wasn't good enough for you. Just like nothing I've ever done has been good enough for you. How I live my life, who I fell in love with, how I brought up my daughter. No, not even who I chose as my friend. At bloody six years old! Not bloody appropriate!"

"You've got it wrong."

"How? How have I got it bloody wrong? I was six years old!"

"I've told you, it's just not how it was."

"So you tell me!"

"All right! All right. I'll tell you." Joy took a deep breath. Closed her eyes. "The reason I couldn't let you play with Tung-Li . . ."

She paused, took another breath. Outside

the door, one of the dogs scratched and whined to be let in.

"The reason I couldn't let you play with Tung-Li is because . . . I couldn't bear it. Because it was too hard."

She opened her eyes, and looked straight at Kate. They were glistening, bright with tears. "Because he was your brother."

Chapter Fourteen

Joy Ballantyne was so ill with morning sickness, her mother told her friends afterward, that her husband had fired two cook-amahs in succession, convinced that they must be trying to poison her. The first Alice had taken somewhat personally, having gone to some lengths to secure the services of the number one amah herself—a task that had involved fighting off advances from no less than one of the Jardine family—but even she had to admit that Joy's frequent vomiting and inability to move from the sofa for weeks was not what one normally associated with a healthy pregnancy.

Because from a little over six weeks, when Joy informed Edward of his impending fatherhood, she had become progressively more ill, her complexion blanching, and taking on a peculiar yellowish-gray hue, and her normally springy hair becoming dull and lifeless, despite her mother's endless attempts to set it. She found it difficult to move, complaining of motion sickness, equally wearing to talk, and almost impossible to socialize, as the vomiting outbursts would often come violently and without warning. Living in that block full of people didn't help, Alice remarked. "All those cook-amahs frying up garlic and goodness knows what in the day. Pig intestines hanging out to dry. Fried turnip paste. That revolting fruit that smells like something rotting." "Yes, thank you, Mother," Joy had choked, and leaned over to relieve herself in her washing-up bowl.

Alice had cheered up considerably since discovering she was about to be a grandmother (because of her physical condition, it was not a secret Joy had been able to keep for long) and had, with an almost indecent satisfaction, leaped into the role of matriarch at number fourteen Sunny Garden Towers. She replaced the last number one amah with a girl from Guangdong, Wai-Yip, rather younger than most cook-amahs but with a reputation for English cuisine, and, as Alice pointed out, a younger woman was likely to have more energy for the children. "Because I'll tell you now, Joy, they don't just wreck your body, they absolutely exhaust you. So you'll need someone who can take them off your hands." She had also appointed the wash-amah, Mary, from Causeway Bay, and made sure she pointed out to Edward on almost every occasion the starched superiority of his shirts.

Joy, meanwhile, had wept silent, bitter tears, resentful of this alien parasite inside her, deeply depressed by the unrelenting nausea and frustrated by her own incapacity. Most of all she cursed this unwanted usurper for coming between her relationship with Edward: for the fact that she could no longer accompany him to social functions, for her appearance, which she knew disappointed him, even if he didn't say it, and for the fact that already it had somehow divided them, turning her not into a partner, but into an impending mother, to be fussed over and protected by womenfolk and doctors, to be banned from riding or playing tennis or any of the other physical things they had enjoyed together. He was already seeing her differently; she knew it. It was apparent in the cautious way in which he approached her after work, to plant a gentlemanly kiss on her cheek, instead of gathering her boisterously to him, as he used to do. It was there in the way he eyed her, as she shuffled from room to room, trying to look like she was coping, as her mother raised her eyebrows and remarked that "she'd never seen anyone look so pasty." But the worst had come at ten weeks, when, evidently frustrated by the lack of physical closeness between them (she did usually accommodate him four or five times a week, after all), he had leaned over to her side of the bed and began gently touching her, his face looming over hers for a kiss.

Joy, who had been half asleep, had woken with a sense of panic. She had not told him the worst; that the very smell of his skin now made her want to be ill. When he had done nothing but kiss her cheek, she had been able to hide it under a forced smile. Now, the rhythmic touch of his hand made her queasy, his mouth upon hers made her dizzy with nausea. Oh, God, please don't do this, she prayed silently, as he moved on top of her, clamping her eyes shut in an effort to block out the mounting sensations within. And then, when she knew she could hold off no longer, pushed him roughly away from her and ran to the bathroom, where she was lengthily and noisily sick.

That had been the beginning of it; he had not wanted to hear her tearful explanations, had silently removed himself to the guest room, hurt emanating from him in palpable waves. He had not wanted to talk about it the following morning, even when the servants had been in the other room. But two nights later, when she had lain awake wondering why he was back so late from the dockyard, he had muttered two words: "Wan Chai." And Joy had been filled with fear.

After that, Joy had never again asked her husband where he disappeared to, three or four nights a week. But despite being slack-jawed with exhaustion, she would lay awake in her double bed, waiting for the sound of the front door opening, and for him to stumble, usually drunk, into the guest room, where he had taken up near-permanent residence (apart from the nights when he was really drunk, in which case he would forget that he no longer shared her bed, and she would be forced out instead, nauseated by the alcoholic fumes). In the mornings, they didn't talk; Joy at her illest, and unsure what to say, and Edward suffering under the effects of the previous night's consumption, and apparently in a permanent rush to get to work. There was no one she could talk to about it; she somehow didn't want Alice to have the satisfaction—and it would be a satisfaction—of seeing her and Edward reduced to the kind of polarized unhappiness so apparent in the couples around them, and, with Stella in England, there was no one she really thought of as her friend. Edward had been her friend; she had never contemplated needing anybody else.

So she became thinner and thinner, at a time when, the naval doctor remarked, she should really be putting on weight, and sadder, so that she knew Edward found it easier to go out than to stay in and look at her reproachful face.

And then, at about sixteen weeks, she had woken up one morning and found that it had almost disappeared; that she could contemplate the thought of food without groaning, that she quite fancied a walk outside, unencumbered by the fear of encountering foul, unexpected smells. Glancing in the mirror, she found that some color had returned to her cheeks, a little brightness to her eyes. "There you are," said her mother, with only the slightest edge of disappointment in her voice. "You've started to bloom. Now you can smarten up yourself a bit. Look a bit more cheerful for everybody."

But there was only one person Joy wanted to look cheerful for. That evening, when Edward came home, she was not just awake, but dressed in his favorite dress, and lightly sprinkled in the scent he had bought her for Christmas. A little afraid, but more afraid of what might happen to them if she didn't, she had moved swiftly toward him as he had opened the door, and silently placed her lips on his, her arms tight around his waist.

"Please don't go out tonight," she had whispered. "Stay with me." And he had looked down at her face, and his eyes had suddenly looked both terribly sad and terribly relieved, and he had held her tight to him, so that she thought briefly that the air might be crushed out of her, and they had stood there together, unspeaking, enfolded in each other, until the tension of the last weeks had finally eased away.

"Well, you both look chirpier this morning," said Alice, when she arrived the next day to find them tucking into breakfast. And then her face closed off again, as she worked out why.

Christopher Graham Ballantyne was born at the naval hospital some five and a half months later, following a short, straightforward labor that, Edward joked afterward, had had less to do with the baby's determination to emerge, and more to do with his mother's determination to be up riding again as soon as possible. He was a large, placid baby, adored by both parents, who nonetheless were very pleased to have Joy's body to themselves again, and did not let the arrival of their son impinge too drastically upon their social life or riding habits. Not that this bothered Alice; not just because it was considered a bit strange for parents to spend too much time with their children, but because it allowed her to devote herself to him, fussing over him, dressing him in pale, beautifully made outfits with silk-covered buttons, and parading him in his huge, imported Silver Cross pram, keen to show off his evidently superior appearance and personality traits to the other pram-pushers of the colony. Joy would watch Alice's adoration of her son with a mixture of maternal satisfaction and some bemusement; her mother seemed far more able to express unconditional love to this child than she ever had to her. She didn't remember enduring the endless cuddling, the ceaseless baby talk, and attention that Christopher now received as a matter of course. "Don't worry about it," said Edward, who was just glad to have the majority of his wife's attention. "They're both happy, aren't they?"

And for the next two years they all were; Edward in his role supervising the engineering works at the dockyard, Alice in her role as unofficial childminder, and Joy, although a doting mother, once again at her husband's side, determined never to let that kind of distance creep between them again. Edward was, if anything, more loving, more attentive, perhaps grateful that Joy hadn't metamorphosed into the kind of anxious, flapping child-obsessed mother he had feared. He didn't mind not going off to sea, like some officers, who got restless when posted too long in one place. He liked to be with his family. With his wife. He never spoke of the Wan Chai period, as Joy secretly called it, and she never pressed him to explain what he had been doing there; she now knew enough of what that part of town was like to have far too many unwelcome suspicions as it was. Let sleeping dogs lie, that was the expression she used. They were all happy; happier than she had expected to be, given the events leading up to Christopher's birth.

Which was why, when she woke one morning to the familiar, clawing sensation of nausea, her heart tightened with fear.

"Well, your suspicions are correct, Mrs. Ballantyne," said the naval doctor, washing his hands in the little oval sink. "Just coming up to seven weeks, I would estimate. Your second, isn't it? Congratulations."

He had seemed rather shocked when Joy burst into noisy, unchecked tears. She sat, her face pressed into her palms, unable to believe that the worst was happening.

"I'm sorry," he said, resting a hand on her shoulder. "I had assumed it was planned. We did talk about . . . methods, after your son was born, after all."

"He didn't really like them," said Joy, wiping at her face. "He said it spoiled things for him."

She began to cry again. "We thought we were being careful."

After several minutes had passed like this, the doctor had become a little less consoling, reseating himself behind his desk, and informing his receptionist pointedly by telephone that he would be ready for the next patient "very shortly."

"I'm sorry," said Joy, rummaging for nonexistent handkerchiefs in her handbag. "I'll be fine in a minute. Really."

"A baby is a blessing, you know, Mrs. Ballantyne," he had said, his eyes sharp under his half-moon spectacles. "There are plenty of wives who would be very grateful for a healthy addition to the family. And sickness is a reliable sign of a healthy baby, as you know."

Joy rose, silenced by the subtle admonition in his words, rose to go. I know that, she thought silently. But we didn't want another baby. We weren't even sure we wanted the first one.

"You might not be so sick this time," said Alice, who had been greatly pleased at the prospect of another grandchild. She appeared to equate her daughter's fertility with an increase in her own status. It had, at least, given her a role; something she had not had since Joy had grown. "Lots of women aren't."

But Joy, already conscious of the hidden smells of the colony, already arrested by the sight of the carcass-filled dust cart, the pungent offerings of the street hawkers, the visible fumes of traffic, knew what was coming. And felt the helpless paralysis of a small animal caught in headlights, waiting for the worst to hit.

This time, if anything, it was worse. Joy, swiftly placed on bed rest, was unable to eat anything except boiled rice, fed to her in spoonfuls every two hours, to try to stem the vomiting. She vomited if she was hungry; she vomited if she ate. She vomited if she moved, and vomited, often, if she did nothing but lay under the whirring fan, wishing, as she frequently did, that a large truck would come and roll over her and put her out of her misery. She could do little but murmur words of comfort to the toddling Christopher, when he clung to her supine body (how could she explain that the smell of his hair made her sick?) and soon felt so ill that she forgot to care about what Edward thought. She simply wanted to die. It couldn't feel any worse than this.

This time, even Alice was worried; she frequently called out the doctor, who prescribed drugs that Joy refused to take, and became alarmed at the rapidity of her weight loss. "If she gets any more dehydrated, we'll have to put her on a drip," he said. But his manner suggested that while it was all undoubtedly unpleasant, Joy was simply going to have to put up with it. It was all part of being a woman after all. "Why not put on some makeup," he said as he left, patting his sweating forehead with a folded handkerchief. "Brighten yourself up a bit."

Edward, while initially sympathetic (he would sit and stroke her hair, and remind her unconvincingly that any time now she would be "up and about again") grew swiftly tired of his role as unofficial nursemaid, and, while evidently trying to be patient and understanding, could not hide his apparent suspicions that she was rather making a meal of things this time.

"She's usually pretty hardy," Joy heard him say to one of his colleagues, as they sat

out on the balcony, swatting at passing mosquitoes. "I can't understand why she keeps
crying about it."

He didn't try to make love to her at all this
time; simply moved his stuff without fuss
into the guest room. It had made her cry all
the more.

It didn't help when various other young
wives and mothers stopped by to tell Joy of
their own experiences. Some, inevitably, had
sailed through it and remarked cheerfully
that they "hadn't been the slightest bit ill," as
if that should be of some comfort to her. Others, the worst kind, said they knew how she
was feeling, when she knew they patently
didn't, and suggested various remedies that,
they assured her, were bound to have her up
out of bed in no time; weak tea, crushed ginger, mashed banana—all of which Joy tried
dutifully and threw up equally enthusiastically.

Days gradually blurred into each other,
dissolving into the wet season; still, humid
days following interminable, sweat-drenched
nights, and Joy found it harder to pretend to
her son that Mummy was fine, or to her husband that she would soon be better (she had
repeated this like a mantra, hoping it might

prevent him from disappearing to Wan Chai). Physically weakened and sunk deep in depression, she ceased to note the days, counting them off as a coming return to normality, but lay in the half light, listening dully to her own breathing and trying not to throw up the water that Wai-Yip brought her, freshened every hour.

When it got to sixteen weeks and there was no discernible improvement in her condition, the doctor had decided that it would be best for all concerned if she were admitted to hospital. She was properly dehydrated now, he said, and it posed something of a risk to Baby. They were all terribly concerned about Baby, who was always referred to as such. By now, Joy could cheerfully not have cared if Baby lived or died, but then neither did she care if she herself lived nor died, and accepted her mother's instructions that she be moved without argument.

"I'll look after Christopher," Alice had said, her brow furrowed with concern. "You just concentrate on getting better." Joy, for whom most things passed by in a nauseous fug of irrelevance, noted her mother's anxious face, and tried to squeeze her hand in return.

"You mustn't worry about anything," Alice

said again. "Wai-Yip and I will take care of everything." Joy had simply closed her eyes as she was gently loaded into the ambulance, grateful that she didn't have to think anymore.

Joy stayed in the hospital for almost a month, until there had been a sufficient easing in her nausea to allow her to eat at least the blandest foods by mouth, and she could walk, unaided, the entire length of the women's ward. She had spent almost two weeks on the drip, which, she was forced to admit, had made her feel almost immediately better, but the prospect of food was still a risky one, tied up with the possibility of unheralded and explosive sickness. Some days it could be something as innocuous as dry bread that prompted it; other days, the better days, she might even be able to force down a piece of boiled fish without concern. White foods, that's what the doctors said, and the blander the better. So Alice, who visited every day (although to both women's dismay she wasn't allowed to bring Christopher, who was considered "too wearing for Mother") brought fresh-baked scones, pale bananas, and even meringues, anything that she and Wai-Yip could devise between them.

"She's been awfully good, I have to say," she told Joy, as she sat beside her bed, dressed in a smart blue suit with a pussycat bow, and nibbling on a scone. "Doesn't talk much, but works ever so hard, even when, frankly, she looks exhausted. I think these mainland girls don't have the attitude of the Hong Kong ones, you know? Much less full of themselves. That Bei-Lin, I've told her. I'll replace her with a Guangdong girl now, you see if I don't."

It was, Joy thought afterward, the closest the two women had ever been; Alice laden with responsibility for both her child and grandchild, took her duties seriously, and didn't make Joy feel guilty for doing so. Joy being ill through some kind of "women's troubles" was somehow a validation for her, it showed both that Alice was needed, but also that her awkward, unconventional daughter had turned out right in the end. She was suffering to bring her husband another child, wasn't she?

Joy, meanwhile, had lost her fight. In her stay at the hospital, beaten down by her illness, and the relentless, gently domineering ministrations of the medical staff, she had slowly become passive; accepting of the various treatments and invalid rules laid upon her, grateful for her mother's help, a slave to the hospital routine. She just wanted someone else to deal with it all. Here, she could lay on crisp white sheets, under the whirring fan, listening to the soft shuffle of the nurses' feet on linoleum, the starched swish of their skirts, and the low murmur of voices from the other end of the ward, away from the noise and sweat and smells of real life. Although she felt a dull ache of longing for her child, it was tempered by relief that she no longer had to cope with his constant requests, his physical neediness.

Ditto her husband.

But after another month had gone by, and she began to feel a little more like her old self, Joy felt a growing need to return home, a desire to be with her family again. Her mother brought Christopher twice, on the days that they were allowed to sit outside in the lush gardens, and her heart broke when Alice had to peel him from her, screaming and pleading, at the end of visiting time. More important, she began to feel concerned about how seldom Edward came.

He had been awkward with her, had not even attempted to kiss her cheek the last two times he arrived, and had paced around her bed, glancing out of the window, as if expecting some disaster to befall, so that Joy eventually had to ask him simply to sit down. He didn't like hospitals, he had muttered. It all made him uncomfortable. He had meant the women's ward, she was sure, and she understood, because all-women environments usually made her uncomfortable, too. But he had snapped at her when she had asked him whether he really was all right, and told her irritably that he wished she would stop fussing, so that when he left, Joy had wept copious tears into her pillow.

"Has—has Edward been out much, do you know?" she had asked her mother afterward. Alice stayed at the apartment often, worried that Wai-Yip would not be able to comfort little Christopher in the appropriate manner.

"Out? Not really. Oh, he went to a reception at the Commander's house last week. And racing at Happy Valley on Thursday. Was that what you meant?"

"Yes, that's it," said Joy, leaning back on her pillows with barely hidden relief. "The Commander's do. I just wanted to make sure he hadn't forgotten that one."

Edward didn't go out much at all, said Alice. She had actually told him he should get out more, "enjoy his little bit of freedom" (which was a bit rich, thought Joy, coming from the woman who once beat her own husband around the head with an egg whisk for coming home in the early hours). But Edward would eat his evening meal, prepared for him by Wai-Yip, stop in to his son's room to say good-night, and then hide himself away in his study, working, occasionally head for Happy Valley, or perhaps go for a late night walk around the Peak.

"I need to come home," said Joy.

"You need to look after Baby," said Alice, touching up her powdered complexion. "No point you rushing back when we can all manage fine without you."

She was eventually allowed home at twenty-two weeks, with the promise that she would rest properly, avoid exertion, and drink at least two pints of water a day, at least until the humid season was over. Edward, in shirtsleeves and slacks, came to meet her in the Morris 10, and greeted her with a more affectionate hug, so that Joy immediately relaxed, convinced that from now on things would improve again. Christopher, after an initial brief reserve, clung to his mother's newly stockinged legs and demonstrated his disapproval of all the upheaval by waking three or four times a night for the first week Joy was home. Alice, meanwhile, seemed to struggle with relief and disappointment that her daughter was no longer an invalid and therefore in need of her help.

"I'll stop by for the first week or two anyway," she said, as Joy opened the door to her apartment, feeling strange and alien in her own home. "You'll need the help. And Christopher needs to maintain his routine. We've got a very good routine going, he and I."

Joy looked around at the immaculate parquet floors, and teak furniture of her home, trying to make it feel like hers again. It seemed like somewhere she had known a long time ago, rather than a place she belonged. Wai-Yip, who had brought through a tray of cold drinks, looked up at her, nodded a brief greeting, and then walked away. Even she's gotten used to me not being here, thought Joy. She's probably trying to remember who I am. She walked softly to the mantelpiece, above which sat the blue horse on white paper, now framed in a pale mount with an ornate gilt frame. She gazed at it for a minute, and then looked over at Edward, who was watching her, apparently also trying to get used to the sight of her in their home.

"It's good to be back," she said.

"We missed you," said Edward, his eyes on hers. "I missed you."

Suddenly not caring about the raised eyebrows of her mother, Joy walked swiftly across the room to her husband, and buried her face in his chest, feeling his solidity, remembering the scent that she loved. He placed his arms around her, and lowered his head, so that his cheek rested on her hair.

Alice looked pointedly away, until Christopher ran back into the room, and tried anxiously to squeeze into the limited space between his parents, his chubby arms outstretched as he yelped, "Car-ry, car-ry."

As it had been during her last pregnancy, Joy and Edward became close again, once she recovered completely from morning sickness. He was unusually affectionate, even for him, often bringing her back flowers, and boxes of Swiss chocolates he had traded with officers on the incoming vessels, and was loving to the point where Alice would get openly irritated, and tell him "do put her down. It's not good for Christopher to have to watch all that." He had also rediscovered his habit of following her around, from room to room, so that on occasion Joy found herself locking herself in her bathroom, pursued by both male members of her family. So if he had lost a little of his sense of humor along the way, become perhaps a little more watchful, Joy put it down to problems in the dockyard. She knew Edward was under a lot of pressure at work, because his naval colleagues told her when they came to dinner. Boring old Edward, they said. Took it all far too seriously. No fun at all, lately.

Katherine Alexandra Ballantyne was born a week early at the same hospital where Joy had spent most of her summer months, in a labor that was almost, the doctor said, indecently short. "Not slow out of the starting gates, that one," he joked to Edward, who, having finally been allowed in, was gazing, enraptured, at his new daughter. The doctor was also a racing man, and the two had met occasionally at the evening meetings at Happy Valley.

Joy, meanwhile, lay back among the pillows, her elation mixed with a deep, deep relief that the nightmare of pregnancy was now over.

"How are you feeling, my darling?" Edward said, stooping to kiss her forehead. "A little tired. But looking forward to coming home," she said, smiling weakly. "Make sure you tell old Foghill to get my horse ready for me."

He had grinned approvingly at that.

But there was less riding for Joy this time around, for the initial months at least. Katherine was, as Alice frequently noted, a "difficult baby," slow to pacify, frequently colicky, and liable to wake several times in the night, and managed swiftly to exhaust the combined forces of her mother, Alice, and Wai-Yip, shredding the "traditional" theories and remedies of the two latter women with the efficacy of a cheese grater.

Edward, oddly, was the most patient with her, often taking over for an hour when he returned from work, and forgoing his usual gin and tonic to take her for a quiet stroll around the Peak (at least it would have been a quiet stroll if Katherine had ever stopped screaming). He was tender with her, when Joy was too exhausted to feel anything but exasperation, and she in turn, seemed to behave better for him, her milky eyes blinking at him with some kind of instinctive recognition.

"There, a daddy's girl," said Alice, who was frankly glad to devote herself to little Christopher. "You were just the same." She managed to make it sound almost unhealthy.

"I don't care whose girl she is, as long as she stops crying," said Joy. She had not had a full night's sleep now for almost two months. Wai-Yip was meant to be responsible for taking care of her in the night, but the baby's cries still woke Joy, managing to trigger some primeval response system, and she had obviously exhausted Wai-Yip, too, because often Joy would rise to find the girl fast asleep and oblivious on her cot bed.

Joy didn't think she had ever been so tired; her eyes were permanently gritty, and lightly red-rimmed as if by an unfortunate choice of makeup, her vision often blurry. Sometimes she was so exhausted that she would hallucinate that she had seen to Katherine when she hadn't, so that Christopher would come and wake her, and announce rather seriously that "Baby was crying *again*." She tried to make light of it to Edward, desperate for them to recover the closeness of their pre-Katherine days, and since the doctors had allowed the physical side of their marriage to resume, she had made sure not to refuse him once, despite her own exhaustion. "I'll be more like myself once she starts sleeping," she would say to him apologetically, conscious that she must be as exciting as an old blanket.

"You're fine. I just want to be close to you," he would say, from above her, and she would become almost tearful with gratitude.

He had agreed to the doctor's "methods" this time.

So consumed had Joy been by the demands of her family, that she had only barely noticed how exhausted her young amah had become. Twice, Joy came in to find her sleeping in the day, a state of affairs her own mother thought scandalous, although Joy, who herself now lived in a permanent state of torpor, felt rather more sympathetic and declined to chastise her. "She did enough for us while I was in hospital," she told Alice, as Wai-Yip shuffled to the kitchen to fetch them their lunch. "She's been very good, as a rule."

She jiggled Katherine on her knee, trying

to stave off another crying jag. At three months, the doctor said, she should be getting less colicky, but no matter how hard Joy looked for the signs, she still seemed alarmingly predisposed to tears.

Joy, who had been leafing through a magazine, looked up as Wai-Yip laid the two plates on the table, and with a small bow, exited from the room.

"I'm going off that girl," Alice said, her mouth set in an ungenerous line. "I think she's cheating you. Nothing I dislike more than a dishonest help."

Katherine, unable to contain herself any longer, let out a piercing wail. Joy began to bounce her furiously on her knee, desperate for her not to wake Christopher, who had only just gone down for his nap.

"What do you mean?" she said.

"Have you not looked at her lately? The weight she's put on! She was as thin as a flagpole when she came here. She must be eating you out of house and home."

Joy shook her head, unwilling to get exercised over a few bowls of noodles. If one had good staff, it was worth overlooking a few foibles. There were few who didn't try and recoup something. Joy had recently been told by Leonora Pargiter on the second floor that while she was out, her amah had been renting out her brand new electric food processor. Made a fortune, apparently.

"I'll leave it this time. She was probably starving in China," she said, placing Katherine over her shoulder and patting her so enthusiastically that the baby's eyes bulged. "This may be the first time she's had a decent diet in her life."

She had felt less charitable when, a month later, as Joy and her mother sat on the balcony, enjoying a brief moment where both children were asleep, Wai-Yip had approached her, and told her, tearfully, that she had to return to China.

"What? For how long?" said Joy, horrified at the thought of losing her. Katherine had just begun to get attached to her. The previous two nights, Joy had been able to go out with Edward, leaving her in Wai-Yip's arms.

"I don't know, miss." The girl looked down. Two large, salty tears plopped noiselessly onto the wooden floor.

"I knew it. Didn't I tell you she was taking advantage?" said Alice, sipping at her sherry.

"Wai-Yip? Are you all right?" Joy looked at

the hunched figure in front of her, suddenly guilty that she had not taken her exhaustion seriously enough. "Are you ill?"

"No, miss."

"Of course she's not ill. You've paid her so much she can afford to go on a holiday. Probably off on one of those new cruises."

"Wai-Yip, what on earth is the matter?"

"Miss, I cannot say. I must leave, return to my home," she said, still not meeting Joy's eye.

Alice had turned from the view, and was looking hard at the young servant, her gimlet eyes studying her closely. She shifted slightly in her seat, as if trying to observe her from several angles.

"She's got herself into trouble," she announced. "Look! She's gotten herself into trouble!" It was said triumphantly, this time. "No wonder she's been putting on weight. She's gone and gotten herself in the family way. Oh, you disgraceful child. You'll have to go, you know, no question about it."

At this point, Wai-Yip began to sob, her shoulders still hunched around a shape, which Joy now had to admit, had filled out quite considerably, although had remained largely hidden under loose cotton clothes.

"Is this true, Wai-Yip?" Joy's voice was gentle, probing.

"I so sorry, miss." Wai-Yip's shoulders shook, her face stayed buried in her work-worn hands.

"You don't have to apologize to me," she said. "It's you who is going to have to cope with it. I take it you are not married?"

Wai-Yip glanced up at her, as if briefly uncomprehending, then shook her head.

"Of course she's not married. Probably been putting it about to some American serviceman. That's what they're all after now, a passport to the United States."

"So what will you do?"

"Please, miss. I want to come back to my work. I work very hard."

"And what is she going to do with the baby?" Alice, who now had her arms crossed, sniffed dismissively.

"I don't know, miss . . . maybe, my mother . . ." Here, she began to cry again.

Joy thought about the prospect of another baby in the house. Edward wouldn't like it, that was for sure. She knew he was keen for a little normality to return to their lives as it was. Which meant him and her, and as little disturbance as possible. But she felt rather sorry for Wai-Yip, who didn't seem to be much more than a child herself (Joy realized, a little to her shame, that she had never bothered to ask her age). And she did work terribly hard.

"You let her bring a baby home, and there'll be no end to it," said Alice, shaking her head.

"I'll have to talk to my husband, Wai-Yip. You understand that."

The girl nodded, bowed her head, and slunk away. They could still hear her sniffing down the corridor.

"You'll regret it," said Alice.

According to Chinese legend, there were once ten suns in the sky, and their combined heat scorched the earth. When an archer, Hou Yi, managed to shoot down nine of the ten suns, The King of the Earth gave him a magic potion that would make him live forever. The archer's beautiful wife, Chang Er, unaware that the liquid was magic, drank the potion, and began rising high into the night sky until she reached the moon.

The archer missed his wife, the Moon Lady, and asked the King of the Earth to help him get to her. The King allowed the archer to fly up to the sun, but he still could not get to the moon except when it was full and round.

Like pregnancy, thought Joy, absently. Becoming a big fat moon brings us all down in the end.

It was the night of the moon festival, when Chinese families across the colony took to the streets in slow-strolling groups, to mark the lunar celebrations with glowing lanterns and offerings and exchange sweet biscuits and cakes baked in its auspicious circular shape. Joy had watched from her balcony, captivated, as she was, every year, by the sight of thousands of tiny moving lights edging down to the inky harbor for the firework displays. In the clear sky, they stood reflected in the stars, two separate sets of constellations winking at each other from earth and heaven. Even Alice, who hadn't previously shown any inclination toward the various Chinese festivals (it was apparently another indication of Chinese "perversity" that they couldn't celebrate the new year at the same time as everyone else), had nonetheless given Christopher a little paper moon lantern, and he had run from room to room, demanding that the lights be turned off so that it glowed, a fragile little beacon in the dark.

Edward was uncommonly cheerful when he came home, not just kissing Joy, but swinging her around in the hallway, so that Christopher laughed and begged to join in, and Alice announced, purse-lipped, that it was high time she was off. He had brought back an elaborately decorated red tin of moon biscuits, given to him by one of the Chinese engineers, and was eager to tell Joy about plans for the dockyards, which, if they came off, looked likely to mean a promotion.

"Will you still be posted here?" said Joy, trying to keep the anxiety from her voice as they sat down at the table.

"Of course. It doesn't involve going any-where. But it might well mean better quarters for us—a nice house, perhaps, instead of apartments. Wouldn't you like that, darling? A house? With a little garden, perhaps? It would be nice for the children."

"I suppose it would," said Joy, who had actually begun to rather enjoy living in the apartments.

"We don't have to go, you know. I just thought you might enjoy the extra space. Now that we have two little ones."

She supposed it made sense. Her mother was always saying how much easier it would be if one could wheel Katherine's pram to the end of the garden and forget about it for a while.

Joy smiled. "I think your promotion sounds wonderful. Clever old you."

Edward reached a hand across the table and took ahold of hers, squeezing it fondly. "Things are going to get better for us, darling. You'll see."

She had gazed at him, at his sleek, reddish hair, dipped toward her as he ate, wolfing his food in a way that was so irrevocably male, and felt an overwhelming tenderness, not dissimilar to the one she felt for her children. He was so attentive, so considerate. She knew she was lucky, especially when one considered what some of the wives put up with. And now that he had agreed to what the doctor had suggested, they need never have another baby again. They could just carry on as they were, getting closer, and closer, and happier. . . .

Joy was aware that she was daydreaming, and pulled herself a little more upright, in order to attack her food. It was chicken casserole; not up to Wai-Yip's usual standards, she thought, chewing meditatively. Then, perhaps that was no surprise.

"You'll never guess what we found out today," said Joy, raising her fork to her mouth. "Wai-Yip is having a baby. Completely took me by surprise, I must say. I didn't even know she had a boyfriend."

Edward's head shot up. His blue eyes looked temporarily startled, before conducting a microcosmic search of her own. In a nearby apartment, someone dropped something metallic on a wooden floor, sending a cymballic crash reverberating along the corridor. He didn't seem to notice.

Joy's fork stilled as he moved. She leaned forward and stared at him, studying this new expression. There was the faintest bleaching of the normally high color in his cheeks.

"You knew?"

Edward looked back at her, blinking hard for a couple of seconds, and then, unusually, he looked away from her. He seemed to consider whether to say something, and then, eventually, took another forkful of his chicken instead, lifting it carefully to his mouth.

There was a brief silence.

Joy kept staring at him.

"Edward," she said, and her voice held a sudden chime of fear. "Edward. Please . . ."

Edward seemed to recover slightly. He swallowed his mouthful without any visible effort, and then lifted his napkin to his lips, wiping them slowly and methodically.

"Your mother was quite right about her. She's become unreliable. She'll have to go." He paused. "I'll give her her notice after the weekend." He didn't look at Joy as he spoke, but kept his eyes fixed on his plate.

Across the table, still transfixed by her husband, Joy began to shake, at first with a delicate tremor, and then more violently. She was still shaking when Edward stood up, and, his voice suddenly strangled as he attempted not to look at her, announced that he was going to his study.

Joy spent that night in the guest room, unchallenged by her husband. She shook until she pulled the embroidered white sheet over her head, and then, laying curled up under the big fan, half-illuminated through the shutters by the blue glow of the full moon, she had begun to howl, great racking sobs of grief cascading through her body like seismic tremors. Edward, sleepless in the room next door, had, at around three o'clock, quietly come in, whispering fervent apologies under his breath, and trying to place his arms around her. But she had grown ferocious, and batted him away with her fists, taking great swings at his head, his shoulders, any part of him she could reach, until, himself weeping, he had backed out of the door.

Then, until dawn, Joy had lain very still on the bed.

Thinking back.

Thinking.

Her mother guessed, of course. She guessed as soon as Wai-Yip brought the baby back to the apartment. It wasn't hard; while sharing the usual squashed features of the newborn, Tung-Li had an unusually aquiline nose, and a distinct reddish tint to his hair. To her credit, Alice never spoke about it to her daughter, perhaps gleaning from Joy's curt announcement that the number one amah would be accompanying them to the new house, that any valedictory announcements about all men being the same, or how those Chinese girls would get their hooks into anybody, would be ill-received. Mindful of Joy's dangerously rigid demeanor, she also kept quiet about the certainty that the neighbors would talk, despite her own terrible reservations. What would people think? Joy didn't seem to care.

Joy had informed Edward of her plans three long nights after the moon festival dinner. She had joined him at breakfast, her hair neatly set, and wearing a crisp blue short-sleeved shirt and white slacks, and had poured the tea without once looking him in the eye.

"I've told Wai-Yip she's not returning to China," she said, her voice low and measured. It was the first time she had spoken to him.

Edward looked up, a piece of toast halfway to his lips.

"What?"

"I've spoken to a couple of people. If she goes to China, she'll be disowned. She and the baby. She will find it impossible to get work, and the baby will be ostracized because . . . because of its appearance. With things as they are, with the communists and all, well, they might well starve."

Edward had not moved.

"I've decided—she's our responsibility. Your responsibility. And I won't have that child's welfare on my conscience. You will have to make sure the new house is big enough . . . that we don't have to see it. You should be able to manage that."

There was a lengthy pause. Edward had risen from the table then, and walked round to her chair. There, he kneeled, and pressed his face into her hand, lifting it from her lap.

"I thought—I thought you were going to leave," he said, his voice suddenly breaking.

Joy said nothing, her jaw trembling slightly as she kept her face fixed toward the window. She could feel his hot tears on her skin.

"Oh, God, Joy. I love you so much. I'm so, so sorry. I just got so terribly lonely. I—"

Joy's head snapped back around. She pulled her hand away from him.

"I don't want to talk about it." she said. "Ever."

Chapter Fifteen

Sabine sat on the upturned crate in the summerhouse, a moth-eaten blanket across her shoulders, and her shirt pulled tightly across her chest, shivering in the cold. She had been in there almost half an hour. She had listened, through the sound of her own crying, to Thom's urgent calls for her down at the stable yard, had watched as the dusk became night, smothering everything in its blackness, and had sat, sobbing quietly in her musty haven, so paralyzed by her own shock and grief that she couldn't make her quaking fingers rejoin the buttons and holes on her now crumpled shirt.

She hadn't known where to go; had just followed her own overriding urge to run away from Thom, to escape the bitter taste of her own humiliation. So she had headed first down to the bottom fields, then walked, lost in her own misery, up the back road to the village, finally settling on the summerhouse as a place of shelter. And now she was stuck; if she returned to the house, she would have to explain it all to her mother. If she stayed here, having left her jumper over the gray's stable door, she was likely to freeze. One thing was certain; she would have to leave Kilcarrion; there was no way she could stay after what she'd done.

Sabine wiped her nose with the back of her hand, dissolving into snotty tears again as she remembered what she'd done: her placing of his hand on her breast; his look of horror as she had done so. What must he have thought of her? She was as bad as her mother; nothing but a whore. What had made her do it? She had ruined everything now. But another thought fought for space: Was she really so hideous? Would it have hurt him so much just to kiss her back a little?

Sabine had not turned on the electric light, fearful of drawing attention to her whereabouts, but she could just make out the hands of her watch, which showed it was almost five-thirty. Down in the yard, she could hear the clanging of doors and buckets as the horses were given their evening feeds. Her grandmother would be busying herself somewhere, brushing off the dogs or consulting Mrs. H about the best way to reorganize the freezer. In the house, Lynda would be counting the last half an hour until she could load herself into her glossy little red car and go home. She would probably be watching one of her soaps. Her day was so punctuated by them, even Grandfather received his various pills according to their schedules.

Thinking about her grandfather made Sabine wipe more fervently at her eyes. He was probably wondering where she was; she had hardly seen him at all today. He probably thought she had become like her mother: thoughtless, uncaring. Selfish. But she couldn't go back into the house. There was nowhere she could go. Nowhere she could rely on anyone, anyway. She sat, kicking at a pile of old flowerpots, not caring as they cracked and fragmented, hardly able to see them through eyes swollen through crying. Then she lifted her head, like a hound scenting the air.

Annie's. She could go to Annie's. She would understand. And if Annie was having an "off" day, she could just ask to use her telephone, and get Bobby to come and pick her up. She had to tell him only half the story, after all.

Sabine shook off the blanket, and, after checking cautiously that there was no one around to see her, slipped through the deserted gardens toward the back gate, trying not to let the hiccup and shudder that inevitably followed her tears slow her pace.

For some reason the three street lamps that lined the main thoroughfare of Ballymalnaugh were all unlit that night, and Sabine found herself grateful for the clear skies as she half-ran, clutching her sides, up the road, hearing only the sound of her own footfall echoing on the tarmac. The only other light came from the windows of those houses she passed that had open curtains, revealing little tableaux of family life: the young couple prostrate on a sofa in front of the television, their small child playing on the floor; the solitary old lady reading the paper; the table, set for tea, while an unwatched television cast an aurora borealis of moving shadows in the corner. Sabine saw them all, running past, and felt lonelier than ever. I shall never have a proper family, she thought, making herself cry again. I shall always be on the outside, looking in.

She slowed as she reached Annie's house, trying to catch her breath and wiping at her eyes, so as not to look too alarming. She didn't want Annie to think anyone had died, after all. She had done enough damage for one day.

The downstairs lights were on, but the curtains were closed, just as they had been the last few times Sabine had ridden past. She paused before she walked up the path, finally doing up her shirt buttons and wondering briefly whether, after what Mrs. H had said about Annie's needing to go for counseling, she should really go in at all.

But as Sabine stood uncertainly on the steps, the door was thrust open from the inside, throwing a bright shaft of orange light out into the garden. A tall, thin man with dark hair and shiny cycling shorts, silhouetted against it, moved as if to run past her down the steps, and then, spying Sabine, stopped and clutched at her shoulders.

"Thank God," he gasped. "Oh, thank God. We need an ambulance."

Sabine froze.

"An ambulance. Have you got a mobile phone?"

She gaped at him.

He shook his head, irritatedly. "Look, I'm just a guest. Anthony Fleming. I just came back this evening, against my better judgment, I might add, and I found Mrs. Connolly—and—well—she needs an ambulance. Urgently. Do you have a phone? This one seems to have been cut off."

Sabine's heart stopped, and she looked past him into the brightly lit house. She knew Annie had been depressed, but she hadn't thought about the possibility . . . Sabine shuddered. She had a sudden vision of a girl at school who had slit her wrists in the toilets two years ago after she was bullied. The blood had spurted as high as the ceiling, one of the fifth formers had told her.

"Is she—is she—?" Her voice faltered.

"Well, I'm no expert, but it looks like she's not got long left," said the man. "We can't waste any time. Where is there a phone?"

Ignoring his protestations, Sabine pushed her way in through the door, hardly aware of the chaos of the front room, the smell of dust and stale food that confronted her. She had to see Annie. She kept walking determinedly, her chest tightening with fear as she tried to ignore the unearthly sounds coming from the kitchen. No one had told her about noise; when people killed themselves in films, they were always silent about it.

But there was no blood, not on the ceiling, anyway, just a sort of discolored water all over the pale-blue lino of the kitchen floor, and Annie sitting in the middle of it, clutching onto a cupboard door with both arms, as if trying to haul herself over it.

"Annie?" she said.

"Oh, *Goooooddddddddd.* . . ." Annie, seemingly oblivious, let out a long, low moan. She looked like she was concentrating on something Sabine could not see. She looked puce with effort. She did not appear to be dying.

"She's not dying," Sabine announced to the man, who had reappeared behind her.

"Of course she's not dying," he said impatiently, his hands flapping as if he were shaking water from them. "She's having a bloody baby. But I'm a loans clerk, not a doctor. And I told you—we need to get an *ambulance.*"

Sabine stared at Annie, reeling slightly as she attempted to take in the significance of what the man had just said. Then "stay with her," she said, lurching for the door. "I'll get help." And her blood pumping in her ears, she began sprinting back up the road toward Kilcarrion.

Kate leaned heavily against the desk, staring at the sepia-tinted photograph she still held in her hand, at her own broad toothy smile, open, unknowing. At Tung-Li's moon face staring back at her, his apparent awkwardness before the camera now infused with a greater symbolism; his unusual features—because they were unusual, now Kate looked carefully at them—now explained.

"Why didn't you tell me?" she said, eventually. Her voice, when it came, sounded frail, tremulous.

Joy, who sat beside her on the chair, her head bowed, lifted her face wearily.

"There was nothing to say. What would I have told you?"

"I don't know. Something. Something that perhaps would have explained—oh, I don't know." She shook her head. "Oh, God, Mummy . . . all this time . . ."

It was dark outside, and the two wall-mounted lights cast gloomy, chiaroscuro shadows on the walls, highlighting the lengths of now-near-empty shelves, the few remaining boxes still to be sorted. An old framed map of Southeast Asia had come off the wall and stood, its glass fractured within its frame, against the wall.

"What happened to him?" said Kate, still staring at the photograph. "To both of them?"

"They didn't go back to China. When we came back to Ireland I found Wai-Yip a good position with a Black Watch family up in the New Territories. I think she was much happier there, really. She was nearer to her family. And things were . . ."—Joy took a deep breath—"simpler."

Kate stared at the photograph again, and then placed it carefully on top of the box, leaving her fingertips lightly upon its surface. She paused, as if deciding whether to turn it over, but left it face upward.

"I can't believe this . . . ," she said, almost to herself. "I can't believe Daddy . . . I thought you were perfect," she said. "I really thought the two of you had this perfect love."

"No one's perfect, Kate."

The two women sat in silence at right

angles to each other, listening to the distant sounds of activity in the stable yard. For once, Kate noted, it didn't seem to stir Joy into some kind of action.

"Why did you stay?" she said, eventually. "It was practically the sixties by then, wasn't it? People would have understood. We would have understood."

Joy frowned, a hand raised to her hair.

"I did think about it. But there was still quite a stigma about it, back then. And despite everything, I decided I was doing the right thing. I thought this way you children would grow up with a proper family. Without having to cope with people whispering, and pointing, and talking. . . . And we had built a life together. I suppose we liked the same things."

She turned to look at Kate, and her expression softened. "Both of us loved you so much, you know. Your happiness was everything to us. And although your father hurt me terribly . . ."—here she winced slightly, and Kate realized with a sense of shock how close to the surface that betrayal still sat—"I decided that my own feelings were actually not the most important thing, in the end."

There was a lengthy silence, as Kate sat in the cold, unloved room, trying to bend her long-held beliefs around this new knowledge. She felt briefly, irrationally, angry, as if it had been her exclusion from this secret that had caused all the problems between them.

"Does Christopher know?"

"Of course Christopher doesn't know. And I don't want him to know. I didn't want either of you to know." Joy sounded, momentarily, like her old, brusque self. "You're not to say anything to him. Or Sabine. There's far too much rubbish about telling everybody everything, these days."

Her voice, although truculent, held something else. Something almost tearful.

Kate stood, looking at her mother for a few moments, slowly recognizing the love story that she had missed. Then she stepped forward and for the first time since she had been a child, took ahold of Joy, gently enfolding her in her arms, allowing her mother time for her habitual stiffness to be replaced by something more yielding. She smelled of horse, and dog, and something sweet and lavendery underneath. After some moments, she patted Kate's shoulder absently in return, as if comforting an animal.

"All these years . . ." Kate said, into her quilted jacket, her voice breaking. "All these years, and . . . I could never live up to you."

"I'm sorry, darling. I didn't mean for you to feel that way."

"No. I didn't mean that. All those years, and I didn't know that you were suffering. I didn't know what you had had to put up with."

Joy pulled back and wiped at her eyes, straightening her shoulders.

"Now, I don't want you exaggerating," she said, firmly. "Your father is a good man. I didn't have to put up with so much, as you call it. He loved me, in his way." When she looked at Kate, her gaze was defensive, faintly challenging. "He—he just—"

"Couldn't help himself?"

Joy turned away from her, toward the window.

Kate glanced next door, to where her father was dozing in his drug-fueled slumber, feeling a cold fury toward the man who had betrayed the only person she had ever thought him capable of loving. "And you never made him pay for it," she said, bitterly.

Joy followed her daughter's glance, and then reached out, taking her hand. It was roughened, weathered by ages of determined activity.

"You're not to say a thing to him. You're not to bother him. Your father did pay, Kate," she said, and her voice held a melancholy certainty. "Both of us paid."

There was no one in the downstairs kitchen, or the drawing room, so Sabine, now almost light-headed with adrenaline, ran through the house, slamming doors and yelling for Mrs. H, making the dogs bark and scrabble in pursuit. "Where the hell is everyone?" she yelled at them, throwing open and shutting the doors of the pantry and the boot room. The house felt still, watchful. The snug and breakfast room were also uninhabited, their silence amplifying the sounds of her brief entry, making them reverberate around the furniture.

Her lungs now tight from her exertions, Sabine ran up the stairs two at a time, her boots catching on the threadbare stair carpet so that she slipped and slithered on her way up, having to clutch at the banister twice to stop herself from falling. All the time, the vision of Annie loomed before her, bowed over by her own suffering; her expression distant, as ever, but this time somehow focused. Somehow primeval.

Oh, God, where was Mrs. H? Annie needed her mother. That much was clear to anyone. She certainly needed someone more than Anthony . . . whatever his name was. Sabine paused briefly on the landing, looking for the vacuum cleaner, or some other clue that Mrs. H had recently been there. Then she stopped.

Lynda.

Why hadn't she thought of Lynda?

She would know what to do. She could take care of it all. Sabine threw open the door of her grandfather's room, her mouth already open and prepared to deliver her urgent message. But she met only the blank, unpixilated gaze of the off-turned television set, and a neat array of plastic cups and pill bottles, a silent reminder that the nurse had already left for home. Her grandfather's skeletal profile emerged from the layers of bedding and pillows, undisturbed by the commotion, deep in chemically induced slumber.

She didn't even bother to close the door. With a sobbed expletive of exasperation, Sabine now ran along the corridor, flinging open each door, and shouting for Mrs. H, her mother, her grandmother, anyone as she did so, fighting with each step a rising sense of panic about the scene she had left behind. What if that man went away? He had looked like he was desperate to leave. What if everyone had gone out? She could call an ambulance, but she didn't know how to help. And a little part of her didn't really want to go back to that noise, that blood, all by herself.

They were in the study. Sabine thrust open the door, not really expecting to find anyone in there, and had stopped, panting, as she confronted the sight of the two women, holding on to each other.

She stood for a second, trying to take in a scene that she knew couldn't possibly be real. Still conscious of the evening's events, she looked away from her mother. Then she remembered herself.

"Where's Mrs. H?"

Her grandmother had pulled away from her mother, and pawed at her sticking-up hair.

"She's gone to town. To see someone about Annie, I think." She looked almost embarrassed to be found in such an intimate embrace.

"I've got to speak to her."

"Well, she won't be back here this evening. She left early. I think Mack came to pick her up." The two women stared at Sabine, who was now hopping from leg to leg in agitation.

"What on earth is the matter?"

"We need to get her. It's Annie—she—I think she's having a baby."

There was the shortest of silences.

"What?"

"A baby? Are you sure?"

Outside the door, infected by the excitement, one of the dogs had begun to bark.

"Annie can't have children," said Joy, unconvinced.

"Sabine? Are you sure?"

"Look, come *on*. I'm not making it up," said Sabine, pulling at her grandmother's sleeve. "She's in the house. With one of the guests. But there's stuff on the floor and everything and he says he's only a loans clerk but she hasn't got long to go and we need to get an ambulance and Annie's phone isn't working."

Joy and Kate exchanged looks.

"He's all by himself," said Sabine, reduced to near tears by their stupid, frozen faces. "Annie needs help. You've got to come *now.*"

Joy placed her hand against her face,

thinking, and then strode toward the door, propelling the younger women before her. "Kate—you run down there with Sabine. I'll ring an ambulance and gather up some things here. Oh, my goodness, I'll try and ring Mack as well. I'm sure we have one of those mobile telephone numbers for him somewhere. I'll get Thom to find it."

"You lead the way," said Kate, as she followed her daughter's rapid descent down the stairs, almost falling over the dogs as she went. "Oh, that poor woman," she said, putting her hand out to pat Sabine's shoulder. "Thank God you found her."

Anthony Fleming was doing a little dance on the step outside Annie's house, a curious jig, accompanied by the merry waving of arms, a Morris dancer, out of time with some mental tune. At least that was how it looked from afar; when Sabine and Kate got close, sweating, and breathing hard from their sprint, it revealed itself as an anxious shifting of weight, a desperate, fumbling plea for help from arms that clutched hold of Kate's lapels when she ran up the steps.

"Are you a doctor?" he said, his face pale and anxious.

"The doctor's on his way," said Kate, coughing. "Where is she?"

"Oh, God . . . oh, God . . ." Anthony Fleming began wringing his hands.

"Where *is* she?"

Ignoring him and Sabine, Kate pushed her way through the living room into the kitchen, and casting around until she spied her, swiftly crouched down by the squat form of Annie, who was now hanging on to the base of a kitchen stool, rocking backward and forward, and letting out low, keening noises that made the hairs on the back of Sabine's neck stand on end.

"You're all right now, you're all right, Annie," Kate repeated, holding on to her, smoothing her hair. "You're doing really well. It's all going to be fine."

Sabine stared at the kitchen, at Annie's long skirt, which lay discarded and soaked in the corner by the sink, at some stained scrap of pink fabric that may have been her knickers. There was pale, watery blood everywhere. It made her think of the time her grandfather had fallen into the vegetable casserole. She realized she had begun to shake again.

"I don't know anything about babies,"

Anthony Fleming kept repeating, his hands wrestling with each other. "I do only bank loans. I came back only because she had somewhere safe to put my bike."

Sabine couldn't answer him. She just kept staring at Annie, who, lost in some private world, was now hanging on to Kate, her eyes open yet unseeing, her face occasionally contorted as she let out another bovine cry. Kate, glancing behind her at her daughter's shocked face, tried to smile.

"It's all right, darling. Honestly. Looks worse than it is. Why don't you go outside and wait for the ambulance to come?"

"I'll do that," interjected Anthony Fleming, who was already making for the door. "I'll wait for the ambulance. I'll wait outside."

Kate cast an irritated glance at his departing back. She kept looking at her watch, marking the distance between Annie's anguished noises.

"Okay. Okay . . . *erm*, Sabine—go and find me some towels, okay? And some scissors. And if you can, boil me a kettle and sterilize the scissors in some hot water. All right?"

"You're not going to cut her open, are you?" Sabine, still frozen at the kitchen door, felt her chest compress with fear. She didn't think she could cope with the sight of any more blood.

"No, darling. It's for the cord. Just in case the baby comes before the ambulance does. Go on, we don't have an awful lot of time."

She turned back to Annie, stroking her hair, murmuring words of encouragement, heedless of the fact that she herself was now covered in the bloodied liquid, from where she had been supporting Annie on the floor.

"I need to push," said Annie, her hair stuck in sweaty tendrils around her face. These were the first words Sabine had heard her say. "Oh, God, I need to push."

"Sabine. Go *now*."

Sabine turned to run from the room, unsure where she was going to find any scissors—Annie's house didn't look like anything would be where you would expect it, anymore—and bumped into Joy, who was holding a bundle of towels.

"The ambulance should be here any minute," Joy said. "Thom's trying to get ahold of Mrs. H. Where are they?"

"Have you gotten scissors?"

"Yes, yes. . . ." Joy was following the long lowing sound, which, this time, raised up into something unearthly, nearer a scream. "We've got everything. In the kitchen, are they?"

The noise, when it came again, was too horrible. It made Sabine chill, like the sounds of the hounds howling in the night. It sounded like Annie was going to die.

Her face crumpled.

Joy turned to face her, her own expression suddenly softening, as she caught sight of her granddaughter's fear and reached out a hand to comfort her.

"It's all right, Sabine. Really. Birth is just a bit of a brutal business."

"Is she going to die? I don't want Annie to die."

Joy smiled and squeezed her, before turning toward the kitchen. "Of course she won't die. A minute after that baby is born, she won't remember a thing about it."

Sabine watched from behind the door as Joy moved past her and crouched down next to her mother, handing over the towels, and helping arrange Annie's limbs on the floor, stroking her legs and murmuring something cheerful as she did so. Kate said something about "transition" and she and Joy looked at each other briefly, and their faces had an expression of not just mutual understanding and concern, but a faint hint of impending joy, as if they both knew something that they couldn't yet acknowledge. Sabine, watching it, found herself suddenly tearful again, but not because she felt excluded. She felt comforted.

"Okay, Annie," said Kate, who was now at Annie's feet. "You get ready to push. You say when you feel the next one coming."

Annie paused, stared wide-eyed at her feet, and then, with her chin to her chest, let out a lengthy roar, at first through clenched teeth, and then through a mouth so wide open that Sabine, peeping round the door frame, found her own mouth unconsciously mimicking its action.

Joy was wincing as she tried to hold Annie's upper half, her face flushed with effort. Kate pushed Annie's knees up, and wiped her face with a cold flannel. She was half crying now.

"You're nearly there, Annie. I can see the head. You're really nearly there."

Annie's eyes opened, briefly, to look at Kate. They were exhausted, bewildered.

"Deep breaths, Annie. Just keep your chin down, and it will soon be over."

"Where's Patrick?" said Annie, blearily.

Kate glanced at her mother.

"Patrick is coming," said Joy firmly, her own face pressed up next to Annie's, her arms supporting her under her shoulders. "Patrick is coming, and your parents are coming, and the ambulance is coming. So you're not to worry. You just concentrate on that lovely baby."

"I want Patrick," said Annie, beginning to cry. And then her tears became strangled, as another contraction gripped her body, and her sob turned into another huge roar. And she gripped at Joy's arms so fiercely that Sabine could see her grandmother grimacing, and Kate was still down in front of her, her hands pushing Annie's ankles, so that her knees were up, her voice offering words of encouragement.

"It's coming, Annie. Go on, push now. It's really coming. I can see the head." Her mother's voice was now shrill with excitement, her face lifting to Annie's with a broad smile.

Annie fell back against Joy, exhausted.

"I can't do it," she said.

"You can, you're nearly there," said the two women in unison.

"Just pant, Annie," said Kate. "Keep panting for a minute." She looked at her mother, adding quietly. "That's right, isn't it Mum?"

Joy shrugged imperceptibly and nodded. They half smiled at each other again.

"Okay, now one more push," she said. Sabine couldn't see past the counter to see what Kate was doing. She was secretly grateful. And then Annie began to yell, a long, wavering, strangulated note, and Kate began to yell, and Joy, who was still wincing because of the hold Annie had on her arms began to yell, and Sabine found she was crying now, without realizing it, because just when she thought she couldn't bear it, suddenly there was a brief, wet slithering and a shout of blood and joy and her mother was holding this thing, this thing with its two purple arms thrust high in the air, like a football fan, and Joy was kissing Annie, and laughing, and Kate was wrapping it tenderly in a towel and placing it on Annie's chest, and the three of them had their arms around each other, and through it all Sabine kept watching Annie's face, with its raw expression of joy and pain and relief, oblivious to the blood and gore, oblivious to the noise, oblivious to Anthony Fleming, who was standing at the door *ah-hemm*ing into his hand and asking everybody to excuse him but the ambulance was here.

And then her mother, as if suddenly remembering her, looked up and reached out to her, and Sabine walked over and kneeled down with them and gazed at this thing, which was covered in blood and wrapped up in a beach towel, smelling of sweat and iron. And as she looked down she couldn't see the pools of blood, the sodden towels, the knickers, the mess it had made of her own trousers. She just saw two tiny milky-dark eyes, gazing steadily back at her in that ancient way that suggested knowledge of all the secrets of the world. A tiny, downy mouth shaped small, silent words, telling her everything she had never known about what life meant. She realized with a brief burst of clarity that she had never seen anything more beautiful in her whole life.

"A little girl," said Kate, her eyes wet with tears, squeezing her daughter's shoulders.

"She's so perfect," Sabine said, reaching out a tentative hand.

"My baby," said Annie, gazing at her disbelieving. "My baby." And then suddenly, without warning, she began to sob, great, wrenching sobs that ravaged her whole body, shaking her head forward, pummeling her under the weight of their withheld grief that went on and on and on, so that Kate had had to briefly take the baby back, to protect her from Annie's anguish. And Joy had leaned forward, clutching Annie's head, crying: "I know, I know," and then, as Annie's tears eventually began to subside, had told her, so quietly that Sabine could only just make it out above the exclamations of the people coming in. "It's all right, now, Annie. It's all right. It's all over."

And then Kate, her own hands shaking, had helped pull Sabine up from the floor, and with their arms tightly around each other, they had both walked silent and blinking out into the night, where the ambulance men, under the spinning siren of blue light, officious in their neon uniforms and monitored by hissing radios, had started to unload the stretcher.

Chapter Sixteen

There were very few real surprises left in life, said Mrs. H, but the birth of her grandchild had been one, for sure. She said this many times, to many people, but it didn't stop her eyes filling with grateful tears every time she said it, and the fact that she often said it to the same people was not minded by anyone who knew her. Little Roisin Connolly was good news, and news that good could happily bear the burden of repetition.

Patrick had returned to Annie the night of the birth, deeply shocked but overjoyed at the arrival of the new baby, overwhelmed with relief at finally having an explanation of his wife's increasingly strange behavior over the past months. Annie, who had never come to terms with her daughter's death, had become temporarily unbalanced by the shock of her new pregnancy, the doctors said, and had coped only by ignoring it, and distancing herself from those around her. It was not an uncommon response, apparently. Despite this, Mrs. H had seemed rather embarrassed not to have realized that her own daughter had been pregnant, and had blamed herself for the trauma of Roisin's birth, but Mack and Thom and everyone else told her not to be so daft—and Annie herself later pointed out that if she had been able to keep it from her own husband, what little chance did her mother have of guessing? Mrs. H was vaguely appeased, but could often be seen studying the waistlines of various local women, keen to be the first to guess any future pregnancies, and several times causing mild offense by asking.

Annie had spent several weeks in hospital—to keep Roisin company, as she had arrived a little over a month prematurely and had to spend some time in an incubator, but also to give Annie time to adapt to her renewed role of motherhood under the watchful eye of the health authorities. She had, after an initial period of delayed grieving for Niamh (the two babies, it was agreed, were heartbreakingly similar in appearance) recovered astonishingly quickly, suffering none of the postnatal depression that the doctors had warned could be a feature in a case like this. And she got her counseling, although Mrs. H said to see her with her little baby, and her husband's arm around her, was all the counseling anyone needed. Annie even talked about Niamh now, pointing out how similar Roisin was in feeding, or winding habits, and how dissimilar in the shape of her tiny seashell fingernails, or the color of her hair, and sometimes she even told off visiting relatives for crying when she did so, saying that while she wanted to remember that she had had two daughters, "she wouldn't have Roisin growing up in Niamh's shadow."

Sabine visited her several times, holding the tiny child carefully in her arms, marveling at how quickly she had lost her squashed and bloodied appearance and become something alert and pink and sweet-smelling. She didn't want to have her own baby, though, she told Annie. Not until they could make boys have them. Annie (who, as Joy predicted, seemed astonishingly to have forgotten all the pain and blood) had laughed at that. She laughed quite often these days; her eyes glinting with mischief when she teased Sabine about Bobby McAndrew, and with delight when her little daughter did something apparently remarkable, like wave a starfish hand in the air, or sneeze. Sabine secretly thought Roisin was still a bit of a blob. But she didn't say anything. Annie had asked her to be a godmother, and even she knew that wasn't a particularly godmotherish thing to say.

Patrick, who was almost always at the hospital "making a nuisance of himself," the smiling nurses said, just sat and gazed at his daughter, his big, dark face radiating a soft beam of satisfaction, his hands no longer anxiously reaching to stroke or comfort his wife, but most often comfortably entwined in hers. He hadn't done any work for weeks, said Mrs. H, but then you couldn't have everything.

He had wept tears of gratitude at Sabine, Joy, and Kate when he had finally arrived at the house, holding on to them, and shaking his head disbelievingly, so that Sabine had been a little embarrassed for him, but Kate had hugged him, herself tearful, and kept saying that she was "so, so happy," as if it had been she who had given birth. A child, Joy had told Sabine, still a little emotional herself, was the greatest gift anyone could possibly have. One day she would understand. Sabine thought privately that she probably did understand. She had never witnessed anything like Annie's expression when she had first laid eyes on her new daughter—that explosive mixture of joy and pain and relief. Thinking about it now made her want to get emotional, not that she ever let anyone know. There was quite enough sentimental stuff going on these days as it was.

Thom never told Kate about Sabine's failed attempt to seduce him. Or perhaps he did, and her mother had decided not to say anything to her about it. Either way, Sabine was grateful, and a little wrong-footed by not knowing who it was she should be feeling grateful toward.

She had first seen him again on the night of Roisin's birth; he had come running down the road shortly after Sabine and Kate had emerged from the house and were standing by the ambulance, not really knowing what they should do next. He had skidded to a halt in front of them, his eyes darting from one to the other, a hand on each. "Is everything okay?" he had said, looking terribly serious. "Is Annie okay? Are you okay?" He had looked very hard at Sabine when he said the last bit, and she had nodded, too full of the drama of the baby's arrival to still feel humiliated. It had all suddenly seemed such a long time ago, an almost dreamlike scenario, as if it had happened to someone else. She had waited, suddenly tense, for him to kiss her mother, or wrap his arms around her or something, but he hadn't. They had just sort of looked at each other, and then Kate had told him quietly to go on inside, to go and see Annie. And after he had gone in she had paused, and then steered Sabine toward home, saying: "I don't know about you, sweetheart. But I could certainly do with a drink."

And then she had seen him the next day, when Thom had waited till Sabine came to the yard, and then asked if she wanted to go for a ride. Just the two of them. She had looked over the gray's door to find him already brushed off and saddled, as if she were being given no choice. Sabine had felt more awkward then, even though it was obvious from the tone of his voice that he wasn't going to make a pass at her or anything; the thought that he might say something about the previous evening was somehow more excruciating.

But he had behaved like nothing had happened, had chatted about horses, and Annie, and the new baby, and how stunned everybody was, and had taken her on a long, meandering ride across the countryside, encouraging her to jump a couple of ditches that she wouldn't have managed on her own, and laughing when she refused point-blank to attempt a Wexford bank. Yes, she said, trying not to laugh back at him. She knew she had done it before. But it was different, seeing things in cold blood. He had nodded at that, and said she wasn't wrong. Like she had said something much wiser than she had meant.

It wasn't even as if anything big had happened between them on the ride. But when she came back, she felt relaxed again, as if Thom were restored to her—as someone to talk to, at least. Besides, she thought, having studied him quite hard when she knew he wasn't looking, she thought she might not fancy him so much now, especially after her mother told her how close Thom had come to being her father. You couldn't look at anyone the same way after that.

Predictably, it was less simple with her mother. The day after the baby, Kate had still been all emotional and quivery, saying she couldn't eat breakfast, and drifting off into daydreams that made her eyes fill with tears. She had also, rather self-consciously, hugged Joy at the breakfast table, which Sabine found a little excessive, although Mrs. H said afterward that it was "just lovely" that they were all friends again, especially after all this time. (Then again, Mrs. H thought everything was "just lovely" for weeks—she even said it once when Lynda announced that she had picked up a parking ticket in New Ross.) Sabine, who had felt increasingly embarrassed at how frightened she had been at the birth, and how much they had all hung on to each other, had decided to be very cool about everything. It was only a baby, after all, she said, when they threatened to go on about it for too long. It had been rather irritating, the way her mother and grandmother had exchanged glances and smirked when she did, like they had always shared some kind of empathy, and knew what she was doing.

Kate had, however, gotten something right. She had come up to see her several days later, as she was getting changed, and, sitting on Sabine's bed, had asked quite bluntly whether she would prefer to stay in Ireland or go back to England. Sabine, her thick blue jumper halfway over her head, had said through the wool (secretly glad that she didn't have to see her mother's face) that she quite liked Ireland, and that she thought that she could do her next exams here just as well, and rather surprisingly her mother hadn't cried at all. She had sounded sort of upbeat, and said that if that was what Sabine wanted, then that's what they should do. Then she had left. No soul-searching, no droning on and on about how she wanted to be her friend, and just wanted them to be happy, blah blah blah. Just matter-of-fact. Sabine had been quite shocked to emerge from the jumper to find her already gone.

Then a couple of days later, when they were alone in the drawing room, she asked Sabine what she would feel about them selling their house in Hackney and moving over here, to be near Granny permanently. You mean, you want to be near Thom, Sabine thought, but she was too surprised that her opinion apparently counted to be too mean about it.

"I thought we could buy one of the cottages up the road," said Kate, who looked more cheerful than Sabine had seen in ages. "Something nearby. Just a two-bedroom thing. Because we'd have plenty leftover from the sale of the London house. And there's no reason why I can't work from here. We could have fun choosing something."

Sabine, suddenly wary, had wanted to ask her if Thom was going to move in with them, but Kate had preempted her.

"Thom is going to stay where he is for the time being. I think there's quite enough upheaval in this family for now. But he will be spending a lot of time with us, if that's okay by you."

"So, what is it? Didn't he want to move in?" said Sabine, failing to keep the hint of derision from her voice. It was like history repeating itself all over.

"I haven't asked him, darling," said Kate. "I thought it was about time you and I had a bit of fun by ourselves." She paused. "And we both know where to find him, don't we?"

Joy had been surprisingly okay about her Mum and Thom, too. Sabine had told her grandmother almost warily, expecting some gruff expression of disapproval. But Joy, who had curiously seemed to know already, had not even looked up from what she was doing, had said that Thom was a good man, and that she was sure he knew what he was doing.

She hadn't actually said the same of her mother, Sabine realized afterward. But as Mrs. H said, you couldn't have everything.

Bobby, meanwhile, had made some crummy joke when she told him she was staying; something along the lines of her "not being able to leave him alone." But when he stopped cracking jokes, he did say that she'd have a grand time getting to know what he described as "the rest of the gang." And he told her about a Hunt Ball in two weeks' time that they could go to, and a party at Adamstown this weekend where there was going to be a live band, and where, he said, they would have the best laugh. He seemed pretty pleased, really. She didn't like to tell him she had started to develop the teensiest of crushes on his elder brother.

Edward Ballantyne died three weeks to the day after Roisin Connolly's birth, slipping quietly and efficiently away between the lunchtime news and the first of Lynda's afternoon soaps. It was all right, Lynda told Mrs. H afterward. She always made sure she video'd all her episodes at home, in case of just such an eventuality. Mrs. H was rather tight-lipped with Lynda after that.

Sabine, who had been out riding with Bobby at Manor Farm, had been inconsolable when she returned, blaming herself for his "being on his own" when he went, despite the fact that even she had had to admit that he barely seemed even to wake up anymore. But Joy had let her into his room, and sat next to the bed, and held her until she stopped crying, and Sabine had had to acknowledge, as her grandmother said, that he looked much more peaceful now. At least what remained of her grandfather; it was as if the little essence of him that had remained had drifted away altogether, leaving just this placid, sunken old face and almost-cold hands, which sat on the scarlet quilt like relics of another life. Sabine had thought briefly of Thom's hand when she first touched one; but Thom's hand, while not a living thing, was somehow infused with his own zest for life. Her grandfather's hands were like dusty, crepey museum exhibits, carrying only the most distant echoes of times past.

"You shouldn't have made her sit with him," said Kate, who had been waiting in the corridor, pale and grim-faced, when they finally emerged. "She'll have nightmares."

"Rubbish," said her grandmother, who was curiously composed and dry-eyed. "It's her grandfather. She had a right to say good-bye to him. Do you good to say good-bye to him, too." But her mother had shook her head, and, one hand to her face, had disappeared into her room for a couple of hours.

Christopher and Julia had arrived that evening: Julia already dressed in black, and so tearful that she had to be repeatedly comforted by Joy. "I can't bear it," she said, sobbing into the older woman's shoulder. "I'm no good with death." As if anybody was, said Mrs. H, disapprovingly. Julia also took pains to tell Joy at every opportunity that "she knew how she felt." It was less than a year since she had lost Mam'selle, after all.

Christopher, meanwhile, had just looked rather pale and corpselike himself and spoke like he had a mouthful of corks. He had rubbed Kate's back awkwardly when she had finally come downstairs, and said he hoped that things wouldn't get "difficult." Sabine knew he was talking about the furniture with labels on, but Kate simply said that she was going to "leave everything up to Mummy." It was her house, after all, now. Her things. It wasn't as if either of them were in dire financial straits. And Christopher had nodded and left her pretty well alone, which seemed to suit both of them.

Joy, meanwhile, had busied herself with the funeral arrangements, declining all offers of help, but not in the slightly rigid, brusque manner she had employed while her husband was dying. Now, while still briskly efficient, she had become gentler, as if all her hard edges had been rubbed off, and a little meditative. "She'll lose it later on," Julia sniffed, mournfully, watching Joy's departing back as they sat in the drawing room after supper. "Delayed grief, that's what it will be. It didn't hit me properly about Mam'selle until we buried her."

But if the grief came, Joy didn't show it. And Lynda especially seemed almost offended by the lack of hysteria in the Ballantyne household. "I've got some sedatives, just in case," she would say to anyone who passed as she packed up her belongings to leave. "You have only to say the word." Julia took one in the end. She didn't really need it, she confided to Kate afterward. She just thought it somehow gave the right impression. She didn't want Lynda telling everyone in Wexford that the Ballantynes were uncaring, after all.

Despite Julia's impressions to the contrary, Sabine was rather shocked at how sad her mother became after Grandfather's death. Not her usual, annoying, show-offy sadness, which manifested itself in all sorts of tears and tugging at her hair and smudged mascara. (That would have made Sabine cross; she felt that she had somehow greater grief rights than her mother when it came to her grandfather.) She was just really, really quiet, and pale, so much so that when

Sabine caught sight of her near the summer-house being hugged by a sympathetic Thom, her first response was not anger, or even irritation, but relief that somebody might be doing something to help. She still found any form of physical contact with her mother inexplicably difficult, and would withdraw from her embrace as soon as she could without causing obvious offense.

But her mother's sadness infected her; Sabine had cried hugely for two days and then felt secretly better. Her mother looked peculiar, and a little bit frustrated, like she was struggling with things she couldn't convey.

"How come you are so sad about Grandfather?" she said, eventually, as they sat in the study, packing the last two boxes in silence, a cooling mug of tea beside each. The room, now reduced to a few skeletal shelves and unevenly faded wallpaper, was going to be redecorated and resurrected as a bedroom. As one of the few remaining dry rooms in the house, it needed, Christopher said, to be utilized effectively, perhaps for a bed-and-breakfast. There would be a hole in the market, after all, now that Annie and Patrick were closing their doors for a while.

("Don't worry," said Mrs. H, at Sabine's appalled response. "She'll soon frighten them off.") So Sabine and her mother had jointly taken charge of the final boxes in the study; Sabine, having picked out her favorite photographs, was now sorting through the leftover bits of correspondence, secretly hoping that she would find a really juicy love letter. The photographs, which were now in chronological order, were going to be mounted in a leather album, her mother had decided, as a present for Granny. Most of them, anyway.

"I'm not being rude, or anything, but it wasn't as if you ever talked about him much when he was alive."

She eyed her mother, aware that her words did not sound quite as gentle spoken out loud as they had in her head.

Kate placed the lid on the sturdy brown box, and paused for a minute, wiping dust from her nose.

"There were things . . . ," she began. And then paused. "I . . . I suppose I just wish Daddy and I had understood each other a little better. We wasted so much time . . . and now it's all too late. That makes me a bit cross and a bit sad."

Sabine leaned on the desk, fiddling with an old pen, unsure how to respond.

Kate turned toward her.

"I suppose I just wish we'd had a chance to be better friends. We really stopped being close when I was not much older than you."

"Why?"

"Oh, the usual. He didn't approve of how I lived my life. He approved even less once I had you. Not that he didn't love you," she added quickly.

Sabine shrugged. "I know." She harbored a secret belief that her grandfather had loved her, by the end, more than anyone.

They sat in silence for a while, Sabine sifting through the faded documents, only really bothering to read the ones that were handwritten. There were lots of postcards, addressed to Kate and Christopher, in her grandfather's now-familiarly angular, austere handwriting, telling them the names of various ships he had been on, and weather conditions of places he had been. He seemed to have gone away for a bit after Kate was born, but she couldn't find any addressed just to Grandmother.

Kate, meanwhile, sat staring out of the window, apparently still lost in thought.

"I've been remembering how lovely he was to me when I was a child," she said into the silence, so that Sabine looked up sharply.

"He was always taking me places: down to the dockyards, to see his work, up on the Peak tram, out to the little islands around Hong Kong so that Christopher and I could go exploring. He was a pretty good father, you know."

Sabine looked at her, noting her mother's faintly defensive tone.

"He was all right. For an old stick." She tried to hide the catch in her voice. She still found it quite hard to talk about him.

"I guess I would have liked him to have been proud of me," Kate said, sadly. "It's pretty hard, feeling like you get everything wrong in the eyes of those you love."

She glanced at her daughter, a smile playing around her lips. "Yes, believe it or not, even at my age."

Sabine looked at her mother for a while. Then she reached out a hand.

"I don't think you get everything wrong," she said, her voice low and rushed, as if betraying a confidence. "I know I'm not very nice to you sometimes, but I do think you're okay, as a mum. As a rule. I mean I know that you love me and stuff. Which is important."

She had started to blush.

"And I bet Grandfather was proud of you," she continued. "I bet he was really. But he just couldn't show it. They were never very good at emotions, Grandmother and Grandfather. Not like you and me. Honestly." She paused, and squeezed her mother's arm. *I know.*"

Downstairs they could hear Julia's shrill voice as she helped Mrs. H rearrange the drawing room for after the funeral. There was the scraping sound of furniture moving, and a pause, as Julia again apparently burst into tears.

Kate looked at her daughter's hand, then looked up and smiled slowly.

"You're probably right," she said.

Edward Ballantyne was buried on a day so wet that the roads around the cemetery flooded, forcing the smaller group of mourners to wade through water ankle-deep in order to get near the grave, which, to everyone's relief, was on slightly higher ground. It had rained solidly for two days, turning the skies the color of wet ashes, the grass to mud, and obscuring the various bouquets under the steam of their protective cellophane. Several of the older people from the village, having retreated to the knave of the little church, tutted at the incivility of the weather, muttering about omens and symbols, but Joy had simply smiled oddly to herself, ignoring her wet shoes, and said that to those inquiring that she thought it "fitting." She even told Sabine matter-of-factly to go and put her Wellingtons on if she liked, so that her granddaughter, tearful at her first funeral, had looked shocked and asked her mother whether Joy was "okay." "Remember what you told me. About emotions," whispered Kate, and Sabine, after some pensive thought, had seemed vaguely satisfied.

He had a good turnout. Surprising, really, said Mrs. H, from under her own umbrella, considering how rude he had been to most of the village at some time or another. But Thom, arm in arm with Kate, had shaken his head and whispered that people knew better than that. Besides, it was about respect, he told Kate, who had herself been quietly amazed at the number of mourners in the church. There were few who didn't admire what he and his family had done for the hunt, and those that didn't had come for Joy. "It's a blood thing. They know good breeding when they see it," he had said quietly, and squeezed Kate's arm.

"They know a good wake when they see it," muttered Mrs. H, who on Joy's instructions had bought two whole legs of ham, a side of salmon, and enough alcohol, according to Christopher, to sink a small ship. She had observed the already lightening mood of the village mourners behind them, the distant but discernable swell of chatter as, duty over, they anticipated a good do back at the big house.

Kate huddled closer under Thom's umbrella, awkward in her new black coat, grateful that the rain splashing onto her face would wash away any suggestion of tears. She had found it impossible to stay furious with her father; her mother had seen to that. He was only human, she had said firmly, her old hands gripping her daughter's as she had raged against the old man on the night of his death. Just as Kate was. And more to the point, she said, it was not Kate's place to be angry.

But that had meant that Kate was left with

only the options of grief and sorrow at her father's departure. And a lingering guilt that, had she tried harder, she might have been able to draw one fragile line back across the gaping hole that had existed too long between the two sides of her family. "Sabine did that for you," Thom had said. "Just be glad of that." But it was too early to be very glad about anything.

The vicar's voice, a dull murmur under the persistent hiss of the rain, had talked of dust and ashes, and somewhere behind them Julia, supported by Christopher, had begun to sob noisily until, apologizing profusely, she was taken away. They could hear her protesting her inability to bear it halfway back to Kilcarrion.

The remaining mourners seemed to take that as a sign to start peeling away from the graveside, too, and walked off alone or in pairs, under a variety of dark or gaudily inappropriate umbrellas. Annie and Patrick lingered nearby, baby Roisin invisibly pressed to her mother's chest, Patrick looming over the two of them like a protective bear. They now stepped forward. "You let me know what I can do, now," said Annie to Joy, as the vicar with a final nod and touch of her arm, walked as briskly as he could back to the shelter of the church, his robes billowing behind him.

"And I mean it, Mrs. Ballantyne. You've done enough for me."

"You're very kind, Annie," said Joy, as the rain ran in torrents down the curves of her umbrella. "I'll do just that."

"She won't you know," Annie could be heard to mutter fondly, as they walked slowly away. "Stubborn as a mule, that woman."

And that left only Thom, Kate, Sabine, and Joy, a tall, stern figure in a black suit that appeared to have last seen good use in the late 1950s, standing quietly beside the grave, not even looking up as the vicar disappeared into the church.

Thom had turned toward the departing Patrick and Annie, evidently deciding his place was with them, first propelling Kate toward her mother. But Kate, at the sight of her mother's resolute, black back, had suddenly begun to cry, and Sabine had motioned to him that he should take her with him. If Grandmother was really upset, then the last thing she needed was Kate crying all over her.

* * *

Joy, oblivious to the mud rising slowly over the sides of her shoes, stood beside the dark earth, encrusted with its floral burden, not really looking at anything. She had half-expected to cry, had rather feared embarrassing herself in front of all those gawping people. She knew she had probably rather disappointed them by not doing so. But the thing was, she actually felt rather better, as if a huge cloud had been blown away.

Sorry, dear, she told him silently, as soon as she acknowledged it. You know I don't mean you. It had been rather easier talking to Edward now that he was gone, as if not seeing him there, in his pain and incapacity, a physical reminder of their life before, had freed her up to love him uncomplicatedly again. She knew her manner had lightened, that Julia and Mrs. H and all the rest were treading carefully around her, believing this to somehow be the calm before the storm, that they were predicting perhaps it would be tonight, at the wake, that she would retire, suddenly felled by grief. She had told him silently that she might do that, just to keep them happy. She wanted to give him a good send-off, yes, but she didn't want to spend too much time playing the hostess, keeping the near strangers happy. She still didn't really like parties, even now.

Edward would understand that.

Joy blinked, suddenly aware that she had let her umbrella fall forward and that rainwater was now trickling down her back. She looked up at the sky, wondering absently whether the paler patch of gray would infect the rest, then turned to find Sabine beside her. The young girl was staring up into her face, her eyes swollen, her own expression concerned, and she slid her young arm determinedly through hers as if comforting both of them.

"Are you all right?" she said.

"I'm fine, Sabine." Joy stared down at where the coffin lay. It really didn't seem to have anything to do with Edward at all.

"Are you sad?"

Joy smiled. Thought for a minute.

"No, darling, not terribly. Not for him, anyway."

She took a deep breath. "I think your grandfather was ready to go. He was rather an active chap, and I don't think he liked sitting around doing nothing. I couldn't wish for him to be alive longer than he was."

"But, won't you miss him?"

Joy paused.

"Of course I'll miss him. But we had some lovely times, your grandfather and I. And I'll have those forever."

Sabine seemed satisfied.

"And I suppose you don't have to worry about him anymore," she said.

"No. None of us do."

The sky was definitely clearing a little. The rain came down in finer threads, as if no longer convinced by its own invincible right to deluge, and already considering its next destination. The two women turned, and began walking back down the hill.

"I've got something for you," said Sabine suddenly, reaching into her pocket. "It was in the last box of stuff in the study. I thought you should have it today. I mean, I don't know anything about religious stuff, but Mrs. H says readings can be a comfort at . . . well, times like these."

She handed her grandmother a scrap of paper, handwritten and faded by age. She had to move closer under Joy's umbrella to try to save it from getting wet, but even then at least two of the words got splashed, sending the ancient ink bleeding outward in miniscule tendrils of blue.

. . . that by the assistance of his
  heavenly grace
you may govern and preserve
the Peoples committed to your charge
in wealth, peace, and godliness;
and after a long and glorious course
of ruling a temporal kingdom
wisely, justly, and religiously,
you may at last be made partaker of an
  eternal kingdom,
through the same Jesus Christ our Lord.
  Amen.

"It's your writing, so I thought it might mean something to you. Is it all right? I mean, it is a religious thing, isn't it? I know you're not really a Godbotherer or anything, but I thought it might be fitting for Grandfather."

Joy stood, gazing at the little piece of paper, as it became gradually softened and darkened by the droplets of water, and felt a large lump lodge itself somewhere back in her throat.

"It is your writing," said Sabine, a little defensively.

"Yes, it is my writing. And it is sort of religious," Joy said, eventually, her voice cracking. "But, yes, it is all right. In fact it's . . . it's very . . . appropriate. Thank you very much."

Sabine looked up, and then smiled approvingly, grief clearing from her young face like the clouds above them.

"Good. As I said, I'm usually a bit rubbish at that kind of thing," she said, and then, arm in arm, a little unsteadily as they tried to negotiate the rough ground, the old woman and her granddaughter splashed their way back toward the house.